T0246020

Advance Praise for *Belonging*

"Fordyce captures the complexities of both love and forgiveness as well as the painful ways the events of the past can't help but color our present-day lives. *Belonging* is a wise, uplifting, and deeply compassionate novel with characters so vivid they feel like part of your own family."
—Stacey Swann, author of *Olympus, Texas*

"*Belonging* is a moving and original story of a girl coming of age and learning who she is in a family wracked with tension, set against a California landscape from the seventies to the present, chronicling the history of that time and place as much as its indelible characters. Jill Fordyce is a sensitive and beautiful writer and a novelist to watch."
—Malena Watrous, author of *If You Follow Me*

Belonging

A Novel

JILL FORDYCE

Post Hill
PRESS

A POST HILL PRESS BOOK
ISBN: 979-8-88845-174-8
ISBN (eBook): 979-8-88845-175-5

Cover design by Diane Luger

Post Hill Press
New York • Nashville
posthillpress.com

Published in the United States of America
1 2 3 4 5 6 7 8 9 10

For Craig

Love once said to me: "I know a song,
would you like to hear it?"

—*Saint Teresa of Ávila*

PART ONE

Chapter One

DECEMBER 1977

On the morning of December 20, 1977, a wall of dirt pushed by a warm wind began to barrel through the canyons surrounding California's southern San Joaquin Valley. When Jenny Hayes arrived at school, the Christmas decorations that hung outside the cafeteria swayed back and forth in a cold, light wind. But by late morning, the air turned oddly warm, the wind picked up, and a dust plume that rose to five thousand feet began to blanket the town of Bakersfield.

Jenny was in a windowless bungalow on the outskirts of the schoolyard, listening to her eighth-grade photography teacher give an overview of the first semester.

"You have all the technical skills now," Mr. Rosenfeld said. "When we come back from break, you are going to *find your eye*. How do you do that? You notice what you notice, trust what you notice, and photograph what you notice."

As her wiry, bearded photography teacher spoke, Jenny realized that all she noticed the entire semester was the boy sitting two rows in front of her. Instead of paying attention to darkroom instructions, she stared at the back of Billy Ambler—his broad shoulders, the dark curls that touched the top of his perfect ears, the way he held his camera like he knew what he was doing.

"By June, you'll have a catalog of your own photographs. For your final, you'll select the three that most reflect your individual eye."

As Mr. Rosenfeld turned to write on the chalkboard, tiny pellets of debris began pelting the sides of the bungalow. The wind began to howl and screech—a ghostly sound closing in on the classroom. After a loud crash that sounded like a metal trash can slamming into a building, he put down his chalk, shook his head, and said, "*What* is going on out there?"

He walked to the door and opened it just enough to see that daylight had been replaced by a murky brown sky. A fierce wind was driving dirt and debris through the schoolyard. Mr. Rosenfeld pushed the door closed, turned to the class, and said, "We appear to be in the middle of a pretty big dust storm. We may have to stay put for a while." He continued to try to talk over the sounds of both the storm and the increasingly anxious group of eighth graders. "Starting after break, you'll be given class time to go out into the field and take pictures. And I don't want anyone wandering off alone, so you'll each pick a partner."

Billy turned in his seat, looked at Jenny, pointed at her and then at himself, and whispered, "You and me?"

Jenny smiled, tucked her hair behind her ears, and nodded. She was hoping he'd be her partner. They'd met the year before, when they sat across from each other in the art class they took as a precursor to photography. She liked him right away. He was earnest and polite, asked questions, and took notes—a star athlete who spent hours on his art assignments. During the unit on drawing, she saw him in a composite like this: baseball cap, greenish eyes, long eyelashes, strong hands, open book.

About a month ago, he began waiting for her at the end of photography, so that he could walk her to her next class. He'd lean against the wall outside her classroom until just before the bell rang, lingering long enough for her to wonder if he might be thinking of kissing her, or maybe she was just thinking of kissing him.

"Before we leave today, I want to give you one final thought," Mr. Rosenfeld said. "What you choose to photograph and how you photograph it will tell people a lot about you. My wife complains that since I'm always the photographer at family parties, I'm never in any of the pictures, but I tell her, I'm in every single one."

The lights flickered and the bungalow felt like it was listing to one side, unable to hold back the wind. The telephone rang in the classroom and Mr. Rosenfeld said, "Aha, saved at last." When he hung up the phone, he turned to the class. "The principal says we have to evacuate the bungalows. Bus service is canceled because the buses are at risk of toppling over. It's apparently a very violent dust storm. Your parents will be picking you up in the cafeteria as soon as they are able to get here. Okay, let's line up and get out of here. Let's do this orderly, people."

Mr. Rosenfeld stood by the door and waited until the sound of the wind died down to open it. The class tumbled outside and huddled together. The first thing Jenny noticed was how warm it had become since the hour before when she had walked into photography class. The second thing she noticed was that the winter sun, masked by dirt, hung above the schoolyard like a dull orange and brown ball. Billy took his camera from his bag and snapped pictures of the dirty sky, the crooked bungalow, and the basketball court littered with tree branches. When he turned and pointed the camera at Jenny, she touched her hands to her face and heard the click of his shutter before she had a chance to look away. While Billy was putting his camera back in his bag, Mr. Rosenfeld told the class to move along. Jenny fell in with the line of students, pulled her sweatshirt over her mouth and nose, and wondered who would come to pick her up.

In the crowded cafeteria, she found her cousin, Heather Moretti, who was a year younger than her and in seventh grade. They sat in a corner with their heads together—Jenny's straight, dark brown hair mingled with Heather's curly blonde. Heather turned to Jenny and said, "Every time I breathe, I get dirt in my mouth."

"Pull your sweater up over your nose," Jenny said. "Do you see Henry anywhere?"

Heather shook her head and Jenny scanned the crowded cafeteria for her best friend, Henry Hansen. She had a chocolate cupcake with white marshmallow frosting and sprinkles in a box in the bottom of her backpack for him. She'd baked it the night before for his birthday. The homemade birthday cupcake was a tradition she started the day he turned ten on December 20, 1973; today he turned fourteen.

The parking lot was filling up with wood-paneled station wagons that came from the neighborhoods and tumbleweeds that had blown in from the adjacent highway. Teachers were taking turns going out to the line of cars in the parking lot and back inside to call out the names of those whose parents had arrived. It was chaotic and loud, the sound of the wind now overpowered by the noise of two hundred students stuffed into a cafeteria designed to hold one hundred.

When a teacher called out to Jenny and Heather together, Jenny felt relieved, knowing that Heather's mom, her Aunt Hope, was there for them. As they walked toward the door, Jenny heard Henry's laugh and turned to see him standing against the back wall of the cafeteria. She held onto Heather's arm and said, "Hold on a sec, okay? I want to say goodbye to Henry."

Jenny walked across the cafeteria and handed Henry the cupcake from her backpack. "Happy birthday."

"I was wondering where you were." Henry pushed his long auburn bangs to the side and looked down at her with his blue-green eyes. "Thanks for the cupcake."

"You're welcome. Extra sprinkles, just the way you like." Jenny looked over her shoulder at Heather standing by the door. "I'm leaving with Heather now. Aunt Hope's here. Who's getting you?"

"My dad, I guess. He's taking long enough. I might just walk home."

Jenny looked at the lightweight sweatshirt and jeans he wore over his tall, skinny frame, and said, "Don't go out in the storm. I'm sure you can come with us. I'll go ask Aunt Hope."

"I'll be fine. Go on." Henry moved his hand toward the door in a scooting motion. "Call me later."

Jenny knew Henry well enough to know his mind was made up. She reluctantly left him standing there eating his cupcake, contemplating going out in the storm. She and Heather zipped their jackets over their heads and ran for the parking lot.

The pale green station wagon was warm and smelled like the flowery perfume her aunt, Hope Moretti, had been wearing for as long as Jenny could remember. Aunt Hope didn't look like she'd been out in a dust storm. She looked like she always did: fresh-faced, shiny blonde hair, a headband that matched her skirt. It was a tense drive home, with tumbleweeds and dirt whipping by, and the wind pulling at the station wagon. The Christmas carols playing on the radio were interrupted by the startling dull buzz of the Emergency Broadcast System, and a monotone voice announced: *nearly two hundred mile an hour winds, road closures, five feet visibility, stay inside.* Jenny listened and kept her eyes on Aunt Hope. Her careful driving and easy chatter calmed Jenny, and she felt like nothing bad could happen to her while Aunt Hope was in charge.

When they got home, Aunt Hope gathered Jenny and Heather close to her, and made a run for the front door. Jenny and Heather's grandmother, Nonna, was waiting for them inside. Jenny was happy and relieved to see Nonna, her maternal grandmother, and the person she counted on the most. On the day of this epic dust storm, they needed to be together. Nonna was wearing a beige pantsuit with a silk scarf around her neck, and her dark hair had been set and coated with hairspray. As Jenny and Heather walked in the door, she wrapped her arms around them, held them against her plumpish chest, and said, "There's my girls." She kissed the top of their heads—Jenny's brunette and Heather's blonde. "Chocolate and vanilla."

Jenny looked around the warm house. The Christmas tree was in the corner of the family room, its colorful lights creating a soft glow. Stacks of gifts wrapped in brown craft paper and plaid ribbons sat beneath the tree. Handmade stockings for Aunt Hope, Uncle Joe, Heather, and their cat, Cherry, hung from the mantel. In the kitchen, the tiles were all different tones of yellows and oranges and stretched up the walls like the rays of the sun. Jenny noticed everything in Aunt Hope's kitchen each time she was there—the light from the window, the smell of a homemade meal, the sounds of the teapot whistling and the dishwasher running. She was comforted by this loving home, filled with family and good food. It also made her feel a little sad, aware that it was something she lacked.

Aunt Hope served them hot tea and warm slices of banana bread. A small TV was tuned to the local news. *Trees and fences down, power outages, swamp coolers blown off roofs, canals filled, cattle buried.*

"This reminds me of the dust storm we had in 1926. The sky was dark mid-day, just like now, and they say the dust cloud rose to a mile high," Nonna said, blowing on her tea.

"How old were you then?" Jenny asked.

Nonna looked to the ceiling and tapped her chin. "I was thirteen, exactly your age."

"How old was Uncle Gino?" Heather asked.

Before Nonna could answer, Jenny said, "Where is Uncle Gino?"

"He's stuck downtown at the store. Power lines are down. I just talked to him before you girls got home."

"Is he okay? Is he alone?" Jenny asked.

"He told me he has a box of cookies and a pot of coffee, and we both know that's all my little brother needs." Nonna winked at Jenny. "Gino is ten years younger than me, so he was three years old during that 1926 storm."

Jenny adored her great uncle, Gino Vitelli, Nonna's youngest sibling. He'd given her a part-time job at his antique store, and during the days spent there together, he shared stories about her great-grandparents leaving Italy in 1902 and putting down roots in the middle of California. He told her what it was like growing up in the old yellow Victorian where he still lived today—the music and food and gathering, the trees that were planted, the flower and vegetable gardens he loved.

Aunt Hope turned toward Nonna with a wooden spoon in her hand. "Marion, want to help with the lasagna? It's your mother's recipe."

Nonna took a drink of her tea and tied an apron around her waist. Although Aunt Hope was Nonna's daughter-in-law—married to her son, Joe, and not even Italian—she took pride in learning Nonna's recipes and carrying on all the Italian traditions. Aunt Hope was from a wealthy farming family that had been in Bakersfield since the late 1800s. She attended private schools and met Joe one summer when she was home from Vassar, and he was interning in the corporate office of her family's farm. Today, Joe ran the whole operation, leaving before dawn each day to travel to fields outside of town, just like Aunt Hope's father used to do.

Nonna stirred the tomatoes, onions, and garlic simmering in a pot on the stove and added a hearty dash of cinnamon. The scent of garlic and rosemary, with just a hint of sweetness, filled the house and felt like another layer of protection from the outside world, from the wildness of the storm.

Belonging

Although the wind had died down by late afternoon, the sky remained so dark that the transition to evening went unnoticed. Just before dinnertime, Jenny's dad appeared in the doorway. Jenny was helping Aunt Hope peel carrots for the salad, and when she saw her dad standing there, she hung her head and closed her eyes. Aunt Hope gave him a quick hug and said, "I'm making lasagna and garlic bread. Why don't you stay, Bob? There's plenty."

"Well, you know, we'd love to, but Janice already made dinner for us." He put a hand on Jenny's head, "You girls been out of school all day?"

"Yeah, most of it." Jenny put the carrot down and wiped her hands on a dishtowel.

"How about if I pack some up for you? I made enough for a small army, and it's even better on day two." Jenny felt relieved by Aunt Hope's offering. She knew her mom didn't make dinner. Now she'd have a warm meal tonight, and it would be the delicious lasagna she'd been smelling all afternoon.

But her dad said, "Thanks, Hope. Don't go to any trouble. We have to get home now. Roads are closed everywhere, and it may take a while. Come on, Jenny. Get your things."

As Aunt Hope and her father were talking, Jenny watched Nonna quietly cut off half a loaf of banana bread and stick it in the front pocket of her backpack. Jenny hugged Nonna and Aunt Hope goodbye, flicked Heather on the shoulder, and followed her father out to his car. The air was gritty and thick, and the front seat was coated with a layer of dirt. Tree branches, tumbleweeds, and garbage littered the streets. In the car, Jenny said, "You think Mom made dinner?"

Her father rubbed his hand over his mustache and said, "No. But she wouldn't want your Aunt Hope to know that."

"Why didn't you let her pack us some lasagna? We won't be able to get anything tonight. Everything's closed because of the storm."

"I don't think your mama would want her handouts. We'll figure something out."

Jenny leaned her head against the dirty window and pulled her sweatshirt so far up over her nose, it covered more than half her face. She knew that "*we'll* figure something out" meant *she'd* have to figure something out. She looked out at the familiar streets that now seemed like a ghost town. Everything was closed down, windows boarded, no cars in the parking lots. The only thing that had an open sign in the window was the Mexican restaurant with the bar that her mother sat in starting at about lunchtime most days. Her dad suggested that they stop there in case her mother was inside.

"I don't want to go in."

"Well, I don't want to leave you out here alone, darlin'."

Jenny pulled her sweatshirt down and said, "I'll be fine." She reached for the door locks. "I'll lock the doors behind you."

Jenny ran through a couple of scenarios while her dad went into the bar alone. In one, he carried her mother out, over his shoulder like a caveman, and laid her across the back seat, passed out and limp. In another, he dragged her mother by the elbow, while she kicked and spat at him, and when he tried to put her in the car, she would fight back. He would eventually win, but then she was in the car with them like a trapped animal, punching the seat and banging her leg against the car door. She'd seen both before. Before she could imagine the third scenario, the one where her mom was kissing all over her dad and calling him *baby*, she saw her dad come out of the bar with his arm around her mother's waist.

Jenny unlocked the doors and got in the back, while her father helped her mother into the passenger seat. Her mother turned and looked at her and said, "Hey, you," in a slurry, sweetie voice. She turned up the radio, put her bare feet up on the dash, and her hand in her father's hair. When she leaned over and kissed his neck, lingering an uncomfortable length of time, Jenny realized it was scenario three. She wanted to jump out of the car, into the desolate and dusty street. She knew this was better than watching her mother kick at her father and slam her fists on the dash, but just barely.

When they arrived at their two-story Cape Cod style house on Lupine Lane, Jenny noticed that a portion of the white picket fence that surrounded the small yard was down, and one of the black shutters was in the middle of the lawn. She got out of the car to retrieve it, stopping to touch the leaves on the lemon tree, and noticing that, instead of being waxy and green, they were dusty and gray. She picked up the shutter and placed it by the front door.

Her father called to her and said, "Can you come over here and give me a hand?"

Jenny walked back to the driveway and saw that her mother was passed out against the passenger side window, a rag doll with a mop of black hair, eyes closed and mouth open. She got in the front seat and held onto her mother's arm so that she wouldn't fall out of the car when her father opened the door. This task repulsed her, but she'd done it often, so she just held her breath while her father lifted her mother from the car and stood her up in the driveway. Jenny grabbed her mother's purse and shoes and watched as her mother opened her eyes, looked at her father, and said, "Hi, baby."

Her father said, "Let's get you up to bed."

Her mother stood up straight and flung an arm at him, the back of her hand smacking the side of his head. "Stop touching me!"

Her father reached for his keys and started for the house, leaving Jenny alone in the dark driveway with her mother. Jenny was unsurprised by his stoic departure. Whether her mother was kissing his neck in the car or taking a swing at him in the driveway, he remained impassive. She didn't know if it was a conscious strategy he employed to keep things from escalating, or if he was just paralyzed, knowing the crushing level of cruelty of which her mother was capable.

Her mother said, "Where are my shoes?"

Jenny held them up. "I have them. I'll put them away for you."

"Put them on my feet! I'm not walking into the house barefoot!"

Jenny hesitated for only a second or two, thinking of the darkness and the dirt.

"Don't just stand there. Put my fucking shoes on!"

As Jenny knelt and complied, the familiar shame she felt from being literally at the feet of this woman flooded her. She was so good at it, though. She merely bent, slid a shoe on each foot, said nothing. She held her breath again as she walked her mother up the stairs and into her bedroom. Having her mother touch her, listening to her heavy breathing, smelling her wine breath, made Jenny feel physically ill.

11

She went back downstairs and found her father sitting in front of the dim light of the TV in the family room, a visible redness on the side of his face. There was a barren Christmas tree in the corner and a box of ornaments on the floor. On the coffee table, there were piles of unopened mail, piles of gossip magazines, baskets filled with piles of miscellaneous things that no one would put away. Jenny had tried to undo the piles many times, but they always came back.

"Should I try to find something for dinner?"

Her father looked up at her, nodded, and said, "Sure."

The kitchen had been fashionable a decade before, but now, it just looked neglected, like everything else in the house. The garbage can was overflowing with empty wine bottles and fast-food wrappers. The refrigerator held only a small carton of milk, a six-pack of Coke, a cube of butter, and two large bottles of white wine. She opened the vegetable drawer, hoping there was a potato she'd forgotten about, but found only a small bunch of carrots.

Jenny's dad was a produce broker, and once a week, he would bring home fresh vegetables or fruits he would pick up from different farmers. Jenny never knew what he'd bring home, but it was food, so she was determined to learn how to cook it. She found an old copy of *The New Doubleday Cookbook* in Uncle Gino's store and discovered there was a simple recipe for everything, and there was an hourglass symbol next to recipes that were quick and easy to prepare. The first carrot recipe with an hourglass next to it was called "Boiled Carrots," so she put a pot of water on the stove and began to peel again.

She found two foil TV dinners in the freezer, filled the teapot with water, and took out the small red jar of Taster's Choice. When the teapot whistled, she fixed her dad his instant coffee the way he liked it, with a lot of milk and a little sugar. She removed the TV dinners from the oven, dished them onto plates, and took the boiled carrots from the stove. She put a generous slice of butter on top of the carrots and brought her father his dinner and coffee in the family room. Pushing aside a pile on the low coffee table in front of the TV, Jenny put her dad's plate down, and said, "Are you okay?"

Jenny's dad nodded, stubbed out his cigarette, and took a drink of his coffee. "Good coffee. Thanks, baby." He pointed to the news. "They say the storm moved around twenty-five million tons of grazing land. And the sun was blocked as far north as Colusa County."

In the same way she was unsurprised by his departure from the driveway, she was unsurprised by his response—or lack thereof—to her question. They never talked about any of it—her mother's drinking and mood swings, negligence and violence—and tonight would be no different. Saying *Are you okay?* was as much of an acknowledgement as either of them would ever offer.

Jenny looked at the image of a giant plume of dust that flashed on the TV screen and thought that it looked like a dirty tidal wave. The newscaster noted that there was other news to report on a day that had been dominated by the weather: President Carter and the First Lady hosted a Christmas celebration at the White House, a Soviet astronaut walked in space, Vietnam agreed to release three young Americans seized off the Vietnamese coast. Jenny patted down a patch of her father's dark brown hair. Sometimes she teased him that he looked a little like a clown, the way the sides stuck out when he hadn't had a haircut in a while.

"Time for a haircut?"

Jenny let her hand rest on the top of his head. "I think so."

She took her dinner and went upstairs. At the top of the stairwell, her parents' room was to the left, and her bedroom was to the right, a mere twenty or so feet down a narrow hallway. Jenny's bedroom was a bright space she'd decorated herself the summer she turned ten. She'd painted it the color of a tangerine, inspired by Aunt Hope's kitchen, and by a book she read that said that the color's resemblance to the sun would make the room feel warm and happy. A cork bulletin board held a photo of her and Henry in a booth at the fair, a newspaper clipping of nuns at a death penalty protest, a homemade kite she and her dad made for a science project, and several prayer cards that all depicted the Virgin Mary.

Jenny turned on KUZZ, the local country radio station owned by Buck Owens. She usually played the radio from the time she woke up until she fell asleep at night, the music creating a buffer around her room. On winter mornings, she'd tune in early to hear if there was a fog delay, which meant the school buses wouldn't be running until about 10:00 a.m. when the fog had dissipated and it was safe to drive. None of the local stations were playing music tonight; they were still talking about the dust storm. *Sand flying so fast that it sawed through fence posts and uprooted orchards of fruit trees. One hundred ninety-four mile per hour winds.* She wiped off the layer of dust that had formed on her window seat and sat down to eat the boiled carrots and TV dinner. She looked out at the yard. The wind was gone, and now there was just the aftermath—strewn branches, toppled garbage cans, and a pile of tumbleweeds.

She took a bite of cold mashed potatoes and imagined eating lasagna and garlic bread in the happy kitchen at Heather's house. Then she pushed the TV dinner aside and reached for the banana bread Nonna had put in her backpack. She was grateful Nonna understood about her mother, about the food. Nonna knew there would likely be nothing for dinner, but to pack the lasagna would've been an affront, the consequences of which were worse than hunger, and a secret stash of banana bread could fill the void. She would not tolerate Jenny being unfed and uncared for, but she also knew enough to keep her assistance covert. She walked this line between tolerance and intrusion, which wasn't always easy to see.

Before bed, Jenny picked up the phone and called Henry's house. When he answered, she said, "You made it home. I've been waiting for you to call."

"I told you not to worry. Are you home now?"

"Yeah."

"Is your mom up?"

"No."

"Well, that's good. What'd you have for dinner?"

"Banana bread. What'd you have?"

"The power was out so we had cold sandwiches and chips. And birthday cake. What are you doing tomorrow?"

"I'm not sure. Christmas shopping?"

"We could go to a movie."

"Maybe. What's playing?"

"Hold on, let me look."

Belonging

Jenny could hear Henry walking through his house: music, people, dishes, and the crackle of the newspaper as he unfolded it in his lap. "*The Goodbye Girl* is opening. *Close Encounters* is still playing. Why is Richard Dreyfuss in everything?"

"What else is there?"

"*Saturday Night Fever.*"

"We can't get into that."

Henry waited a beat, lowered his voice, and said, "We can buy a ticket for *The Goodbye Girl* and go into the wrong theater."

Jenny thought it was just like Henry to suggest such a thing. In kindergarten, when they were assigned to a low table with tiny yellow chairs with two other kids whose last name began with "H," there were many days that Henry wasn't at the table. Instead, he sat on the tall chair in the corner, wearing the dunce cap for being too loud during circle time or refusing to sit still during sharing or getting up from his mat at naptime. Often, when Henry was sent to sit in the dunce chair during recess, Jenny would sit beside him, sentencing herself to the corner as well, her face burning with anger that he had to wear that hat. Henry didn't seem to care, and Jenny fretted that he'd get in even more trouble by making faces behind the teacher's back. When they were outside, Henry was wild and free, the most fun person on the playground. Jenny was shy and slow to make friends, but everyone loved Henry, and being with him out on the playground, she felt free and fun, just like him.

When they were in second grade, Henry's mom came to school every Wednesday to collect book order forms with his baby brother, Christopher, on her hip. Sometimes, she'd bring Henry a lunch from McDonald's, and when she did, she always brought one for Jenny too. They were best friends, unlikely but inseparable. In fourth grade, Jenny began walking home from school with Henry on Fridays for dinner and a movie with his family. She was enamored by their traditional nature: a dad who was an accountant and came home from work in a suit and tie with a briefcase; a mom who baked and volunteered at church and school; a sibling; dinner on the table; a nice, clean house on the golf course; everyone gathered around the TV with a bowl of popcorn on a Friday night.

Jill Fordyce

When Henry's parents separated during their fifth-grade year, Jenny didn't understand it, and Henry wouldn't talk about it. She was afraid his mother would move away and take Henry with her, and she couldn't imagine a life without Henry. A few days after she heard the news, she sat on the front steps of his house and studied his wispy auburn hair, freckles across the bridge of his nose, eyes that were too pretty for a boy. She tried to smell him without him noticing. He smelled like cinnamon cookies and soap and Band-Aids. She listened to him laugh like a high-pitched squawking bird. Then, one by one, she put each of his features, his smell, and the sound of his laugh away inside of her, and turned an imaginary lock. As it turned out, Henry's mother moved to a condo nearby, got a clerical job at one of the oil companies, and soon remarried. His father stayed in the house on the golf course and began working from home in the afternoons so that he'd be there for Henry and Christopher. When he took up baking, it made Jenny feel tender toward him, because she could see how much he wanted things to stay the same for his sons after the divorce, even if all he could do was have a plate of cookies on the kitchen table when they came home from school.

Jenny wasn't sure if she'd have the guts to follow Henry into *Saturday Night Fever* or if she even wanted to, but they planned to meet up at two o'clock the next day at Stockdale 6, the six-theater movie complex that had been a fixture in their lives since it opened four summers before. She told Henry she'd think about it. When she hung up the phone, she turned up the radio. KUZZ was playing music again. As Dolly Parton's sweet voice filled her room, Jenny thought about how much the refrain of "Light of a Clear Blue Morning" sounded like a prayer. She looked out the window and watched a tumbleweed roll across the yard, joining a small mountain of tumbleweeds pushed up against the cinder block fence. She took her camera from her backpack and climbed out onto her rooftop, a flat rectangular space, covered with a layer of black tar and green gravel. She could still smell the dust, even taste it in her mouth. She aimed her camera straight up at the yellowish-brown moon and pressed the shutter.

In bed that night, she thought about sitting on her knees in the dirty driveway, placing shoes on her mother's feet. She thought about how her father turned and walked away, leaving her alone when he couldn't

16

take it anymore, but somehow believed she could. Then two dark images appeared in her mind. She wasn't even sure where they came from: cattle buried up to their necks in dirt, unable to move, and fruit trees standing upside down, their roots exposed to the elements.

Chapter Two

JANUARY 1978

Eleven days after the dust storm, Jenny woke to intense itching on both of her arms. In her half-sleep, she scratched at what felt like large mosquito bites that ran from her wrists all the way to her shoulders. She sat up in bed, pushed up the sleeves of her flannel nightgown, and saw the large, raised red welts. In the mirror in the corner of her room, she saw that the welts were also on her face. She lifted her nightgown, discovered they were on her legs as well, and panicked as she began to itch everywhere.

Jenny put herself in the bathtub and sat there, arms crossed over her small chest, and let cold water run over the hot bumps. There was relief from the itching for a short period of time, but it was a trade-off; it was a cold January morning, and she was in a cold bath. Her teeth chattered and her body shook, and soon she felt her own hot tears on her face. She looked down at the welts that covered her body and became afraid of what was happening beneath her skin. She knew she had no choice. She stepped out of the tub, wrapped herself in a towel, and walked into her parents' bedroom.

Light was coming through the bent and broken plastic blinds above her mother's bed. The nightstand was piled with gossip magazines, candy wrappers, empty glasses, and cigarettes.

Jenny stood over her mother and whispered, "Mom."

Her mother didn't wake up, so she touched her shoulder and gave her a little shake. Her mother awoke, startled and gasping.

Jenny jumped back, equally startled, and said, "Sorry I scared you." She sat on the edge of the bed and held her arms out. "I have a really bad rash."

Her mother reached for her pack of cigarettes and a lighter on her nightstand. She lit a cigarette, took a long drag, and touched the bumps on Jenny's forehead. Jenny was holding her breath when her mother blew out the smoke and said, "A lot of people are getting valley fever after the dust storm. Get dressed. We'll have to go to the doctor."

"I'm so itchy."

"I don't know what to tell you."

"Can we call Nonna?"

"Why?"

"She might know what to do."

"I'm calling the doctor. Why don't you just get back in the bath?"

Jenny had heard of valley fever—everyone who'd ever lived in Bakersfield had either heard of it or had it—an illness caused by a fungus found in only a few areas of the country, one being the structural depression in the middle of California known as the San Joaquin Valley. The fungus blooms and forms tiny spores that lay dormant in the soil until they are stirred up and become airborne. When inhaled, the spores enter the lungs and cause a pneumonia-like infection.

Back in the cold bath, Jenny heard her mother making phone calls—but not to the doctor and not to her grandmother. She heard her call Linda and Judy, her two best drinking buddies, fixtures on the porch in the summer and on barstools in the kitchen the rest of the year. *I think she has valley fever. When Joe had it in '54, it started as a rash. It's all over her body. It's been just about two weeks since the dust storm.* When she finally heard her mother talking to Nonna, Jenny noticed how her voice changed. The conspiratorial giddiness she shared with Linda and Judy was replaced with a flat tone and a hint of exasperation.

An hour later, Nonna met them at the pediatrician's office, where a doctor took a two-pronged instrument and poked Jenny's forearm. He swabbed the blood and told her that if the marks turned into bumps, she had valley fever. When the doctor left the room, Jenny looked down at her arm, the pale scar that ran across the inside of her elbow, the two pokes from the doctor, and she thought how much it looked like she'd been bitten by a snake.

While her mother flipped through a women's magazine from the previous spring, Nonna rubbed her fingers over the bumps that were already forming on Jenny's arm. Sitting between her mother, with all of her hardness—her slim, toned figure, flat chest, fair skin, and short black hair—and her grandmother, with all of her softness—her heavy bosom, olive skin, and loose brown bun—Jenny thought about how much they seemed like strangers to one another. They didn't look alike, except that they both had the same brown, almond-shaped eyes. They didn't talk or touch or really even look at each other. They never shopped or had dinner or went to church together. In fact, the link between her grandmother and mother was so tenuous and bitter, Jenny wondered how her grandmother had been able to be so prominent in her own life.

After a few moments, Jenny held out her arm and said, "I have it."

The doctor came back in, confirmed that Jenny had valley fever, and had them walk across the street to the hospital for chest x-rays. There, she donned a heavy cape and answered "no" when the nurse asked if she'd begun menstruating yet. Afterward, the doctor held up the chest x-rays, pointed to a large shadow on her right lung, and said that the shadow, coupled with the severity of her rash, indicated that she had a very serious case. Jenny looked at the dark mass that had invaded her lung and wondered if this meant that, at some point, if the black overtook the pink, she would be unable to breathe. She wondered how that spore of dust containing the valley fever got there. Did it go up her nose or into her mouth? Why did it decide to stay in her lung? How was it able to thrive and grow there? The doctor said Jenny wouldn't be going back to school after Christmas break, and she might be in bed for the remainder of eighth grade. He said he wanted to see her weekly, and if things didn't turn around by April, he would be recommending hospitalization for an experimental treatment. *April?* Jenny looked at her mother when the doctor said this and wondered if the miserable look on her face was one of compassion or inconvenience. She looked at Nonna and saw an expression of alarm that she tried to mask as soon as she noticed Jenny looking at her.

Belonging

Nonna asked the doctor, "What do we do about school?"

Jenny's mother tipped her head back and shot Nonna a look that Jenny didn't understand; it was as if her mother was about to laugh—but tinged with anger and irony—a look that said *what a joke!* The doctor said that, in cases like these, the school district can usually arrange for a tutor to come to your home, and he would provide them with a note making that request. Nonna thanked him, and on the way out of the office, Jenny's mother took hold of Nonna's elbow and spat out the words, "It's interesting you're so worried about her education."

Jenny looked over at her mother and grandmother, alarmed by the nastiness of her mother's tone, and the fact that she was touching Nonna.

Nonna said, "It's the rest of junior high, Janice."

Jenny's mother ignored her and made a point of walking ahead of them to the car. Outside the car, Nonna hugged Jenny. "I'll come over this afternoon. I'll make some soup and bring you some magazines, okay?"

Jenny held onto Nonna and felt comforted by the feel of her warm, soft body and the smell of her gardenia perfume. When she got in the car, Nonna walked over to the driver's side window and motioned for her mom to roll it down. Her mom lowered the window and said, "What?"

"We have to talk. I'll be at your house daily. I need to be able to speak to her doctors and have access to her medical records. I think there's a form for that."

Nonna spoke in a calm, deliberate voice, and Jenny could tell that she was trying to find the balance between firm and matter of fact. Nonna wanted to make sure her mother knew the seriousness of the request, while not triggering her. It didn't work, though. Her mother closed the window and sped out of the parking lot, leaving Nonna standing there alone. Jenny sat in the passenger seat, frozen and afraid, as her mother took angry turns and slammed on the brakes and sped through the downtown streets.

When they got home, Jenny went up to her room and sat in the window seat. She looked out at the silvery grass and fog and tried to push aside the thoughts of having a black mass in her lung, of being hospitalized, of not breathing. She thought of being stuck in her room for months, with no one to talk to, no one to cook. Her dad was gone more than he was home, and she doubted his ability to help with anything anyway. She wondered who would take care of her if her mother didn't let Nonna come over, and she knew Nonna couldn't be there all the time anyway. She lived on the other side of town and worked part time at the Hallmark store.

Jenny thought about missing her weekend work at Uncle Gino's antique store, where they would spend the days telling stories, eating cookies, and listening to the oldies station, while they sorted and tagged items he found at estate sales and swap meets. She thought of missing photography class, and for the first time since she'd been alone in the bathtub, felt like she would cry. She would not be wandering around taking pictures with Billy every day, and probably someone else would. It was as if the life she knew before the dust storm was gone, suspended indefinitely, and this new life was filled with uncertainty and worry.

A week later, the rash had been treated and faded away, and Jenny just sat in her bedroom all day long, feeling lethargic and light-headed and bored. Her fear about having no one to care for her, at least in the beginning, didn't bear out. Her usually empty house became filled with concerned people—the tutor sent by the school district, neighbors, her mother's friends. Nonna came over every day after work, and Aunt Hope brought over whatever she made her own family for dinner, Jenny's illness providing the opening to help without offending her mother. Uncle Gino brought her books and cookies and, occasionally, prayer cards he'd found. Once in a while, her father would sit on the end of her bed, and they'd make kites together out of tissue paper and balsa wood to pass the time.

Jenny realized that the valley fever had become sort of a social event—the ladies from the bar had moved to her living room. On most evenings, she would sit in her bedroom listening to their chattering downstairs, and at some point, would wander into the kitchen, take some of the food that was left, and bring it back to her room, usually without notice. This is how she overheard her mother dramatically saying things like *her lung could collapse* and *there's no cure* and *she could be sterile*. She didn't know what "sterile" meant, so she looked it up in the dictionary in her room. Jenny didn't think her mother meant that she was "free of germs," so she zeroed in on the next definition, the one that said "incapable of producing offspring." Not 100 percent sure what that meant, she turned to the word "offspring" and read the word "children."

One day in late January, as Jenny balanced a paper towel full of oatmeal cookies in one hand and a bowl of minestrone soup in the other, she heard her mother talking about a boy who got valley fever from the dust storm. It was in his blood, and his body was covered in boils, and then he died. Jenny tried to hum loudly so she wouldn't hear, but it was too late. She'd already imagined dying with boils all over her body. Back in her room, she ate the cookies before the soup and rearranged her collection of Virgin Mary figurines: Mary in carved wood, Mary in painted plaster, Mary in terracotta clay, Mary in green glass. Then she took out the box of prayer cards she kept in her bottom drawer.

On the day of Jenny's First Communion, Nonna presented her with three prayer cards. The first depicted Jesus standing before a colorful stained-glass window and read: *Whoever comes to me will not be hungry, and whoever believes in me will never be thirsty. John 6:35.* The second had an image of Mary standing against a dark sky. It read: *But Mary kept all these sayings, pondering them in her heart. Luke 2:19.* The third was of Saint Clement, and it included the Prayer for All Needs, which read in part: *Deliver the oppressed. Pity the insignificant. Raise the fallen. Show yourself to the needy. Heal the sick. Bring back those of your people who have gone astray. Feed the hungry. Lift up the weak. Take off the prisoners' chains.*

With these three cards, a collection was born, and the seeds of a faith that revealed the following simple tenets: you will never go hungry, be fierce in your beliefs, help those who cannot help themselves. Jenny went to Mass every Sunday with Nonna and Uncle Gino. She began finding prayer cards in pews at church and tucked into books and boxes at Uncle Gino's store. Occasionally, Uncle Gino would bring her an entire bag of prayer cards, gathered at estate sales. Some of them had beautiful illustrations. Many had pictures of old people. A few had pictures of young people. Some had prayers and poems. Others had bible passages. She could almost always find one to soothe her.

Jenny opened the box and picked up a card that had creases in it, like it had been held over and over again. On the front was an image of a young nun with a dove hovering above her shoulder. On the back, it said: *Let nothing disturb you, Let nothing frighten you, All things are passing away: God never changes. Patience obtains all things. Whoever has God lacks nothing; God alone suffices—Saint Teresa of Ávila.* Jenny held the prayer card in her hand and thought of what her mother said about the boy who had died and settled herself with the knowledge the valley fever was in her lung, not her blood, so there probably would never be boils.

Shortly after Jenny became ill, Mr. Rosenfeld sent an assignment home with her tutor. He was teaching a unit on documentary photography and thought it might be interesting for Jenny to take some photos that captured her experience at home with valley fever. He clipped a note to the cover of a book by the photographer Mary Ellen Mark, asking Jenny to study her style and content, and challenging her to come up with her own. Jenny flipped through the book. She'd never seen pictures like this before, of people not posed in any way, often in their most intimate spaces—lonely bedrooms, plastic backyard swimming pools, kitchen tables. She was moved by the photographer's bearing witness to people in places so personal and real, capturing images that, but for her camera, no one else would ever be able to see.

Inspired by the book and the assignment, Jenny began photographing everyone who came to visit her and everything that captured this time and place. She photographed Heather braiding her hair in front of the mirror; Henry sprawled across her bed, reading from the journal he kept for Miss Wilson's English class; Billy backlit in her window seat. She photographed the donuts her father left on her nightstand, the birds on the rooftop waiting for her to feed the donuts to them. She photographed her favorite passages from *Our Town*, the book assigned for English, highlighted in yellow, words that made her feel something. She felt as if her desire to chronicle and capture time, people, places was not unlike Emily's at the end of the play, when, in death, she pleads with the living to stop and look at everything.

This photo assignment also gave her a different way of seeing her own life, and she began to uncover truths that she maybe did not want to discover. For example, with the camera as her ally, she learned that plenty of people were worried about her mother's ability to care for a gravely ill child. She took photos of Nonna sitting on the cot she'd set up in her room, so she could watch over her at night; of her father at his makeshift desk in his workshop, so he could work from home; and of her tutor holding an open folder in her lap, not realizing there was a visible note inside that said *concern about neglect*.

Chapter Three

APRIL 1978

B y April, Nonna was spending several nights a week on her cot in the corner of Jenny's bedroom. She brought her own floral bedding and a pillow from home, giving it a feel of permanence. When Jenny asked why she was sleeping over so much, Nonna said it was so they could have some fun while she was stuck at home, *a slumber party just for us chickens*. But Jenny knew that when Nonna was around, she slept better, she ate better, she didn't ache so much, her worry dissolved, and for the most part, her mother just stayed away. She knew that Nonna kept her safe—body, mind, and soul.

To pass the time, Nonna played music for her, old and new. She taught her about the Bakersfield Sound and told her to take pride in the fact that she was born and raised in a place that generated its own authentic and raw genre of music. The Bakersfield artists sang about real things, like the life of the workingman, the need to put food on the table for a family, the displacement felt by moving far from home. Nonna's favorite artist was Merle Haggard, and it didn't take long for Jenny to fall in love with him too. He was a poet, and he captured home in a way no one else did. He sang about cotton fields, tumbleweeds, trains, and the Kern River, about farmworkers, dust, and valley fever.

One day Nonna came straight from work, wearing a pantsuit the color of a lemon drop with a kelly green silk scarf tied around her neck and carrying an album. Her dark hair was pinned in a bun at the base of her neck, and she wore simple jewelry: pearl earrings, a silver watch, and her wedding ring—a small diamond set in an antique silver band. She looked so pretty. Jenny picked up her camera and took a picture, focusing her lens on Nonna's soft brown eyes, loose strands of hair around her face, tiny wrinkles that framed her eyes and mouth.

Nonna sat on Jenny's bed and handed her Carole King's *Tapestry*. "This is for you to listen to and study. Underline your favorite lyrics and we'll talk about them. There's a lyric sheet inside." Jenny looked at the cover—a barefoot woman sitting in a window seat next to a cat. She studied the interaction of shadows and light and wondered if she could duplicate it in her own window seat. She took *Tapestry* from the album sleeve and put on track four. Nonna unzipped her boots and scooted next to Jenny in her stocking feet. Sitting this close, Jenny could smell her gardenia perfume and hairspray and a hint of a Coffee Nip. When Carole's voice and the piano keys reached a crescendo at the same time during "Home Again," Jenny felt goose bumps on her arms. At the end of the song, she looked up at Nonna and said, "The words are so simple."

Nonna put her arm around her. "That's true. How does the song make you feel?"

Jenny wasn't sure how to articulate it at first. She tapped her chin and looked at the ceiling. "Sad and happy at the same time."

"Yes! Do you know what that is?"

"What?"

"It's *hope* and *longing*. You'll find them together in almost any good song—and it isn't always in the lyrics. You can hear it in the melody too, in a bow being pulled across the strings of a violin, or even in the timbre of the vocal."

Nonna couldn't sleep over that night because she had to work early in the morning. When it was time for her to leave, Jenny knew her mother had been sitting downstairs all afternoon with a jug of wine and thought it might be best to walk her to the door. Ever since Nonna began coming to her house daily and staying over some nights, she'd noticed that the tension she witnessed between her mother and Nonna at the doctor's office had grown. It was as if something had been simmering between them for years, but until now, they'd just been able to avoid each other, or there were always enough people around to keep her mother's anger under wraps.

When they reached the bottom of the stairs, Jenny was relieved to see that her dad was home, sitting across the bar from her mother with a bag of fast food and a Coke. Nonna said goodbye to her mom and dad, and Jenny walked her to the door with her arm around her shoulder. At the door, Jenny was telling Nonna how excited she was to play the whole album, when her mother yelled in a sing-song voice, "*You-can-go-now!*"

Jenny's father said, "Janice."

In the same mock cheerful cadence, her mother shouted, "*Jenny-needs-her-rest-and-no-one-else-wants-you-here!*"

Jenny looked at Nonna with her eyes wide, surprised that her mother would lash out at Nonna in front of both her and her father. They overheard her mother say something about Nonna caring more about her granddaughter than she ever did her own daughter and her father say, "Janice, please." Then they heard the barstools scraping and sliding against the faux brick floor, the sound of her father trying to take her mother up to bed. Jenny looked at Nonna and saw that her eyes were downcast, that shame had appeared on her face. She put her hands on Nonna's soft cheeks. "I'm sorry, Nonna."

"No, I'm sorry." Nonna hesitated at the door, and Jenny knew that she was uncomfortable leaving her alone in the house.

"Mom's going to bed, and Dad's here. You can go home. You have to work early. I'll be fine."

Nonna waited a little longer. When they heard her parents' bedroom door shut, Jenny repeated, "I'll be fine." Nonna kissed her goodbye, and Jenny watched as her lemon-drop colored pantsuit disappeared into the dark.

Back in the house, behind her parents' closed bedroom door, she heard her mother say, "and you're no different" and "I don't want her here anymore" and something about being so tired of having Jenny home all the time. She heard an object hit a wall, the bathroom door slam, muffled arguing. In her room, Jenny sat frozen, worried that her mother would barge into her room and continue her tirade. She put on the Carole King album to drown out the noise and looked for a prayer card that she wanted to give to Nonna next time she saw her.

Belonging

By the middle of the next day, Jenny had listened to every song on *Tapestry* and selected her favorite lyrics. That night, Nonna slipped up the stairs to Jenny's room. She sat in the window seat and looked over the lyrics Jenny had underlined.

Jenny said, "After I picked out my favorite words, I realized they all have it."

Nonna looked up at her and smiled. "What do they have, honey?"

"The hope and longing. The happy and sad. It's in all of them."

Nonna closed her eyes briefly and said, "Yes, it is."

Before Nonna went to sleep, tucked into the cot beside her, Jenny handed her a prayer card with a painting of a lit candle in the dark woods. She remembered the card when she saw Nonna's downcast eyes the night before, her solemn face as she stood at the door, her yellow pantsuit disappearing into the dark. Jenny could see that her heart was troubled by something she could not say out loud, and she wanted her to know that God loves her even when she is angry with herself. The back of the prayer card read: *if our heart condemns us, God is greater than our heart, and knows all things. 1 John 3:20.*

A week later, Jenny was awakened from an afternoon nap by the phone ringing. At first, she thought the phone was in her dream, but as she sat up in bed, she realized it was real. She didn't know she was home alone. At the beginning of her valley fever, her parents were home in the late afternoon—her mother on a bar stool in the kitchen with Linda and Judy, her father in his workshop. But by late April, after nearly four months of illness, her mother had returned to her bar stool at the Mexican restaurant down the highway, and her father had returned to work.

Jenny walked into her parents' room, moved some fast-food wrappers off the nightstand, and picked up the phone. On the other end, she heard beeping sounds, the tapping of keys on a typewriter. A woman asked to speak to a relative of Marion Moretti. Jenny said she was her granddaughter. The woman asked if her mother or father was home, and Jenny said no. The woman asked how old she was, and Jenny said, "Thirteen and a half." The woman paused for a moment and said she was very sorry to tell her that Mrs. Moretti had died of a heart attack in the parking lot of the Hallmark store in the Crossroads Shopping Center. She'd been transported to Mercy Hospital by ambulance. She'd been "gone" for about an hour.

Jenny sat down on the bed. *Gone?* An image popped into her mind of Nonna standing in a row of birthday cards and photo albums in the Hallmark store, walking out the door to the parking lot, and then *poof!* The woman on the phone continued to talk, but Jenny couldn't hear her anymore. Her teeth began to chatter like she was cold, but she didn't cry or scream or make any noise at all. She just sat there unable to control her teeth from clacking together. Her whole body began to shake, and then she felt a wail come out of her that didn't sound human. She was never going to see Nonna again?

Her mind went from the magical image of Nonna disappearing from the Hallmark shop to an image of Nonna laying on the dirty asphalt in the parking lot. She felt a searing pain in her head. Is that how Nonna died? Was that her last view of the world? She thought about how Nonna must have suffered, from both the heart attack and the blow of her body hitting the pavement. She couldn't stop seeing how dirty it was, and Nonna's precious face, laying there amidst garbage and oil and spit-out chewing gum. While her body shook, she dialed her dad's work number. Someone at the warehouse told her he was on sales calls and didn't know when he'd be back. She went downstairs to see if her mother had left a note saying when she would be home. She found nothing. She picked up the phone in the kitchen and called Aunt Hope. How would she tell her? What would she say? She decided right then that it just wasn't true, that Aunt Hope would say, *Nonna is sitting right here, honey. You must have had a bad dream.* And Nonna would get on the phone and say, *Oh, honey, I would never leave you.*

Heather answered the phone and started chatting away, thinking that Jenny called to talk to her. Jenny cut her off and said, "Heather, can I talk to your mom?"

"What's wrong? Are you alone again? What's happening?"

"I just have to talk to your mom."

Jenny heard Heather sigh and yell to her mom, and then the sound of Aunt Hope's heels clicking across the kitchen floor.

Belonging

"Jenny? Hi, sweetie. What's up? Are you okay?"

The concern in Aunt Hope's voice made her finally begin to cry, and Aunt Hope said, "Oh, my goodness. Honey, what is it?"

Jenny said, "Is Nonna there?" She held on to a shred of hope that she was in a bad dream but braced herself for the answer she knew would come.

"No, I haven't seen Nonna today. What's wrong, honey?"

Jenny began to sob. In between her cries, she was able to say, "A lady called from the hospital and said Nonna had a heart attack and died. They need someone to go down there."

Jenny heard Aunt Hope gasp and call out to Uncle Joe. "Oh my God. We'll go right now. Jenny, are you alone?"

"Yes."

"I'll be right over. Uncle Joe will go to the hospital. I'll bring you to our house."

"You should go with Uncle Joe. I'm not feeling well. I just want to stay home." Jenny knew she couldn't put herself in Aunt Hope's kitchen right now, or in Heather's bedroom, or anywhere they could watch her or try to comfort her. She didn't want any witnesses. She didn't want anyone to touch her. She just wanted to be alone.

When she hung up the phone, she went into her bedroom and was met with the unexpected anguish of seeing Nonna's cot, perfectly made up with her floral comforter and her soft feather pillow, and a pair of her shiny boots on the floor. She picked up Nonna's pillow and smelled it, and the pain of being able to smell Nonna without feeling her was something she'd never felt before. She was reaching for someone she couldn't touch, for arms that could not hold her, for a love and comfort that were gone. She opened her window and stepped out onto the rooftop. Sitting on the loose green gravel, she held onto Nonna's pillow, and looked up at the early evening sky, the faint quarter moon, and wondered where Nonna was now. She watched the porch lights turn on next door, then the pool lights, the water shifting from darkness to a glowing pale blue. She sat back against the house, closed her eyes, put her face in Nonna's pillow, and rocked and sobbed.

Her need for Nonna was so great. Nonna was the person who nurtured and adored her, who held her and made her feel cherished. She thought of the last time she saw Nonna. It was on her way to her bridge group last night. She was wearing one of the pantsuits she had in almost every color, and last night she wore it in navy, with shiny red patent leather boots. Her hair had been set with rollers and sprayed so that it sat on her head like a helmet—her "bridge hair." She'd dropped off some rigatoni and cauliflower fritters in the kitchen and sat next to Jenny on the bed and played her the new John Prine album. She was so excited about all the words, so many words. Jenny sat on the rooftop long enough to become cold, and then went back inside and got under her covers. She stared at Nonna's cot, and in her mind, she kept hearing "Bruised Orange (Chain of Sorrow)," a John Prine song about certain types of pain that you carry all through your life. Unable to sleep and no longer wanting to be alone, she picked up the phone and called Henry and asked if he could come over.

Henry arrived at about nine o'clock with a plate of cookies and said, "My dad said to bring these to you." He put the plate down on her window seat. "I'm sorry about Nonna."

Jenny pulled on the ends of her hair with both hands. "How could she just die?"

Henry sat next to her on the bed. "I don't know."

Jenny put her face in her hands and began to cry again. Henry patted her on the back and looked around her room and said, "Where do you keep your box of prayer cards?"

"In my bottom drawer."

"What do you usually do with them?"

"Sometimes I look for one that will help me. Sometimes I sort them, spread them out around the room."

"Should we look for some about heaven? Would that help?"

"I don't know."

"Let's try."

Jenny sat on the floor next to Henry and emptied the box between them. They were quiet as they read through the prayer cards, looking for anything that could ease the pain and emptiness she felt.

Belonging

Henry held a prayer card in his hand, studied it for a while, and said, "What was Nonna's favorite song?"

Jenny tapped her chin, looked at the ceiling, and shook her head. Tears welled up in her eyes again. "I don't know. I can't believe I don't know."

Henry stood and walked to the pile of albums on Jenny's dresser. "Are these Nonna's?"

Jenny nodded, and Henry pulled Jean Shepard's *Lonesome Love* from the pile and put it on. Before the album was over, they had both fallen asleep on the floor, piles of prayer cards beside them.

Sometime after midnight, Jenny heard her parents' bedroom door slam shut, the loud wailing of her mother down the hall, and opened her eyes to find her dad standing in the doorway of her room. The Jean Shepard album was skipping and whirring; the plate of cookies sat half-eaten on the window seat; and Henry was asleep next to her on the floor, his arm draped across her shoulder, his hand clutching one of her braids. Her dad gestured to Henry on the floor and said, "I'll bring him home." Jenny moved Henry's hand and gently shook his shoulder to wake him. She got up and pulled the needle from the album, and Henry stood and stretched. He patted her on the back and said he'd be back tomorrow and followed her dad down the stairs.

As soon as she heard her dad's car drive away, anxiety joined her sadness, as she realized she was now alone in the house with her mother. She listened for any sounds coming from her parents' bedroom. She hoped to hear the thud of her mother dropping into bed, but instead, she heard pacing, a glass being set down, crying. She was unable to settle herself, listening for the turn of a doorknob, for footsteps in the hall. She straightened the blankets on Nonna's cot. She organized Nonna's albums. She zipped and unzipped Nonna's boots. She thought about her wedding ring. Who removed it? Where was it now? She imagined someone sliding Nonna's precious silver wedding band from her finger and placing it in a plastic bag of her belongings at the hospital.

She picked up the one prayer card that Henry had set aside. It had an image of Jesus holding the lost lamb. On the back was a quote from Luke 15:4–7: *Which of you men, if you had one hundred sheep and lost one of them, wouldn't leave the ninety-nine in the wilderness and go after the one that was lost, until he found it?* She held it for a while, wondering why Henry chose this particular card when it had nothing to do with heaven; then again, it was just like Henry to not follow any assignment, even his own. She picked up the card she had selected. It was one she knew well, the Prayer of Saint Francis, which read in part: *Grant that I may not so much seek to be consoled as to console; to be understood as to understand; to be loved, as to love. For it is giving that we receive, it is in pardoning that we are pardoned, and it is in dying that we are born to Eternal Life.*

When she heard her dad arrive home a half hour later, she got into bed and held onto Henry's prayer card. She decided he must have selected it because he knew she was lost but refused to let her believe she was alone. She said a prayer of gratitude for his friendship, and for her own healing, both physical and emotional, infected lung and broken heart. She prayed for Nonna, imagining her on the hilltop in *Our Town*, talking to all the people who died before her. She imagined her hugging Nonno, who she'd lost more than a decade ago; greeting her childhood friend, Edith, who'd died of polio; saying hello to her sister-in-law, Beatrice. She fell asleep wondering if it was true that sunny days and rainy days and snow would somehow, someday make her not miss Nonna so much.

A couple of days later, Uncle Joe, Aunt Hope, and Uncle Gino came over to take the cot out of Jenny's room. Uncle Joe sat with her mother downstairs, while Aunt Hope and Uncle Gino went up to Jenny's room. Aunt Hope and Jenny carefully folded Nonna's bedding and put it in a basket. Uncle Gino folded up the cot and rolled it into the hallway. Then the three of them held each other and wept as they looked at the empty space in Jenny's room. Jenny passed Nonna's pillow around, and they each held that too.

The next week was the funeral, but Jenny's mother told her she couldn't attend. Jenny needed to go so badly that she went behind her mother's back and begged her father to let her go. She walked out into his workshop and said, "Please take me to Nonna's funeral."

He said, "I'm sorry, baby. We don't think it's a good idea, with the valley fever and all."

"It's just sitting in church. I'm not contagious. It's no different than sitting in my room. I need to go. I have to be there."

"Jenny, the funeral will be hard enough on your mother as is. We won't be able to handle the funeral and you at the same time."

Jenny didn't understand what that meant. Her parents had never "handled" her. Since Nonna died, she'd kept her feelings to herself; she hadn't burdened them at all. She didn't let them know she cried herself to sleep every night, that she felt a loneliness she'd never felt before. They didn't notice that she'd barely eaten and hadn't showered or brushed her hair or changed her nightgown for days. She didn't tell them she was struggling with her faith, wondering why God would take Nonna when she needed her so much. Attending Nonna's funeral was the only way to properly say goodbye and honor Nonna's life. The thought of not being able to do so made her feel like she couldn't breathe. So, she refused to relent, kept pleading, but in the end, her father merely raised a hand to halt her voice, turned, and left her alone in his workshop.

On the day nearly everyone she knew went to pray and say goodbye to Nonna, Jenny's father brought her a donut that she would feed to the birds. Henry came over and they lit a candle on her rooftop, read aloud the Prayer of Saint Francis, and played a few hymns from Merle Haggard's gospel album. When her parents came home, she heard muffled arguing from their bedroom again. She heard her father say her name. She heard her mother tell him that he'd "better be careful." She heard her father say something about "neighbors." Her mother responded, "you would never do that" and her father said something about "someday." There was a slammed door, loud footsteps on the stairs, the sound of her dad's car engine.

The next morning, Uncle Gino brought Jenny a pile of leftover prayer cards from Nonna's funeral, and a small book called *The Greatest Thing in the World*. He told her that the book was very old, written in 1874. He said that he turned to it in times of grief and loss because it makes a powerful case that our love for someone, and their love for us, is eternal. Jenny thumbed through the book and saw that he had underlined the passage: *To love abundantly is to live abundantly, and to love forever is to live forever.* She marked the page with one of Nonna's prayer cards, looked up at Uncle Gino and said, "I'm worried I didn't get to pray for

Nonna in church. What if she doesn't know why I wasn't there? What if she didn't get my prayers?"

"Oh, my dear child." Uncle Gino sat on the bed next to Jenny and put his arm around her. "People can always feel the love and prayers you send them. That's just the way it works. It doesn't matter where you are or where they are. They can be in heaven or on Earth. You can be in a church or in your room. You don't have to hold them or speak to them or see them. You can just sit by yourself and love them and know that they will feel your love wherever they are. Your Nonna feels every stitch of your love. I promise."

Jenny hugged Uncle Gino and told him about the ceremony she and Henry held for Nonna.

"What joy Nonna must have felt seeing you on your rooftop playing Merle Haggard for her!" He held her face in his hands and said, "Your Nonna loved abundantly. And so do you. It will carry forward. It will outlast our lifetimes."

When Uncle Gino left, Jenny studied Nonna's prayer card. On the front was a picture of Nonna just like she looked on her bridge days. Her head was tilted to the side, and she smiled broadly. Jenny had seen the picture before. It was on the wall at the Hallmark store when Nonna was employee of the month. She wished it had been a more natural picture of Nonna. On the back were the words, *Marion Vitelli Moretti, November 7, 1913–April 21, 1978,* and a poem about a fallen leaf and "the bright sun's kindly rays" and hearing God's promise "in every robin's song." Jenny wished it had been one of Nonna's favorite prayers or a Hail Mary or even a song lyric. She wished for something more dignified, more like her Nonna. She sat on her bed and laid the prayer cards out in rows, Nonna's smiling Hallmark face looking up at her over and over again.

Chapter Four

MAY 1978

In May, a blood test revealed that Jenny's valley fever had gained momentum. She was referred to Andrew Martin, a young air force doctor who'd had some success with a new treatment. Immediately after meeting Jenny and looking at her serology, Dr. Martin admitted her to Mercy Hospital, where Nonna died just a month before.

Dr. Martin recommended that Jenny receive an intravenous treatment of the drug Amphotericin B. He explained to her parents that the drug would probably kill the valley fever fungus, but due to its many side effects, it was considered a drug of "last resort." Jenny wondered what that meant. Would she die without the treatment? Would the valley fever live in her body forever? Could the treatment hurt her more than help her? As Dr. Martin reviewed the "consent to treat" papers with her parents, Jenny heard the words: *Intravenous. Aggressive. Convulsions. Nausea.*

She watched them sign the papers without reading them, and for the first time during her illness, she feared for her life. Grave and consequential decisions were being made about her body by parents who were both neglectful and indifferent. She no longer had Nonna as a backstop. She was not yet fourteen, but it occurred to her that *she* should be asking the questions. What questions would Nonna ask? She thought of calling Henry to see if he could sneak her out of the hospital. She thought of all the things she hadn't done yet. She'd never even kissed a boy. That afternoon in her hospital bed, she went from trying to advocate for herself, to wanting to flee, to giving up and giving in to the fear that she might die very young. At the height of her worry, an old, familiar numbness took over, and she left her own body. She rubbed the scar on her inner elbow and just let herself disappear.

Later that night, Dr. Martin sat on the edge of Jenny's bed and touched the veins in each of her hands. He had thick black hair and twinkly blue eyes, and Jenny thought he looked a little like John Travolta. He looked right at her and said, "This is going to work, and you are going to be a strong and healthy girl again."

Jenny felt tears pop into her eyes and turned her head away from him.

"It's okay. There's no need to be afraid. Ask me any questions you like."

She looked down at her hands and asked, "How does the IV stay stuck in my skin? Won't it hurt?"

He smiled and told her, "You'll have a topical anesthesia, so you won't feel it, probably at all. Maybe just the tugging of the skin around it."

Jenny touched the tops of her hands, as she thought of how to word her next question. She looked up at Dr. Martin. "Could I die?'

Dr. Martin shook his head and said, "Not on my watch." He explained to her carefully and thoroughly, in words she could understand, how the treatment was going to get rid of the valley fever. He told her about the side effects and also how rare they were. He said he would not have recommended the treatment if he believed it would do her harm. Jenny felt relieved and understood that she could rely on this doctor, that she wasn't alone.

She was quiet for a minute, and asked, "Will I be able to have babies?" It was a question she'd tucked away the day she looked up the words *sterile* and *offspring*, but this was her opportunity, and she knew Dr. Martin would tell her the truth.

"How many would you like?" Dr. Martin asked.

"Maybe about four."

"Well, that would be a very big family. You'll have to get healthy and put some weight on first. And you'll have to finish school. And find a husband."

Jenny found herself smiling despite the fact that she was in a drab hospital room on the night before a needle would push poison into her veins and decided that she loved this doctor. Besides looking like John Travolta, he was calm and smart and he listened to her. Before he left her room, he told her that the treatment would not affect her ability to have babies, that she could have as many as she wanted. He said that he and his wife had two children, and he winked when he said he couldn't imagine four.

As she sat in the hospital room alone that night, she couldn't stop thinking about the IV. She hated the idea of something threaded into her skin that she couldn't take out. She hated the word *tugging*. Unable to sleep, Jenny went to her suitcase and took out the box of prayer cards she'd brought from home. On top were all the cards about orphans she'd become interested in since she'd lost Nonna. She dumped the prayer cards out and placed them in neat rows on her bed. When she was done, she slid under the covers, leaving the prayer cards spread out on top of her. The colorful squares formed a quilt and she slept covered in prayers.

The next morning, she held her breath and said the Hail Mary in her head while a nurse stuck a needle into her hand and taped it to her skin. Her parents were there when they hooked up the bags and she received her first dose of Amphotericin B. Her father sat in a chair in the corner of the room, looking at the floor, his hands clasped in his lap. Her mother held onto his arm, her face buried in his shoulder.

Within a half hour, Jenny was nauseous and having violent convulsions. She prayed as she shook and was afraid of being unable to control her own body. Then, she startled as her mother rushed toward the bed, threw herself on top of her, and pinned her down. Her mother's black hair swished across her face and her hands circled her own like handcuffs. Nauseous and spinning, Jenny was now confined, weighed down, and all she could smell was cigarettes and dirty hair. She wished she could push her mother off. But she was also somehow touched by her mother's attempt to stop her from shaking. So as her head spun and her body shook, revulsion and need did battle inside of her. She squeezed her eyes shut and just kept saying the Hail Mary.

When the bags were empty, their contents dumped into her veins, the nurse moved her mother off the bed. Jenny dragged the IV stand into the bathroom and threw up. As soon as she got back in bed, wet hair sticking to her face, she asked the nurse, "Can you take the needle out now?"

She felt the tugging of the tape and her skin being pushed down as the nurse removed the needle. When it was out, the nurse iced and bandaged Jenny's swollen hand and told her they'd switch to the other hand tomorrow. About thirty minutes later, her parents slunk out of the room, her dad unable to meet her eyes, her mother overly chatty with hospital staff. Jenny decided to ask Dr. Martin if it was okay that her parents not come to any more treatments. She wanted to believe that her mother throwing herself on top of her was an act of love. What she really believed, was that it was an act, *period.* Janice Hayes was acting the part of the heroic mother. This belief was confirmed when she watched her mother tell Dr. Martin *how awful it was to see her daughter suffer* and noticed that the words were delivered with a glint of excitement in her eye, her mouth upturned as if she were about to smile.

That night, Uncle Gino appeared at her door, round and olive-skinned like Nonna, gray hair tucked behind his ears. Seeing him standing there, holding a bag of cookies, she felt comfort for the first time since being admitted to the hospital.

He said, "Hello, *mi passerotta*," a term of endearment which means "little sparrow" in Italian, something he'd been calling her since she was a baby.

"Hi, Uncle G."

"Do you feel up to a little company?"

Jenny nodded and said, "Sure."

"One treatment down?"

"Yeah."

"I sure miss you at work. I have so many boxes to sort." Uncle Gino handed Jenny the bag of cookies and sat down in a chair by the bed.

She opened the bag, handed a cookie to him, and said, "I miss Nonna so much."

"I know, sweetheart. I do too. You know what helps me sometimes?"

"What?"

"I pick a favorite day I spent with Nonna, and I replay it in my mind, every stitch of it, and when I'm done, it feels like we've been together again. Can you think of a day with Nonna you'd like to replay?"

"So many."

"Pick one. And I'll sit here and do the same, and I bet it'll feel like she's right here with us."

"Okay, I pick my last sleepover at Nonna's house, in the summer, before school started."

"Excellent. I pick the day Nonna helped me plant my rose garden and we had a picnic in my front yard."

Jenny smiled at him and said, "Excellent."

She closed her eyes and imagined herself falling asleep at Nonna's house, the smell of rosemary, cinnamon, and coffee drifting from the kitchen into her warm room. She imagined Nonna sitting on the edge of the bed in her nightgown and gardening boots, whispering, "They're out. And they're eating all our vegetables. Get your boots on." She pulled on the gardening boots Nonna kept at her house for her, and together, they marched into the garden in their cotton nightgowns. Nonna shined the light on the neat rows of carrots, onions, and lettuce. Jenny had never seen so many snails, and she watched as Nonna started stomping away. *Crunch, squish, crunch, squish, crunch, squish.* Jenny followed, doing her part, until the garden was a glistening mess of snail guts and shells. When they got back into the house, Nonna put some Saltines and Velveeta on a plate and put on a Johnny Cash album. Together, they ate the crackers and cheese and danced and twirled in the kitchen.

Lying in her hospital bed, Jenny wished she could make the memory last longer. What had they done the next morning? *Nonna served her cappuccino in a tiny white cup. They folded laundry in front of the "Million Dollar Movie." Jenny refilled the bowl of Coffee Nips. Nonna cut a single orange-pink rose from her garden and put it in a bud vase.* Jenny opened her eyes and saw that Uncle Gino's were still closed. His cheeks were pink, he had a small smile, and he had cookie crumbs on his shirt. He looked just like a sweet, chubby angel.

After enduring the third day of Amphotericin treatments, Dr. Martin practically skipped into Jenny's hospital room and announced that the valley fever was gone. She wouldn't need any more treatments, and she could go back to school and graduate with her class in June. She stayed up half the night in her hospital room and imagined sitting behind Billy in photography class, walking home with Henry, sleeping over at Heather's. She also thought about all she'd endured since the dust storm, and she knew she would be going back to school a different person than when she left. She had experienced both the loss of Nonna and her own serious illness. She had questioned and confronted mortality in a way that most young people never have to do. While she took comfort in knowing that a band of loved ones—Henry, Uncle Gino, Heather, Billy, Aunt Hope, and Nonna—surrounded her and helped her through this dark and frightening time, a very persistent voice inside of her told her that she should rely only on herself. She drew strength from the image of the "fierce" Mary—the one who was fearless, the one whose primary characteristic was to persevere. She resolved to stop playing dead and stop numbing herself. She promised to never again leave her own body.

After the valley fever, she also saw her parents in a new light—the months at home, Nonna's death, and her hospitalization giving her knowledge that she didn't possess before. She saw how early in the day her mother started drinking, how hard her father worked to please her mother, how secondary she was to her parents' own relationship and lives. She saw their lack of preparedness for anything, their failure to seek or to learn. Perhaps the most compelling thing Jenny observed was how other people reacted to her mother's lack of care. For the first time, she understood that she was missing something most people never had to think about—the natural, rooted feeling of a mother's love. She wondered what that would be like, if it would've fundamentally changed her, and she figured that she wouldn't know until she had children of her own. She knew that one day, she would make her own family and her own home. Her children would be cared for and loved. They would have hot meals and full cupboards and Sunday dinners. They would be read to and tucked into bed and kissed goodnight. Her home would be clean and open and filled with light, and it would feel completely different from Lupine Lane.

On the Saturday before Jenny returned to school, Uncle Gino took her to the Union Cemetery, so she could finally see Nonna's grave. Jenny was moved by the cemetery's history and the knowledge that Nonna's whole family was there, beneath thatches of grass, stems, and roots, shaded by poplar and oak trees. Slightly elevated above town, it reminded her of the hilltop cemetery in Grover's Corners, where Emily sat in a chair and reviewed the most typical and beautiful day of her life with all those who went before her.

"This is how you will always be able to find our family," Uncle Gino said, as they approached the elevated cross on the far west side of the cemetery. "When you are facing the cross from the road, we are just behind it, at the right hand of the Father, so to speak. Let's walk the block."

Uncle Gino explained that the block included the sixteen graves between the cross and the pathway—all of which held members of her family, most of whom died long before she was born. He told her that the stones all faced east to west in anticipation of the dead rising upon the return of Christ. She wasn't prepared to see the joint gravestone that held a place for Uncle Gino next to his wife, Beatrice, who he'd lost in a car accident in 1953. Uncle Gino touched her name, next to his name and said, "Good morning, my Honey Bea."

She already had tears in her eyes when they arrived at Nonna's grave. Jenny was shaken by the broken rectangle of grass in front of her headstone, earth that hadn't yet grown back together after her burial. She put her hand on the rectangle of dirt surrounding Nonna's grave and said, "Uncle G? Where do you think Nonna is right now?"

Uncle Gino put a hand to his heart and said, "Why, she's right in here. Can't you feel her?"

Jenny closed her eyes and put her hand over her heart. "Sometimes. I wish it were all the time."

"You know how people say, 'I know that song by heart' or 'I know that recipe by heart'? Don't you think we know Nonna by heart?"

Jenny tapped her chin and looked at the sky. She pictured Nonna's almond-shaped eyes and gentle smile. She searched for the scent of her gardenia perfume and Coffee Nip candies and listened for the sound of her soft voice. Soon, she realized it was all there. She looked at Uncle Gino and said, "I do know Nonna by heart. Do you?"

Uncle Gino smiled and said, "I do." He put a hand on her shoulder and asked if she remembered the story about Saint Francis, Saint Clare, and the roses.

Jenny shook her head.

"Well, when Saint Francis was leaving on a long journey, Saint Clare was sad, and asked him when they would be together again. It was winter and snowing out, and Saint Francis said, 'When summer returns and the roses are again in bloom.' And just then, roses bloomed all over the snow."

"I remember that now. Saint Clare picked the roses and gave them to Saint Francis."

Uncle Gino smiled and said, "Do you remember what it means?"

Jenny sat down against Nonna's headstone and closed her eyes. She listened to the sound of plastic windmills whipping in circles on a grave of a boy across the way. There was a breeze, and she could smell citrus trees and roses. She opened her eyes and said, "It means that we will never be separated from people we love, no matter how far away we are."

On the way home from the cemetery, they stopped at the bakery and picked up a box of cookies and went to the antique store, so that Uncle Gino could set up a new window display. He flipped on the lights and the ceiling fan inside the store and turned on the oldies station. He told Jenny to look around and see if there was anything she'd like. She wandered through the aisles, while Uncle Gino set up an easel in the window and sang along to "Moon River."

While rummaging through a box of quilts, Jenny looked up and noticed a painting hanging on a wall. She stared at it for a long time—a vivid scene of a household that nearly shouted at her. She took it down and rubbed her hand over the acrylic. She lifted it to her nose. It smelled like mothballs, like it had been packed away in a closet for years. The painting depicted a large family gathered around a stone fireplace. There was a table set for dinner, a cat asleep in a chair. There were four children—a girl dancing, a boy holding a bird, another boy playing the violin, a baby being cradled by a woman. There was an old man carrying firewood. The room was warm and full of books and color. The table was filled with food. There were windows open to blue sky and green fields. Jenny turned the painting over and looked at the back. The artist had signed it and written the title: "*Belonging.*" Uncle Gino walked down the aisle and found her holding the painting.

"There you are. What are you looking at, dear?"

Belonging

Jenny held up the painting and said, "I'd like to buy this."

Uncle Gino reached for it and said, "Hmm. What do you think this is? A farmhouse of some sort? A party scene?"

Jenny said, "I think it's my house."

"Your house?"

Jenny touched the edge of the painting and said, "Yes. The house I'm going to make some day. It's going to be like this."

Uncle Gino closed his eyes for what seemed like a long time. When he opened them, he placed his index finger on the end of her nose and said, "I believe you."

He carried the painting to the counter and studied it again before wrapping it up. "Is that me carrying the firewood?"

Jenny nodded and said, "Yes, that's you."

When she got home that afternoon, she retrieved a hammer and nail from her father's workshop and hung the painting over her bed.

Chapter Five

MAY 1978

On the day Jenny returned to school, Henry and his dad picked her up with a plate of hot cinnamon rolls that Mr. Hansen had baked that morning. Jenny was nervous after being away for so long. So much had happened in the corridors and classrooms while she was home in bed. It was like walking into a movie after missing half of it. She didn't cross paths with Billy until photography class. He was already in his seat in the second row, looking over some proof sheets, when she walked in the door. She took her old seat near the back and opened her notebook. Her last entry was from the day of the dust storm. Tucked in the front was the project she'd prepared documenting her time with valley fever.

That week in photography class, they were allowed to leave the schoolyard every day to take pictures for their final. The project gave Jenny and Billy nearly an hour a day to wander around together photographing whatever they noticed, each sharing what they loved about photography. Billy loved the technical aspects—composition, lighting, and aperture. He loved to stand in the darkroom and watch an image materialize, revealing himself to be serious and thoughtful. Jenny loved capturing something exactly as she saw it, reproducing and printing it. It was a moment in time that could be taken from her memory and placed in her hands, revealing herself to be romantic and watchful.

The project also gave them a lot of time to talk. Every day, they walked from school to a nearby park. The park was small—just a circle of grass, a few shady trees, and an old swing set. They sat under a large old oak tree and Billy told Jenny about working with a pitching coach and a trainer every day after school. He told her that his dad wouldn't let him play on the school basketball team for fear he could get injured. He told her about his plans to photograph the Tehachapi Loop someday. Jenny told Billy what it was like being in the hospital, the lonely months at home, how much she really liked *Our Town*. She told him about the painting she'd found in Uncle Gino's store. When she told him about Nonna dying and not being able to go to the funeral, he put his hand on her shoulder. They talked about summer vacation, which was now just about a month away. Billy would be working in the sheds, boxing canta-loupes and watermelons, and playing in a summer league. Jenny would be working at the antique store, and she and Henry bought summer movie passes at Stockdale 6.

That Friday, the Spring Dance was held in the same dusty cafeteria where they'd been cooped up the day of the dust storm. Henry was lead-ing a conga line through the lunch tables. He'd asked a girl to dance, and she had to haplessly follow him around as he held her hands on his hips, kicked his legs from side to side, and added more girls to his line. Jenny was sitting on a bench, watching him, when Billy sat next to her.

"Hi," he said. "Want to dance on a slow song?"

Jenny turned toward Billy and noticed that his eyes looked more pale green than hazel tonight. She spread her fingers over her skirt and said, "Sure."

While they sat side by side, she felt his arm against hers, smelled his sweet aftershave, and wondered if there was any way he could see how fast her heart was beating. The next slow song, Billy took her hand and walked her out to the dance floor. When Jenny heard the melody coming over the speakers, she got a little shiver. Ronnie Milsap was singing about falling in love and it being almost like a song. She carefully placed her hands on Billy's shoulders, and when he pulled her closer, she tucked them around his neck. They were barely moving, and his hands were holding her so lightly that she could really only feel their heat against her back. It was like he was holding a glass doll.

They were quiet for a while and Billy said, "Do you want to come to my game tomorrow?"

Jenny looked up at him, surprised by the invitation.

"I like you, and you've been gone for so long. I was just hoping I could see you tomorrow. I have to play baseball, though, so maybe you could come to my game?"

Jenny put her head against his chest and said, "I like you too."

When the song ended and the thumping beat of something faster began, Jenny reluctantly stepped away from Billy and said, "Thanks for the dance. I'll come if I can get a ride—to your game tomorrow." Billy held onto her hand and started to say something when Henry swooped in and swept her away in his conga line. "Come on! Miss Wilson is chaperoning! I'm showing her what a playboy I am!"

Jenny held onto Henry and looked back at Billy, who tilted his head to the side, waved, and started walking toward the door.

When she got home that night, Jenny sat up in her room and wrote in her journal for the first time since she'd returned to school. She wanted to remember exactly what this night felt like. She wrote about dancing with Billy, the butterflies in her stomach, the way he held her, how his fingertips touched her hair. She wrote about the color of his eyes, how she could feel his heart beating, how she didn't want the song to end. She wrote that she might even love him and listed all the reasons why her feelings for him were different from her feelings for anyone else in the world. It was as transparent as she'd ever been, every bit of her almost fourteen-year-old self revealed on the page. She scribbled the lyrics to the Ronnie Milsap song in her journal. The ending was so sad, but she liked the idea of loving someone and it feeling almost like a song, plus it was the first song she and Billy danced to, and she wanted to remember that.

The next day, Heather arrived with a bag full of her own clothes, determined to dress Jenny for Billy's game. She picked a pair of cut off jean shorts and an eyelet blouse and said, "Here, try these."

Jenny slid out of her own loose clothing and put on Heather's. As she stood in front of the mirror, Heather walked up behind her and lifted her ponytail.

"Why don't you wear it down? And curl it?"

"For a baseball game?"

Belonging

"Billy Ambler *asked* you to go to his game. That makes it more like a date."

"A date? I might not even get to talk to him. He's playing."

"Trust me. Oh, and when he does talk to you, lick your lips a little. It'll make him want to kiss you." Heather let down Jenny's hair and pulled her into the bathroom where she'd already plugged in a curling iron.

She took a bottle of perfume from her bag and said, "Here. Spray this in your hair, so when he hugs you, he smells it. And put a little bit on the tip of your nose, so when he kisses you, and his nose is right by your nose, he'll breathe it right in."

"Oh my God, Heather! We are not hugging or kissing!"

"We'll see."

Aunt Hope drove them to the ballpark, gave them money to buy Cokes and sunflower seeds, and said she'd be back in two hours. They walked along the dirt path until they found the field where Billy's team was playing and took a seat on the wooden bleachers. Billy was pitching and Jenny watched as he calmly stood on the mound, focused and alert. She thought of the way he held his camera, confident and assured when he pointed his lens and took a photo, and realized it was the same way he held the ball and threw it over the plate.

After the game, Billy walked over to the bleachers, sat down next to Jenny and said, "Hey. Thanks for coming." He took off his hat, put a hand on Jenny's bare knee, and gave her a little sweaty kiss on the side of her mouth. It wasn't on the cheek and it wasn't on the lips, just the corner of her mouth. She hadn't even licked her lips and there it was, her first kiss.

Billy left his hand on her knee and said, "Do you want to get something at the snack shack?"

"Sure." Jenny got down from the bleachers, and Heather sat there eating sunflower seeds. "Aren't you coming?"

"I already have a Coke and seeds. I'll just wait here for you."

As they walked down the path toward the snack shack, Jenny turned to Billy. "You're a really good pitcher."

Billy swung his arm out in front of him, stretched it, reached back and took her hand and said, "Thanks."

Jenny put an image of them in her mind—him in his dirty pinstriped uniform, her in Heather's pretty blouse and cut-offs, walking hand in hand on the path, like they were a couple.

They were sitting at a table next to the snack shack, drinking cans of Dr Pepper and sharing fries, when Heather walked over to say her mom was there to pick them up. Jenny took a last long look at Billy sitting across from her and wished she had her camera. It was exactly the type of image she'd learned to capture, one that would let her hold onto the smell of the warm spring day, the sounds of the baseball park, the color of Billy's eyes. She smiled at Billy, said goodbye, and walked toward the parking lot with Heather. When they were out of earshot, Heather turned to her and said, "Were you smooching some more behind the snack shack?"

"No, just one smooch, right in front of you."

That afternoon, Jenny grabbed her camera and hopped out her bedroom window onto the rooftop. A mourning dove landed not far from where she sat, and she snapped pictures of its soft gray feathers against the green gravel. While she studied the bird, she thought about Billy—holding hands at the baseball game, his hazel eyes under his baseball cap, the tiniest little kiss. She thought about how lucky she was to be healthy and back at school for the remainder of eighth grade. She wondered if Billy was going to be her first boyfriend. She'd never felt so much hope in her whole life.

When she lifted herself back through her window at sundown, she was startled to find her mother sitting on her bed. She was even more startled when she saw her journal opened in her mother's lap. Her mother held it up and said, "I think I'll just hold onto this for now."

"It's my journal. I need it for school."

"You let your teacher read this crap?"

Jenny felt her face grow hot, as shame and embarrassment crept over her. She imagined her mother reading her most personal thoughts with a sneer, gobbling up the information, mocking her childish crush. Jenny reached for her journal, but her mother snapped it back.

"Miss Wilson doesn't usually read them. She just looks to see how many pages we've written."

"I'm on to you. You should know that. And I'll be watching."

Belonging

Her mother flung the journal back on her bed and walked out of the room. Jenny sat and tried to catch her breath. Ever since she became healthy, not confined to her bedroom, a regular teenage girl, she'd noticed how her mother had gone from neglect to an overbearing interest, especially when it involved boys. She wondered how, in the span of five minutes, she went from feeling as joyous and hopeful as she could ever recall to being terrified and ashamed, and she knew the answer to that question had just walked out her bedroom door.

When it came time to select images for the photography final, Jenny went through the images she'd captured for her valley fever project. As she looked at the photos, she realized that her photography had become bolder and more insightful. She'd learned to recognize and reveal subjects at their most natural and contemplative, and the printed images captured the specific time and place and felt alive.

There was the picture of her and Heather in front of her bedroom mirror. Heather is on her knees, braiding Jenny's hair. Heather's long blonde hair, fair skin, and blue eyes; Jenny's dark brown hair, olive skin, and brown eyes. Heather's freckles; the two dimples beneath Jenny's lower lip. There is an expression of care and certainty on Heather's face, an expression of sadness on her own. The contrast is stark—in both appearance and emotion. She remembered the moment, how she'd thanked Heather for braiding her hair; Heather simply replying: *Your mom should be doing this. This is something that moms do.*

There was a series of pictures of Henry sprawled across her bed reading from his journal. Long limbs, pink cheeks, and auburn hair. He's mid-cackle in most, regaling her with his fictional journal entries, an endeavor he embarked upon to prove that Miss Wilson actually did read their journals, and the ones she liked the best detailed their teenage love lives. She recalled her initial discomfort when Henry read aloud his fictional entry about an evening he shared with a *sexy red-headed hooker named Cinnamon and her big pink boobs.* And how that discomfort turned to giddiness, the two of them dissolving into laughter. She

51

remembered thinking that he was the boldest and funniest person she'd ever known, and she was grateful he was her best friend.

There was the picture of Billy, who surprised her one day, appearing in her doorway with some notes from photography class. She remembered being embarrassed by her childish nightgown, her sickly appearance, her bare feet. But he sat in her window seat and was backlit like Carole King, and she asked if she could take his photo. He is beautiful and shy, and the sun shines around his curly hair, his small ears. What she remembered most about that day was that he'd asked her when she was coming back to school, and he'd said, *I miss you.*

There was a series of pictures of the donuts her father left on her nightstand every day, before leaving to work. Maple bars, sprinkle donuts, glazed. He was so sure that donuts would make her feel better that she didn't have the heart to tell him when she lost her appetite for them altogether. Instead of throwing them out, she began tearing them into small pieces and tossing them out the window for the birds on her rooftop, and she began photographing them too. Her favorite photo was of the birds gathered in anticipation of their daily donut, circled around her ankles on the gravel rooftop, eagerly looking up. In the frame, there is nothing but birds, the edge of her nightgown, and her two bare feet.

There were photos of Nonna—sitting on her cot, playing music, carrying plates of food. There were photos of her father—making kites, cutting across the lawn to his workshop, smoking cigarettes on the back patio. There were photos of Uncle Gino—arriving with a gift, eating cookies, napping on Nonna's cot.

For her final, she settled on the photo of Heather braiding her hair, and she called it "Chocolate and Vanilla." The photo was sad, but it was also true, and Jenny liked that it captured this act of care and love. Her second photo was one of Henry laying across her bed, his journal in one hand, the other wildly gesturing. She called this one, "Henry and Cinnamon." Her third photo was of the birds gathered around her on her rooftop, and she called it "Self Portrait." This last photo was the most difficult to choose. Months ago, she thought the image was sullen, that it evoked a poor, lonely child with nowhere to be other than a gravel rooftop, and no one to be with, other than the birds. Now, she saw a girl with purpose, standing tall, feeding the birds that gathered around her. It reminded her of one of her favorite stories about Saint Francis. He was preaching to a group of birds as if they were villagers who spoke the same language. He told them that God gave them their beautiful feathers and wings to fly. The birds responded by stretching their necks and extending their wings. From that day on, Saint Francis preached to all living beings, and even insisted that the birds and animals celebrate Christmas with feasts of their own. With this story in mind, Jenny no longer saw a lonely child, but an image of a strong and faithful girl, honoring the mission of Saint Francis.

Billy chose photos he'd taken in the park, one of a little boy holding a red balloon and crying, and one of an old woman reading to an old man on a park bench. He called them "He Wanted a Purple Balloon" and "Reading Aloud." He was secretive about his third photo, though, so Jenny didn't see it until Mr. Rosenfeld hung each student's prints on the walls of the classroom. She would never forget what it felt like when she saw Billy's last photo. It was the picture he took of her the day of the dust storm, her face filling the frame. Hair blowing, eyes staring straight at the camera, a faint ray of sunlight shining through the dark sky onto her face. Billy called it: "Jenny."

She noticed two things when she saw this photo. First, she looked so much younger on the day of the dust storm. There was a wonder and innocence that maybe weren't there anymore. She knew so much less, and it was revealed in her own large, dark eyes. The second thing she noticed was the way she was looking at Billy. It happened so fast—looking up, seeing his camera pointed toward her, and understanding that she meant something to him. He'd looked for her, out of everyone in the schoolyard. He'd captured her expression, unspooled the image in the dark room, held it in his hands, and made this delicate moment of realization permanent.

On the first Saturday of summer, Billy appeared on Jenny's doorstep in his pinstriped baseball uniform with a gold box in his hands. When she opened the door and saw him, she felt flushed and excited, but also embarrassed. She did a quick glance over her shoulder at the dirty family room and stepped outside, closing the door behind her. It was ten in the morning, and it already felt like it was one hundred degrees outside.

"Hi," she said. "Happy summer."

"I'm starting summer ball today."

Jenny looked up at him. "Maybe I could come and see you play again."

"I hope so." He handed her the gold box and said, "Here. It's your graduation present. Open it. I wrote you a note inside."

She opened the box and took out the note. She felt shy reading it in front of him, but it seemed that he wanted her to. In Billy's all-capital letters handwriting, it said: *Dear Jenny, Happy graduation! Thanks for being a great photography partner! I think the picture of you is the best. I like the way you look in the light. Love, Billy. P.S. We're going to have a great summer!*

She took out the three pictures Billy had selected for his photography final. He had handwritten the titles on the back of each one. "Your pictures," she said. "I love them." Jenny put her arms around his neck and said, "Thank you. It's the best present ever."

Billy smiled and jogged down her driveway, saying he had to get to the field, but he'd call her later. Jenny went up to her bedroom and sat on her bed, unfolded the note, and re-read it. She looked at each picture again. She remembered how Mr. Rosenfeld told them that, in every single frame, you can see the photographer, what he cares about, what's important to him. As she held the picture Billy took of her, she didn't just see herself. She saw Billy, and this one photograph revealed that he liked her as much as she liked him.

Henry showed up in her room later that day with a 45 of The Rolling Stones' new single, "Miss You."

"Have you heard this?" He held it up: Mick touching his hand to his forehead, the band bathed in purple light.

"Of course. They play it on the radio all the time."

"But have you heard the B side?"

Jenny shook her head and Henry dropped the needle and they sat on her window seat and listened to the slow twangy intro to "Far Away Eyes." Henry bobbed his head from side to side and broke out in a broad smile when Mick began to sing about driving through Bakersfield. He let out one of his high-pitched howls. "The Stones are singing about Bakersfield!"

"Why is he singing in that accent? Does he think that's how we talk?"

"I think he's imitating Buck Owens or someone."

They listened to the whole song, and in the end, Jenny thought it was beautiful and wished the delivery had been more sincere. Henry put on the song again, and Jenny took out the gold box and showed him the gift from Billy. Henry held the picture called "Jenny" in his hands for a long time, looked back at her, and then back at the picture.

"What is it?" Jenny asked.

"You have a boyfriend," Henry said, reaching out and touching the top of her head.

"Maybe so."

When it was time for Henry to go home for dinner, Jenny took the 45 from the record player and handed it to him. He put it in the sleeve and handed it back to her. "I bought it for you."

"Oh, you did? Thank you."

After Henry left, she listened to "Far Away Eyes" one more time. She looked at the note and pictures from Billy again, put them back in the gold box, and decided to keep both the photos and the 45 in her drawer next to her prayer cards and her copy of *Our Town*.

Chapter Six

APRIL 1980

During the spring of her sophomore year, Jenny worked as a hostess at King's Table, a cafeteria-style restaurant near the high school. It didn't pay much, but she could walk there, and she could help on the weekends at Uncle Gino's antique store. Her paychecks went straight into the college fund Henry's dad helped her set up, and the manager let her take whatever food she wanted every day after her shift. She'd fill a to-go box and she'd have all the food she needed until her next shift. She didn't have to rely on anyone for meals, and she was able to take enough to feed her dad too.

One afternoon in April, Jenny clocked out, made her box of food, and walked the three blocks back to school for Billy's baseball game. By the time she got to the field, it was already the third inning. She thought Billy would be pitching, but he was on second base. She noticed Billy's dad, Ray, a tall man with an athletic build and dark hair, holding a clipboard and pacing along the third base line. In the remaining innings, Billy threw out a player at home, and he hit a line drive to the left field fence for a double and a game-winning RBI. After the game, Jenny met Billy outside the locker room.

"Hey," he said, reaching an arm around her waist and kissing her on the cheek.

"Hi. You had a good game."

Billy shook his head and laughed a little and said, "Ha! Clearly, you missed the first few innings."

"That's true. I did. What happened? Did you pitch?"

Belonging

Billy tossed his bat bag into the back of his truck. "I tried to. I walked a guy. I beaned a guy. I gave up two hits. I basically sucked. They moved me to second and put Kyle in to pitch."

Jenny put her hand on his cheek and swept his hair out of his eyes. "Everyone has an off day, Billy." She leaned down and opened her box of food. "Here, do you want a snack?"

Billy shook his head. "I'm okay."

On the way home, Jenny turned on the radio and sat close to Billy. Her favorite Kenny Rogers song was on, and she turned it up and put her hand on Billy's knee as he drove. They'd been together for two years now, almost exactly. Jenny sat next to his mom at baseball games and had Sunday dinners with his family. Billy drove her to the cemetery and kept her company while she visited Nonna. They'd begun talking about getting married someday.

When they got to Billy's house, his mom and dad were in the kitchen unloading groceries together. Billy's dad set down a box of cereal when he saw them and said, "Jenny, do you mind helping Peggy in the kitchen while I take Billy out back for a bit?"

Jenny knew that the question was rhetorical, a formality—*Do you mind?*—but the truth was, she did mind. Billy had been holding his arm all the way home, and she'd noticed that the interior of his elbow had a patch of yellow and gray bruises. When she asked him about them, he told her that sometimes they just appear and they were no big deal, but she didn't think that was true.

"Oh, he's not throwing anymore, is he?" Jenny asked.

Billy let his chin fall to his chest, grabbed his mitt, and just walked out the sliding glass door. His dad followed, picking up his clipboard and a bucket of balls on the way. "We're just throwing a few. We'll be back before you know it."

After the door slid closed, Jenny turned to Billy's mom and said, "He has bruises on the inside of his elbow."

Billy's mom put a hand on her shoulder. "I'll make sure he ices it tonight."

It wasn't the first time Jenny had been a part of this scene. Over the past couple of years, she'd come to know his family well. Billy's dad had once been a baseball star too, and he pushed Billy in a way that seemed unreasonable to her but that Billy seemed to blindly accept as part of being Ray Ambler's son.

Ray was raised in a tin-roofed house in Florida, the son of a fisherman and homemaker. His father hadn't shown any interest in his baseball career. He rose and left before Ray went to school, drank in the evenings, and never went to his games. Ray arrived in Bakersfield in the early 1960s to play on the Phillies minor league team. He was a backup catcher who barely saw playing time. When he was let go by the team, he'd already met Billy's mom at the apartment complex in the southwest part of town where they both lived, so he decided to stay. He got a job selling automated adding machines, discovered he was a very good salesman, and soon became responsible for the entire region.

When Billy was born, Ray wanted to do things differently with his own son. He wanted to acknowledge his talent, give him the best tools, help him fulfill the dream that had eluded him, and he had the time and money to make it happen. When Billy was old enough to hold a bat, he began training him. At ten, he hired a private pitching coach. At twelve, people started talking about Billy the way they once talked about Ray. By Billy's freshman year, colleges were already sending letters. Billy was never allowed to play any other sports, or even ride a skateboard, because Ray didn't want him to get injured and jeopardize his baseball career.

Jenny walked to the window and watched Billy wince as he threw a fastball to his dad. She'd seen this before—his dad working him out when he was already in pain. Usually, the pain is what made him have a bad game in the first place. His velocity would drop, and he would become less effective because he was subconsciously protecting his arm. His dad would work him harder, and the cycle continued; Jenny was never sure if Billy ever really healed. When they came in about twenty minutes later, Billy's dad was slapping him on the back, saying his adjustment made all the difference. Billy was sweaty and holding his elbow.

During dinner, Billy's dad talked about all the colleges interested in him and campus visits he was planning for the summer—some of them as far as the Midwest. It brought up the inevitable, that someday Billy would move somewhere far away. Someday there would be more to his life than school and baseball and Bakersfield and her. After dinner, Jenny helped Billy's mom in the kitchen, while Billy took some pictures in the backyard. He was on top of the swimming pool slide, looking toward the oil fields, when he called Jenny to come outside.

Jenny climbed the ladder to the slide and Billy held the camera over her eye.

"Take a look," he said.

Billy was shooting the unusual coupling of the colorful lights on the oil rigs as the sun hung low in the sky. The background was orange and gold, and the foreground was dotted in primary colors.

"The lights look so pretty." She wrapped her arms around his waist and said, "You're going to colleges this summer?"

"Nothing's set up yet. We'll probably just go to California schools. You should come with us."

Jenny didn't answer him. When she imagined him on the campus of one of the big Pac-10 schools he always talked about, she never saw herself with him. And when she tried to imagine herself on a college campus, somehow it always got blurry. She put her head on his shoulder and looked back toward the setting sun and the blinking lights of the oil fields.

When Billy dropped Jenny off at home, her mother was sitting at the bar in the kitchen with Linda and Judy, talking and laughing. Linda had Farrah Fawcett hair and buggy eyes that made her always look startled; Judy reminded her of a bobblehead doll because her head wiggled back and forth on her long neck after too much wine. Jenny waved hello and went straight upstairs.

Later that night, Jenny was studying in her room when her mother leaned against the door, her arms folded across her chest, and said, "I think at some point you should consider spending time with someone other than Billy."

Jenny looked up, startled, and regrouped, realizing that the turn had taken place from the happy drunk with Linda and Judy to the mean drunk who had no one in the house to stop her.

"The only thing that boy has going for him is throwing a ball. What happens when that's over? Seems like a tragic waste of time to me."

Carefully choosing her words, Jenny said, "I have plenty of friends."

"You do? Like who? Henry? He's a freak. He's not normal. Heather? She'll be pregnant before she gets to beauty school."

Jenny listened to her mother describe her boyfriend, her best friend, and her cousin in the same harsh way she categorized everyone—a waste, a freak, a slut. She didn't want to engage or defend, knowing they were alone in the house. She didn't want to reveal the way her mother's comments made her feel—sickened, angry, disgusted. She put on a face of pure stone, eyes that were dead, emotionless, and calmly said, "I should get back to my homework." Jenny had learned this tactic from her dad and had maybe unconsciously adopted it. She knew how to stop all her feelings and utter the right words in the right tone to survive any encounter.

Her mother snorted and shook her head and said, "You are one cool customer. Most people don't know that about you. They just see this studious girl with minimal personality. But I see you. I've always seen you. You are cold as they come. Your father and I have known that since before you could talk."

Jenny felt the prick of tears but fought them off. She held onto the stone face and said nothing. When her mother turned and walked out of the room, Jenny felt the rage inside her body. She stared at her flashcards, but couldn't focus. She kept hearing the words: *waste, freak, cold.* It wasn't the first time her mother described her as "cold." She was cold when she sat expressionless and listened to names she was called. She was cold when she found it difficult to be touched by or even in close physical proximity to her mother. She noted that, this time, her mother had looped her father into the harsh assessment. She imagined that, if he'd been home to speak for himself, he probably would've just gone along with it. He'd say almost anything to appease her mother, even if it was a cruel judgment pronounced upon his only child.

She opened her window and went out onto the gravel rooftop and sat down. She leaned her head back against the house, just below the light from her window. Spring evenings always brought a different smell to Bakersfield, one that was less musky, cleaner. She could smell lemon blossoms and honeysuckle, dirt and grass, chlorine from her neighbor's swimming pool. She thought of dinner at Billy's house and wondered if she was supposed to have a real plan for college already. She reached into her room and pulled the phone outside and dialed Henry. When he answered, she said, "Have you thought about where you want to go to college?"

"Sort of. Somewhere cool, with you. Why?"

"Billy's going on campus visits this summer. And that made me think it's time to figure it out for myself. I need to know that I'm getting out of here."

"What's wrong? Did something happen tonight?"

"Just the usual stuff. My mom came in and said some mean things. She called me cold. She said my dad thinks I'm cold too."

"God, I hate that bitch. Put her voice out of your head."

"I'll try. I always try."

"Good. Now where should we go to college? East coast? L.A.? San Francisco?"

"I don't know how I'll have enough money for any college, much less one on the east coast."

"Let's just fantasize for now. We'll figure out the money later. I'm not going without you."

"Okay."

"Come on, cheer up. Don't think about that old hag. We're leaving her in the dust."

When Jenny hung up the phone, she stepped back through her window into her room. She was troubled by the things her mother said. She didn't know how she would ever save enough money for college. She took out her box of prayer cards and decided to organize the Marys according to type: Mary holding the baby Jesus, Mary in a garden of roses, Mary revealing her Immaculate Heart, Mary at the foot of the cross, Mary watching Jesus's ascension. There was a row for birth, a row for beauty, a row for the trusting heart, a row for sorrow, a row for faith. She studied each version of Mary, together revealing the most quietly confident woman she had ever seen—a woman who was afraid of nothing at all—and she resolved that she would find a way out.

In bed that night, Billy called and asked why she sounded so sad. She never told him about these encounters with her mother. She just asked if it would be okay for him to stay with her on the phone while she tried to fall asleep. Billy said, "Sure," and she put the phone on the pillow next to her face and listened to him talk. He talked about developing his pictures of the oil fields and his baseball game this weekend and getting new tires on his truck and the foster kittens his mom was thinking about and the history project he was working on and whether she wanted to see the Loretta Lynn movie and fly fishing and how he really wanted to take her out to see the Tehachapi Loop and eventually she fell asleep, and he did too.

Chapter Seven

AUGUST 1981

Jenny looked over at Henry as they walked down a dark street toward the noise of a house party. There was the faint smell of sprinklers, cut grass, and settling dust in the air, and it was hot out despite the fact that the sun had gone down hours before. Henry was wearing a tight pair of white jeans with a sun-gold bowling shirt he found at a thrift shop. On the front pocket, it said "Pete." He'd bleached the tips of his dark auburn hair and wore it short in the back and long in the front—the opposite of all the boys on the baseball team who had mullets. Henry noticed Jenny looking him over and said, "What?"

"I'm worried about your outfit."

"You're always worried about something. Should I be wearing Wranglers and boots? A football jersey?"

"You know that's not what I'm saying."

"Then stop worrying."

The house was ranch style with a large covered patio in the back. When they walked into the backyard, Jenny saw a loud group of guys in sleeveless t-shirts and trucker hats hanging by the gate. She didn't know them but had seen them at parties like this before. These were the boys from the north edge of town, boys who chewed tobacco and drank beer from the time they were twelve years old.

"Hey, pretty boy!" one of the boys shouted as Jenny and Henry walked by. Jenny gave Henry a look with wide eyes and raised eyebrows as if to say, *I told you so.*

"Nice hair!" shouted another. "Hey, *Pete!*"

Jenny held on to Henry's hand. "Are you sure you want to do this?"

"Fuck them. Let's go out back and see the band."

"Henry—"

"Come on, how often do we get to see a punk band in Bakersfield?" When Jenny didn't answer, Henry said, "That's right. Never."

They walked through a small grove of trees toward a kidney-shaped pool. The water was still, and there was a layer of dirt and leaves on the bottom and a dozen June bugs floating near the glow of the pool light. They found an old lounge chair and sat, waiting for the band to arrive.

"One more year and I swear I'm never coming back here."

"Henry, it's not so bad. Someday you might even think it was sort of nice to grow up here."

Henry let go of one of his loud cackles and threw his head back. "These people are *not* nice. This place is *not* nice."

"A night like this is nice. I love the smell of the chlorine in the pool mixed with the hot summer air."

"Well, that's real sweet, pumpkin, but it doesn't quite make up for all the boredom and bigots."

Jenny scooped a June bug out of the pool where it was wriggling on its back and placed it on its legs on the warm cement. They sat a while longer as the makeshift stage was taken over by a group of girls dancing to 38 Special. Someone said the band wasn't going to show, so Jenny and Henry began to make their way back through the yard toward the gate. They passed someone throwing up in the bushes. A couple that had a fight at every party was having a fight. Jenny and Henry turned to watch as the girl jumped on the guy's back and tried to punch him in the head, while he ducked and tried to throw her off.

Henry leaned over and said, "Oh look—nice people."

When they got to the gate, the boys who'd shouted at Henry earlier were standing there, huddled, blocking the exit.

"Hi. Sorry. We just need to get by," Jenny said.

One of the boys walked up to her, stood too close, and said, "But, we haven't had any fun with Pete yet."

Jenny braced herself, took Henry's hand, and tried to walk past them. She led with her shoulder and kept her head down. As she pushed the gate open, she felt Henry's hand pull from hers with a hard yank. She swung around and saw him flat on his back in the dirt.

"Henry!" She bent down to help him up but was knocked over. The boys were kicking and spitting and pulling at Henry's hair. Jenny got up and threw herself on top of Henry, straddling him on all fours. As she tried to protect him, she was caught in the fray. She felt a cowboy boot to her ribs and gasped and the next thing she knew, she was lifted up and away, leaving Henry alone and exposed. As Billy draped her over his shoulder, she shouted, "Don't leave Henry!"

Billy put her down by his truck and went back through the gate with two of his friends from the baseball team. In the backyard, the crowd had already dispersed. Billy extended his hand and helped Henry up. Henry had a bloody lip and an open cut the size of a dime above his left eye. They got in the truck, and Jenny pressed a towel to Henry's eye. When she lifted it to see the wound, blood gushed into his eye and down her arm. She quickly reapplied the towel and said, "That's a really bad cut. It has to be stitched." She ran her hand across his ribs and could feel his heart beating fast. "And you should have an x-ray."

Billy drove, staring straight ahead, with one hand on the wheel and the other in Jenny's hair. "Maybe you should have an x-ray too."

"I'm fine. Nothing hurts."

"What about your lung? Shouldn't you check your lung?"

Jenny took a sharp inhale of breath and touched the area just below the right side of her rib cage. "No, it's fine. My lung is healthy now."

At the hospital, Billy and Jenny sat beneath fluorescent lights and vents blowing cold air while Henry was being treated. Jenny wrapped her arms around herself and shivered. Billy retrieved a sweatshirt from his truck, handed it to her, and sat back down without speaking. She thanked him, took his hand and said, "Hey, what's going on?"

Billy turned to face her. "What if we hadn't been there tonight? What if I'd stayed at practice five minutes longer, or even two minutes longer?"

"I know. I'm sorry. Henry was so excited about seeing the band—"

"Jenny," he cut her off. "You need to be more careful when you're out with him. I mean, going to a party on the wrong side of town dressed like that—it's not smart. He doesn't have the best judgment, and sometimes it seems like you blindly follow him."

Jenny shook her head and let go of his hand. "Not *blindly*," she said, and although the word triggered her—she rarely did anything blindly—she was moved by his instinct to always protect her.

Jenny put her arms around him and said, "Thank you for being there tonight. You're right, I don't know what would've happened if you didn't come when you did. I'm sorry. I love you."

"I love you too."

Henry came out with a large gauze bandage above his eye. "It'll be better than a tattoo, don't you think? A scar from a fight over my eye for the rest of my life? Think of all the girls I'll impress."

Jenny watched Billy give a small fake smile—the best he could muster, she knew. She went to Henry and placed a hand on his face. She knew he was doing the best he could as well, using humor and bravado to protect himself. They drove home in silence, and Jenny felt the peculiar anxiety of sitting between two people who were only together because of her and who were each suppressing the toll taken by the events of the evening. Henry, she knew, was both traumatized and embarrassed by the incident, and couldn't wait to get out of Billy's truck. Billy was angry that Henry had put Jenny in danger. Jenny sat between them, feeling all of Billy's anger and disappointment and all of Henry's hurt and shame. When they pulled up to Henry's house, Jenny walked him to the door. She looked back at the truck and said, "I'm sorry about Billy."

"He's just worried about you. You should go or you'll be late."

Jenny got back in Billy's truck and sat close to him. As they drove away, she held her face in her hands and began to weep, all the tears she'd kept in for the last couple of hours now pouring out of her. Since the moment Henry hit the ground, she'd been on autopilot, the crisis demanding that she act with no room for her sadness.

"I can't stop seeing the way he looked laying there in the dirt, helpless, and those boys kicking and hitting him. And they spit on him too." Jenny sobbed, unable to shake the image of Henry, descended upon, trapped, and beaten.

Billy put his arm around her shoulder and held onto her.

"I wasn't scared. I mean, at first, I was scared for Henry, but when I was on the ground, over him, I wasn't scared at all." Jenny wiped her tears and glanced up at the clock on the dashboard. "Oh, God. We're late."

"I'm sure it'll be okay. I'll walk you in."

Jenny shook her head, unwilling to let Billy see what likely awaited her inside—the irony of her mother, who was always passed out at dinnertime—waiting up for her, pouncing upon her arrival. When they pulled into her driveway, Billy kissed her lightly on the lips and ran his hands down over her hair, smoothing where it had become disheveled.

"I love you," she said.

"I love you too. You sure you don't want me to come in?"

"Yeah."

Jenny opened the front door to her house, quietly closed it behind her, and walked toward the stairs. She jumped and threw her hands across her chest when she heard the flick of a lighter and her mother say, "You're late."

She turned and saw her mother sitting in the dark in a black nightgown, her face eerily illuminated by the burning of her cigarette. "I know. I'm sorry. We had to take Henry home."

It didn't occur to her to tell her mother what had happened that night. She knew it would be like feeding flies to a spider. It was just the kind of horrible information that sustained her. Jenny could imagine her repeating it, twisting it, even using it against her.

Her mother stood, walked up behind her, and touched her hair where Billy had just straightened it. "You look a little sloppy. Have you been out parked somewhere in your boyfriend's truck?"

"No, he just drove me home."

"What do you have on under that sweatshirt?"

"A t-shirt, why?"

"Let me see it."

"Why?"

"Because I want to know what you were wearing while you were out partying."

"But I wasn't. We just went to a party to listen to music."

"Why won't you take off that sweatshirt?"

Jenny felt humiliated as she took off Billy's sweatshirt and stood before her mother in a gray t-shirt with pearly buttons and 501s.

Her mother lifted an envelope and threw it at her. "I need to check your wardrobe now that I see how you've been posing."

Jenny opened the envelope and took the picture out. It was a photo Billy had taken of her at the park, wearing a halter top and shorts, a photo she'd left in her desk drawer. Now she knew that her mother had been in her room, rifling through her things. An image arose of her sweeping through the bedroom, like a witch in her black nightgown, opening drawers, her hands touching notes from Billy, her pictures, her prayer cards.

"Do you like posing seductively? Do you know how trashy you look?"

Jenny looked at the picture and her face grew hot. She didn't know. The truth was she didn't know. She looked *trashy*? She thought she was just wearing what all the other girls wore on a hot summer day. Her mother ripped it in two and tossed it in the trash. Jenny wanted to tell her that she had no intent to be seductive, that all the girls dressed like that. She wanted to tell her that she wasn't even *posing*, that Billy had just picked up his camera and taken her picture. She wanted to proclaim her innocence. But she'd learned a long time ago that there was no sense in telling her mother anything. So, at a few minutes past curfew on a night where she'd witnessed the senseless beating of her best friend, she did what she'd learned to do to survive in this household: apologize and say goodnight. When her mother went upstairs, she looked at the picture in the trash and noticed that her head had been completely torn from her body.

In her bedroom, she picked up the phone and called Henry. "Are you okay?" she whispered.

"I'm a little sore."

"In your ribs?"

"Yeah, and my eye is sort of throbbing."

"What about your heart?"

"Still beating."

"That's not what I mean."

"I don't care what those assholes think of me. They're completely ignorant. They're *assholes*. I don't care."

Belonging

"I don't understand how people can do something like that."

"I know you don't. Get some sleep and try not to think about it anymore tonight."

When she hung up the phone, she went out the window and sat on the rooftop. A rare breeze lifted her hair slightly off her face as she stared into the darkness. The only sound was the collective hum of air conditioning units droning through the neighborhood. She thought about her mother asking her to take off her sweatshirt, tearing the photograph, calling her trashy. Her mother had always been absent maternally, unconcerned with all the things that other mothers were concerned with, like grades and groceries and dinner, but there was something about Jenny being a teenage girl, with breasts and long legs and full lips, that piqued her interest. She'd become overly intrusive, and her scrutiny was constant. Her standards were from a different time. She didn't want Jenny to wear spaghetti straps or cut-off jeans or sandals with heels. She glared at her if she ever saw her touch Billy, even just holding his hand. The words *trashy, slut, tramp, whore, floozy* were flung at her so often that Jenny almost believed that they were true, even though she was a virgin and had only kissed one boy her whole life. She wondered how much of it had to do with her mother's own teenage years, and the fact that she'd married her father and given birth to Jenny at nineteen.

She thought about seeing Henry being kicked and punched and spit on, about throwing herself into the fray. She realized that she was more afraid walking into her own house than she was confronting Henry's attackers. She remembered what Henry said by the pool, and she knew he was right. She started to imagine driving away from Lupine Lane, from Bakersfield. They would find a way to go away to college.

Before she got in bed that night, she took her prayer cards out of the drawer. She searched for the Saint Teresa prayer she'd turned to so often. *May I be at peace. May my heart remain open. May I be aware of my true nature. May I be healed. May I be a source of healing to others. May I dwell in the Breath of God.*

The next day, Jenny arrived at Henry's house to watch *The Graduate* together. Henry opened the door with a new gauze bandage taped above his eye. He reached out and touched her right side, under her rib cage. "How do you feel?"

"Okay. You?" Jenny looked past Henry, toward the kitchen. "What did your dad say?"

"He's pissed. He wants to press charges."

"What do you want to do?"

"I don't know. Disappear?"

Jenny took his hand. "I know who those boys are. Should I tell your dad?"

"Please don't. Let's just watch the movie, okay?"

Jenny walked toward the kitchen and said, "I'll just say hi to your dad first. I'll be right in."

Mr. Hansen was making grilled cheese sandwiches, and he turned from the stove when he saw Jenny and said, "How are you feeling today?"

"I'm fine."

He flipped the grilled cheese on the griddle. "Can you fill me in? Did Henry say something to someone or do something? What started it?"

"We were just leaving the party. He didn't do anything. Those boys were just looking for trouble. We were probably just in the wrong place at the wrong time." Even as she said it, she didn't believe it, but what could she say to Mr. Hansen? That Henry was wearing the wrong clothes? That it might have been his frosted hair? That they called him a "pretty boy"?

"You think so?"

Jenny nodded, "I do."

She brought the plate of sandwiches to Henry in the den, and they sat and ate grilled cheese and watched *The Graduate*. It was one of the few films that they liked equally, if for different reasons. Henry loved the dark humor. Jenny loved the way that Ben loved Elaine. In the scene at the end, when Ben raises his arms above his head and pounds on the glass overlooking the church, she was reminded of the risen Christ above the altar at church. And when a very young Richard Dreyfuss said his two lines—*Shall I get the cops? I'll get the cops*—it was a confirmation of their own private joke that he was, indeed, in every film.

Belonging

During one of the scenes filmed on campus, Henry said, "I've decided that this is where we should go to college."

"Berkeley?"

"No. This isn't really Berkeley. It's USC. In L.A."

As they watched Benjamin walk through the leafy campus, Jenny said, "It looks just like college."

Henry laughed at her and said, "Yes, just like college."

"What would you want to study there?"

"Oh, who cares? That's what college is for, to figure out what you want to do. You can study in that library like Elaine. I can take you to the clubs—the Starwood and the Whisky, and Al's is right downtown, not far from campus."

Henry was naturally smart, maybe even brilliant, plus his family had money for college. He would get in where he wanted to go, and he'd take his time figuring out his major. As he talked excitedly about going away to school together, his mention of the Starwood, the Whisky, and Al's was a reminder that Henry had spent a lot of junior year drifting away from her. She wasn't sure if it was weekends he'd begun spending in L.A., the crowd of punk kids he'd started to hang out with, or was it something else? When "The Sound of Silence" played at the end of the movie, she looked over at him, his bandage, the frosted tips of his long bangs—and thought about the song, how it laments the silence between people.

Chapter Eight

SUMMER 1982

The night of the senior prom, while their classmates partied in adjoining rooms at a discount motel, Jenny and Billy drove about thirty miles east of town to watch the trains on the Tehachapi Loop at sunrise. Billy had been talking about bringing her there since the summer after junior high—one of the seven wonders of the railroad world. It was so quiet in the mountains; they could hear the clicking of the tracks from miles away. As the train emerged from the tunnel, the sun was rising, and Billy stood in awe at all the light and motion. Jenny was moved by his anticipation and curiosity, as he waited for the moment the train climbed the mountain in a circular motion, the front crossing over the back about eighty feet above the tunnel.

They stopped at a diner in Tehachapi for breakfast, and talked about the summer ahead, their last summer together in Bakersfield. Billy would be leaving in the fall to play baseball at Arizona State. He'd declared a civil engineering major, and it was his ambition to build bridges and buildings someday. Jenny would be off to USC with Henry and had declared an English major with a Political Science minor, hoping that would best prepare her for law school. While there was a great deal of excitement about going to college and moving away, Jenny felt the grip of something else at the same time: the desire to stay put, to not leave this particular summer, in the year that they both turned eighteen, in the only town they'd ever known. She loved Bakersfield, its flat green lawns and strip malls, its leafy neighborhoods and dusty downtown streets. It was ironic and sad that, even as she did everything that she could to leave her home, she felt melancholy about leaving her hometown.

Over blueberry pancakes and biscuits and gravy, Jenny and Billy talked about everything they wanted to do during the summer and realized what they really wanted was for it to be last summer, with the whole of senior year stretched out before them. Their plans were simple. They would do what they did every summer. Lay by the pool at Heather's house. Drive to the Panorama Bluffs and watch the sunset. Listen to Uncle Gino tell stories at the antique store. Get an ice cream cone at Dewar's. Watch the trains run through the center of town. Sit on the swings at the park at the end of a Saturday night.

Their plans were bittersweet, offered up in anticipation of an ending. But whenever Jenny was sad about their impending separation, Billy would remind her that in only seven years, they'd be married, and they'd never have to be apart again. It had been his idea to get married in seven years. He'd reasoned that she'd have finished law school, and he would've had a few years to save money. Seven years was as long as they could wait and as soon as made sense. Jenny admired the way Billy could put aside the sadness and just be hopeful for their future together, and she tried her best to do the same.

Three weeks after the prom, they were seated in the school auditorium in alphabetical order for graduation practice. Just like at the kindergarten table, Henry Hansen and Jenny Hayes sat side by side, with no one in between them. As the vice principal droned on about when to walk, where to stand, and what not to wear, Jenny whispered, "Want to go to a movie this weekend?"

She watched as he hesitated, deciding what to tell her. This was part of their new dynamic senior year. Instead of the openness, trust, and comfort that defined their relationship, Henry had become closed off, distant, and secretive. He had, it seemed, intentionally begun to pull away from her, and she knew that, at times, he lied to her as well. She accepted whatever he told her, though, figuring it would save him from having to lie more.

Finally, he said, "I'm going to a concert in L.A."

Jenny didn't ask who he was going to see, or who he was going with, or when he'd be back. She just let it drop.

That night, Jenny and Billy went to a party hosted by a girl in their class at a Spanish-style house on the golf course. Most of the seniors were there, jumping in the pool, huddled in groups on the lawn, dancing on the covered patio. Billy led Jenny to the makeshift dance floor and pulled her close to him. She put her head against his chest and put the image away inside of her: warm summer night, Alabama on the stereo, the smell of grass and Billy's shirt, the feel of his arms around her. She tried not to fast-forward to the end of summer, to leaving each other, to living in different states, to not being able to feel or smell him.

After the party, Billy drove them to the park they'd been going to since eighth grade, and that they now referred to as "our park." Billy sat down in the grass and leaned against the big oak tree. Jenny sat close to him and rubbed her thumbs over his cheekbones. She touched his hair and pressed her nose to his neck.

Billy smiled and said, "What are you doing?"

"I'm memorizing you. When I'm in my dorm room, I want to be able to close my eyes and feel like you are there."

Billy leaned his forehead in and rested it on hers. His eyes were her favorite color. "Sea glass," she said and leaned down and smelled his shirt. "Grass, Tide, and your Baron cologne."

Billy put his face in her hair and said, "Cocoa Butter and lemons."

Jenny placed her hands on his shoulders and said, "Lay back."

As Billy stretched out under the oak tree, Jenny began to trace him with her fingertips. She started with his eyebrows and traced a line up through his curly hair, down his face, neck, shoulders, arms, hands, legs, all the way back. Then she kissed his eyelids, and he opened his eyes. Without moving her eyes from his, she brushed her lips over his mouth, and he said, "My turn." Jenny lay back in the grass and Billy started to trace her the same way. He was slower, though, and she found herself just wanting him to kiss her eyelids, so that he could move down to her lips.

As they lay in the park, Billy took something from his pocket and placed it in her hand, closing her fingers around it. Jenny sat up and opened her hand. In her palm, there was a little gold ring with pink garnets in the shape of a heart.

"Billy, it's so beautiful. But we weren't supposed to get each other graduation presents. We have to save money to visit each other."

"It's not a graduation present. It's a seven-more-years ring."

Jenny slid the ring on her finger and stared at it with her eyes damp. Seven more years. Sitting in the park on a warm summer night listening to the sounds of frogs and crickets and distant drag-racing, looking at the boy she loved more than anything, knowing they'd soon be apart, seven more years seemed like forever. The whole time Jenny was pushing and planning for a way to go to college, she had set aside thoughts about missing Billy. In theory, it made sense for them to each pursue their own dreams, neither holding the other back. They would go away, grow, and come back together, because they loved each other, and they belonged together. But in practice, she knew that waking up day after day, without being able to see or touch Billy, would feel empty, and that her longing for him would be constant.

"A promise ring," she said.

"Yes. I promise that no matter how far away we are and how much time goes by, I'll never forget, and I don't want you to forget."

"Forget what?"

"Forget this."

Jenny's eyes widened, realizing he wasn't just talking about sitting in their park on a summer night. He was talking about all the growing up they'd done together, everything they'd been to each other, their whole story.

"How would I ever forget?"

"I don't know, but stuff happens. Especially with distance."

"I promise I won't forget."

"Me either." Billy kissed her, took her hand, and led her to the swing set. At the end of the night, they always sat side by side on the swings. Jenny closed her eyes and felt the warm air against her face. She opened them and held her left hand out and watched as the light from the full moon reflected on the ring that held Billy's promise.

After the park, Billy drove her to Heather's house. Jenny kissed him goodbye and turned and waved as she walked through the gate. It was dark in the backyard, and she made her way to the sliding glass door with the help of the glowing light from the pool. Inside the house, she smelled homemade biscuits and something sweet and fruity. Heather was in her bedroom, listening to the radio and flipping through a magazine. Her hair was in rollers and the room smelled like nail polish and popcorn. Heather looked up from her magazine and Jenny sat on the edge of the bed.

"Hey. Where'd you go after the party?" Heather asked.

"To our park."

"That's sweet."

"Yeah."

"Are you hungry? My mom made biscuits today, and raspberry jam."

Jenny followed Heather into the kitchen, where she flicked on the light above the stove. They ate biscuits and jam and Heather poured them glasses of milk. Jenny held out her ring for Heather to see.

"Wow, Jenny. He gave you this tonight?"

"Yeah. It's a promise ring."

"It's so pretty." Heather held Jenny's hand and looked at it. "And delicate." She was still holding her hand when she said, "So, what's the plan when you leave for college?"

"What do you mean?"

"I mean, are you going to date other people?"

"Why would we want to date other people? He just gave me a promise ring. We're getting married. I don't need to date in college."

"It might be good for you, though."

"I don't want to date. I love Billy."

"I know. I just worry about you."

"Don't worry about me."

"What about him, though?"

"You think he wants to date in college?"

"I don't know. But Jenny, you've been together since you were in eighth grade. Neither of you have had any experience with other people."

"Yeah, so." Jenny hesitated and then said, "Are you asking me this because we're not sleeping together?"

"Well, no, but I do think it's sort of unrealistic to expect him to go off to college and not have sex when everyone else is."

Jenny covered her eyes with her hands and thought about all the times he'd tried to convince her it would be okay. Once, in his truck, her dress and his jeans were on the floorboard before she stopped him. He was lying on top of her, kissing her neck, running his hands over her body. There wasn't a plan about it—they'd just gotten carried away—and then something brought her back. Maybe it was the noise of another car on the riverbank, maybe it was a scripture about virginity, maybe the song on the radio ended. Maybe it was the sound of her mother's voice saying the word *slut*.

"Billy loves me," Jenny said. "We'll figure it out."

At one a.m., Jenny pulled an oversized t-shirt from Heather's pajama drawer, slipped it on, and got into bed. The album rock station was playing a sad, plaintive song about reaching a crossroads and leaving home. Unable to sleep, she thought about all the reasons she'd refused to sleep with Billy, trying to take inventory of what was true and what was not. There was the shame her mother heaped upon her, and there was what she'd been taught in church about remaining chaste until marriage. The night in Billy's truck, she had to admit that there was an urgency between them that felt *impure*. There was the risk of pregnancy. She didn't know how to get birth control and didn't know how she'd hide it from her mother if she did. If she got pregnant, she wouldn't be able to go away to college, and she'd be a teenager with a baby, just like her mother.

There were also fears she couldn't articulate yet, fears that had something to do with being that close to anyone, even Billy. She knew how confusing it must be to him and how frustrating. She loved him and she wanted to be with him, but she had so much to sort out, and she wanted to feel ready. She wanted it to be perfect. She listened to the sound of the air conditioning clicking on and fell asleep in the glow of the pool light, with Heather beside her and Gregg Allman on the radio.

The week Jenny turned eighteen, Henry wanted to take her to the opening day of *Fast Times at Ridgemont High* at Stockdale 6. It was 106 degrees out on that August afternoon, so they opted for the matinee at three p.m., during the most intense heat of the day. Jenny invited Heather to go with them, and when Billy's baseball game was canceled, he met them at the theater too. Thirty minutes before the show, kids were already sitting on the hot cement outside the cold theater lobby, waiting for the doors to open. Jenny had her camera with her, and while they stood in line, she asked Heather to take a picture of her standing between Henry and Billy on the sidewalk in front of Stockdale 6. She wanted to hold onto the image of the three of them together on the day they'd sit in the cool dark of the theater on a hot August afternoon for the last time before they left for college. When the movie ended, they lingered in the theater to watch the credits so Henry could see the names of all the songs. Heather invited them over for a night swim, and the plan was to get swimsuits and meet back at her house.

At eight, when Henry still hadn't arrived at Heather's, Jenny called his house to see what was keeping him, and there was no answer. At eleven, when Billy dropped Jenny off at home, she called Henry again, and again, there was no answer. She decided to drive to his house to check on him. There were several cars in his driveway, and Henry answered the door with a beer in his hand. X was playing loudly on the stereo inside, and through the open door, Jenny could see a handful of punk-looking kids in thrift store sundresses and ripped jeans. Henry looked surprised to see her and stepped out on the front porch and closed the door behind him.

"What's going on?" she said. "Are you having a party?"

"Just a few friends."

"We thought you were coming to Heather's."

"I'm sorry. I should've called you."

"Who are all these people?"

"Just some friends. Do you want to come in?"

She could tell he was bluffing by the way he tossed the comment out and pushed open the door in a way that could only be described as acting. She knew him well enough to know that the invitation was not sincere, and he knew her well enough to know that she'd never say yes. Still, Jenny looked over his shoulder at the girl with pink hair smoking in his dad's chair and thought of calling his bluff. She watched him watch her pondering going in. Then, tired of both of their games, she sat down on the porch and said, "I was worried about you."

Henry sat next to her and put a hand on her shoulder. "I should've called. I'm sorry."

"Where's your dad?"

"He took Christopher to the beach."

"Can I ask you something?"

"What?"

"Is it going to be like this when we get to college?"

"Like what?"

"Like you making plans with me, and getting a better offer, and forgetting the plans with me and not even telling me about it."

"It's not like we had a big plan. We were just going to swim at Heather's. And I told you, you can come in."

"Yeah, but you didn't mean it."

Jenny watched as Henry tried to think of something to say. She'd said the truth, and he knew it. He didn't ask her to come in again. He didn't respond to her comment that he didn't mean it. He just walked her to her car and went back in the house.

On the drive home, Jenny felt heavyhearted as she passed Stockdale 6. They'd seen their last movie there, they were leaving town, they were growing up. She thought about all the movies she and Henry had seen together with the summer movie passes they bought every year since fifth grade. She remembered *Young Frankenstein* and *Heaven Can Wait*, *Grease* and *Rock 'n' Roll High School*. She remembered seeing *Ode to Billy Joe* three times and still didn't understand exactly what happened. It was the summer she turned thirteen. It started as a sweet coming-of-age love story, but then, Billy Joe tells Bobbie Lee that he's been with a man and that it was a "sin against nature" and a "sin against God" and he jumps off the Tallahatchie Bridge, just like in the song.

Jill Fordyce

She thought about the day after the dust storm, when she and Henry walked to Stockdale 6 amidst the dirt, tumbleweeds, and tree branches strewn along the highway. She could see them standing there, him wily and her unsure, buying tickets to *The Goodbye Girl*, but sneaking into *Saturday Night Fever* instead. They shared popcorn; Jenny covered her eyes during a lot of the movie; Tony Manero tried to break free of his family, his heritage, his religion; and some other poor guy fell from a bridge.

Chapter Nine

SUMMER 1982

With the help of Henry's dad, Jenny found a way to pay for college. She was awarded a few small scholarships and agreed to one big government loan that she'd be paying off well into her thirties. She had no doubt, though, that it would be worth it. The moment she and Henry stepped onto the USC campus she knew this was where she wanted to be. It was as if the college campus she'd imagined actually existed, and it was only about one hundred miles away from home.

She could have gone to freshman orientation with Henry and Mr. Hansen, but Jenny was touched when her dad told her he'd taken a vacation day so that he could drive her to L.A. The morning of orientation, as they drove over the Grapevine, Jenny's dad pointed up at the steep, winding road above them.

"You see that? That's the old Ridge Route. The way the sound travels through there, you can hear cows mooing from the other end of the valley. There's nothing around for miles and miles, but you can hear the cows. When I was a boy, we'd pull off the road to listen to them."

"Can you still hear them?"

"I'm not sure. The valley is much more populated now." He took a sip of his coffee and continued to narrate the archaeology of the area, noting the ancient sea floor, pointing to the San Andreas fault.

"What are you going to do while I'm in orientation?"

"Oh, I'll just park and wander around the school. I've never been on a university campus before."

Jill Fordyce

When they got to USC, Jenny's dad dropped her off at the Figueroa Street gate, and they agreed to meet after orientation at the fountain in front of the library.

The campus had a hum to it, even in the summer, and Jenny felt a surge of excitement, independence, and freedom as she thought about what the next year would hold. She would finally be in college. It was something she'd thought about from the moment she discovered it was her ticket out.

During the lunch break at orientation, Jenny went into the financial aid office to check on one of her scholarships. A counselor pulled her file, looked at a notation on top, and asked her to sit down in a conference room.

"Is everything alright?" Jenny asked.

"Well, your file's incomplete. We still don't have your parents' tax returns. It says here that we've sent the request three times and the deadline has passed. Any chance you brought them with you today?"

He never sent the tax returns? Jenny felt sick to her stomach. She'd talked to her dad about this. She'd told him she needed a copy of their tax returns in order to get her student loans. She gave him a stamped envelope made out to the USC Financial Aid Office, and a note on the top that said, "mail tax returns" and "important" and the due date six months ago. Her face became flushed and hot. She couldn't believe she'd left something this important in his hands and hadn't followed up with a phone call to the financial aid office. She wondered why she hadn't seen the three requests the counselor mentioned. Did he put them in that pile of mail that no one ever opened? Or did he toss them in the trash to hide the fact that they hadn't been sent? She thought, *How hard is it to put a copy of your tax returns in an envelope and mail it?* Then, it occurred to her that maybe he didn't send the tax returns because they didn't exist.

"What if, for some reason, I can't get my parents' tax returns?"

"The government loan, and some of your scholarships, require it."

Jenny paused, unsure of what she should share. She thought she would cry right there in the financial aid office. The counselor stood up and walked to a file cabinet. He handed her a form and said, "Is it possible for you to declare yourself an independent?"

82

"What does that mean?"

"This is an IRS form you can fill out. If you meet the requirements, the government will only need your tax returns."

Jenny thanked him, put the form in her orientation folder, and walked out of the financial aid office. Her excitement about being on campus had now turned to embarrassment, fear, and anger. She watched other kids and parents walk around campus, seemingly without a care in the world. When she saw her own father sitting at the fountain in front of the library, wearing a new USC t-shirt and holding a bag from the bookstore, she wanted to turn and walk the other way. But he smiled and waved when he saw her and pulled a USC sweatshirt from the bag. She accepted his gift and sat next to him, having no idea how to address the failure that had occurred.

He reached over and patted her knee and said, "You'll be a Trojan soon. How was orientation?"

Jenny didn't answer right away. She was trying to figure out what to say about what she'd learned. Then, she just blurted it out. "You never sent the tax returns?"

He rubbed a hand over his mustache and said, "I'm afraid we haven't prepared them yet. Can't send something that don't exist."

"So, you just never told me? What did you think would happen? Did you think I'd just somehow magically get my financial aid?"

"I'm sorry, baby. There's just nothing we can do. We haven't filed."

"Can you do it now? I mean, can you just file and not pay or something? I found out today that I'll lose my scholarships and loan if I don't have the tax returns."

Her father shrugged and put his chin to his chest, a gesture she'd seen many times before and recognized as a mixture of shame and defeat. "I'm afraid it's a little more complicated than that."

"What do you mean? How complicated can it be?"

"There are things you don't need to know about—some tax problems. I'm handling it."

"When?"

Her father ran a hand over his new t-shirt, looked down at his feet and said, "I'm working on it."

Jenny held her head in her hands. He had failed the one task she gave him in her quest to go to college—a task that she was sure was pretty simple for most families. Somehow though, her pity for him began to suppress her anger. He was so hapless, so disappointed in himself. She couldn't look at him anymore, so she just stood up and said, "We should get on the road."

On the drive home, she closed her eyes, started devising plans, and eventually dozed off. She was aware of the sounds around her—the whirring of the car descending the steep grade of the road, the static of the L.A. radio station as they left signal range, Willie Nelson singing a sad song about not loving someone as good as he should have. She awoke when she felt the car come to a halt and heard her father open his door. Jenny got out of the car and looked out at the brown and purple and golden hills that went on forever. She felt like they were the last people on earth, or that they'd landed on some other planet. There was nothing but barren hills for as far as she could see.

"Where are we?" she asked.

Her father waved her toward an outcropping of rocks and said, "Sit down and listen."

Jenny sat and listened intently, but all she could hear was the wind. After several minutes of sitting in silence, she heard the mooing of a faraway herd of cows. It was like they were ghosts—there was nothing around for miles, but the cows sounded like they were right there. Listening to the invisible cows, Jenny thought, *It's no wonder he thinks he can do magic.*

When they got back home at about eight p.m., Jenny's mother was sitting on the front porch with Linda and Judy, bug-eyed and bobble headed. Her father leaned over to give her mother a kiss, and her mother made a big scene of it, holding onto his face and making smacking noises.

"Jenny got her schedule today. She's almost a real college girl," her dad announced. He turned to Jenny and said, "Why don't you show your mama your schedule?"

Jenny bristled at the suggestion, and it looked like her mother did too. She'd just told him she might not even be able to go to college now. Did he forget? Didn't he understand what his failure could cost her? She was also disturbed by his effort to have her share her schedule with her mother. Ever since Jenny started receiving acceptance letters, when it became clear that she was going away to college, her mother had vacillated between fury and avoidance. She'd either be yelling at Jenny about something, or pretending she was invisible. It was as if she realized that Jenny's fate was no longer something she could control, but it was also more than that. The specific idea of college seemed to trigger her, and Jenny didn't know why. She knew that her mother didn't go to college. She knew she was born when her mother was only nineteen. She wondered what role that played, what role *she played*, in her mother not going to college. As her father prodded her to show her mother her class schedule, Jenny thought, *Why is he doing this? Why won't he just give up the charade?*

"I'm just going up to get ready for bed now. It's been a long day. Maybe tomorrow." Jenny didn't wait for a reply. She looked back at her father before walking into the house. He'd wandered over to the lemon tree in the middle of the lawn and pulled a lemon down. He was still in his new USC t-shirt, and he had that look on his face again, the one that said, *I'm just doin' the best I can, darlin'*, the one that made her want to hold him like a baby.

Up in her room, she called Henry and asked if his dad could help her fill out the IRS form that would make her an independent.

"My dad can take care of that for you in two minutes. Why don't you come over now? He's making an apple crisp."

Sitting at the kitchen table in Henry's house and eating apple crisp while his dad helped her complete the tax form sounded like the perfect thing to do. It would ease her mind and fill her belly at the same time. But that would also mean walking back downstairs, explaining to her parents where she was going, seeing her father's shame, and giving her mother one more chance to switch moods. She told Henry she'd come over tomorrow after work. Before they hung up the phone he said, "You're going to USC. We will not let them stop you."

The next afternoon, when she pulled up in front of Henry's house, she had a feeling that something was off. The feeling was so intense that when

85

she got out of her car, she left the IRS form behind. The front door to the house was wide open. Henry's twelve-year old brother, Christopher, was sitting on the front lawn. There was yelling—Henry's mom. What was she doing there? Then there was a boy sitting in a car across the street with the windows down. He looked like he was about twenty, handsome, clean cut, with short blond hair.

As Jenny walked up the drive, Henry was walking out of the house, a duffle bag over his shoulder, his father chasing after him. Henry stopped, startled, when he saw Jenny standing in the driveway. He pointed his finger at her car. "Go home. Leave. Now!"

She grabbed his elbow as he tried to walk by her. "What's going on? Where are you going?"

"You shouldn't be here. Go home."

Henry's dad shouted, "Henry! Don't leave!"

Henry kept walking, without looking back. His father, wearing an apron over his work clothes, went after him. Henry's mother came flying out the front door, pale and wild-eyed. She went to Christopher, who was crying, took his hand and walked him quickly back into the house. When she saw Jenny standing there, witnessing this scene, she blinked and turned her head, as if she could make her disappear. The boy got out of his car and opened his trunk. He wore nice jeans and a button-down shirt, and for some reason, Jenny knew he wasn't from Bakersfield.

"Jenny, go home!" This time it was Henry who was holding Jenny's elbow and he squeezed it hard and looked at her with damp eyes filled with rage. When she started to cry, he let go, and said it again quietly. "Please, please just go home."

Henry threw his bag in the trunk and didn't look at Jenny or his father when he got in the car with the boy. When they drove off, Jenny went to Henry's dad. This morning, he'd told her he'd be around all afternoon, and that he'd be happy to help her. What happened in the last five hours? Jenny looked up at him and said, "Where is he going?"

He wiped his eyes with the back of his hand. "L.A., I guess."

"Who was that boy?"

Henry's dad put a hand on her shoulder and said, "Honey, I think you have to have this conversation with Henry."

Belonging

Henry's dad turned and walked toward the house, leaving Jenny alone in the driveway. She could hear the loud wailing of Henry's mom from inside. Jenny got in her car and sat there, not knowing where to go or what to do. She drove around for a little while, and then found herself in front of Uncle Gino's store. A bell rang when she opened the door, and Uncle Gino looked up from behind the cash register.

"Well, hello darling! Have you come to sort and tag? Or just to visit?"

Jenny took a deep breath and said, "Actually, I don't know. I guess I could sort and tag." She took a box from behind the register and began to unpack it. It was mindless work and felt like exactly what she needed.

"What's going on?" Uncle Gino asked. "You look like a little lost lamb."

What could she tell Uncle Gino? She didn't want to tell him about orientation because she didn't want to reveal her parents' failure. She didn't want to tell him about Henry's house because she knew it was a scene she shouldn't have witnessed, and she wanted to protect Henry and his family. She said she was just tired from the trip to L.A. and continued to sort, while he set up a display of antique dishes on a table beside her.

Because the work was mindless, it allowed her to sit and review the year she and Henry had spent trying to hold on to their friendship, while he became increasingly secretive and distant. Henry had always treated going away to college together as if it were a given, a necessity. His father accepted this as well and was committed to helping Jenny get to USC. Mr. Hansen helped her apply for every scholarship and grant they could find. He read her essays and applications, and made sure deadlines were met. He had even paid some of her application fees without telling anyone. But despite all of this, Henry spent a lot of senior year avoiding her, at least socially. She'd ask him to go to a movie or get ice cream, and he'd almost always say he was busy. He had a whole new group of friends that she didn't even know. He never stayed in town on the weekends. He didn't come by King's Table to help himself to a free soft serve while she finished her shift like he used to. He didn't honk the horn outside her house to pick her up for a drive. In fact, if they hadn't planned to go to USC together, she might even question how their friendship would endure after this year.

Jenny replayed the scene in front of Henry's house over and over again. She thought of Henry's dad saying, *You should have this conversation with Henry*, and realized that Henry was probably in a relationship with the boy parked in front of his house, that he may even love him. She reflected on the long, close friendship she and Henry shared, the openness and intimacy that—up until this year—had defined it. The scene she'd just witnessed compelled her to admit to herself what she'd probably known for quite a while. Henry was gay and didn't want anyone to know. At first, when Henry started distancing himself from her, she'd presumed it was because he was hanging out with his new punk crowd. Eventually, she started to believe that wasn't it at all, but she had no frame of reference and could not ask Henry the questions she began to ask herself. How many times had they fallen asleep holding on to each other? Why was there never any type of desire between them, despite their deep emotional connection? Why had he never had a girlfriend? Why was he so secretive about his love life? Her thoughts were interrupted by Uncle Gino standing over her with his hands on his hips, saying, "I have an idea."

"What is it?"

"I cut some roses in my garden today. Some rosemary too. Let's bring them to the cemetery."

"That sounds nice."

"First, we have to talk about something." Uncle Gino reached for an envelope behind the counter and said, "It pains me terribly to say this dear, but I have to let you go."

Jenny laughed and took the envelope from him. "Yes, I guess you do. Is this my letter of termination?"

Uncle Gino smiled at her and said, "It's your last paycheck."

"You already gave me my last paycheck."

"Okay, then it's your bonus. I've been putting aside a little for you every month over the last five years. I think it will come in handy at USC."

Jenny opened the envelope and there was a check inside for $5,000. She'd never seen so much money. She wanted to hand it back, unsure of how she would even go to college without her student loan. "Uncle Gino, this is way too much. I can't accept this. You keep it for the store."

Belonging

"You earned it. I'm so proud of you. I will miss you dearly, but I am so very proud of you."

Jenny hugged Uncle Gino and accepted his gift, deeply touched by his generosity and faith in her. "I will miss you more. Thank you."

Uncle Gino turned out the lights and locked up, and Jenny sat in the coolness of the dark store. She took a last look around as the overhead lights flickered off and the ceiling fan whirred to a halt. She took a deep breath and tried to store the smell inside of her: old books, mothballs, dried flowers, frosted cookies, stale coffee. She was going to miss the antique store, the sorting and tagging, the cookies, and the oldies station. Mostly, she was going to miss Uncle Gino.

She scooped up the roses and rosemary from the counter and they drove two miles to the cemetery. They always brought roses to Nonna's grave because they were a physical representation of her life on earth. She was a woman who grew roses of every color. The roses also symbolized their enduring togetherness, the lack of separation between the living and the dead, Saint Francis's gift to Saint Clare. *We will be together again when the roses bloom.* The rosemary, Uncle Gino taught her, was a symbol of love and remembrance. Jenny sat on the grass in front of Nonna's grave, while Uncle Gino wandered around, touching the headstones of his wife, parents, and siblings, leaving a sprig of rosemary on each.

There were so many things Jenny noticed every time she was in the cemetery. Mourning doves and church bells. Plastic windmills and balloons. Rows of identical smooth white stones for soldiers killed in Vietnam and Korea. Beautiful handmade stones in Potter's Field, where the people who couldn't afford to buy a tombstone, were buried. The poplars and palms, oaks and eucalyptus, that were as old as the cemetery itself.

Uncle Gino asked again if everything was okay, and Jenny was tempted to tell him that she had to return his check because she may not be going to college anymore. But she remembered the way his eyes twinkled when he handed it to her, and she remembered her dad standing by the lemon tree, his chin to his chest. And she decided that she would remain quiet, and she would figure this out. She looked back at Nonna's stone and put the image away—green grass, blue sky, yellow roses, and the granite headstone that read *Marion Vitelli Moretti, loving wife, mother, and grandmother, 1913–1978.*

Chapter Ten

SUMMER 1982

Henry never told Jenny what happened at his house that day, and Jenny never told him what she believed, knowing how fiercely he was holding onto his secret. So, when he returned from L.A. after the weekend, she pretended she didn't see it and he pretended she didn't see it, and they each, separately, pretended it never happened. Henry's dad also never mentioned it again, but he showed up at her door the following day and helped her complete the IRS form. He filed it for her and made sure her student loan was approved. She would be off to college in just a couple of weeks.

On a Saturday afternoon in August, she was home alone, cleaning out her room, deciding what she would take with her and what she would leave behind. The floor was covered with the contents of her closet. The late afternoon sun streamed through her white plantation shutters, and her favorite John Cougar song was on the radio. Her parents were at the beach, at the same place they rented in Ventura every August. She heard a slight tap on her door and looked up to see Billy standing in his dirty summer league uniform. He leaned over and kissed her, and she pulled him down next to her. He was so warm and smelled like grass and dirt and sweat. They lay back on her bed, her head on his shoulder.

"What are you thinking about?"

He waved his arm around her room. "This. You leaving."

"Will you drive me to L.A.?"

"Don't you think your parents will want to take you? I could ride with your parents."

Belonging

Jenny held him and said, "I want you to take me."

Billy's naïve question made Jenny realize just how much she'd elected to not share with him, for years really, but in particular, over the last month. She didn't tell him she needed her mother's signature on the IRS form and that she had refused. She hid the hellish limbo she was living in, each day dodging her mother's rage, while simultaneously trying to please her, so that she would sign the form, so that she could go to college. It all ended one evening while her mother was out. Her father handed her the IRS form, purportedly signed by both of them—her dad's signature, blocky and slanted, her mother's signature, a feminine version of blocky and slanted. The relief she felt was so great, she began to sob. She hugged her dad and thanked him for his forgery. He kissed the top of her head, and said, *Now you go make me proud, darlin'*. Jenny didn't tell Billy any of this. She'd decided very early in their relationship to not let him in on the darkness of her home life. She wanted to appear whole and unburdened, and she didn't think that was possible if he knew the truth.

Billy looked around the room at the photos that chronicled their last four years, most of them of him, and the painting she loved that hung over her bed. "It'll be sad," he said.

"It'll be sad wherever we say goodbye."

Billy took off his hat and tossed it on the floor, started to kiss her again, and moved on top of her. Jenny had one hand in his hair and the other on the small of his back. With his knee, he moved her legs so that he was lying between them. He pulled his jersey off and pushed up her shirt. Her heart was beating fast, and she felt a little dizzy. They lay there kissing, her legs wrapped around his, his hands beneath her t-shirt. Her eyes were closed, and she heard him start to undo his belt and she said, "What are you doing? Stop."

"Come on, Jenny. Why?"

She pressed her fingertips to his chest. "You know why."

"No, I don't. I really don't know anymore."

Billy rolled over on his back and lay there, catching his breath. Jenny pulled down her shirt and sat up. With Billy lying shirtless on her bed, she could see that there was a mottled patch of bruises again on the inside of his right elbow. She reached out and touched his face and said, "I promise

I won't make you wait till we're married, but I'm not ready. Especially now, when you're headed to Arizona, and I'm headed to L.A.—for four years."

Billy sat up and said, "I just don't see how you would ever regret it. You know how much I love you. You know how long I've waited for you. Christ, Jenny. I'm so tired of waiting."

"I know. I'm sorry. I love you too."

"That's just it. We *love* each other. We've been together since we were thirteen years old. We're getting married in seven years. We should be able to trust each other enough to do this."

"I do trust you, and I can't imagine ever loving anyone the way I love you. I want to be with you—completely. Don't you know that? I do. I just can't yet."

Billy exhaled heavily and closed his eyes. "You know what I think? I think it'll just make us even closer."

Jenny held both of his hands in hers. "Can we just see how this year goes? How we do away from each other?"

"We're back to that again. One more year."

"What if we make a plan for it? Like something to look forward to. We could go to a hotel together next summer. At the beach. And we can stay all night and sleep next to each other. How about that?"

Billy lay back on her bed again and stared at the ceiling. "Next summer is so far away."

"We won't be near each other most of that time anyway." Jenny laid down next to him and wrapped an arm around his waist. "Should we make it a plan, then?"

Billy didn't say anything for a minute. He ran his hand over her hair and kissed her and said, "Sure."

"I love you."

"I love you too."

She touched the bruises on his arm, and said, "Billy, how long have they been back?"

He looked down at his arm and said, "I don't know. They usually show up a day or two after I pitch."

"You didn't pitch this week."

He pulled his jersey back on. "My dad had me throw a lot yesterday."
"Does it hurt?"

"It's just sore. It's nothing to worry about." Billy kissed her and said, "I'm going to Kyle's later. He's having a party. You want to go?"

"Not really. I have to pack. Just come by after if you want, okay?"

"Okay, I'll stop by on my way home."

That night, Jenny fell asleep on top of her bed with all the lights on, waiting for Billy to come back. She had a dream that she was driving straight up a silo that stretched high into the sky—her car perpendicular to the ground. She had to drive fast so her car wouldn't fall off. When she reached the top, she realized she was on a small square landing, surrounded by ocean and sky. She stepped out of the car and jolted awake before she could fall. She sat up and looked at her clock radio. It was 1:45 a.m. Immediately, she thought, *Where's Billy?* He never stayed out that late. He never went to bed without calling. He said he was coming over after the party. She felt panicky, from both the dream and the absence of Billy. She decided to go look for him.

When she got to Kyle's house, she saw several cars in the driveway and Billy's truck parked a few houses down. She opened the screen door and walked into the dark living room. It smelled like stale beer and pot, and her flip-flops stuck to the dirty linoleum. There was a couple making out on a couch and someone passed out in a chair. Eddie Rabbitt was playing on the radio. She heard someone yell "hey" from the kitchen and turned to see Kyle hop up from his chair. He put his arm around her and started to walk her out the door as soon as she walked in.

"Where's Billy?"

"He's asleep. He's staying here tonight."

She could tell Kyle was trying to use a casual tone, but his eyes looked nervous. She knew something was wrong. "Where is he? I want to see him."

"There's a bunch of guys sleeping back there." His eyes wandered toward a closed door at the end of the hallway. "He's passed out. I doubt I could even wake him."

"Passed out? He barely drinks. Can you just tell him I'm here? I can bring him home."

Kyle kept looking toward the closed door and didn't answer. Jenny followed his eyes and saw the door open. A girl Jenny recognized walked out of the bedroom with her sandals in her hand. She was older—a college girl home for the summer. She used to be a cheerleader at their high school. The girl looked at Kyle, Kyle looked at the girl, and Jenny knew. She had to see for herself, though, so she started to walk down the hallway toward the closed door. Kyle stood in front of her and wrapped his arms around her, stopping her from moving toward the bedroom.

Someone broke a glass in the kitchen and when Kyle turned to see what happened, Jenny slipped by him. She went to the end of the hallway and stared at the closed door. Her body started to tremble as she turned the knob and pushed the door open. Billy had his back to her. He was facing the window to the front yard, buttoning his jeans. His baseball cap was on the floor. His shirt was crumpled on the messy bed. She closed the door before he could turn and see her and ran out of the house.

It was ninety degrees outside, but her body shook and her teeth chattered. As she drove home, she didn't cry, but she couldn't control the shaking of her arms and legs. It crossed her mind that she shouldn't be driving and then she thought, *Who cares?* When she got home, Heather was sitting on the front porch in a nightgown with curlers in her hair. Seeing Heather waiting for her, Jenny started to sob. She walked the opposite direction, away from Heather, and sat down on the front lawn next to the lemon tree. Heather followed, sat in the damp grass beside Jenny, and wrapped her arms around her.

Jenny said, "Why are you here?"

"Kyle called me."

"What did he say?"

Heather hesitated, and Jenny dug her fingers into the grass and dirt and shouted, "I have to know! Tell me!"

"I know. I'm sorry. Kyle told me you ran out. He said Billy was really drunk. They'd been doing whiskey shots."

"Billy doesn't ever do shots."

"Well, that may be why he got so drunk." Heather took Jenny's hands and started wiping the dirt and grass from them. "Kyle said that Michelle

Belonging

Duncan was all over him. He put Billy in a room to sleep it off, and she followed."

Jenny thought of the look that Kyle and Michelle exchanged. It may have been meaningless to them—a simple wordless admission of what happened in the bedroom. To Jenny, the look said *life as you know it is over*. She knew that before she forced her way down the hallway to see for herself.

Jenny sobbed and said only, "I don't understand" over and over again. She didn't understand a lot of things. She didn't understand how Billy could ever be with someone else. She didn't understand how he could be with someone he didn't love. She didn't understand how the day they sat on her bed and talked about trust and love and getting married could turn into a night where trust was broken, love didn't matter, and getting married seemed like a long-ago teenage fantasy. She couldn't believe she'd been so foolish, thinking she could plan their first time, thinking he'd wait another year.

When Heather finally got Jenny up to bed, she laid down next to her and held her. Jenny curled up into a ball and replayed the day in her mind. She thought of Billy in her doorway in his summer ball uniform. She thought of kissing him, how he smelled like a summer day. She remembered him saying how much he loved her—how much he would always love her. She could hear him begging to be with her, and her saying no, again. She thought of her ridiculous plan to meet him at the beach next summer. She couldn't get the made-up image of Billy laying on top of Michelle out of her head. The hurt was so severe, the loneliness so complete, it felt like she'd slipped into a horrible dream.

She knew where she was—she was deep in the hole. Billy's the one who made up the name for it—Fourth of July when they were sixteen. They were at a pool party at Aunt Hope and Uncle Joe's, and her mother was drunk. She pulled Jenny by the elbow to a shady corner of the yard, and as Jenny stood in her wet bathing suit, she hissed that she'd been watching her all day. She told her she was "overly familiar" with Billy's body, that her bathing suit was too revealing, that she looked like a slut, and that she was embarrassing to her and her father. It was the only time Billy had ever witnessed the direct aftermath of her mother's rage, the way

95

Jenny completely shut down. Usually, these episodes happened in private, and Jenny would have the time and space to pull herself back together. Plus, she'd done such a good job of keeping Billy from seeing what went on in her house. That day, as they walked out of the party, Billy saw how she stared straight ahead, emotionless, and wouldn't talk, wouldn't let anyone touch her, even him. He said, "It's like you're in a dark hole. Please let me pull you out."

Now she was deeper in the hole than she'd ever been before, and Billy wouldn't be there to rescue her. When her dad got home Sunday night and asked her what was wrong, she simply told him that she and Billy had broken up. He put his arm around her and said something like, "I'm sorry, darlin'. But maybe this is for the best, with you leaving for college and all." That was the extent of their talking about it, except he'd come in every night after work and sit on the edge of her bed, look at her sad, swollen eyes and say, "I just don't know what to do for you, baby."

The rumors swirled for the last few weeks of summer. *Billy was a virgin. Michelle was a very good teacher. Jenny walked in on them. Billy didn't really remember it.* Jenny would never forget it. Her last image of Billy would be of him standing by the window, buttoning jeans that she imagined Michelle had unbuttoned. She refused to see Billy again and packed up everything that had anything to do with him. She locked up her house so that he couldn't try to see her and prepared to do what she'd always been preparing to do—leave home. She tore down all the pictures in her sunny room, from all the dances, parties, and baseball games, and tossed them in a large box. She made a pile on her bed of notes, cards, and letters from Billy. She took down all the photos she'd taken of Billy over the years, from the boyish thirteen-year-old who told her he liked her, to the tall, young man who said that he loved her. When it was all scattered about, the room had blank walls and empty bookshelves. She opened her bottom drawer and took out the gold box containing the three photos Billy gave her for eighth grade graduation: "He Wanted a Purple Balloon," "Reading Aloud," and "Jenny." When she looked at the last photo, she felt a tremendous sadness remembering the significance of the moment and the beautiful boy who captured it.

Belonging

She was holding the box in her hands when Henry pushed open her door.

"How'd you get in? I locked everything downstairs."

"I took the screen off the kitchen window and crawled through." Henry looked down at the pile of things on her bed. "What's going on?"

"I'm getting rid of stuff."

He picked up a picture of Jenny and Billy at graduation just a couple of months before and said, "Looks like you're getting rid of everything."

"I don't want any of this!" Jenny threw her arms in the air and raised her voice at Henry.

He put his arm around her and patted her back. "It's okay. I know."

"Will you help me? It'll be faster if you help me."

"Sure." Henry helped Jenny dump everything into the box, until the only thing remaining was the gold box containing Billy's photos. "Are these the pictures? The eighth-grade ones?"

"Yes, and I don't want to see them again. Just put them in like that."

"Jenny, are you sure? You're so hurt and angry right now. What's the harm in saving them until some day when you're not so hurt and angry? You really want to throw them out?"

"Yes! Put the box in the box!" Jenny stopped and looked down at her left hand. "No. Wait." She took the little garnet ring she loved so much off her finger. She looked at it for a long time, tears running down her face. She opened the gold box and put the ring inside it with the photos. "Okay, now. Get rid of the box."

Henry looked at her with his eyes wide. "Jenny."

"Please. Now."

Henry did as he was told, and that afternoon when he left, he carried the box with him, and she watched through the window as he set it out on the curb with the garbage.

Until the morning she left, Billy would call and come by multiple times a day trying to get her to listen to him. He'd knock at the door, yell up at her window, plead for her to come down. Jenny left the phone off the hook, locked all the doors to her house, and kept her shutters closed. She barely left her room. She wanted to open the door and let Billy in. She wanted to hold him. She wished she could wake up and discover that it had all been a nightmare, that the night of Kyle's party, when she dreamt of driving up the silo, she fell into this, and now she could wake up, and everything could go back to the way it was before. But she knew this was not a dream. She was in a new reality, and she understood that she would never let him back in, and also, that she may never recover. She didn't know if she would ever be able to love or trust any boy, other than Henry, again. Her only comfort came from the fact that they would be leaving for L.A. in just a matter of days. They would start a new life in a new town, and she would not look back.

On the last night Jenny was in Bakersfield, Aunt Hope, Uncle Joe, Heather, and Uncle Gino took her out to one of the Basque restaurants in town to give her a proper send-off. The Basque restaurants, with their long tables, bottles of red wine, simple food, and family-style meals, were an integral part of life in Bakersfield, gathering places since the first one opened in 1893. It was the first time Jenny had left her house since the night of Kyle's party. She put on a sundress and applied makeup around her puffy eyes. She tried to shake off her sorrow and move herself into gratitude, for the chance to go to college, for the ability to start over, for the love of this family who wanted to celebrate her.

After dinner, her dad called from the beach and said he was very proud of her. He said he was sorry they weren't there to take her to school, and they'd see her at Thanksgiving. She thought her mom might get on the phone, might say something to her on the night before she left for college, but her dad said she was already asleep. Jenny was only slightly surprised, having noticed yet another shift in her mother. This one occurred in this final month, when it became clear that Jenny would actually be leaving. Her mother recoiled, and just began to avoid her altogether.

Billy arrived at Jenny's house sometime after ten o'clock and sat on her front porch for most of the night. He stood beneath her window and called her name over and over again. It was the middle of August and her neighborhood was empty, so there was no one around to stop him. She wouldn't answer. She wouldn't come down. She had trusted Billy. She had relied on him to always do the right thing. She had complete faith in his love for her. All of this was gone now, his betrayal a fatal blow to all that she held to be true about him. It occurred to her that maybe he'd never been that earnest and faithful boy she believed him to be. She had nothing to say to him, and she wouldn't give him the chance to say anything to her. She didn't want to feel any of his pain. She didn't want him to see any of hers. She didn't want to soften. She turned up the radio in her room so she didn't have to hear him. When Ronnie Milsap came on, she unplugged the radio and put it in one of her suitcases, putting a stop to the music that always played in her bedroom. The last song on her childhood soundtrack would be the saddest of them all, and now she sat in silence.

When it was well past midnight, and she thought Billy was done, she tried to go to sleep. The minute she lay down, she heard him again, and put her pillow over her head. At daybreak, she heard the engine of Billy's truck and walked to the window, thinking she'd finally see him drive away. Instead, in the gray dawn sky, she saw Billy get out of his truck, slam the door, and retrieve a bat from the back. With the bat in hand, he hopped the fence that surrounded her front yard and ran toward the birch tree beneath her window. He took the bat and swung it, striking the large tree over and over again. It made a horrible crushing sound, and Jenny stood in the dark and watched as Billy just kept swinging. Then he stopped, turned, walked across the damp grass, and threw his bat in the back of the truck. Jenny watched as he got in his truck, laid his head down on the steering wheel, looked back up at her window one last time, and drove off.

That morning, Jenny said goodbye to her tangerine room and her gravel rooftop, the cinder block fence and the lemon tree. She packed the box of prayer cards she'd kept by her side constantly over the last few weeks, took down the painting from Uncle Gino's store, and she and Henry left for L.A. together. They did one last loop around town and drove under the iconic gold "Bakersfield" sign that crossed over Union Avenue. Jenny turned to Henry and asked, "Are you going to miss home?"

"No way."

"Not at all?"

"I don't think of it as leaving home. Home is wherever we say it is, and I'm bringing my favorite person with me."

Jenny looked out the window and knew that, despite Henry's certainty, she was leaving a big part of home behind. Not her house or the

TV dinners or the daily confrontations with her mother. Those were not home. Home was Uncle Gino and his antique store, Aunt Hope's kitchen and Heather's flowery bedroom, the patch of grass on Nonna's grave. Home was wherever Billy was—the baseball field, his truck, their park. She wasn't sure how she could actually forget him, but she decided that she'd try. She'd let all her mental snapshots of him move through her one more time, and then she'd bury them for good. *He's thirteen, backlit in her window seat. He's fourteen, and they're slow dancing at the junior high dance. He's fifteen, looking for her in the stands at his baseball game. He's sixteen, and they're driving around listening to Kenny Rogers. He's seventeen, watching the sun rise behind the Tehachapi Loop. He's eighteen, handing her a little garnet ring and promising to wait for her.* When the snapshots were done, she vowed to never let them back in, and she buried Billy so far down that eventually she didn't think of him at all.

Chapter Eleven

DECEMBER 1985–JANUARY 1986

Winter of their senior year at USC, Jenny accompanied Henry to the passport office, and at Henry's insistence, they both got passports, although she had no plans to go anywhere but a law library for the next few years. She'd selected a school named for Saint Clare, with a rose garden and mission bells, and a commitment to social justice. Henry was leaving for Europe after graduation. With a degree in communication and a minor in international relations, he was ready to see the world. He said he was leaving for the summer, but his flight was one-way, and Jenny suspected that he might just find a job and stay there.

As they drove over the Grapevine for their last Christmas vacation as college students, they shared the cupcake she'd made for his twenty-second birthday; Jenny pointed out the San Andreas Fault and other geographical features she'd learned from her dad; Henry patted her on the knee and gave an exaggerated yawn. When they neared town, Henry suggested that, before going home, they get a drink at the old Padre Hotel in Bakersfield. Jenny had driven by the Padre many times, but had never thought to go in. Opening in the spring of 1928, it had once been an opulent place, but she had never known it that way. She only knew it as the condemned building with the giant neon sign on the roof that read "Alamo Tombstone" and protest signs in the windows that said *Freedom of Speech? O Yeah—Reprisals* and *Infamy Rules Our Town*. The third through eighth floors had been closed and vacant for decades. Rumor had it that the ghosts of people who died in a fire roamed the seventh-floor hallway, including a little girl in prairie clothing and a butcher in a bloody apron.

Henry had somehow discovered the bar on the bottom floor and wanted to share the red velvet walls and the view from the fire escape with her. They found a table in the corner, ordered salty dogs, and watched as the crowd became an uneasy mix of college kids home on break, farmhands in cowboy hats, and men who wandered in from the alley. When they finished their drinks, Henry announced it was time to go to the seventh floor. When Jenny hesitated, Henry said, "Oh, come on. I promise you'll be glad you came with me."

Jenny realized this was something Henry said to her a lot, and it was usually true. Just a few weeks ago, he used this very line to get her to follow him into a mosh pit at the Hollywood Roosevelt Hotel, where Hüsker Dü was playing. He persuaded her with the fact that the band covered the Mary Tyler Moore theme song and maintained that the crowd couldn't be that scary if the band paid homage to Mary Tyler Moore. It was a reasonable theory, but it didn't prove to be true, and Henry ended up standing behind her in the mosh pit, his arms extended to shield her from the kids smashing into each other. It was only when they played "Love Is All Around" that she turned to him, took his hands and raised them in the air, and together, they jumped up and down and screamed along with the band.

They stepped out of the elevator into the eerily quiet hallway. It smelled like no one had opened a window in fifty years—like damp old carpet and rotting wood. They walked down the hall, lit only by a line of emergency lights on the ceiling. Henry tried a couple of locked doorknobs and led Jenny to the floor-to-ceiling window that opened to the fire escape. He pulled the lever and stepped out onto the metal fire escape seven stories above town.

Jenny stalled, but then she felt the fog on her face and saw the Christmas lights on the houses downtown and the Santa Claus on the marquis that wrapped around the old Fox Theater, and she climbed out onto the fire escape and sat beside Henry. In the distance, the green, blue, and red lights from the oil rigs on the edge of town flashed. Jenny heard the whistle of a faraway train, a Buck Owens song rising from the bar below. She pressed her forehead against the cold railing and watched as a man in a cowboy hat carrying a small Christmas tree walked down the foggy street alone.

"Our hometown," Henry said.

When it became too cold to sit outside any longer, they climbed back in the window, and went back down to the first floor. In the bar, someone shrieked, "Henry Hansen!" Jenny and Henry turned to see a group of guys about their age gathered against the red velvet wall. One of them came over and shook Henry's hand. He was blond and handsome and had a scarf wrapped around his neck.

"Are you home for Christmas? How's L.A.?" Without waiting for Henry to answer, he turned to Jenny and said, "Hi. I'm Scott."

Jenny introduced herself, and Henry said, "Scott and I have been friends since high school. He went to Highland."

Scott waved his friends over, and they all moved into a booth together. Jenny didn't recognize any of them, but they all knew Henry. She noticed Henry was avoiding eye contact with her, that he was nervous and fidgety sitting next to Scott. Looking around the table at Henry's friends that she'd never met—or even heard of—and sensing Henry's discomfort, Jenny decided that these might be his gay friends or friends that knew he was gay. She sensed it was her presence in this group making him uncomfortable. Even after nearly four years of college together, this was still something they never talked about. Henry never told her anything about his romantic life, and Jenny still never asked questions. She didn't want to be out drinking anyway, so she tapped him on the shoulder and said, "I think I'll just go home. I promised Uncle Gino I'd be at his house early tomorrow to cook."

"Are you sure?"

"Yeah. You stay and have fun."

Henry tossed her his car keys and told her he'd get a ride. She drove through a light fog past the Christmas lights on the closed businesses downtown, the darkness of the riverbed, the flashing lights of the oil rigs. As she neared the southwest part of town, the fog became thick and dense, and she could see only a few yards in front of her. This type of heavy fog, she realized, was as much a part of her childhood as her tangerine walls, valley fever, and the country music on the radio.

She parked Henry's car in front of her house. December 23rd at nearly midnight and there were no lights on. In the dark driveway, she felt the wet fog on her face, smelled the sweet smoke from a fireplace, and thought about how much she'd missed this valley, its earthy smell and misty air.

The next morning, Jenny went outside to retrieve the newspaper and was surprised to see Henry walking up the driveway, looking a little sheepish. She figured it was because she'd met his friends last night, which she knew made him uncomfortable.

"Hey, you're up early. Do you need your keys?"

Henry stood with his hands plunged deep in his pockets, his eyes downcast. "Can we go inside for a minute?"

"Henry, what's wrong? Are you okay?"

"I'm fine. I have something to tell you, though."

Jenny put her arm around his back and led him in the side door. He sat down on the couch while she grabbed his keys. The troubled look on his face made her wonder if he was going to tell her something about Scott, or about him and Scott, or one of the other boys she met at the Padre.

Henry pushed his hand through his hair and said, "I saw Billy last night."

Jenny felt a shiver on the back of her neck and put a hand to her heart. "He's home? Did you talk to him?"

Henry looked right at her and said, "Jenny, he's getting married."

"Getting married?" she asked, her face getting hot and her heart beating too fast. "To who?"

"All I know is her name is Tara and he met her in Oregon."

"He just told you that?"

"Well, we talked for a couple of minutes, like what's up, you know, and he said he left Arizona State and is playing ball in Oregon, and that he's getting married."

"When?"

"Next month."

"Next month?" Jenny got up and started walking around the room. "Why? Is she pregnant?"

"I don't know. It was weird, us running into each other. Billy and I are linked only because of you. It's not like he wanted to stand around and talk to me. He said he's going to be here through New Year's. Maybe you should go see him."

Jenny stopped pacing and stood in front of Henry. "Did he ask about me?"

"He was with Kyle and a bunch of other guys."

"So, that means no?"

"Why don't you call him?"

Jenny walked Henry to his car, went up to her room, and closed the door behind her. She hadn't seen Billy since the night on her lawn almost four years ago. She remembered how he'd called her repeatedly during her first semester at USC, and how she ignored his phone calls. Eventually he gave up, and when he did, she was relieved. She knew he would, of course, move on, that he would live his life without her, and that it would probably always hurt. But she was thoroughly unprepared for this—Billy getting married—just a few years after they'd decided to wait for seven. It hit her all at once, and the loss felt as fresh as the summer she left for school.

She stayed in her room the rest of the day. She thought about what she had done, what Billy had done, what they had been to each other, and how unfathomable it was that they both had let the relationship go. Part of her believed she deserved this unhappy ending—after all, she'd been the one who refused to even talk to him. She'd been the one who buried every memory of him. They'd spent nearly every day together since the summer she turned fourteen, and she'd refused to ever see him again—for a long time, even in her thoughts.

Over the last year or so, time and distance, and maybe maturity, had allowed her to feel some empathy for Billy, and she began to understand what that night and the aftermath must have felt like for him. She imagined him the day after Kyle's party, or even right after Michelle left the room, realizing what he had done—and what it would do to her. He knew she trusted him completely, as much as she was able to trust anyone. She thought how painful it must have been for him, knowing that he not only destroyed the relationship, but quite possibly put her in the hole for good. She thought about how she let him stand there alone in her yard, pleading for her to come out of the house. She was filled with shame and regret for refusing to listen, to open, to soften. It was if her own actions after that night, so severe and cold, had somehow nullified his betrayal.

There were times when she thought she should just pick up the phone and call Billy, that maybe they could find a way to be part of each other's lives again, even if in a small way, like someone you could send a Christmas card to or call on his birthday. But she never did, and she wasn't sure why. At first, she thought it was because of some sort of fear—fear of what she'd feel when she spoke to him, fear of actually dealing with that night, fear of hearing about his life without her. After some time, she realized it was more than just fear. She loved Billy, had never not loved Billy, and the only way she'd been able to get through the heartbreak was to actively put him away. To be in touch in any way would necessitate bringing him back, and she was never willing to do that. Now, confronted with the fact that he was getting married, she needed them to do what they never did before: say goodbye in a way that would honor what they'd meant to each other, the mutual love and care that, for many years, sustained them. In the early evening, she picked up the phone and dialed Billy's parents' house.

Her eyes filled when she heard his voice. "Hi, Billy."

"Jenny? Hey. What a surprise. How are you?"

"I'm good. I'm here in town for Christmas. I heard you saw Henry last night." Jenny hesitated for a moment and said, "He said you're getting married." The minute she said it, she wished she'd made at least a little small talk first.

"I am."

"I can't believe it. You're getting married." She wanted to say: *to someone else?* She wanted to shout *but you're only twenty-one!* Instead, she said, "I don't know what to say. I'm just so surprised."

"Yeah. It all happened pretty fast."

"And you're getting married next month?" Jenny twisted the phone cord around her wrist and stared down at the shag carpet in her old room.

"Yes."

Now she knew—she knew that after Christmas, Billy would go back to Oregon, and soon after that, he would be someone else's husband. She needed to see him before he put on a wedding ring. She convinced herself that it was the logical thing to do—a way to be complete. She didn't have any expectation that Billy would see her and change his mind. She just wanted them to look at each other and remember. She wanted to close the book. It didn't occur to her that her request would be forward or even unexpected; it felt like a necessity.

"Can I see you?" she said. "I mean, I'd like to see you. Could I come over? Or do you want to meet somewhere for a drink or something?"

Billy hesitated and then said, "I can't."

"After Christmas, then?"

Billy didn't answer her right away, and in the silence, she became confused. It all got muddled together, the past and the present, the boyfriend he used to be, the stranger he was now.

Billy said, "No, I mean, I can't see you. At all."

Her face flushed. She thought it was a simple request, to sit across from each other, to see his eyes, to have him see hers, to wish each other well. Now she realized it wasn't a simple request at all. She remembered refusing his pleas to see her, and she understood that he was now doing the same, and this is how it would go. Before she could stop herself, and before she realized how much anguish his answer would cause her, she asked, "You can't see me? Why not?"

"Jenny, I'm getting married in a month. She knows our history. She doesn't want me to see you. I can't do it."

"You talked about it? Why?"

Billy paused and said, "She was worried about me coming home for Christmas and seeing you."

Jenny was surprised the subject had even come up. They hadn't seen each other in years. She said, "Why? Why would it matter? You're getting married."

"It matters to her."

Jenny sat there trying to imagine what it was like—Billy telling another girl about her, about them. It made her feel so vulnerable and exposed and sad. "You won't see me?"

"I'm sorry."

She thought of all the things she wished she could say to him. She wanted to tell him about the regret she felt for refusing to see or talk to him after that night. She wanted to say that, as much as she tried, she was never able to forget him. She wanted to say, *I need us to say goodbye. Please can we look at each other again?*

They sat there for a while, neither saying anything.

Billy said, "Jenny, I had to move on. I tried to make you hear me for a really long time. But you erased me. Remember?"

Jenny put her head down and listened to Billy describe what she had done to him. *Erased*. It made her feel so sad and sick. "You're right. That's what I did. I'm sorry. I just wasn't equipped to deal with the hurt, so that's what I did."

"I know. I'm sorry too."

"I know." Jenny paused for a minute and then said, "Does this mean we'll never see each other again?"

"No. Why would you say that?"

"Well, how? How would we see each other? You live in a different state and you're marrying someone who doesn't want you to see me. So, I guess I don't understand how that would work—how we would ever see each other again."

"I'm sure we will."

Jenny knew his assurance just wasn't true. There was no way they'd see each other again without a plan to see each other. And there would be no plan to see each other when he would be marrying someone in a month, in another state, who didn't want him to see her now. She wondered if he knew that too and was just trying to be nice—or simply leave the subject behind.

Billy awkwardly tried to redirect the conversation. "So, are you good?" he asked.

Because his words came out in a way that felt more impatient than inquisitive, she wasn't sure what he meant. "Do you mean am I doing well, or do you mean am I ready to hang up the phone?"

"I mean, are you happy? Is your life good?"

"Oh." She thought of what to say. Her life was good. She was graduating from college soon. She was getting ready for law school. But happy? She wasn't sure how to answer him, so she just said, "Yeah, I'm good. Are you?"

"Yeah, I'm good."

Billy's tone revealed something different, and for the first time, it occurred to her that he might not be entirely happy about his impending marriage. She also knew him well enough to know that, if he felt that way, he would hold it close to the vest. He would be honorable. He would say nothing to disparage his future wife, or the situation he must have found himself in. So, after all her questioning and floundering, she decided to finally try to be graceful. "I hope you'll be happy. I mean it. I want you to be happy."

"Thank you."

Jenny didn't want to hang up the phone, but didn't really have anything else to say, so she just sat there again. Billy said, "Do you want to hang up now, since we're not really talking anymore?"

"I'm afraid to. I'm afraid that if we hang up, we won't ever talk again. Can we just sit here a little longer?"

"I'm sure we'll talk some time, but sure, I'll sit here with you."

They were both quiet. Jenny was trying to think of something to talk about that would keep them in conversation, without getting too deep. She imagined that Billy might be doing the same. Finally, Billy said, "Are you still planning to go to law school?"

"Yes. I'm hoping to go to Santa Clara in the fall."

"Good luck. I'm sure you'll do great." They sat on the phone for a few more minutes and then Billy said, "I should probably hang up now. My mom's putting dinner on the table."

Jenny squeezed her eyes shut. She could hear the sounds of Billy's house—a football game, the sliding glass door, the timer on the oven— and she pictured herself as a teenager there, setting the table with Billy's mom, putting her plate right next to his so they could hold hands. It was a sweet image, now turned excruciating. She thought, *If I'm not ever going to talk to him again, I want him to know*, and she said, "I love you, Billy."

Billy paused as if thinking of what to say back to her and then said only, "Thank you."

Jenny knew before she uttered the words that they would not be reciprocated. But hearing Billy say *thank you* instead of *I love you too*, presented such an immediate finality. After he said goodbye, she heard the hard click of his telephone being placed back on the receiver and thought, *The end*. The dial tone buzzed in her ear, and she just sat there. She thought of the box of photos and letters she'd thrown out and realized that the only memories of Billy she had were the ones in her mind, the ones that survived burial, and she would likely never see him again. She had no physical representation of their relationship. She ached for the photographs she'd put in trash, for the love letters he'd once written, for her little garnet ring. She crawled out onto the roof in the frigid December night air and began to scream and cry. She threw a tantrum worthy of a small child, something she hadn't allowed herself to do her whole life.

On Christmas day, Jenny took a bag of bird seed from her suitcase and sprinkled it on her rooftop. When the birds began to land and enjoy their meal, she said, "Merry Christmas, birds." She sat by the Christmas tree and unwrapped a few small gifts from "Santa" that her father had wrapped in special "North Pole" paper with glittery ribbons, just like he did every Christmas. She watched him present her mother with gifts he couldn't afford. She delivered a Christmas present to Henry's doorstep, wished him a Merry Christmas, and he held her for a long time.

A week later, on the drive back to school, Henry and Jenny didn't talk much. She was deep in the hole, and not even Henry could reach her. She was struck by the fact that mistakes she and Billy made as teenagers would now affect the whole of their lives. She was torturing herself with *what ifs*. She leaned her head against the window and stared out at the brown fields.

Belonging

When they got to school, she had Henry drop her at the campus bookstore, where she picked out a handmade card with a sketch of a bride and groom. Inside, she wrote the following simple note to Billy: *I know you will be a sweet and devoted husband. I picture you someday with a house full of beautiful children. I hope you have a really happy life. Love, Jenny.* She slipped a prayer card inside that she'd found in a box of devotional items at Uncle Gino's store. It had delicate edges cut like lace and old-fashioned gold lettering that said: *Above all these things, walk in love, which is the bond of perfection. Colossians 3:14.*

After she mailed the card to Billy, she went to a table in the corner of the Philosophy Library and laid her head down on her books. She'd opened the door to memories she'd kept out for years. She thought of being with Billy in their park the summer she left, how she touched his hands and ears and lips, and smelled his shirt and hair and skin, wanting to be able to feel him next to her even when they were far away. She wished she'd never memorized him. She had no idea what to do with her memories, with the love she felt for him. She remembered what Uncle Gino told her the day after Nonna's funeral, about being able to send love to people from wherever you are to wherever they are. From then on, whenever she thought of Billy, she sent him all the love she felt for him, and imagined him receiving it, not knowing what it was, but just being happy, feeling it.

A few weeks after they returned from Christmas break, Jenny and Henry went to the Norris Theatre to see *Splendor in the Grass*, the first film in the Introduction to Cinema class they'd signed up for together. *Splendor in the Grass* proved too close to home for Jenny—the tragic story of Bud and Deanie coming of age, falling in love, and breaking each other's hearts. The worst part was the end, when years later, Deanie sees Bud on an old dirt road and he utters these seven words: "Hey, you want to meet my family?"

As the credits rolled, Henry took a tissue from his backpack and handed it to Jenny. "She's better off without Bud, don't you think?" he said. "I mean, who'd want to live out there with chickens in the kitchen? And now she gets to marry a doctor from Ohio!"

Jenny smiled at Henry's attempt to console her, and as they walked through campus after class, he put his arm around her. It was a cold, clear L.A. evening, and they were in their last few months of college. They stopped and sat on the fountain in front of Doheny, just like Dustin Hoffman did in *The Graduate*. Ironically, *The Graduate* was another film they would study in their cinema class, and they would have the dream-like experience of watching it on campus. They would learn that, while some reviewers believed the film was a time capsule of that generation of young Americans, others thought it was not definitive because it failed to mention the Vietnam War or the antiwar protests that were such a central part of their coming of age. They would also learn that the long shot of Ben and Elaine in the bus at the end was designed to show the uncertainty of their future.

Campus was quiet, just the occasional whirring by of kids on bicycles, faint music coming from the window of a dorm room, the doors to the library opening and closing, allowing light to seep out into the night. Henry said, "Hey, do you want to go to the Whisky with me tonight?"

Jenny shook her head and blew her nose. "Not really."

"Come on. I heard Robert Palmer is playing a private show."

"If it's private, how do we get in?"

"I know a guy who can get us in."

Jenny laughed, because of course Henry knew a guy. He knew a guy at the *Times* who gave him press passes so Jenny could meet Jackson Browne at a benefit in Malibu. He knew a guy at an independent theater in West Hollywood, who let them go to movies for free. He knew a guy who waved them into a roped off area on the library stairs while Bishop Desmond Tutu spoke about South African apartheid. He knew a guy who introduced them to the Red Hot Chili Peppers after a show in Hollywood, where during their encore they only wore tube socks—and not on their feet. He knew a guy who unlocked the stairwell to the Bovard Tower, so they could climb to the top and look out over campus and the lights of L.A.

Belonging

Behind the Whisky, Henry exchanged a few words in Spanish and handed five dollars to a busboy in a white apron, who let them cut through the kitchen to the club. Robert Palmer wasn't on yet, and the crowd looked like industry people—older and disinterested and sitting. Jenny and Henry leaned against the stage until Robert Palmer came on and then danced through his hour-long set that began with "Johnny and Mary" and ended with "Addicted to Love."

That night, when she got back to her apartment, Jenny took out her box of prayer cards and put a handful on her bed. With college almost over and so many unknowns, she felt untethered. She believed that graduation signified the end of adolescence, her ties to childhood and home. Henry leaving the country and Billy getting married put an exclamation point on this belief. She knew she wouldn't be going back to Bakersfield, except to visit. She thought about Uncle Gino, Heather, and Aunt Hope, and felt sad that they'd never live in the same town again. She didn't know what the future held. She picked up one of the prayer cards and held it. It had an image of a sunrise, and on the back, it said: *Weeping may stay for the night, but joy comes in the morning. Psalm 30:5.*

PART TWO

PART TWO

Chapter Twelve

AUGUST 1990

Jenny cracked her window and stuck a hand out to feel the hot air as she passed the cattle and palm trees that bordered Harris Ranch on the I-5, the long, straight highway running through the middle of California. She was listening to a tape Henry made for her—all the U2 songs he thought she should know. It arrived in the mail just before her trip with a note that said: *They're Catholic! And they write poetry! You love Catholics and poets!* Jenny was on her way back to Bakersfield for Heather's wedding, where she would be standing beside her as the maid of honor. She hadn't been home since the summer after college graduation, when she and Henry made one last trek over the Grapevine together, cleaned out their childhood bedrooms, and said a sad goodbye before Henry boarded a plane to Europe, and she left for law school. Now, she was a twenty-six-year-old lawyer, and Henry was working for the Brussels Independent Film Festival.

As she neared town, Jenny turned off U2 and tuned into KUZZ. The DJ announced that it was 108 degrees outside and cued up Garth Brooks' "The Dance." The melancholy song and the feel of August in Bakersfield after years away made Jenny feel wistful. While she felt hopeful for the happy weekend ahead, there was also longing for part of her life that was gone. *Hope and longing*, the same as any good song, just like Nonna taught her.

When she parked in front of 822 Lupine Lane, she got out of her car and stared at her childhood home. The black shutters and the white picket fence were both in need of paint. The lemon tree was a mass of dark green shiny leaves and yellow fruit. The birch tree beneath her bedroom window had grown taller and thicker. She felt the intense heat on her face, and inhaled the scent of leaves, grass, dirt, gardenias, chlorine, cows. She walked across the grass and pulled a lemon from the tree and held it up to her nose. The scent was so familiar and entwined with her childhood that it registered in her body, and she could feel the boredom and promise of a summer afternoon.

She opened the front door, and the cold air conditioning blew at her. The house had the same stale smell. The family room was dark, and the piles were there. She heard the whir and drop of the icemaker and a TV in the distance. The scene, the smell, the sounds were all exactly the same as when she left. She felt like she'd stepped back in time. She went upstairs to her old room. It was also just as she left it, except for bags of her mother's old clothes that now took up a corner. The tangerine walls had never been repainted; the corkboard was empty. She hung her bridesmaid dress in the closet and opened her shutters. Looking out at the gravel rooftop, she remembered the night she'd climbed out her window and screamed and cried. Her prediction had been true; after that night, she never saw or talked to Billy again.

Jenny changed into a simple sleeveless yellow shift, touched up her makeup, and sat down on her bed, stalling. The last time she stayed in this house, she had just graduated from college. Since then, she had seen her parents infrequently and made only the obligatory phone calls on birthdays and holidays. She knew very little of their day-to-day lives, and they knew none of hers. She was nervous to see them and unsettled by the feeling of being in the house. She sat in the window seat and recalled her silent prayer to Saint Teresa. *May I be at peace. May my heart remain open. May I be aware of my true nature. May I be healed. May I be a source of healing to others. May I dwell in the Breath of God.* She took a deep breath and went down the hall to her parents' room.

From the doorway, Jenny saw her mother in a black silky bathrobe, putting hot rollers in her hair. Her father was sitting on the bed in his dress pants and a white undershirt, his hair wet and slicked back. He had the remote control in one hand and a Marlboro in the other. He stood when she walked in and said, "Well, look at you."

Belonging

Jenny went to him and gave him a hug. His smell was just as she remembered—cigarette smoke, Prell shampoo, sawdust, coffee. Her mother walked across the bedroom with her drink in her hand. She had her same trademark look—short black hair, hoop earrings, and frosty brown lipstick that she'd worn for years. Jenny stiffened, worried about an unavoidable embrace or some other awkward show of affection. She should have known better. Her mother merely touched her linen dress, holding the fabric between her thumb and forefingers and said, "We don't have much time. You should get changed."

Jenny said, "This is what I'm wearing. I bought it for the rehearsal dinner."

"It's cocktail attire. You look like you're going to church." She took off her bathrobe and walked across the bedroom in black underwear and a sheer black lace bra and retrieved a pack of cigarettes from her purse.

Jenny's dad stared at the local TV news. *Search parties are looking for a Canoga Park man who disappeared while tubing in the Kern River. Six people have died in the river this year.* Her mother took a drag of her cigarette and exhaled the smoke, forming a little cloud around her.

Her father went to the closet and took out his dress shirt and jacket. "Is that a new suit?" Jenny asked. "You look nice."

"Your mother said everyone in town will be there, and I've got to look presentable."

Her mother, still undressed, walked up behind her father, ran a hand along the back of his shoulders and said, "He does clean up well."

Jenny wanted to creep out of the room, get in her car, and head back up the I-5 blasting U2. Instead, she tried to make small talk. "Have you seen Aunt Hope? I bet she's so excited for the wedding."

Her mother wagged an index finger at her. "You'd think that her daughter was marrying Elvis, instead of some country singer we've barely heard of. Everywhere we go, that's all I hear about—the fancy house, the damned song, her perfect life."

She slipped on her black cocktail dress and walked into the bathroom, where she released her hot rollers, filled the room with hairspray, and sat in front of the red glow of her sunlamp. Jenny touched her fingers to her forehead and recalled the prayer she'd just said in her bedroom. *May I be at peace.*

On the drive across town to a Basque restaurant, Jenny's dad put the Dodgers game on the radio. Her mother powdered her face, now red from the sunlamp. Jenny had given up trying to make conversation, so they just rode in silence with the occasional whack of a bat, the calling of balls and strikes. Jenny looked out the window and kept her hand on the door handle. She'd been gone for four years, and yet, they fell into the same exact patterns from her childhood: her mother's bitterness, her father's oblivion, her own silence and desire to flee. *May I be healed.*

While her eyes were adjusting to the darkness of the restaurant, Jenny spotted Heather buzzing across the dining room, darting between people there to wish her well. Her blonde curly hair fell to her waist, and she wore a short white dress that showed off her long, tanned legs. When she finally reached Jenny, she grabbed both of her hands and pulled her into a tight hug.

"You look so beautiful," Jenny said.

"Thank you. You too."

"My mom said I look like I'm going to church."

"How would she know what the inside of a church looks like?"

Jenny laughed and realized how much she'd missed being with Heather. They talked on the phone all the time, and Heather visited often, but it just wasn't the same as living in the same town. The door to the dark restaurant opened and Jenny spotted Uncle Gino in the brief flash of sunlight. His silver hair was pulled back into a ponytail behind his brown, deeply lined face, and he wore a faux diamond stud in his ear. Jenny put her purse down at the table and crossed the room to greet him. He was warm and smelled like Old Spice and maybe a little garlic.

"Well, wonders never cease." Uncle Gino released Jenny from the hug and held her at arm's length. "I told Heather she has to get married more often since it's apparently the only way to get you home."

"I know. It's been too long. I miss you." She reached out a hand and touched his earlobe. "You got your ear pierced. I like it."

"All of the dealers from L.A. have them. I thought I'd try it out. Do I look silly?"

"No, you look handsome."

Jenny noticed her father get up from the table with a pack of cigarettes in his hand and head toward the front door. While Uncle Gino mingled, she went outside and found her father smoking on a bench in the parking lot.

"Hey," she said and sat down next to him.

He scooted over to the end of the bench. "You'll get smoky sitting here by me."

"I don't mind. We haven't even really talked yet."

"Well, how are you, darlin'?"

"Excited for the wedding, and to be home. I've really missed this place."

"You missed *this* place?" He raised his eyebrows at her, took a drag of his cigarette and turned the other way to exhale the smoke. "Tell me what you missed about this place."

"Well, I missed the heat and the smell of hay and the sound of the sprinklers when you first wake up in the morning. The flatness of the horizon. Hearing country music from the window of every passing car. Uncle Gino's antique store. Stockdale 6. Your lemon tree." She paused and tapped her chin and glanced up at the sky. "Going to sleep sticky sweaty until the air kicks on like a great surprise. Basque food. The river. Dr Pepper with crunchy ice. Lots of things."

He reached over and pointed to the pale scar that ran across the inside of her arm, just above her elbow. "You still have that scar."

"I have all sorts of scars. It's because I have olive skin."

"You must have been pulling really hard for it to leave a mark like that."

"I don't remember it," she said, running her finger along the line.

It was true, she would've never known how she got the scar unless he told her. And she knew that he did, so she would believe it was an innocent mistake instead of an intentional wound. When she was about two years old, in an effort to have her stop sucking her thumb, her mother placed a plastic tube on her arm, so that it wouldn't bend, so that she couldn't reach her thumb to her mouth. Jenny pulled hard enough, though, trying to reach her thumb, that the rough edge of the tube sliced

121

into her skin. Her dad said that he cut off the tube right when he got home from work. He said she'd only had it on for a few hours, but she suspected that she may have worn it for days. She wasn't sure why she thought that, except for a shadowy memory of laying on a floor, unable to comfort herself, holding onto a white stuffed rabbit with large pink eyes. She was struggling in both daylight and dark, and she somehow learned to play dead. It was the first time she could remember being able to make herself disappear, going to the place that Billy later named "the hole." Even now, she could see the toddler on the floor, abandoned and separate from the self she had vanished.

Her father stood and tossed his cigarette on the ground and stepped on it. "We should go back in," he said, as he started to walk back toward the restaurant. "Mama will be looking for me."

Jenny closed her eyes and sighed. She wasn't ready to go back in yet. She heard the rumble and whistle of a train. She looked out at the horizon, brown soil meeting purple sky, and thought of all the songs that evoked the landscape of Bakersfield in a way that was poetic and beautiful—the immense flat spaces, cotton and potato fields, orchards and oil fields, the canals and the Kern River. It was a city born from a desire to *make waste places bloom and blossom with grass and grain and cheerful homes*, named for a man who planted fields of alfalfa, corn, potatoes, and beans, and allowed immigrants to camp on his land and take what they needed. Why didn't her dad see the beauty? Did you have to leave and come back to see it? She'd been told once or a hundred times that Bakersfield was "the armpit" of California. She figured the people who said that had never been here, never stepped barefoot on its flat green lawns, never felt its warmth, never heard its music. To her, Bakersfield felt more like the soft underside of the wrist, where you felt for the pulse, or maybe the palm of your hand. Sometimes, she'd be standing in her front yard in Santa Clara, and she'd get a whiff of wet dirt or cut grass, or the winds shifted just right, and she could smell the cows down in Gilroy, and she could see herself as a child—on Nonna's back patio, in Uncle Gino's garden, on a school bus on a fall day.

Jenny took a deep breath and walked back inside. She made her way to her table and sat down next to Uncle Gino. Waitresses in black uniforms with red aprons came out carrying bowls of vegetable soup, green salad, beans, salsa, and crusty French bread, followed by serving platters of French fries, pickled cow's tongue, spaghetti, and tomato salad—all served family style as "the set-up" in a traditional Basque meal. Uncle Gino reached for a platter and put several slices of pink tongue dotted with garlic and parsley on his plate. Jenny looked down at her watch. It was almost time for her toast. She excused herself and went to the old-fashioned powder room in the back of the restaurant.

She brushed back her brown shoulder-length hair and put on a smidge of pink lip gloss. She straightened her yellow dress, which stood in contrast to her dark brown eyes and olive skin. As she checked her reflection and began to mouth the words of the toast that she'd practiced so many times, her mother appeared behind her in the mirror and removed her lipstick from her clutch.

"What are you doing?" she asked.

"I'm practicing my toast."

"Who, exactly, are you trying to impress?" She leaned toward the mirror and applied her frosty brown lipstick. "You know, the toast doesn't have to be perfect. You'll probably be giving one at all her weddings."

"I wish you wouldn't say that."

"I'm just not buying it. Sorry."

"Well, could you keep that to yourself tonight? She's your brother's daughter."

Her mother gave her a look of pure disdain. "I see you're still better than everyone else." She tossed her lipstick into her purse and said, "I'd be careful if I were you."

Jenny took a step back, her body registering the threat. What would happen if she wasn't careful? Her mother turned and left the bathroom, and Jenny took a moment to compose herself. *May my heart remain open.* When she returned to the table, Uncle Gino clanked his spoon on his glass, and soon the room joined him. When it was quiet, she held Uncle Gino's warm, rough hand, and stood to give her toast.

"For those of you who don't know me, I'm Heather's cousin, Jenny. I'm here as her maid of honor, a role I've been preparing for my entire life."

Everyone laughed and Jenny winked at Heather, who had moved onto Rickey's lap.

"Heather has always known what she wanted in life—to be a devoted wife, to create her own loving home, to fill that home with as many children as it would hold. And, if the lyrics to 'Ready to Grow Old with You' are true, she told Rickey this the night they met."

Jenny's reference to Rickey's number one song caused an uproar in the room. It told the story of the night he and Heather met at the Buck Owens Rodeo Dance—an annual event held at the fairgrounds that included live music, barbecue, two-step dancing, and the announcement of the rodeo queen. The Rickey Sutton Band was introduced as a newcomer to country radio, and a personal favorite of Buck's. After they played their set, Rickey approached Heather, who was sitting side stage—a privilege afforded her as a former rodeo queen—and asked her to dance. One dance became five, and according to the song, by the time the sun came up behind the Ferris wheel the next morning, Heather had named all their children.

When the clapping and hollering died down, Jenny raised her glass and said, "Heather and Rickey, here is my wish list for you: that you always speak each other's virtues; that you hold hands every day; that each time you part, you wave goodbye until you can't see each other anymore; that you never forget how essential kissing is; that you have a home filled with the sounds of happy children and music and laughter; and that you are surrounded every day by people who love you."

Everyone raised their glasses, and Jenny turned to Uncle Gino, who'd finished his champagne before the toast, and he squeezed her hand instead of raising an empty glass.

· As guests began to mill around, Uncle Gino collected leftovers from the table. He set aside a full loaf of French bread and a handful of foil-wrapped pats of butter. He emptied serving plates of food into to-go boxes. A waitress, who seemed to know Uncle Gino, put the boxes of chicken, fries, and pickled tongue, and the loaf of bread and pats of butter, in a large paper bag and set it down next to him.

Jenny put her hand on Uncle Gino's shoulder and said, "Would it be okay if I take you home and keep your car tonight?"

Belonging

"Of course, darling. I'm ready when you are."

Jenny went into the bar to say goodbye to Heather and Rickey, then walked across the street to the dirt field where Uncle Gino's old Cadillac was parked. The radio was set to the oldies station, and they listened to Patsy Cline as they passed all the local landmarks—Buck Owens's recording studio, the old clock tower, the ice cream shop that had been there since 1930.

They parked in front of the yellow Victorian house that had been in their family for over eighty years. Uncle Gino walked in the front door and turned the dial on the air conditioning unit until it clicked on with a slow rumble and a whoosh of cold air. The house had all the smells she remembered: leather chairs, old books, roses. The floors were dark, shiny oak, and the walls were covered in a Victorian era wallpaper, pink roses surrounded by green leaves. On the bookshelves, there were rows of old photo albums. They chronicled the beginning of her great-grandparents' life in California: her great-grandmother planting fruit trees, herbs, and a vegetable garden; her great-grandfather standing under the arbor he'd built in the backyard; families gathered around the two long picnic tables under the arbor, saying grace, giving thanks, and sharing meals.

Jenny went into the kitchen to unload the food from the restaurant. A half pot of coffee had been left on since morning. The drying rack on the counter held one plate and one cup, one spoon and one fork. A framed copy of "The Italians in America" hung above the kitchen table.

Uncle Gino pulled a glass from the cupboard and filled it with ice and water. He put some milk in a bowl, opened the screen door to his patio, and put the bowl outside for the stray cats that wandered downtown. The sound of dropping ice into a cup and pulling open a screen door combined with the smell of old coffee and leftover fried chicken gave Jenny a feeling of longing that was both familiar and distant. She hadn't felt it in a long time, and it arose just by standing in the air-conditioned old house on a late summer night.

After she kissed Uncle Gino goodbye, Jenny drove west onto a wide tree-lined street that held the large pale yellow ranch style home that Nonna and Nonno built together in the 1930s, where they raised their two children: Jenny's mother, Janice, and Heather's father, Uncle Joe. She parked in front and wished she could bother the current occupants to let her stay the night in the room at the back of the house that Nonna made just for her—with the bookshelves filled with books and records, water-color paintings of garden fairies, and windows facing the rose garden.

Jenny got out of her car and stood in the street, looking at the house. She could hear the loud chirping of frogs in the ivy that grew alongside the driveway and the *click-click-click* of the circular sprinklers on the lawn. She could smell the rose garden and the chlorine from the pool. She imagined herself at six years old, when she lived with Nonna for a while. She never knew why or for how long, but remembered it was long enough to believe that her parents might not be coming back. It was long enough for her to go from the fear and uncertainty of being left, to embracing the joy of living with Nonna. There were warm spring days in the garden and dancing on the back patio after dinner. She ate oatmeal with cinnamon and apples at the kitchen table with Uncle Gino. She had clean, pressed clothes to wear to school and someone to pack a lunch for her. She was tucked in every night by Nonna in a warm house that smelled like rosemary and corn muffins. She remembered the night it all ended, the dim light of dusk, the records on the floor, the shadows from the trees on the walls. She'd fallen asleep to the soft warbling of the tiny owl that lived just outside her room and was awakened in the middle of the night when her mother plucked her from the bed and threw her in the backseat of her car.

There was one more memory from this house that frequently emerged. She was walking through Nonna's rose garden as a toddler, clutching her stuffed rabbit and holding Uncle Gino's hand. She felt an uneasiness she couldn't articulate—she didn't have the words then, so it lived inside her body, unnamed. But she remembered the smell of roses and the sound of her mother crying from inside the house. And she remembered that when her mother took her home, no one held her for what seemed like forever.

Chapter Thirteen

AUGUST 1990

Heather was sitting in front of a full-length mirror, wearing a white lace slip, her hair in rollers, when Jenny walked into her bedroom. She grabbed Jenny's hand and led her to the balcony. "Look at the sky. And can you smell it? It smells like rain, doesn't it?"

Jenny looked up at the purple and gray sky. The air was damp and muggy and very still, what her father always called "earthquake weather."

"It's beautiful, and yes, it smells like rain."

"Just in time for my outdoor wedding. It hasn't rained since March. It's the end of summer. How did this happen?"

"They're already setting up tents. It will all be fine." She smiled and put her hands on Heather's shoulders. "It'll be perfect."

By the time Uncle Joe walked Heather down the aisle in the late afternoon, loud booms of thunder could be heard in the distance, but there was still no rain. Heather and Rickey exchanged vows in a gazebo under the dark sky, and after both said, "I do," three men with violins stood and began to play the prelude to "Ready to Grow Old with You." As Rickey sang to Heather, Jenny reached for the tissue under her bouquet. She knew she'd cry at the bridge, when he said the names of the children.

never again would I let a day go by
without holding your dreams and making them mine
I'll build you a house
where the river runs out back
where our children will run—Hope, Daisy, Sam, and Jack

As they walked back down the aisle, splits of lightning could be seen just beyond the riverbed. The clouds above them were dark gray and looked like they would burst open at any moment. When the last attendant reached the end of the aisle, the wedding guests started quickly moving toward the tent. Jenny just stood there, waiting for the rain to come. She was so happy for Heather, at the prospect of the life ahead of her. She thought, *I bet it will be just like the song.*

After an hour or so of trying to mingle and dance in her long, lavender bridesmaid dress with the full petticoat underneath, Jenny decided to abandon the petticoat. As she made her way across the tented dance floor, she spotted her mother with a drink in the air, her father trying to keep up. Inside the house, she pushed open the door to the large guest bathroom and was surprised to see a small boy, about three or four years old, sitting by himself on the marble countertop. He was blond, his dress shirt was untucked, and his shoes were on the counter beside him. He was sailing a toy boat in the sink, and when Jenny walked in, he took it out and held it on his lap.

Jenny knelt, bending the wires in her skirt, and said, "Hey, buddy. Whatcha doing?"

He looked at his damp socks and put his thumb in his mouth.

"It's okay," Jenny told him, "I was just looking for a place to take off this itchy petticoat." She reached up and turned off the running water and the boy removed his thumb from his mouth.

"I made a lake for my boat."

"I see that. It's pretty cool. What's your name?"

"Carl."

"Hi, Carl. I'm Jenny." She lifted his hand and shook it. "Where's your mom and dad?"

Carl shrugged and Jenny said, "Do you want me to help you find them?"

"Okay."

"Here, let's put your shoes back on."

Belonging

Jenny straightened the socks on his feet, slipped on his shoes, tied them, and said, "Is that okay? Too tight or anything?"

Carl reached out his wet hand, touched the sparkles on her dress, and said, "They're good."

Jenny drained the sink and took Carl's hand and went outside to the dance floor. It was so crowded under the tent that it was hard for Jenny to see three feet in front of her, so she knew Carl wouldn't be able to see at all. "Is it okay if I give you a lift? So you can see better?"

"Okay."

Jenny held Carl on her hip as they moved through the crowd. Nearing the edge of the tent, he pointed toward the riverbank, and shouted, "There's my daddy!"

She put him down and watched as he took off running under the dark sky. When she realized he was running to Billy, her hands began to slightly tremble, and tears popped into her eyes. She watched as Billy leaned down to lift Carl. She hadn't seen him since the night on her lawn. It had been eight years, almost exactly, that she looked out her window and saw him swinging his bat against the birch tree until he couldn't swing anymore. It had been almost five years since she'd sat in her old bedroom and said, "I love you" into the phone, and he had responded, "Thank you." Now, here he was in a suit and tie, holding his little boy.

The trembling and the tears came from joy and sorrow rising at the exact same time. *Billy is here, and I can see his eyes. Billy has a child, who has a mother, who is Billy's wife, who is not me.* The emotions were overwhelming and confusing. One part of her wanted to gather up her dress and sprint to him; another wanted to run away, down the winding canyon road. When Billy smiled at her, she lifted the bottom of her dress and walked toward him.

"Billy."

"Hey, Jenny."

She looked at Billy's hazel eyes, then at Carl's, and said, "Carl is your son?"

"Yeah, he is. I guess you've already met." Billy reached for her with his free arm and said, "Come here."

He hugged her tightly against his chest, and she could feel how fast his heart was beating. He smelled different, but the same, and she wasn't sure how that could be. She hugged him back and reached down and held onto his hand. The last time she'd been this close to him, they were sitting in her bedroom talking about summer and college and sex and getting married, and she'd kissed him goodbye, thinking he'd be back in a few hours. Standing with him now, she realized they'd never been around each other when they weren't a couple, and holding hands felt instinctual, like they were supposed to be that way.

Billy smiled and shook his head. "How did Carl manage to pick you out of the crowd?"

Jenny looked up at Carl and said, "I think I might have picked him."

The wind had whipped up in the canyon around them, and warm raindrops started to fall.

Jenny said, "Let's get out of the rain. Follow me."

She led Billy and Carl into a mudroom on the east side of the house, and the wind slammed the door shut behind them. They sat down on a wooden bench and Carl wandered around, sailing his boat through the air, studying the antlers Rickey hung on the walls.

"I can't believe Heather didn't tell me you were coming." Jenny looked over at Carl. "What am I saying? I can't believe you have a son."

"Didn't you know?"

"I did. I mean, I'd heard that you had a baby. But seeing him—" Jenny searched for the right words. "Knowing his name, seeing you with him. It's different. You know, not abstract. He's precious. How old is he?"

"He was four in July."

Jenny thought about the timing. She couldn't help it. Now she knew—Billy's wife had been pregnant when she called him that Christmas Eve. Where was she now? It crossed her mind that she could walk into the mudroom any minute.

"Are you still in Oregon?"

"No, I'm living near Santa Barbara, finishing school and coaching at a high school there."

"You're not playing anymore?"

"I haven't played since Carl was a baby. My arm gave out. I became 'ineffective,' as they say."

"I didn't know. I'm sorry."

Billy made sure Carl was out of earshot and said quietly, "My wife, Tara, left me—and Carl—when she found out I wouldn't be playing baseball anymore. I mean, when she realized I wouldn't ever be a star or make a lot of money or anything."

"I don't know what to say, Billy. I'm so sorry."

"I could say the whole thing was a giant mistake, but I know that's not true because of Carl."

"Do you share custody of Carl?"

"No, she followed another guy to another team. Carl doesn't really know his mother."

"Not at all?"

"Well, she left when he was five months old, and she's only seen him twice since."

"I'm so sorry, Billy. I have no words."

"That's so unlike you." Billy smiled, squeezed her elbow, and trying to break the tension said, "What about you? I heard you passed the bar. Congratulations."

"Thank you. I'm now a deputy public defender in Santa Clara."

Billy nodded. "That sounds about right."

Jenny smoothed her dress and said, "I'm sorry. I really should go back to the reception. I have so many maid of honor duties."

"I understand. What if I come back later, after things wind down? I'll take Carl back to my parents' house. We could talk."

This was something Jenny never imagined could happen. The night she told him she was afraid they'd never talk again, she understood that was a real probability. And as a result, she'd never have the answers she needed. They'd never be able to forgive each other face to face. She would never feel complete. The years since had proven this to be true, leaving a wound that had never healed. Now, after all this time, with Billy offering to sit with her and talk, she hesitated. There were so many painful things they had never discussed. She knew how she'd feel sitting alone with him after the wedding. She already felt it. Before she could answer, Carl was tugging on her dress and whispering that he'd found another sink for his boat. Billy lifted Carl and squeezed her hand. "So, what do you think?"

Jenny closed her eyes briefly, opened them, and said, "I would love that."

At the end of the night, Heather asked Jenny to come upstairs with her while she got out of her wedding dress and double-checked her honeymoon packing. Jenny changed into shorts and a t-shirt, brushed her hair back into a ponytail, and scrubbed the heavy makeup from her face. She opened the balcony doors that looked toward the riverbed. The rain had stopped, and the air smelled clean and sweet after the storm. She sat on Heather's bed and said, "I saw Billy."

Heather stopped primping and sat next to her. "Oh, was it okay? I mean, was it weird?"

"Not weird. Just so unexpected. Why didn't you tell me he was going to be here?"

"I thought you knew."

"No."

"Oh. Well, I invited all our old friends."

"Yeah, but Billy. I sort of think that warranted a conversation. I mean, to prepare me?"

"Honestly, Jenny, I was so preoccupied with my wedding, and I didn't know it would matter that much to you. I mean, you moved on, like, years ago?"

Jenny thought, *Yes, of course, that's exactly how it must have looked— she'd moved on years ago.* It was a stark reminder of just how good she was at concealing her feelings. She couldn't fault Heather. She was a master at hiding, and no one, except for maybe Henry, knew she'd never truly recovered from the loss of her relationship with Billy. *She'd moved on years ago.*

It was almost one a.m. when Billy came back. He had on jeans and a button-down shirt that he wore untucked, and when he got close enough, she realized he had on aftershave she didn't recognize and his hair was a little damp. She was perplexed again by both his familiarity and unfamiliarity at once. She'd touched his damp hair thousands of times. She felt like she could easily do so now, but she didn't know anything about him anymore. They hadn't even been in a room together since the summer before she left for college. A lot of life had happened since then—for both of them.

"Your duties must be complete." He looked at his watch. "The wedding was yesterday." Billy looked at her bare face. "You look like yourself now."

"Yeah."

"Do you want to go for a walk or something? It's actually a little cool outside."

"That sounds nice."

They walked down the narrow gravel path by the riverbed with only the small pathway lights to show them the way. They talked about the wedding, being back home, Rickey's song. Billy asked Jenny about practicing law. Jenny asked Billy about fatherhood. She reached for his hand and held it, and said, "Tell me about Carl."

"He just turned four. He loves dinosaurs and trains. He's very curious. He wants to know all about the planets and stars. He'll be in kindergarten next year. He's affectionate and talkative, and not at all shy, but I guess you already know that."

They found a small embankment and sat down. It was so quiet—only the sounds of an owl in the trees and the tumbleweeds rolling in the riverbed. Jenny turned to Billy and said, "I wish I had known all that was going on with you. I wish you would have called me or something."

"I actually did call you once—from a pay phone at a supermarket in Bend while I was still married. I called your house in Bakersfield because it's the only number I knew. I talked to your dad. He gave me your number."

"You talked to my dad? He never told me."

Jenny felt like the wind had been knocked out of her. She couldn't believe her dad never mentioned the call from Billy. She wondered what would've changed inside of her if she'd known that he called, that he hadn't fully closed the door on them, that he still thought of her.

"How long ago was this?"

"About three and a half years ago. Carl was a baby. I dialed your number, and he started to fuss, and I thought, *What am I doing?* I hung up. I mean, what was I going to say?"

Jenny pictured him next to a row of grocery carts, phone in hand, a baby in his arms.

"What *were* you going to say?"

Billy shook his head. "I don't know." He lifted her hand and held it with both of his. "Sometimes, I wonder what would have happened to us if you would have at least let me see you again."

Jenny closed her eyes, opened them, and said, "Sometimes, I wonder what would have happened to us if you would have at least let *me* see *you* again."

"I'm sorry, Jenny. You never got to hear me say it face to face, but I'm so sorry. I know what I took from you. I do."

"Billy—"

"I would do anything to change it. I'm more sorry than I could ever make you understand."

Jenny swiped at the tears running down her face. "I would do anything to change it, too—all of it. And I'm sorry too. I forgave you a long time ago. Don't you know that?"

Billy stared out at the riverbed. "I think of that one afternoon a lot—the last time I saw you. We were in your bedroom, and you were packing for school."

Jenny shook her head and said, "That wasn't the last time I saw you. When you were in my yard the night before I left, I stood in my window and watched you."

Billy bowed his head, and Jenny could tell that he was remembering that night, the desperation he felt, and now reckoning with the fact that Jenny had witnessed it.

"I wish I could've opened the door. I wish I would've let you in. But I couldn't see past my own hurt. I'm sorry."

Billy put his head down on her shoulder and said, "No, I'm sorry. And I shouldn't have expected you to."

Back inside the house, Jenny turned on the radio and sat close to Billy on the couch. He held her face in his hands and kissed her lightly on the lips. She draped her legs over his and kissed him, not the way he'd kissed her, but in a way that she hoped would convey that she had truly forgiven him, and the gratitude she felt that he had forgiven her. After she kissed his lips, she kissed his forehead, his eyelids, his nose, and his lips again.

Billy lay back on the couch and Jenny put her head on his chest and her arms around him. Keith Whitley was on the radio, and she began to doze off, the long day finally catching up with her, and the warmth and security of being held by Billy allowing her to give in to her sleepiness. When she woke a little while later, the sun was starting to rise and the sky was orange and pink, casting a warm light on the tumbleweeds and brush growing in the riverbed. She had her nose pressed up against Billy's neck and his arms were wrapped around her.

"You should get home," she said.

"Yeah. Carl will be up soon."

Jenny laid her head down on his chest and said, "I want to know Carl."

"You will."

She walked around the house and gathered her things. In Heather's room, she scribbled a quick note that said: *I know your life will be just like the song. I'm so happy for you. I love you. Jenny*, and tucked it into the drawer beside Heather's bed.

As Billy opened the door to a blue Jeep Cherokee, Jenny saw the car seat in the back and thought about how natural it was that he had become a young father. Even as a teenager, he was able to provide the calmness and care that she needed—that her own father had been largely unable to provide. When they arrived at her parents' house, Billy parked and kissed her goodbye. They planned to see each other in two weeks and promised to talk every day until then. She wondered what it would be like to be in his home. She thought about bringing him into her home, into the new life she'd made, away from the setting of their past.

Up in her room, the heavy, stagnant feel of the house made Jenny anxious to get on the road. While she was packing her bag, her dad walked in.

"Time to go already?"

"I have to get back for work tomorrow. I didn't see you leave last night."

"Your mama wasn't feeling well. We left while they were cutting the cake."

"I saw you dancing just before. She looked fine to me."

"Well, you know how quickly it can turn."

Jenny was acutely aware of how quickly it could turn. Her mother could go from dancing to raging, from having polite dinner conversation to throwing a glass across the room, from sitting in the passenger seat of a moving car to opening the door and threatening to fling herself out on the highway.

Her father put a hand on top of her head and said, "I sure miss you, girl."

"I miss you too. You should visit me some time. You've never even seen where I live."

Her father hesitated. "You know how mama hates to travel."

"You could come alone."

He shook his head and stared out the window. "Not worth the price I'd have to pay." He touched her shoulder and said, "Sorry, baby."

She let his comment go, like always—her pity for him trumping her own feelings. The truth was, she was so used to it, she didn't even register it as rejection anymore. He'd sacrifice anything and everything to keep her mother from being angry. She couldn't even blame him. She knew that countering her mother would lead to devastating consequences, and he still had to live here.

"Well, I'm headed for Pacheco Pass. No phantom cows there but plenty of ghosts." Jenny thought of the legendary Pacheco Pass hitchhiker ghost—a girl looking for a ride, getting in a car, and vanishing from the passenger seat.

Her father lifted her bag. "You should go say goodbye to mama."

Jenny closed her eyes and exhaled as her dad stood there waiting. She didn't want to see her mother, and she knew her mother didn't want to see her. In the entirety of the weekend, their encounters had been limited to an awkward conversation at home, a silent car ride to the rehearsal dinner, a chilling warning in the restaurant bathroom, and a careful, cho-reographed distance at the wedding.

Jenny looked at her dad, still waiting, and went down the hall to her parents' bedroom. Her mother was asleep, her back to her. "Goodbye, Mom," Jenny whispered and closed the door.

At her car, she hugged her dad and said, "I guess I don't know when I'll see you next."

"You can come home any time. You drive safe now, darlin'. Don't go picking up any hitchhikers."

When Jenny pulled into Uncle Gino's driveway, he was pruning a vibrant orange rosebush, the flowers the color of fruit punch or an October sun-set. She walked down the gravel path toward the garden. "Beautiful roses, Uncle G."

"This variety is called 'Remember Me.' I took them from Nonna's garden. I dug up the whole bush and brought it to my house after she died. Nonna was the real green thumb in the family. She could grow anything. I dug up some of her rosemary too."

Jenny smiled, recalling Nonna in her garden and the smell of rose-mary that always floated through her kitchen. She thought how beautiful it was that a part of her grandmother, something her hands had touched, something called 'Remember Me,' was growing in Uncle Gino's yard. She smelled one of the roses and said, "It may not have just been her green thumb. She had a pretty militant style of pest control."

Uncle Gino chuckled. "I'm familiar with the hard-soled rubber boots she'd wear in her garden at night."

Uncle Gino went into his house and brought out a large basket that held plastic containers of polenta, jars of rigatoni sauce, several sprigs of rosemary, and a stalk of Nonna's rosebush that he'd dipped in honey and wrapped in cheesecloth and foil. He put the basket in the backseat of her car. "I don't want you to go hungry, dear. And I cut a stalk of the roses to plant in your garden in Santa Clara. Some rosemary too. Wouldn't it be nice to have a little bit of Nonna there?"

"It would be so nice. And it'll be a little bit of you, too."

"There's another little present in the basket. Open it when you get home." He took a single yellow rose from a bucket on his porch, tied it with twine to a sprig of rosemary and said, "Bring this to Nonna."

Jenny thanked him and gave him a long hug. Backing out of his driveway, she waved and watched him yank up a weed from his lawn. He waved back, weed in his hand, and shouted, "I'll miss you, *mi passerotta*."

"I'll miss you more!"

At the cemetery, Jenny sat by Nonna's grave under the harsh heat of the August sun. She closed her eyes and imagined Nonna sitting beside her in one of her pantsuits and a pretty blouse, her hair set for bridge. She told her about Heather's wedding, about seeing Billy, about meeting Carl. She placed the yellow rose and the sprig of rosemary against her headstone and sent all her love through the air, just the way Uncle Gino taught her.

Chapter Fourteen

SEPTEMBER 1990

Jenny arrived home to her white stucco Spanish bungalow in Santa Clara by late afternoon. She stopped at the end of the driveway to pick up her mail and walked into the minimally furnished two-bedroom house with white walls and dark wood floors, colorful quilts, and folk art images of Mary she collected since she was a child. The centerpiece of the home was an old Spanish fireplace made of colorful Talavera tiles, flanked by picture windows that framed a grand old magnolia tree. She was met at the door by her cat, Chico, an orange Maine Coon with long whiskers and freckles on his nose.

Jenny tossed her mail onto the kitchen table and reached for the sunset postcard among the catalogs and bills. She flipped it over and saw Henry's familiar scrawl; his handwriting was the same as it had been in fourth grade. *I think of you every day! See you in September?* She looked at the caption and the date—the Yugoslavian coastline three weeks ago. Was he really coming back in September? After college, he'd found a flat and a job in Brussels, a city he loved at first sight, and had been back only once since; this was the longest they had ever gone without seeing each other.

Jenny began unpacking the basket from Uncle Gino. Underneath the food, there was a brown bag with a stamp from the antique store. Inside was a plaster figurine of one of her favorite saints, Saint Teresa of Ávila. She was holding a book; a white dove was on her shoulder. Taped to the bottom was a prayer card. It read: *Christ has no body now but yours. No hands, no feet on earth but yours. Yours are the eyes through which he looks compassion on this world. Yours are the feet with which he walks to do good.*

Yours are the hands through which he blesses all the world. Yours are the hands, yours are the feet, yours are the eyes, you are his body. Christ has no body now on earth but yours.

It was a beautiful passage; one she'd never seen before. She went to her bedroom and put the Saint Teresa and the prayer card on her nightstand. She put Henry's postcard in her bottom drawer, where she kept the stack of postcards from everywhere he had traveled. Next to Henry's postcards were her shoebox filled with prayer cards, her old copy of *Our Town*, and the 45 of "Far Away Eyes." The prayer cards were like a security blanket; she reached for one when she needed comfort, although she hadn't placed them all around her room in years. Her copy of *Our Town* reminded her that the least important day is important enough, and the 45 reminded her of just such a day—a day when she and Henry sat in her room and listened to Mick Jagger sing about driving through Bakersfield.

Jenny pressed the button on her answering machine and was surprised that there was a message from Henry, saying he would be arriving on Friday. She couldn't believe it—she really would be seeing him in September. There was also a message from Billy, asking her to call when she arrived home. Jenny wrote his number down and stared at the unfamiliar 805 area code. She finished unpacking, called her neighbor to thank her for taking care of Chico, started a load of laundry, and eventually, sat by her window and called Billy. She was nervous, and at first, they made small talk—work, school, the wedding, the weather, Henry's planned visit—and then Billy said, "I thought about you all day."

"I thought about you too. I've been trying to picture where you are."

"I'm on my back patio. We have a small yard with a peach tree and a sandbox. Carl's playing with his dump trucks. We're just a few blocks from the ocean, so there's almost always a breeze. I'm putting two hamburgers on the grill. I wish it were three."

"Me too."

"Okay, now tell me where you are."

"I'm sitting in my bedroom. It's not tangerine. It's off-white and there's a window out to my yard. It's open and I can smell the magnolia tree in the back. I have a lace coverlet on my bed that belonged to my Nonna. And my painting, the one from Uncle Gino's store, is above my bed. I've hung it everywhere I've ever lived." Jenny paused as she heard the soft echo of bells coming from the Mission and said, "And I just heard the Mission bells."

Jenny could hear Billy open and close a screen door, take silverware from a drawer, set plates on a table. They talked until it was time for him to sit down for dinner with Carl. When Billy said goodbye, Jenny almost said "I love you." It felt as instinctual as holding his hand the night of the wedding.

Back at work the next morning, Jenny found a pile of messages and some new files covering the neat desk she'd left before the wedding. She was scheduled to be on the dependency court calendar, where typical cases involved children living in trailers full of garbage with drug-addled parents. The cases were difficult and emotional, but they presented Jenny with the opportunity to do precisely the type of work she believed she was called to do.

Her decision to practice law, and more specifically, to become a public defender, was rooted in her faith, the seeds planted while she sat in a church pew with Nonna and Uncle Gino. Every Sunday, she was told about a covenant of love and justice that called for the faithful to act as Jesus did, *to bring glad tidings to the poor* and *liberty to captives*. She was taught that Jesus identified with the hungry, the poor, the strangers, and *the least of these*. There was an obligation to reach out to others with love, to pursue justice, to treat all life with dignity. When she was around twelve, she saw the nuns on the news, singing outside the prison walls the night before an execution. That linked the concepts of justice and faith for her in a tangible way, and she decided that the best way for her to live out her faith was to be a defender of people who could not defend themselves. She not only felt called to do this work, but believed that it suited her. She understood the pain of being silenced and powerless, of being defenseless.

There were times in law school when she doubted her decision to pursue a career in social justice. She was tens of thousands of dollars in debt from student loans; she lived in a small studio apartment in a dilapidated building; and also, few of her classmates were on this same path. Most were competing for internships with high-powered law firms, and while they spent the summers going to Giants games and fancy lunches and working in tall buildings, she toiled away in the back room of a makeshift poverty law office in a strip mall in San Jose.

Every summer, she interned for a nonprofit organization that provided home visits to poor and elderly clients who wanted their wills done. They had no assets to speak of, but it gave them peace of mind to be able to name someone to close up their house after they were gone, to give away a wedding band, or arrange for the care of a beloved pet. Jenny saw the inside of homes where people lived all day in front of a TV, where they asked her more questions than necessary just to have someone around a little longer. She was patient with her clients' need for human contact, always allotting extra time for simple tasks. She knew what it was like being alone all day. During her months at home with valley fever, she was sustained by the visits from Nonna, Heather, Henry, and Uncle Gino. Even seeing her tutor was a welcome relief from the loneliness.

When Jenny arrived home from work on Friday and saw Henry sitting on her front porch with his hair bleached white, she ran out of the car and threw her arms around him. "I can't believe you're here! Look at your hair! It's just like what's-his-name in *Subway*."

"Fred," he said, touching the top of his hair. "And that was a great movie, subtitles and all."

"I know, your favorite."

Jenny couldn't stop looking at the sharp contrast of the white hair and the dark stubble and the bright aquamarine eyes. Henry brushed some of the hair falling from her ponytail behind her ear and kissed her on the cheek. "I missed you," he said.

"I missed you more."

She led him into her small entry, turned on the stereo, and showed him around. "Here you are at my house! What do you think?"

"I think it's perfect. I always thought you might become a nun, and here you are, living in a little church."

Belonging

Henry hung his black leather jacket on a chair. "What's this crap we're listening to?"

"Henry, it's Merle. It's our heritage."

Henry picked up her box of CDs, sat down on the couch, and flipped through them. "You know, I exposed you to all sorts of remarkable music in L.A. Why is it you are still listening to *this*?" He took out a Bryan Ferry CD and put on "Slave To Love," a song they used to play on the jukebox at Al's Bar in college.

Jenny sat next to him on the couch and rubbed her thumb over the scar above his left eye. She closed her eyes and listened to Bryan Ferry's perfectly sorrowful voice. "You know what it is? It's the longing and the hope. He has it too. Hear it?" Jenny opened her eyes and looked at Henry.

"Ah, that explains it, the longing and the hope." Henry put his arm around her. "Whereever did I find you?"

Jenny went into her blue tiled kitchen and returned with a beer for each of them. Henry raised his beer and said, "This appears to be solely longing."

Jenny rolled her eyes and said, "So, why are you here? I thought I'd have to go to Brussels to ever see you again."

"My dad wants to downsize, so I need to help him go through my things."

"He's moving? I miss that house and your dad."

"Me too." Henry pointed to the skirt and blouse she wore. "You almost look like a grown up in that outfit. Did you have court today?"

"Funny. I have court almost every day."

"Well, is it all you thought it would be?"

"It's a lot harder. It's one thing to write briefs about legal issues. It's very different to sit with a client who hopes I can help them, when a lot of the time, I just can't. Monday, I was in court with a woman who's losing her fourth child to social services. She's developmentally disabled, really young, and I'm not even sure she understands what's happening. She was a runaway, on the streets at thirteen. She's disabled and poor and has no voice. She has no one."

"She has you."

Jenny smiled at Henry. She'd missed him so much, his upbeat presence, the role he'd always played in her life, her biggest cheerleader. She looked down at her watch and said, "Do you want to go get some dinner? Let me go change, and we'll go out?"

They decided to go to sushi—Henry's choice—so Jenny drove them to Tsugaru, her favorite restaurant in Japantown. Henry ordered sake bombs for each of them. He dropped a small glass of hot rice wine, glass and all, into a large mug of beer and set it in front of her.

"How's Brussels? Your flat? Your job?" she asked.

Henry looked down at the hot rice wine bubbling in his beer and didn't answer right away. He took a drink and said, "Sometimes I wish you could be there with me."

"We should plan on it. I have loads of vacation time and I have that passport we got together."

"Unused, just like your vacation time."

"So, what do you think? When should I come? I want to see your flat, go to your favorite bars, sightsee with you."

"We'll figure it out."

He said it with a dismissive wave of his hand and Jenny knew he was deflecting her.

"How's your dad? I miss his frosted brownies."

"He's good. Busy."

"Your mom?" Jenny asked.

"It's been a long time since I've heard from her."

"I'm sorry."

"Let's not waste any time on her, okay? Tell me about the wedding."

Jenny clasped her hands together under her chin. "I think the best part was the song."

"Of course it was."

"No, really. Rickey is really good, and the song, I mean, he wrote a song for her that's on the radio and he sang it!"

Henry rolled his eyes. "How's it go? Sing me a few lines."

Jenny sat up taller in her chair and sang the chorus. It was in the middle of singing a little too loudly that she realized she might be a little drunk.

144

Belonging

Henry applauded and said, "Wow. Now tell me about seeing Billy. The whole story."

"Oh, Billy." Jenny tilted her head back and breathed in deeply. She returned her eyes to Henry's. "It was so nice when we were talking about life now. It was like this, like catching up with your oldest friend after a long time away. But then, we started talking about the summer I left, and oh my God—I'm not sure who's more remorseful now, him or me." Jenny hung her head and held her face in her hands.

"Jenny."

"I mean, squandering is not a harsh enough word. I eliminated him from my life. My relationship with him was so precious and he made an awful, drunken mistake and I never even let him apologize. I withheld forgiveness for so long. I gave him no grace."

"Jenny, what he did was devastating to you. I was there, remember? I saw you in fetal position on your bed. For days. And you were a teenager. You both were. The grown-up Jenny can forgive him now. Maybe it was meant to play out this way. Have you ever thought of that?"

"Yeah, I don't know. We'll see what happens."

"What do you want to happen?"

Jenny leaned across the table and whispered, "I want to marry him and have four children."

"Oh my. Wow."

Jenny hung her head again, this time feeling the weight of the alcohol pulling her down. "I guess I'm sort of terrified. I mean, how do I even know who Billy is anymore? Despite the way I feel, so much time has gone by, and a lot of life has happened. Obviously, things are going to be different."

"Different how?"

"I don't know. When I knew him, he was a teenage boy and all we knew was each other. He's been divorced now. He's lived with someone else and loved someone else. He has Carl and he's raising him alone. He's not just a guy who has to go to baseball practice every day."

"Well, you're not just a hostess at King's Table anymore either."

"Ha. I'm just not sure that any of this will work. It's hard for me to just *date* Billy, who I have loved so deeply and been hurt by. And it's not just Billy anymore. He has a child. There's distance, a little boy, and all our baggage besides. That's a lot to deal with, and if I don't think I can handle those things, I have to wonder why I should go down this road at all."

Henry paused and briefly closed his eyes. He seemed reflective, or like he was mentally switching gears. "How can I say this to you? Do you think we only do things that we know will work out? Only enter relationships that we know will be life-long?"

"Of course not."

"I think you do that, Jenny. You wear this little suit of armor everywhere you go. In some cases, it has served you well. In this case, it probably won't."

"I'd just like to know how it'll end, you know? How we'll end up. Like I wish I could close my eyes and know where we'll all be a year from now, or five years from now."

Henry shook his head and said, "There's no way to know until you do it, dear. I wish it could be easier for you. I know you don't trust him yet, and truth be told, you shouldn't. But you love him, so what else is there to do but live with the possibility of hurt? I mean, what if you knew in eighth grade what was going to happen to you and Billy by the time you left for college? Would you have given up all those years if you knew there wasn't a happy ending?"

Jenny said simply, "Maybe." She felt a little fuzzy, and she'd never seen Henry like this. She was aware of his seriousness, and she tried to stay focused. It crossed her mind that he was recalling something else that ended badly, and her eyes wandered upward like they did sometimes when she was trying to figure something out.

"Here's what I think: you need to just jump in with your eyes open, instead of closing them until we all end up somewhere. I'll put it this way—" Henry looked at her and realized she'd drifted off into some other thought or place. "Christ, this would be easier if you weren't drunk. How'd you get drunk?"

"Your fault."

"Two and a half drinks?"

"Sorry."

146

Belonging

"Okay, just try to listen to me. You are one of the bravest, strongest women I know."

Jenny slapped the table and laughed, snorting loudly.

"Oh my Lord." Henry grabbed her hand across the table. "Just listen, okay. Stop your snorting and listen."

Jenny ran her free hand over her face, changing it from smiling to serious, and said, "Okay, I'm ready now."

"You're hysterical. Now listen to me." Henry squeezed her hand and said, "You left Bakersfield at eighteen to go to college where you knew no one, except for me, and as I remember, I wasn't always around. You trusted me and followed me even when I brought you to some pretty undesirable places. You survived years living in the same home with probably the scariest woman I've ever known. You sit in a jail cell with accused felons and stand as their last line of defense against the government. I mean, have you ever thought about that? And, in case I haven't convinced you yet, I remember the time you threw your body over me, to protect me from some rednecks several years back." Henry leaned across the table and kissed her on the forehead. "I think you need to try to be a little fearless where Billy is concerned. I'll reserve judgment on whether to trust him yet. This isn't about him. It's about you, keeping your eyes open, and not fast-forwarding to the end."

When Jenny went to bed that night, she couldn't sleep because she couldn't stop thinking about Henry. She thought of him coming home to go through his old room and wondered if that really warranted a trip from Brussels. She thought of how he deflected her when she suggested visiting, the seriousness of his eyes when he talked about being fearless, how his overall demeanor was softer and more solemn than usual. She determined that he had some kind of ache, and she wondered if he was going to tell her what it was.

Early the next morning, she crept into the living room, expecting to find him asleep on the couch, but he was scribbling away in a composition book, a faraway look on his face.

"You're up," she said. "What are you doing?"

"I've started keeping a journal again."

"If only Miss Wilson knew how she'd inspired you."

Henry smiled, closed the book, and packed it in his bag. "If only."

Jenny put on The Judds' *River of Time* CD and went into the kitchen to make coffee. Track two was her favorite—a romantic story song that spanned the life of a young couple. She brought a cup of coffee to Henry and said, "You know why else I listen to country music? I love hearing a good story—bittersweet—that ends happy."

Henry closed his eyes for a moment and smiled at her in a way she could not read. He patted the cushion next to him. "Come sit with me."

She sat down and put her arm around his shoulder. "What is it?"

"I'm not sure when I'm going to see you again, so I just want to sit with you for a minute."

"I can come and visit. I told you I have vacation time."

"I would like that."

"When? Let's plan it. That way we don't have to be sad now. We'll have something to look forward to."

"Why don't you figure out what works on your trial calendar and call me."

Jenny suspected he was deflecting her again, that he had no intention of ever having her visit. He was acting just like he always did when he was hiding things from her.

"Do you remember all the birthdays we celebrated together?"

"I still expect someone to bring me a homemade cupcake with marshmallow frosting and sprinkles on December 20th, but, alas, you are too far away." Henry put his head on her shoulder and held her for a long time.

"Henry? What is it?"

"I just miss you is all."

"I miss you too. Let's plan my trip."

Henry lifted his bag from the floor and carried his cup of coffee to the kitchen. He stood in the entryway and looked around her sunlit house. At the front door, he held her hand and said, "You know who really lived in the mystery, having no idea of the outcome?"

"Who?"

"Mary."

"Yes, you're right."

"And you know what else?"

"What?"

"She was really brave."

"I know. She was fearless."

Henry hugged her tightly, kissed her once on the forehead and once on the nose, and he was gone.

After work that day, Jenny went to a specialty paper store near the courthouse. As she perused journals of every material, color, and size, she thought about the fictional journal entries Henry wrote for Miss Wilson. To this day, he'd repeat his favorite lines about Cinnamon: *She sat naked on my lap, and I was wrapped in a warm Cinnamon roll. She called me "sugar" and I liked that. She kissed me like a fire-breathing dragon.* Jenny picked out a handmade leather journal with large pages that would accommodate Henry's wild, slanted writing. It was simple, with only a tiny, embossed angel on the back. It was more than she was used to spending, but Henry now lived in another country, with a job and a flat, and friends she'd likely never meet, and part of her wondered if he'd ever come back. She wanted him to have something of her with him, a place where he could reveal himself.

Chapter Fifteen

SEPTEMBER 1990

Billy lived on a palm tree-lined street in the small beach town of Carpinteria. His modest ranch-style house was on the corner, painted cornflower blue. On a Saturday in mid-September, Jenny arrived in the late morning after a five-hour drive south to the central coast. When she saw Billy and Carl waiting for her on the front porch, part of her couldn't believe she was really there and part of her felt like she'd been there all along.

The three of them spent the day on the beach, where they made a meandering sandcastle, ate sandy sandwiches, and collected rocks and shells. Carl taught Jenny how to dig for sand crabs, and they captured and released a bucketful. In the late afternoon, they returned home, and while Carl napped, Billy and Jenny went outside to talk. Since Heather's wedding, they'd talked on the phone every day, sharing all they could about the eight years they'd spent away from each other. They spoke about everything from important milestones to anecdotes of daily life—narratives intended to reach out and pull the other closer. This was working, and Jenny no longer felt the strange newness of reviving an old love. Instead, she felt a comfort and familiarity of a blossoming new love.

There were still things they hadn't talked about, though. Billy hadn't told her about marrying Tara, and Jenny hadn't told him about any of her past relationships, the most significant being her college boyfriend, Paul. They'd agreed to talk about these things in person, understanding that it would be important to see and touch each other while they did.

Belonging

Sitting on Billy's back porch at the end of the day, a coolness settling over the yard, Billy went first.

He started by telling her how he ended up in Bend, Tara's hometown. He'd left college and signed with the Phillies at the urging of his father. The farm team was in Bend, and he met Tara at a party after a home game. They'd been dating a few months when she got pregnant. Tara was elated at the prospect of getting married and starting a family together. Billy was less so; he didn't know her that well, and he didn't feel prepared to be a father. But as Tara began to show, he put aside his worries and decided that he could be happy with a young family. He would marry her before the baby was born, and their relationship would grow as they raised their child. He felt tremendous shame and embarrassment when he realized that Tara's elation about getting married and starting a family had nothing to do with him or the baby. She wanted to be the wife of a major league baseball player, have a lot of money, and leave Bend.

Billy realized all of this after he got injured and his baseball career stalled. When he came home with his arm in a sling, Tara was already halfway out the door. He was afraid of losing Carl, so he tried to make the marriage work. At Tara's urging, he sought multiple medical opinions. He had fluid drained from his elbow. A doctor recommended Tommy John Surgery. He foolishly thought that, if he could pitch again, he could keep his family together. But then he thought about who he wanted to be as a father, and he knew it wasn't a man who salvaged his marriage by throwing a fastball, and it wasn't a struggling minor league ball player, always an injury away from being unable to support his family. He decided it was time to end his pitching career. He told his father first, who he expected to be disappointed, but surprisingly, supported his decision. He knew what it was like to be let go by a team and have to make a fresh start, and he trusted Billy's instincts about his injury and his career. Having a grandson also made him see things differently, and he understood Billy's impulse to make sure he could provide for Carl. Billy said this was around the time he'd called Jenny from a pay phone at the grocery store. He didn't even understand why. They hadn't talked in years. Maybe he just wanted to hear her voice, to remember what it felt like to be so loved.

Within days of telling Tara that he was done playing ball, she packed up and left. Six months later, he was living in Carpinteria, divorced, with sole legal and physical custody of Carl. He didn't regret any of it, though, because it gave him Carl. When Billy said simply, "It was only about baseball. Tara never loved me," Jenny put her arms around him and held him tight. She couldn't imagine how it was possible for anyone to look at Billy's clear eyes and strong hands, to witness his earnestness and sense of purpose, to be the recipient of his abundant care and love, and not love him back.

When it was Jenny's turn, she told him about meeting Paul in college, and shared that her first time was with him. She was twenty, and they'd been together for over a year. She knew that Billy would need to understand what had changed for her, so she told him how different things were when she got to college. For the first time in her life, she felt some personal freedom. She saw how other girls her age lived and realized that a lot of the things she'd always been told were just not true. She was intentionally vague, opting not to tell him that obtaining distance from her mother's voice, from her intrusiveness and shaming, was the primary reason she finally felt free enough to have a sexual relationship.

She told him that they broke up when Paul moved to Vermont for graduate school. He wasn't planning to come back to California, and she wasn't going East. He was sort of a free spirit and didn't even want children. He believed in monogamy, but not marriage. Although they loved each other, spending a life together was never even discussed, so when it ended, it was all very practical, and they remained friends. Jenny said that she thought of Billy a lot around that time. She thought of how he had always been willing to make a life-long commitment to her, even as teenagers, without having the benefit of a physical relationship, or even the knowledge of what one would be like. She told him, "I realized how rare and precious you were."

There was a lot of buildup to this conversation, anxiety about hurting each other, and worry about how it would affect their relationship. But what they revealed only solidified that, though they had spent years apart, they had always, in some way, held onto each other.

Belonging

When Carl got up from his nap, Billy was barbecuing chicken and Jenny was laying out balsa wood, tissue paper, string, ribbon, and glue on the kitchen table. Carl reached out and touched Jenny's elbow, and she turned to see him wearing a faux leather tool belt strapped around his waist. She smiled and handed him a bottle of glue and a spool of string, and he put them in the pockets of the tool belt. They sat together at the table, and she showed him how to build a homemade kite, teaching him about the spine and the spar, the bridle and balance, just like her dad had taught her.

Dinner was eaten on a blanket outside due to the mess of glue, tissue paper, and ribbons on the kitchen table. After dinner, Carl ran around the yard for a while, and he and Jenny put the finishing touches on their kites. Billy read a pile of books to Carl before bed, while Jenny cleaned up the kite mess on the kitchen table. When she was done, she popped her head into Carl's room, and said, "Happy dreams, Carl."

Carl said, "Happy dreams too."

Billy came out a little while later, locked up the house, and peeked in on his sleeping son one more time. He found Jenny sitting on the steps to the back patio, took her hand, and led her down the hallway into his bedroom. His room was warm and dark, and an open window above the bed let in the smell of the ocean and the peach tree in the backyard. They stood by his bed, and he started to kiss her. He leaned down and folded back the covers, took off his t-shirt, and reached underneath hers. Jenny shivered a little when she felt his hands across her bare stomach. She lay back on the bed and pulled him down next to her. The sheets on his bed were soft and white, and smelled like he'd just washed them. The house was quiet, the only noise from the hum of the refrigerator inside and the wind outside, leaves crackling as they scattered across the walkway behind the bedroom window.

"Are you okay? Is this okay?" Billy whispered.

Jenny held his face and said, "I don't want any space between us."

"None?"

"None. Nothing. No space at all."

Billy pulled her t-shirt over her head and started to unbutton her jeans. She reached down and helped to tug her jeans off and started to unbutton his. She lay there, never taking her eyes from his, thinking of nothing, and feeling everything—his hands on the small of her back, her legs laced with his, the warmth of his mouth on hers. Their lovemaking was so cautious and gentle that it seemed like they'd gone back in time and changed their history. It felt like she'd imagined it would have been like if Billy had waited for her, if their first time had been together. As he touched her tentatively, it occurred to her that he was trying to make up to her what they'd missed, that he was trying to recreate it for her. He moved with great care, the sincerity and wonder of a teenage boy, merged with the capability of a grown man who would fulfill her request to have no more space between them.

When it was nearly dawn, Billy whispered that he'd better go down to Carl's room before he woke up. Jenny reached up and put her hands on his face and said, "I felt all of you."

Billy smiled and said, "I felt all of you, too."

Billy kissed her and she watched as he opened the door and crept quietly down the hall. When she heard the soft turn of Carl's doorknob, she closed her eyes and finally slept.

A few hours later, Jenny woke to the sound of wiffle balls being whacked in the backyard. By the time she made it to the kitchen table in a sundress and wet hair, Carl was finishing his breakfast. Jenny buttered the stack of pancakes Billy placed in front of her, and Carl moved from his chair to her lap. He twisted around to face her and said, "Jenny, do you know about the grunion?"

"No, what are grunion?"

"They're fish that lay eggs on the beach."

"Really? How?"

"It happens at night. They roll in with the waves and flop around and lay eggs and go back out. The whole beach looks silver."

"Wow. I want to see that," Jenny said.

Carl grabbed a section of her hair just below her shoulders, and rubbed the ends of it under his chin, like he was painting. "You will love it, Jenny."

After breakfast, Jenny went to pack her suitcase. Standing in Billy's sunlit room, feeling the ocean breeze from the window above his bed, the smell of pancakes and coffee lingering in the house, she wished she could stay more than one night. It had been too late to make the long drive on Friday after work, and she needed to get back for court on Monday morning, so she'd settled for the day and a half she could get.

Carl ran into the room and shouted, "Hey, Jenny, do you have any pets?"

"I do. I have an orange cat named Chico."

"Where'd you get him?"

"I got him at a shelter."

"Why'd you name him Chico?"

"He already had a name when I adopted him. It suits him. You'll see when you visit me."

"Okay. Do you know how to find Venus? I do."

"How?"

"It looks like a bright star. It comes out right at sunset. But also, sometimes in the morning. But now it's at sunset. I know how to find Orion's belt too. And Vega."

"Maybe you can show me sometime."

"How about tonight?" Carl threw his arms in the air.

"I'll be back at my house tonight."

"Okay, well, call me and we can find it together."

Driving back through the hills and farmland, Jenny thought about what it took to bring Billy back into her life. She'd spent years regretting both of their choices to not see each other—hers the night before she left for college, and his on the Christmas Eve she learned he was marrying Tara. But now, she saw how both of those decisions, as reflexive and thoughtless as they were, put them on this course. Carl wouldn't exist if they had stayed together, if Billy hadn't been with Tara. So, while Jenny had regrets, she was also hopeful. They were older now, and Carl, a child she was immediately drawn to, was now a part of her life. She thought of a prayer card she often looked at—a ring of roses around the following words: *May today there be peace within. May you trust God that you are exactly where you are meant to be. May you not forget the infinite possibilities that are born of faith. May you use those gifts that you have received, and pass on the love that has been given to you.*

When Jenny got home that evening, she threw her bag down in the entry, picked up the phone and dialed Henry's number in Brussels. She didn't care how much it would cost. She wanted to tell him that she'd followed his advice—that she'd been fearless, that she was in love, and that she could even see herself being a mother. She was disappointed when she got his answering machine. She left a message telling him to call her, that it was important.

As she waited for him to call back, she sat down on her back porch and started writing down all the things she wanted to tell him about her weekend. She sat there for so long with the phone by her side, that she saw the first twinkle of Venus in the early night sky. She picked up the phone again and called Billy's house. When Carl answered, she told him that she was sitting in her backyard next to Chico and that she could see Venus above her magnolia tree. He told her to hold on a second, and she heard the snap of the screen door, Carl saying something to Billy, footsteps, another door opening and closing, and then he picked up the phone again and said, "Venus is in our front yard, above the flower farms."

The following week, Jenny decided to take apart the office in her spare room, buy two twin beds, and turn it into a room for Carl. She put up a bulletin board and bought books, crayons, and a train set with a circular wooden track. She bought a children's table at a yard sale and placed her Saint Teresa on it. She thought of how Saint Teresa was the perfect inspiration for making a room for a child who was not her own. *Yours are the hands, yours are the feet, yours are the eyes, you are his body.* She remembered her warm room at Nonna's house, with its windows out to the garden and shelves filled with records and books.

When the room was complete, she wrote to Henry, telling him all about the room she made for Carl. Because he'd never returned her phone call, she'd taken the list of things she wanted to tell him, and slipped it in the envelope: *the beach, sand crabs, making kites, brushing my hair under his chin, Billy's house, Venus, grunion, sleeping together.*

That Friday, when Billy arrived alone at her small Spanish bungalow, Jenny kissed his lips and cheeks and forehead. She took his hand, showed him around her house, introduced him to Chico, and led him down the hallway to the closed door of Carl's room. She opened the door and turned on the lights to reveal two twin beds covered in forest green plaid comforters. In between them was a bookshelf with some of her favorite childhood books. On the wall was a bulletin board—empty for now. The child-sized table was pushed against a wall and held a stack of paper and a new box of crayons. In one corner of the room was a bucket of plastic dinosaurs; in another was the circular train track.

She said, "This is for you and Carl. I want you to be able to bring Carl here. I want it to feel like home to him."

When she looked at Billy's stunned face, she realized how dramatic it was that she'd emptied her office and made a children's room for a little boy she'd spent about a day and a half with. As she waited for Billy to respond, she felt a raw vulnerability she hadn't felt at all while she was buying train tracks and shelving books and making up twin beds. It occurred to her for the first time that creating this space may not have just been bold—it may have been presumptuous, even pushy.

"I'm overwhelmed. I don't know what to say."

"Is it too much? Too soon?"

Billy shook his head and said, "No, not at all. I just didn't realize that you were here. I'm here, but I thought it would take a while for you to be here."

"Where is here?"

"Here is you, me, and Carl being a family."

"I'm here." Jenny hugged him and let her head fall against his chest. "Your heart is beating fast."

She took his hand and led him to her bedroom. He stood near her bed and looked at her painting on the wall. "There it is, still hanging above your bed."

She watched Billy study the scene, and wondered if he'd ever understood it, if he realized that it held every hope she'd ever had, a physical manifestation of her desire for a home and a family.

There was a package on the dresser that she was planning to send to Henry. Billy touched the top of it and said, "What are you sending to Henry?"

"A care package. An old picture of us in a photo booth at the fair, a Merle Haggard CD, a copy of *The Greatest Thing in the World*. Uncle Gino gave me one a long time ago. It's a beautiful book. It's about love. I haven't heard from Henry since he left. I'm a little worried about him."

"I'm sure you'll hear from him soon."

She knew Billy wasn't the person with whom to share her worries about Henry. Billy never understood Henry or the depth of their friendship—a relationship that pre-dated their own, sustained her when it ended, and endured even though they lived on different continents. From Billy's perspective, Henry was probably still the boy who brought her to parties on the wrong side of town and who he suspected she confided in more so than him. He was the one who drove off to college with her, leaving him behind. While she wanted Billy to understand Henry's place in her life, their relationship was new and delicate. She resolved that, eventually, she would make the two less separate. She would begin to share more about Henry with Billy. Tonight was not the time to do this, though.

"What's Carl doing this weekend?" she asked.

"My parents arrived yesterday. My dad wants to get him a new mitt before Little League starts."

Jenny thought of Billy's dad squatting in the yard, making Billy work on his form long after he should've thrown his last pitch of the day. "You are a much different sort of father than your dad."

"I learned a lot from him, and I know he tried, but I don't want Carl to ever feel the way I felt—obligated to perform, or like he owes me something. I felt that way, even as a ten year old. My dad is much different with Carl. I think we both want better for him."

As Jenny listened to Billy talk about his childhood, she realized how little he still knew about hers. He spent years coming and going from the side door, up the stairs to her tangerine bedroom. He saw fragments of her life, but she'd never told him what it was like to live there. Her own shame kept 822 Lupine Lane locked away.

She reached out and took his hand and said, "I want to do better someday too."

Belonging

Jenny made a lot of plans for the weekend. She wanted to take Billy on a hike on her favorite trail, eat at the best local taqueria, walk through the Mission gardens. As it turned out, they did none of those things. Twelve years after first falling in love, they were finally in a place and time where it was possible to stay in bed together all day, to sleep next to each other all night. They let the candle burn down to the wick and the music stop playing. They ignored the transitions of days to nights. Outside, the magnolia tree shed its leaves and the Mission bells rang. Inside, there was only the warmth of the bed, the stillness of the room, and the two of them, finally inseparable.

On Sunday, before Billy left, he stood in the doorway of Carl's room and said, "Thank you for making a space for Carl."

Jenny wasn't sure if he was referring to a space in her home or a space in her heart, but she knew she'd made both. She put her hand on his face. "You're welcome."

That evening, Jenny sat at her kitchen table and wrote to Henry again. She included another list of things they had to talk about: *sleeping in the same bed, Carl's bedroom, the books, the balls, and the bulletin board, the train tracks and the T-Rex, Billy's surprise, her newfound joy.*

When Billy and Carl bounded into Jenny's house in late October, they brought a life and energy she hadn't imagined. She had a fire burning in the fireplace and hot apple cider on the stove. The house smelled like an autumn day—the sweet cider mixed with the smoke from the chimney. When it was time to show Carl his room, Jenny felt a rush of emotion, her body registering what it meant for both of them. For her, it was the beginning of the family she'd always wanted. For him, she hoped it would be a tangible symbol of love and security. Carl stood with a small hand covering each eye, as Jenny swung open the door.

Carl took his hands from his eyes and looked around the room. He ran to the bookshelves and said, "Are these books for me?"

Before she could answer, Carl hopped up on the bed. "Is this bed for me?"

Jenny smiled. "Yes, this whole room is for you."

That night, Jenny helped Carl unpack his suitcase. He put his clothes away in the closet, put on his pajamas, and sat at the little table and colored a picture. He dumped the train tracks onto the floor. Jenny read him a stack of books. Chico lounged on the end of the bed, his tail moving back and forth in a slow, steady swish. When Billy declared it bedtime, Jenny lifted the heavy comforter and tucked Carl in. "Happy dreams, Carl."

"Happy dreams too."

Carl asked Billy for one more book, and Jenny left them alone in the room. She put her teapot on the stove and sat down at the kitchen table. Chico came padding out of Carl's room and laid against her feet. She reached down, rubbed the space between his ears, and thought about how full and happy her household felt, with the smell of cider and crayons, the wood floors littered with books and dinosaurs.

When Billy didn't come out after about forty-five minutes, Jenny peeked into their room. As she suspected, he was sound asleep in Carl's bed, with two more books open beside him. She turned out the lights, tiptoed back out, and looked around the family room, dimly lit by the jack-o-lantern lights she'd hung around the window. She stood there for a moment, wanting to retain the feeling of closing up her quiet house on the night it first held her family.

Hours later, Billy snuck into bed beside her. She felt his warmth against her back and turned to face him. She touched his face and met his sleepy eyes.

"Sorry," he whispered.

"Sorry for what?"

"Sorry for falling asleep and missing our night together."

Jenny kissed him and said, "I liked you sleeping."

Billy said, "Close your eyes."

She closed her eyes, and Billy began to trace her, starting with her eyelids, down her neck, shoulders, arms, hands, the side of her body, her legs, and all the way back. While she lay there, letting him touch all of her, she couldn't believe he remembered this simple act of intimacy they shared as teenagers under the oak tree in their park, innocent and inexperienced, trying to find a way to know every part of each other, without having sex. When he finally returned to her eyelids and kissed her, she rolled him over on his back, and said, "My turn," and traced him the same way he had traced her, recalling the trouble she always had going as slowly as he did, wanting to get back to his eyelids, his lips. When she did and she started to kiss him, Billy unbuttoned her pajama top and slid it off her shoulders. They fell into an easy rhythm, attuned to each other in a way she'd never experienced. She felt both completely vulnerable and completely protected. Openness and security co-existed in a way that she'd never felt and didn't know was possible. It was as if there was nothing else but this moonlit room, the heat from their bodies, and a wondrous single-hearted devotion.

Before she fell asleep, Jenny whispered, "Something is different tonight."

"I agree."

"What do you think it is?"

"Maybe you finally trust me. Maybe you let me in."

They spent the next day preparing for Halloween—the pumpkin patch, the costume store, and a spooky train ride. They stopped at the nursery and picked up a tray of Early Girl tomato seedlings, the best variety according to Uncle Gino. That afternoon, while Carl napped, Jenny and Billy planted the tomatoes in her garden. Jenny was quiet, thinking about the day, about Carl. When the tomato seedlings were in the ground and watered, she asked Billy to sit by her on the back porch.

"This makes me a little nervous to talk about, but I've been thinking a lot about it, so I guess I should just put it out there."

"Okay. What is it?"

Jenny exhaled heavily and looked at the ground. "I know it's really soon, but, if we get married, will I be Carl's mom?"

Billy placed a hand on his forehead and leaned into it. "I've thought about that too. I'm not sure what to do."

"Yeah."

"He knows who his mother is, sort of. I mean, he knows who gave birth to him. But he'll be raised by you. You will *be* his mother."

"She's seen him twice since she left?"

"Yeah. One time right before we moved out here and one time when he was two and she was in California for something."

"What was that like?"

"I don't know. Awkward, sad. Carl didn't know her at all, and she just stayed for about an hour."

"Would you consider letting me adopt him?"

"Would you want to?"

"Yes. I want to be Carl's mother. And we wouldn't need to do it anytime soon. We could take our time, figure out what's best for Carl, see what he may be feeling. And I don't care if he calls me Jenny or Mom or something else. I love him and I want to be his mother."

Billy was quiet and put his head down on Jenny's shoulder.

Jenny put her hand on top of his and said, "I have a friend who practices family law. Should I call her and see what the process is?"

Billy nodded and said, "You're going to be such a good mother."

The next morning, while Jenny made the bed, Carl came into her room and asked her about her painting. She told him to climb up and take a closer look. He stood on her bed and asked if the cat sleeping in the chair was Chico. She said, *Yes, it is.* He asked her which of the boys was him. She asked which one he'd like to be, and he said, *The one holding the bird.*

When it was time for Billy and Carl to get on the road, Carl sat on Jenny's lap and said, "Jenny? Why do we wave for so long whenever we say goodbye?"

Jenny laughed and said, "Oh, it's just a rule I made up. Why do you think we wave for so long?"

"To look at each other longer?"

She swept his hair out of his eyes and smiled. "Exactly. So that the person you are waving to knows that you aren't doing anything but saying goodbye to them. When you wave at someone until you can't see them anymore, it fills them up. It makes them feel loved."

That day, as Billy and Carl drove away, Jenny stood at the end of her driveway and waved. Carl rolled down his window and put his hand out, waving to her until they turned the corner at the end of her street.

Belonging

When they were out of sight, Jenny went into Carl's room and saw all he'd done to make it his own in just one visit. Billy had helped him make a mountain out of an old cardboard box and placed it in the center of the train tracks, along with a handmade sign that said "Tehachapi Loop." Books were scattered on the bed. Carl left a pair of shoes and a set of his pajamas on the floor of the closet.

Alone in the house, she put on the astronaut costume Carl picked out for her and took a picture of herself with an old Polaroid camera. She scribbled "Happy Halloween" across the bottom and sat to write a letter to Henry. She'd given a lot of thought as to why she still hadn't heard from him, and over the last month, had begun to believe he'd intentionally stopped communicating with her.

She kept thinking about their last morning together—his solemn goodbye, the way he held her, his ache. He must have known then that he would not write to her again. But why? Reflecting on times past when he'd deliberately distanced himself, she decided that he must be moving forward with his life in a direction that, he believed, could not include her. He didn't want her to visit him in Brussels. He didn't want to share his new life with her. While this made her incredibly sad and disappointed, all she could do was continue to write and send lists, whether he wrote back or not. And she hoped that one day, one of the letters or lists would change his mind.

She wrote about the family she and Billy were creating, and her favorite stories about Carl. She told him that she missed him terribly, and that she hoped he was okay. She said that if he wasn't writing back because he really didn't want her to visit him in Brussels, but felt bad saying so, that was okay—she didn't need to visit. She just wanted to hear from him. Before sealing the envelope, she combed through her prayer cards until she found one of Jesus holding the lost lamb and slipped it inside with the Polaroid picture and the letter.

Chapter Sixteen

DECEMBER 1990

Early Christmas Eve, Jenny drove down the Pacheco Pass with her car packed with Christmas presents. She would be spending Christmas in Bakersfield for the first time since college. Billy and Carl always spent the holidays there with Billy's family, and Heather was insistent that Jenny be at her house for her Christmas Eve dinner. The road was foggy and empty before sunrise, reminding her of all the eerie stories she'd heard about this stretch of highway being some sort of time warp, where travelers reported suddenly driving beside a horse and buggy or seeing an Ohlone village on the hills or reporting a car fire on the side of the road, only to find out there hadn't been one. Exiting onto the I-5 at dawn, Jenny was struck by the beauty of the morning sun reflecting on the wet road and the golden orchards, the brown and gold and blue all intersecting where the land met the sky.

A few hours later, she walked through the large wooden doors of her childhood church in Bakersfield. The church was empty except for a couple of musicians setting up for Mass. The altar was lined with Christmas trees and lit candles, but the rest of the church was dark, the only light coming from the winter sun shining through the stained glass. Jenny hadn't been inside this church in years, and the smell of the incense and pine made her feel like she was a child, squished comfortably in the pew between Uncle Gino and Nonna. In the soundproof sanctuary to the left of the altar, she took a long stick from a jar of sand, lit a candle for Nonna, and knelt to pray.

Belonging

While she had her head bowed and her eyes closed, she heard a door open. She turned and was startled to see Henry's mother. She felt like she was seeing a ghost—she couldn't remember the last time she'd seen her. After the day in Henry's driveway, Mrs. Hansen had avoided her, and now she visibly jolted when she saw Jenny kneeling in the room. She looked back toward the door, like she was deciding whether she could sneak back out without notice.

"Mrs. Hansen, don't leave. I just lit a candle for my Nonna." She stood and took one of the long sticks from the sand and said, "Here, do you want to light a candle for someone?"

Mrs. Hansen nodded, took the stick from her and said, "Thank you."

She lit the candle next to the one burning for Nonna, and they both knelt and prayed. It was hard for Jenny to focus on her prayers while sitting this close to Henry's mother. Henry had never shared with her the complete story of their falling out. She knew it happened the summer after their senior year of high school, sometime around the day in the driveway. At first, Henry told her that his mother was mad because he wanted to live full-time with his dad, which he did around that time. Then, he said it was because he didn't want to go to church anymore, which he stopped doing around that time. During college, Jenny noticed that the rift had grown, that Henry's mother had virtually vanished from his life, but he never offered any further explanation.

Mrs. Hansen stood and straightened her skirt and looked intently at Jenny. "You should pray for my son."

Jenny said, "I will. I always do."

Henry's mother started to walk toward the door, turned back around, and in a quiet voice said, "If you were really his friend, you'd help him."

"Help him how? Is something wrong with Henry?"

Mrs. Hansen sat in a pew and motioned for Jenny to sit beside her. There was a prayer card lying there, so Jenny picked it up. It had an image of Saint Nicholas on the front—a bearded man in a white robe with children gathered around him. She held it in her lap as Mrs. Hansen spoke.

"Years ago, I brought someone to our home to talk to him about a program that could fix him. He wouldn't do it. He was young and angry.

I'm sure he's told you how horrible I am, that I disowned him, but I was just trying to get him the help he needs. I was trying to save him."

Jenny felt a shiver through her whole body and held a hand to her heart.

"I had no choice but to tell him he couldn't be my son anymore. Don't you see how I had no choice? I was trying to save him. But his father enabled him and that was that. I wouldn't give up on him, though. I went to see him after college graduation. I told him he could still be welcomed into heaven if he would just remain chaste. If he doesn't act on his unnatural impulses. He wouldn't listen to me, though. My only hope now is that he will repent. He can repent and choose to live the rest of his life differently."

Jenny held her breath and felt the goose bumps on her arms, as she listened to all the suffering Henry had endured without uttering a word to her. *She tried to "fix him"? She told him he couldn't be her son anymore? She told him he was going to hell?* Jenny spoke calmly and said, "Henry doesn't need help, Mrs. Hansen. There is nothing to fix. He's perfect just as he is, and God loves him just as he is."

Mrs. Hansen shook her head and said, "No. You're wrong. It's not what the Bible says. He'll go to hell for his sins." She bowed her head and started to cry. "And I'll never see him again."

Jenny couldn't believe she actually felt sorry for the woman who condemned and banished Henry, but seeing the pain on her face, she realized that she was suffering from her own type of condemnation. She was condemned to believing that God would banish her son, just as she had. Jenny gripped her hands. "That's very sad, and it's not true. Don't you see? God doesn't exclude. Churches might exclude, but God doesn't. God teaches only love."

Mrs. Hansen pulled her hands away, and Jenny watched her face change. The sadness and expression of futility that drew her in a moment before disappeared. Mrs. Hansen stood over her in the pew and said, "You are sitting in a church! And you have no idea what you're talking about! How can you claim to be a Christian?"

Jenny stood up and stared right at Henry's mother. "I'm sorry, Mrs. Hansen, but I wonder the same thing about you."

Belonging

Mrs. Hansen looked as if she'd been slapped across the face. She took a step back from Jenny. "Let me ask you something. When's the last time you talked to Henry?"

Jenny's stomach turned. She'd overstepped and was about to be punished for it. "I haven't talked to him since September. Why?"

Mrs. Hansen gave her a look of disgust and pity all rolled up into one and turned and walked toward the door. Before she pushed it open, she looked back and said, "You just keep praying for him."

When the swish of the door echoed in the sanctuary, Jenny caught a glimpse of the musicians who'd witnessed the whole exchange in the soundproof room and thought it must have looked like the final scene in *The Graduate*, when a glass wall prevents Benjamin from hearing the words Elaine's father, mother, and groom are shouting at him. Here were two women in the sanctuary of a church on Christmas Eve, lighting candles, praying together, and then exchanging angry words, in silence imposed by glass. She looked down at the prayer card she'd held throughout their encounter. *Keep all children safe from harm; help them grow; give them the strength to keep their faith.*

When Jenny arrived at Heather and Rickey's house for Christmas Eve dinner, Heather pulled her into a quiet room and told her she was pregnant. "I'm due the end of May, and I want you to come home and be in the room with me when the baby's born."

Jenny jumped and squealed and hugged Heather. "I'm so happy for you! I get to see your baby being born?"

"Well, I hope so. I want you to photograph the birth. I want you with me and I want the pictures to be by you."

Jenny held onto Heather and thought about what it would be like to witness the birth of a child, to see Heather become a mother, to chronicle the beginning of the next generation of their family. They spoke excitedly about the due date, starting to show, the nursery, the gender. Jenny wiped the tears from her cheeks and said she'd be honored to be in the room with her, to capture the moment she gives birth.

When they went back out to the party, Jenny noticed her parents had arrived. Her mother was wearing a low-cut red satin blouse and a tight black skirt with stiletto heels and was boisterously greeting everyone. Her father was a few paces behind in the same suit he wore to Heather's wedding. Sitting down to dinner an hour or so later, Jenny was relieved that Heather had put her parents at a different table and that she was seated between Uncle Gino and Carl. When she took her seat, though, Uncle Gino, Billy, and Carl were nowhere to be seen. Just as dinner was served, the three of them joined her at the table.

"Where were you?" Jenny asked.

She was looking at Billy, but Uncle Gino answered for him. "We went outside to scan the sky for Rudolph. It's a bit foggy, though."

"It was so foggy, Jenny," Carl said.

Toward the end of dinner, Jenny's mother approached, squeezed in between her and Carl and said, "Merry Christmas Eve, Carl!"

Startled by her mother's bold intrusion, Jenny reflexively reached her arm out and held onto Carl's knee, forming a barrier between him and her mother. She dropped her gaze to meet Carl's and said, "Carl, this is my mom, Mrs. Hayes."

"Hi," Carl said.

Jenny's mother smiled brightly at Carl and said, "There are some colorful fish in the aquarium. Would you like to see them?"

"We'll take him to see the fish later," Jenny said firmly.

"Oh, enjoy your dinner! Let me take Carl to see the fish."

Jenny said quietly, "Carl doesn't know you."

Carl stood up and said, "Can I go? I want to see the fish!"

Billy pulled Carl onto his lap and said, "Mrs. Hayes, why don't you show both of us?"

"Well, okay. Let's go."

Jenny watched as her mother walked up the stairs leading to the foyer with Billy and Carl and disappeared around the corner. She tried to talk with Uncle Gino until they returned, but she was completely distracted. When she finally spotted them heading toward the stairs about ten minutes later, she felt relieved. Then she watched as her mother, carrying a drink, took the first stair in her stilettos, missed the second one, slid one leg under Carl, and rolled on the floor on top of him. As she fell, her hand swiped Heather's picture wall, knocking down several framed photographs, causing shards of glass to fly. Jenny could hear the collective gasp of the guests in the room. She jumped up to help Carl, who was bleeding from his mouth and crying.

Jenny's dad rushed over to help her mother. She waved him off and said, "Bob, I'm fine!" She got up, straightened her skirt, raised her empty glass, and said, "I'm graceful as ever. Who wants to dance later?"

A housekeeper started sweeping up the glass and retrieving the pictures from the floor. Billy carried Carl down the hallway to the bathroom and propped him up on the same counter where Jenny first met him. He lifted his chin, gently dabbed at his mouth with a tissue and said, "You're gonna be just fine, buddy. You just bit your lip."

"Does anything else hurt?" Jenny asked.

Carl shook his head and rubbed his eyes.

Jenny kissed the top of his head. His lip had stopped bleeding, but his face was puffy and damp from tears. She squeezed Billy's hand and said, "I'm so sorry."

"It was an accident, and Carl's fine. Right, buddy? You feel okay now?"

Carl nodded and Billy picked him up and held him. Carl put his thumb in his mouth and his head down on Billy's shoulder. Listening to Billy state simply that it was an accident, reminded Jenny again of how little he knew about her mother. Witnessing Carl's fragility in her mother's wake, she felt a fury she'd never felt before, and she resolved that this time, she would not remain quiet, and her mother would be held accountable.

By the time they went back out to the party, no one was sitting at the dinner table anymore. Guests were gathered around the fireplace in the living room, while coffee was being served and dessert trays were passed. Uncle Gino was waiting at the door with a bag of leftovers. Jenny walked toward him and said, "Are you heading home?"

"I am. It's getting late for me, dear. I wanted to see you before I left, though. Is Carl okay?"

"He's okay."

"Are you okay?"

"I will be."

After she hugged Uncle Gino goodbye, she turned and saw Billy and Carl standing beside her. "We should probably be getting home, too," Billy said. "Come with us."

"I wish I could. I told my dad I'd stay at home."

"Just go in there and tell him you decided to go home with me."

"I'll see you in the morning. I'll be fine. Go on. Carl needs to get home."

Billy shook his head and hugged her for a long time. Jenny kissed Carl on his forehead and stood at the end of Heather's driveway and waved to them in the fog. When she went back into the party, she overheard her mother say to one of Rickey's relatives, "We were coming down the stairs and he just darted right underneath me."

Jenny had let her mother's outrageous behavior go without comment her entire life, always opting to stay silent to keep the peace. Now, she walked right up to her and said, "That's not what happened."

Her mother turned, startled at first, but then appeared to delight in the thought of a battle, a conflict, something ugly. "It is exactly what happened."

"You're blaming an innocent child for your being unable to walk in heels after drinking too much?"

"Oh God, you're so predictable."

"Someone had to be. I don't want you around Carl—ever. Stay away from him."

Her mother cocked her head to the side and smiled with her mouth while hating with her eyes.

"I don't know why you're smiling. You will never be near my child again."

Her mother let out a loud, fake laugh and said, "*Your* child? Did you just say *your* child? You're playing house! It's clear to everyone but you that Billy is using you. I mean, it was pretty convenient, right?" She shook her head in disgust and said in a pitiful, mocking voice, "You think he loves you? You should be smarter than this."

Jenny stepped back. She'd just fed her mother a fly, and it had been gobbled. She turned and left the room, found her father, and told him she was staying at Heather's. There was no way she would go home with them now.

"I don't know if I can even get her up the stairs alone."

"You've been doing it for years now without me."

"Yeah, but tonight—it'll be so much easier for me if you're there. A buffer, you know."

Jenny looked at his sad, puffy eyes and said, "I can't be your buffer anymore."

"I know, baby. I know that. It's just one night. We can sneak into the Christmas pastries and make some coffee. Mama will just go to bed."

As Jenny listened to her father beg for her to come home, and also acknowledge that her presence would somehow shield him from her mother, she was once again consumed by her pity for him. She imagined him driving through the canyon, her mother either raging or passed out, then dragging her into the house and up the stairs. She thought of him sitting downstairs alone, making instant coffee, putting a pastry in the microwave. In the end, his childlike plea for her to come home so that he wouldn't have to endure the full brunt of abuse from her mother, was too much for her, and she agreed.

At eleven o'clock, Jenny's mother was still carrying on, talking and laughing in the living room. Jenny was surprised by her indifference, that their interaction didn't alter her mood in some way. She acted like nothing had happened. While her father sat miserably on the couch, waiting for her mother to be done, Jenny decided to hide out in the kitchen with Heather.

Aunt Hope was wrapping up foil pans filled with leftovers. She turned to Jenny and said,

"I'm so sorry, honey."

"You knew my mom when she was young. You must know some of her history, don't you, from Uncle Joe?"

"I guess so, yes. But I'm not sure it's my place to say."

"Mom, if you know something, you should tell Jenny," Heather said.

Aunt Hope said, "I know this much. I know your mom desperately wanted to leave Bakersfield. She wanted to go away to college, and Nonno wouldn't allow it. It was a different time. I know it's hard to imagine women being treated so differently. Joe left for college a couple of years later, with Nonno's full support, but your mother wasn't given the same opportunity. Joe said she went a little crazy and took most of it out on Nonna, who she believed should've taken her side."

"I always thought she didn't go away because my dad was playing football at Bakersfield College."

"No, I don't think she knew your dad then. I think they met at Bakersfield College. They hadn't even dated very long when they eloped."

"I can't believe Nonna wouldn't fight for her to go to school."

"In the late fifties, early sixties, wives—especially from conservative Italian Catholic families—didn't really counter their husbands, especially about decisions like this. I imagine it was very painful for Nonna too."

"You think that's why my mom is so angry…why she drinks?"

"I don't know that, honey. But she had big plans that were stopped. She wanted to leave and had to stay. She became a mother at nineteen—" Aunt Hope stopped, realizing how hurtful that comment would be, and said, "I'm sorry, Jenny."

"It's okay. I did that math a long time ago. I know I was born six months after they eloped. I know I was an accident."

Aunt Hope bowed her head and said, "I would never say that."

When her mother was finally ready to leave, she was sloppy and slurring, and looked dangerous enough for Jenny to stay away. She waited in the fog by the front door while her father led her mother to the car. Once he was in the driver's seat, Jenny got in the back. She felt nauseous even before they started down the winding canyon road. Connie Francis's version of "I'll Be Home for Christmas" was playing on the radio, and Jenny watched as her mother's head bobbed from side to side, waiting for her to fall asleep, wondering if she would suddenly turn in her seat, wide-eyed, ready to attack, like a doll in a horror film. When her head finally landed on the passenger seat window with a little smack, Jenny exhaled and stared out the window at the Christmas lights, dim and glowing in the fog.

Belonging

At home, they followed their usual drill. Jenny moved to the front seat of the car to hold onto her mother's arm so that she wouldn't fall out, while her father opened the passenger side door. Her father lifted her mother and carried her into the house and up to bed. Her mother didn't wake up, and for that, Jenny said a silent prayer of gratitude. She watched her father place presents under the tree, most of them for her mother. Outside, a coyote howled, displaced by the development on the outskirts of town.

Her father frowned and said, "Damn coyotes. I'll never forget the morning they got your pet rabbits. All that blood and white fur."

"What are you talking about?"

Her dad lowered his eyes. "I'm sorry, baby. I thought you knew I made up that story about Tabby and Rufus running off to Bunnyland to live with their friends. I mean, you were, what? Twelve?"

"I was ten."

"Well, you're probably old enough now to handle the truth."

"You're right. I am old enough now. I'm old enough for us to be able to talk about a lot of things, don't you think?"

"What do you want to talk about?"

"Someday, I'd like to talk about why you take it, why you stay."

"I love your mother." He took a bear claw pastry from a pink box and held it up, "Want half?"

Jenny shook her head. She couldn't believe she thought his revelation that her childhood pets had been ripped apart by coyotes was the signal that he was finally ready to speak some larger truth. She couldn't believe he still thought a pastry was the cure to all.

"Goodnight, Dad. Merry Christmas."

She looked back at him eating his bear claw, vacant and alone, and she regretted trying to force him to talk about something he'd probably stopped considering decades ago.

In her room, she dialed Henry's number in Brussels, and left a message on his answering machine wishing him a Merry Christmas. As she was getting into bed, she heard a clamor on her rooftop and light tapping on her window. She opened the shutters and saw Billy standing on the roof in the cold. She pushed open the window and reached for him. "Oh my gosh. You could have come to the front door."

"That would not be nearly as fun." Billy held onto the windowsill and pulled himself up and into her room.

Jenny closed the window and wrapped her arms around him.

"We shouldn't have left Heather's without you. You should be home with us." Billy looked around the bedroom that he hadn't been in since 1982. "Where are all your pictures? I used to be the star of this room."

"I'm sorry to say that they've been gone for a really long time."

"Gone, like packed away?"

Jenny held onto both of his hands and said, "No."

"Oh." Billy gave a solemn nod, an acknowledgment that the most painful part of their past had resulted in the abandonment or destruction of all the photos of their young life together. He walked around the room, looking at the blank walls, and said, "Let's get out of here. Get some shoes on. Grab your bag. Let's go."

After years of facing this same decision—to stay or to go, to continue to be a buffer for her father or to take care of herself, to leave this home and this family behind—she started packing her bag. She would leave with Billy tonight, and she wouldn't come back. She didn't even stop to think about it.

It occurred to her that her dad might wander downstairs for a cigarette in the middle of the night and discover that she was no longer in her room. She didn't want him to worry, so she decided to write a note. She took paper from her old desk drawer and thought about what to say. An apology for leaving? An opening to talk? Why she'd left? Merry Christmas? Ultimately, she decided against all these things. She wanted to give her parents the courtesy of not wondering where she was or worrying about her, nothing more, nothing less. So, she left a note on her bed, telling them that she would be staying at the Ambler's house until she went back to Santa Clara on the 26th. The note seemed both terribly incomplete, and also said all that she could say.

"Do you want to use the front door?" Billy asked.

Jenny shook her head and said, "Let's go out my window."

Belonging

Billy opened the window and hopped out onto her rooftop. He helped Jenny down and walked to the edge, ready to lower himself onto a section of cinder block fence. He looked back and saw Jenny sitting on the rooftop beneath the light from her window. "What are you doing? Let's go. It's freezing."

"I need to sit here for just a minute. I think I've been here before on this same night. Is it still the 24th?"

Billy sat beside her and looked at his watch. "Nope. It's 1:15. Christmas day."

Jenny turned to him. "I'm never going to stay in this room again. And I'm never going to cry on this rooftop again. I just want to feel it and see it and put it away, be complete."

She looked up at the stars and down at the dark yard. She stuck her head in the window to her room. It looked dull to her now, like someone had tried really hard to make it a bright spot but could not quite accomplish the task—or maybe it was once a bright spot, but one that had long ago been abandoned. She took a sack of bird seed from her bag and began tossing it onto the gravel and said, "Merry Christmas, birds."

Billy jumped down first, took her bag, and helped her down. Jenny looked back at her dad's workshop. Through the window, she saw his coffee mug and some North Pole paper he'd left out. On the front lawn, she stopped and looked at the birch tree and the lemon tree and the cinder block fence. She picked up a lemon from the frosty grass, dried it off on her nightgown, and brought it with her.

When they got to Billy's parents' house, they peeked in at Carl, who was sound asleep with his thumb in his mouth and a stack of Christmas books beside him.

Jenny turned to Billy and said, "He definitely has visions of sugar plums."

They tiptoed out of Carl's room and went down the hall to the spare room. Jenny took off her shoes and coat and got into bed. She put the lemon from her yard on the nightstand. Billy tucked her in, kissed her, and said goodnight. She felt warm and safe and fell asleep easily.

Jill Fordyce

On Christmas morning, after gifts had been exchanged and the breakfast dishes were cleared, Jenny went into Billy's old room and called her dad. He sounded like he'd been sleeping, and she realized he probably didn't even know she was gone.

"Hi, Dad. I'm at Billy's. I just wanted to call and say Merry Christmas," she said.

"Oh, when will you be home?"

She took a breath and exhaled. "I'm not coming home. But I love you and I wanted to say Merry Christmas, okay?"

"You're not coming home?"

"No."

He didn't speak for a minute, and she knew he was thinking about whether she meant she wasn't coming home today or ever. Then he said, "What'll I tell your mother?"

"Tell her whatever you like. I just can't go back there, okay? Do you understand?"

Jenny heard her father shifting in the bed, the flick of his lighter, and a door closing behind him.

"You're not coming back."

"No, I'm not."

He paused, his silence revealing that he knew she wasn't just talking about today. "Well, I guess I don't know what to say, except I'm sorry."

"I know."

"And I hope you know how much I love you. We both do."

The sorrow and futility in her father's voice made her want to cry. "You know what I hope?"

"What, baby?"

"I hope that someday you can be free too."

When she hung up the phone, she pictured her dad sitting at the kitchen table in his underwear, listening to her finally say what she'd been trying to say since she was about ten years old—that one day, she would leave, and she wouldn't come back. He must have known it had always been an ironic two-for-one-deal living in that house—with one who starved her and one who fed her, one who held her underwater and one who helped her float. She thought about their last night together, how they each fell back into the unspoken roles they'd performed for years. Her mother controlling the mood, even the air. Her father passive, never intervening. Jenny, the bystander to it all, officially declared to be the buffer she'd always been. She thought about the cold, wet air on her face as she leapt off the roof, leaving behind her tangerine room for good.

At the end of Christmas day, Billy drove Jenny to their park. He led her to the oak tree and told her he brought her there to make a new promise. He presented her with a ring, a small diamond set in an antique silver band and asked her to marry him. Jenny recognized the ring right away but wasn't sure how it could be.

Her heart was beating fast, and she had tears in her eyes. "This is Nonna's ring?"

Billy nodded, "Yes. Uncle Gino has been saving it for you. He gave it to me last night, when we went outside before dinner."

Jenny thought of seeing Uncle Gino, Billy, and Carl arriving late to the dinner table, of Uncle Gino saying they'd been out looking at the sky for Rudolph. Now she knew the three of them shared in this secret, and that Uncle Gino handed over Nonna's ring on Christmas Eve behind Heather's house, in the place where she found Billy again, in the place where she first held Carl.

Jenny kissed him and wrapped her arms around his neck. She told him that, yes, she would marry him, and he placed Nonna's ring on her finger.

As Jenny was getting ready to leave town the next day, Billy gave her a photograph of the two of them he had in his childhood bedroom. They're sitting on his front lawn the summer they were fifteen. He'd taken it on a self-timer. Jenny is laughing and he is looking at her instead of the camera. He's in his summer ball uniform; she's in a sundress. When the shutter clicked, he was tucking a strand of hair behind her ear. Accidentally candid, they look exactly how she remembered them.

Billy said, "Now you have a picture of us."

On her way out of town, Jenny drove to Henry's house to see what his dad or Christopher knew about him. When she arrived at the brick house that Henry grew up in, she immediately noticed that it was lifeless. There was no music, no smell of cookies baking. The curtains were drawn, and a dying pine wreath hung on the door. Jenny knocked and half-heartedly waited for Henry's dad or Christopher to open the door. She couldn't imagine they'd gone away for Christmas. Mr. Hansen always had a big gathering to share the Christmas cookies and cakes he spent the month preparing. She opened the back gate and walked around the perimeter of the house. The lawn was covered with brown leaves and rotting persimmons. She remembered how Henry's dad used to gather the persimmons and make bread and cookies and pudding, none of which anyone would eat. Jenny began filling her sweater with as many persimmons as she could carry and wondered what she would bake.

On the drive home, she replayed her encounter with Henry's mother over and over again. She couldn't believe Mrs. Hansen stood in the sanctuary of the church and admitted banishing Henry from her life after failed attempts to "fix" him. He had hidden so much from her for so long, suffered for years without telling her any of it. It occurred to her that she had kept a secret from him too. Somewhere amidst the golden hills, the ghosts, and the fog on the Pacheco Pass, she decided it was time to tell Henry what she should've told him years ago. She hoped it would allow him to open up to her, to understand that it made no difference in her love for him. That night in her house alone, she sat at the kitchen table and wrote him a letter.

Dear Henry,

First, I apologize for not writing this letter sooner. I wish I had. It took seeing your mom in church on Christmas Eve to make me understand what a mistake I'd made over the years, repeatedly turning a blind eye, failing to say out loud what I believed. I'm sharing this now, so we can move forward, honor our friendship, and stay in each other's lives.

That day in your driveway in Bakersfield, I believed that you were in a relationship with that boy. I understood then that you were probably gay. I never talked to you about it because it seemed that you so badly wanted to keep it secret. Here's what I didn't know. I didn't know that your mom tried to "fix" you. I didn't know she left you. I wish I had. I wish I could have been there for you. I acknowledge that my silence probably reinforced your belief that you couldn't share this with me. I am so sorry for the pain you had to endure alone. I should've told you what I believed. That way, you would've understood that it did not and could never change my love for you. I thought you knew that, but after seeing your mother in church, I understand why you think people who are supposed to love you could reject you. I guess we've always had that in common, without even knowing it.

I want to be sure you know that my beliefs are nothing like your mother's beliefs. The core of my faith is love and acceptance. My faith would never make me reject you. I miss you so much. I want you in my life. I hope that you will write me back or call.

I love you,
Jenny

She took out her box of prayer cards and spread them around her room. She selected the simplest of them all, a card that read: *We love him, because he first loved us. 1 John 4:19,* and put it in the envelope with her letter. She washed the persimmons from Henry's yard and found a recipe for persimmon bread. While the bread was baking, filling her home with the smell of cinnamon and nutmeg, she decided to call Henry's house in Bakersfield. When no one answered, she left a message that she was looking for Henry and left her work and home numbers. That night, she dreamt she was in an airport terminal and spotted Henry across the way, smiling with his arms outstretched. She was trying to get to him, moving through the crowd, but he never got any closer; he was always the same distance away.

Chapter Seventeen

APRIL 1991

Carl's first little league game of the season was Saturday morning, so Jenny drove straight from work on Friday and arrived at Billy's late that night. By April, she no longer had to pack for her trips to Billy's house. After Christmas, she just started leaving her things there, taking up about a third of his closet, and claiming two of his drawers for herself. Carl was asleep when she arrived. She peeked in on him and saw that his new baseball uniform was laid out on the floor, next to a note card in Carl's handwriting that said, *one base rule.*

Jenny and Billy sat together on the back porch. It was a cool spring night and the air smelled like peach tree blossoms and the sea. Billy explained the "one base rule." In t-ball, since the kids don't know how to field the ball, the batter can only run one base at a time. Carl needed to remind himself of this; he was used to hitting the ball and running as far as he could.

Jenny smiled and said, "I brought my adoption file. Have you figured out your units yet, when you'll have enough to graduate?"

"I'll be finished in two semesters."

Jenny reached for Billy's hand. "So, I should follow up on the job leads I have here? I mean, we'll have to live here for another year, right?"

"We could wait a year."

Jenny was surprised he thought this was even a possibility. She put her hands up over her eyes. "You want to wait another year?"

Billy kissed her and said, "I don't want to, but we could if it makes more sense for your career. A year isn't that long."

Belonging

The next day, Carl forgot about the one base rule, and the first time he got a hit, he kept running toward second, and the coach directed him back to first, reminding him of the rule. The second time, he stayed on first, but inched off, like he would steal. The coach reminded him that there was no stealing in t-ball. The third time, Carl just stood on first base with his hands on his hips and made bored faces.

After the game, Billy sat with Carl at the kitchen table to talk about sportsmanship. Jenny left them alone and was opening windows to let the spring air inside when she heard a knock at the door. "I'll get it," she shouted.

She opened the door to a woman she'd never seen before, but somehow recognized right away—her long blonde hair and tiny waist and the pretty little nose that looked just like Carl's. She looked briefly at Jenny and then over her shoulder, and said, "Hi. Are Billy and Carl here?"

Jenny stood there thinking, *Is that really her? Is she really here? If I close the door and open it again, can I make her disappear?* She felt sick to her stomach, but outwardly she remained completely calm. "Um, yes. Hold on a sec." Then she said, "I'm Jenny."

Tara looked at her with no sign of recognition and Jenny added, "Billy's fiancée."

Tara continued to look past her into the house and said, "I'm Tara. Carl's mom."

As they stood at the door, Billy poked his head out of the kitchen to see who was there.

When Tara caught sight of him, she said, "Hi, Billy."

Billy stepped out of the kitchen and walked toward the front door. Jenny watched as surprise, and something else, maybe fear, crossed Billy's face.

"Tara. What are you doing here?"

"I was on my way to L.A., and I thought I'd drive out and see you and Carl. Where is he?"

Billy put his hand on the front door and pulled it partially closed and said, "You didn't think of calling first?"

"Sorry. Is it a problem?"

"Could you give us a minute?"

"You want me to wait out here?"

Billy nodded. "Yeah, I do."

As soon as Billy closed the door, Jenny threw her arms up, and said in a loud whisper, "She just pops in? What will this do to Carl? He's not two now! Are you going to let her see him?"

Billy held her arms and said, "I don't want to start something with her. I don't want her thinking she has to fight me. If she thinks she can come and go, which she won't—she's proven that—she'll never think she has to pursue any rights. So, yes, I'll let her see him."

Billy was right. This made perfect sense, but Jenny was consumed by her own insecurities. She was haunted by who Tara was to Billy. They were married in a church. They set up a home together, slept in the same bed. She gave birth to his son.

"You have to trust me. I will handle it." His voice was even and steady, but his eyes were not. He looked nervous and unsure—like he knew he had to make her feel better even if he wasn't quite equipped to deal with the situation himself. Recognizing that Billy needed her, Jenny made a conscious effort to put aside her own worries.

"You don't have to handle it by yourself," she said. "I'll help you. Let's just see what her plans are, okay?"

Jenny didn't want to talk to Tara. She didn't want to look at Tara. But her desire to protect both Billy and Carl was greater than her discomfort. So, while Billy went into the kitchen to tell Carl that Tara was there to see him, Jenny opened the front door and led her into the family room.

When Billy and Carl came out of the kitchen, Carl walked right over to Tara and said hello. Jenny didn't know what Billy had said to him about his mother's visit, but it appeared he recognized her, or at least understood who she was.

"You're so big now!" Tara said to Carl. "And you play baseball!"

"Uh-huh. I played today. I hit the ball good, but you can't get doubles in t-ball." Carl picked up a large puzzle box on the ground. "Want to do this puzzle with me?"

"Okay." Tara sat on the floor next to Carl as he dumped out the puzzle pieces. "Sorry if I interrupted your weekend. I guess I should have called."

Billy said, "Yeah. So, do you know what your plans are?"

Belonging

"I need to be in L.A. tonight."

"You're here for, what? A couple hours?"

"Yeah, is that okay?"

Billy looked at Jenny, who was looking at the ground. Carl was oblivious, trying to put two pieces of the puzzle together. Jenny realized they were waiting for a response from her. "That's fine," she said. She tried to stay focused. She kept telling herself this was a blip, an aberration, not part of their daily life.

No one was talking again, so Jenny said, "Do you still live in Bend?"

"Yeah. I'm thinking about moving to California, though, to be closer to Carl. I've been thinking about that for a while now. He's starting school soon, right? I was thinking I could be home for him in the afternoons."

The words hit her with such force that she lost her bearings for a moment. It was just like all those times in her childhood when her mother would say or do something that would suddenly alter the course of a day or a year, something that—despite all her scanning and preparing—she didn't see coming.

Jenny collected herself, drew in a breath, and said, "He'll be in kindergarten in the fall. And he'll probably go in the afternoons."

"Oh, well, whatever. I just want to be close by. You two are engaged?" Tara asked.

"Yeah, we are," Jenny said.

"Where did you meet?" Tara asked.

Jenny thought, *She doesn't know who I am? Maybe she just doesn't remember my name?* She looked at Billy with a puzzled expression and Billy looked away, avoiding her eyes. Jenny was confused and looked back and forth between them. She was hot and flushed and starting to sweat a little.

Billy said, "We met in Bakersfield."

Jenny made note of his vagueness. She fanned herself and watched as Carl tried to include Tara in his play. She thought, *I know the names of all these dinosaurs. I know Carl's favorite books, what he likes for breakfast. I can spot Venus the minute the sun goes down. I know how the sound of his breathing changes as he falls asleep in my lap.*

Tara said, "Maybe Carl and I could go get lunch together?"

Jenny was alarmed by her suggestion to take Carl out of the house, and she shot Billy a concerned look. Billy raised his hand slightly, as if halting her from saying anything, and said, "There's a burrito stand down the street that Carl likes."

Tara and Carl left holding hands and the minute the door was closed, Jenny said, "You let her go places alone with him? Are you sure that's safe?"

"We can see the burrito stand from my front yard. Do you want to sit outside and watch them?"

"Actually, yes. Did you hear what she said? Did you hear her say—"

Billy cut her off. "Yes, and it will never happen. Never. For whatever reason, today she is interested in Carl. It'll be different tomorrow, or in an hour, as soon as she gets bored."

"How do you think Carl is?"

"I think he's fine. I'll talk with him about it tonight. I think he'll be fine, though."

"What if she really does it, though? What if she moves here and wants to be with him every day after school, or decides she wants a fifty-fifty arrangement with you?"

"It's just not possible."

"Because of the custody agreement?"

"Because she would never want that type of obligation."

"Pretend she did."

"Jenny. Stop."

"Just tell me. What would you do?"

Billy shook his head with his eyes closed and his hands on his hips. He looked so frustrated with her. "Okay, I'm pretending. Tara decides to come over every day and takes me to court to have Carl half the time. What do you want me to say?"

"What would you do?"

"I'd fight her with everything I have."

"What if that's not the best thing for Carl?"

"Is this what it's like when you cross-examine people? It's exhausting."

Billy threw his hands up in defeat, and said, "I'm sorry, Jenny. I guess I just don't know. You're right. I'd have to figure that out. But if we're not here in pretend-land, there's no point in figuring it out because I'd be willing to bet anything that we won't see her again for years."

"She just said in front of Carl that she wants to be with him every day after school, and you think she may never come back?"

"Yes, exactly."

Jenny walked into the front yard and looked toward the burrito stand. From where she stood, she could smell the whole pinto beans mixed with the sea air, and she could see Tara and Carl sitting at a table on the covered patio. She came back in, sat down at the kitchen table, and said, "Can you sit with me for a minute? I know you don't want to talk about this anymore, but I have to ask you one more thing."

Billy sat down and sighed and closed his eyes. "What?"

"She didn't know where we met. She'd never even heard of me."

Billy put his face in his hands and said nothing.

"You said you couldn't see me before you got married because of her. But she doesn't know anything about me or us."

Billy put his hands flat on the table, looked at her and said, "Yes, you're right. I lied. Back then, I lied."

Jenny began to cry. "Why? Why would you lie about that? You wanted an excuse to not see me?"

"Jenny, you have to understand. It's not that I didn't want to see you. It's that I couldn't. I had committed myself to being Tara's husband and our baby's father, and I was so surprised to hear from you. You never even let me talk to you again, so it's not like I thought we were a possibility. Then there I was, getting married, and you call me. And I realized something when I spoke to you. I realized that if I wanted my family to work, I had to leave you in the past."

The words *my family* and *leave you in the past* stopped her cold. She remembered in her bones what that felt like. At the time, it was a devastating final acknowledgment that what they once were to each other was long over, that he had moved on, and that he had made a life without her. It was Bud standing on a dirt road at the end of *Splendor in the Grass*. Billy reached for her, and she pulled away and walked out of the room.

"I said that Tara didn't want me to see you because it was easier than admitting I still loved you. I worked really hard to convince myself I could be a good husband to Tara and a good father to our baby, and I could make it all work. It wouldn't work if I was in love with someone else. I knew how I'd feel seeing you, and I didn't want to feel that way."

Jenny went out the screen door to the back, into the yard, and Billy followed. He reached for her shoulders and turned them so she would face him. Jenny's face grew hot, and the back of her neck was tingling a little. She looked at him but said nothing.

"Why does this upset you so much? It has nothing to do with now," he said.

"It doesn't? You lied to me and said you couldn't see me. You were actually okay with never seeing me again. And you did it so you could make a family with Tara. And now here she is. And you know what else? I don't think I could ever explain to you how shattered that left me. It was the worst feeling I've ever had in my life."

"I'm sorry. I couldn't see you. And I didn't just lie to you. I lied to myself too."

Jenny looked at the sorrow in his face and felt ashamed for pressing him. She knew he was right. He had to avoid her to go on with his life; she knew exactly what that felt like.

"It makes sense, Billy. It does. But that doesn't make it hurt less."

When Tara and Carl came back, Carl had chocolate ice cream on the tip of his nose, his chin, and his hands. He ran in the door and jumped up into Billy's arms, and said, "We got ice cream."

Carl put his sticky hands on Billy's face, leaving a smudge of ice cream on his cheek. Tara walked over to the kitchen sink, wet a paper towel, and wiped the chocolate off Billy's face. Jenny watched in stunned silence—Billy holding Carl in his arms, Tara close enough to feel his breath. She looked down at the ground. She could feel Billy looking at her.

When Billy walked Tara to the front door, she said, "My parents want to be part of Carl's life. They want to spend time with him. And I would like to start spending time with him, too—with both of you."

"If you want to see Carl, write something up and I'll look it over."

"Okay. I'll 'write something up,'" she said, with a swish of her hand. "But I'd like things to be different. I mean, he is my son. We are his parents."

Belonging

Jenny watched the way Tara looked at Billy. She was in awe of her combination of confidence and carelessness—how she believed she could just knock on the door on a Saturday afternoon and pick up where they left off.

Billy said, "If it's good for him to spend time with you and your parents, we can work on that. But you shouldn't have any other expectations."

Jenny recognized this tone. It was a calm intended to mask something else: fear for Carl, panic at the intrusion into their lives, the uncertainty of how to best protect his son.

When Tara left, Jenny and Billy sat on the porch, watching Carl fill his dump trucks with sand. Jenny felt like she might throw up. All that pushing down of everything she felt formed a toxic brew in her stomach.

Billy said, "I think I'll take Carl on a little walk."

"Alone?"

"Yeah."

"Oh."

Jenny swiped at the tears that came without warning and went into the house. She thought Billy might follow her, but he didn't. She sat on his bed and heard him talking to Carl through the open window to the yard. She heard Carl say, "Why isn't Jenny coming?" and she heard Billy answer, "You know earlier, when we talked about your game, and it was just you and me? It's sort of like that."

She heard the back gate open and close and started to sob. Every fear she had swirled inside of her. Why didn't he want her with them? If she was part of their family, if she was going to be Carl's mother, she should be with them. But if she wasn't—if they were just *playing house*—obviously, it made sense to not include her. It was there in the bedroom alone that Jenny began to close down, pull away, and isolate herself. She could feel it happening and wanted to stop it but didn't know how.

One part of her just acknowledged the end of the fantasy—she wasn't Carl's mother, and she would never be the only woman in their lives. It was selfish, she knew, but Tara being absent made it so much easier for her. She didn't have to be a stepmother because there was no mother, and she didn't have to see Billy with his ex-wife; it was almost as if Tara never existed. But the most scared part of her thought she could actually lose them—that the life they were planning could be swept out from under her, and now she'd had her warning. She stared out the back window and tried to ignore the stark imagery in her mind: doors closing, credits rolling, her car driving away. She saw herself tumbling down the dark shaft of the hole.

In the hour that Billy and Carl were gone, she sat in silent prayer, calling on her favorite saints, Teresa and Francis, in particular, to help her up and out. She put on her running shoes and shorts and went for a run, careful to go toward the flower farms instead of the ocean, so she wouldn't run into Billy and Carl. When she got back, they were already home, and Billy was picking up clothes in Carl's room.

Jenny put her head in the door. "How was your walk?"

"Good. Did you go for a run?"

"Yeah, out by the flower farms. How's Carl?"

"He seems fine."

Jenny sat on Carl's bed and looked up at Billy. "What did you talk about? I mean, if I can ask."

"Why couldn't you ask?"

"Well, you didn't want me to go. So maybe it's private or not my business or something."

"Why would you say that?"

"I guess it's the way you made me feel."

"Maybe it's the way *you* made you feel."

"Well, you knew I was upset, and you didn't really seem to care. And you know, there's the whole lying thing sitting right here." Jenny put a hand to her heart.

Billy said, "That's exactly why I didn't want you to go."

"Why?"

"Because we are unsettled right now. I know that, and I needed to get through some things with Carl before I could get back to you and me."

Jenny said, "Yeah, I guess we are. So, how was Carl? What did he say?"

"He was fine. He said Tara was 'fun' and compared her to his babysitter, Megan."

"Did it make him feel bad at all?"

"He doesn't understand enough for it to make him feel bad."

"Maybe not now. But he might someday. Does he think she's moving here?"

"He didn't mention it, and neither did I, because it will never happen."

"But she said it right in front of him. Carl is very smart. He may just be thinking about it inside."

"Jenny—" Billy let out an exasperated sigh and said, "I'll talk to him about it when the time is right, okay?"

"Why do you seem so impatient with me?"

"I just don't want to talk about it anymore today."

They went through the evening doing the things they always did—having dinner, reading books, throwing a ball, straightening up the house—but with an absence of joy. The presence of Tara and all she represented—Billy's failed marriage, the end of his baseball career, Carl's abandonment, Jenny's threat—sat right there in the room with them.

When Jenny got in bed with Billy that night, she couldn't stop thinking. She didn't know how Billy felt and she knew he didn't want to talk anymore. One thought kept floating across her mind. The thought went something like this: *It was Tara who left Billy. He wouldn't have left her. He wouldn't have given up on his family. Now she's back, and she's beautiful, and she's Carl's mom, and she wants to be part of his life. And Billy seems distant, closed off. What if he wants to try to make his family work again? What if that's what's best for Carl?* This line of thinking was intensified when Jenny thought about the lie. She thought, *He could leave me even if he loves me. He could make that decision just like he did before, and I would lose them both.* The thought caused her such distress that she began formulating a plan. *I can just go home. It might be easier on everyone that way.* Finally, she thought, *This is crazy. I'm back in the hole. None of this is true. Maybe he can reassure me.* She rolled over and looked up at the ceiling and said, "Billy?"

"Yeah?"

"I've been thinking," she paused and hesitated. "You know how important it was for you to try to make your family work?"

"Jenny. Stop thinking."

"Please, just listen. You said you loved me then—when I called you before you got married. Remember? You loved me. Just like you love me now. But you decided to be Tara's husband and devoted yourself to your new family. You wouldn't even see me to say goodbye. And you loved me. So, what's the difference now? What if she does come back?"

"Jenny, she has no interest in me and little interest in Carl. We're back in pretend-land. It will never happen."

"It feels like it could happen."

"*You* are the person I want to spend my life with. *We* are a family now. I love you. I'm not leaving. And I'm not letting you leave. I love you and this will all be fine. Nothing has changed. Nothing will change."

Billy was firm, severe even. As a teenager, she loved his matter-of-fact unemotional declarations. His refusal to entertain her fears, to go deeper, made her feel secure, almost like he was a caring adult who knew better. It also protected her from ever having to reveal too much. Now, however, she was a grown woman, actively trying to show him a part of herself, speaking aloud the thought process that got her to this point. The unemotional declaration was not enough. She needed more from him, so she continued to push.

"I don't understand why you wanted to talk to Carl without me."

Billy rolled onto his side and pulled Jenny closer to him. "I know. I'm sorry. It was a bad decision. I was stressed out and I regret it. Can we please move on from this?"

As he held her, Jenny looked at his hazel eyes. She wished he would say more. She wished he understood what she needed from him, but she also couldn't fault him. She'd never shared the way her mind spun, and the bad thoughts stuck. She'd never let him see the dark places she went, the inside of the hole. This is the way they'd always resolved things. She would express a worry or a fear and he would tell her it would all be okay, that they would get through it. But he never really understood her worries or fears because he was so focused on stopping them. What used to be comforting to her, now seemed to form a wedge, a space that kept them from the closeness she desired.

"I wish we could move on from this, but I don't know how."

Belonging

"Jenny, Carl has never known his mother. Part of me wasn't even sure I should've let her in. I have no manual for this. I need to do what's best for Carl, and I don't know what that is. That's all I could focus on—*what does she want with Carl?* And I'm sorry. You should have been with us."

When Billy fell asleep, she held onto him and listened to the sounds of the house—dishwasher running, wind outside, his breathing. She looked around the room, lit only by the moon, and tried to memorize it, a mental exercise in anticipation of loss, a way to make sure she could always access a place she was afraid she might not see again. The open window to the yard. The basket of children's books in the corner. The photos on the dresser—of Carl, of his parents, of her. She observed the shape of Billy's body under the covers, felt his hand wrapped around hers, looked over at his open closet where her sundresses hung. She thought of Emily at the end of *Our Town* saying, *I can't look at everything hard enough*. It was so warm and felt so much like home, she couldn't believe she was thinking about leaving.

The next morning, Jenny was helping Carl make his bed, when he looked up at her and said, "Did you know that Tara is my mom?"

Jenny sat down on the bed and put a hand on his head. "I did, sweetie. Yes. Did you have a good day yesterday?"

Carl sat beside her and said, "Uh-huh. She said she might live by me."

Jenny sat looking at Carl and thinking about the file she brought with her—research about adoption and forms to start the process. Part of it involved terminating Tara's rights entirely. She thought, *How would this work now? How would they explain it to Carl? Carl, Tara is your mom, but she won't actually be your mom, just live nearby. And Jenny, who is not your mom, will be your mom. You can call her Jenny, though.* It was confusing even to her. She couldn't imagine the confusion of a four-year-old boy who'd spent most of his life with no mother at all. She was relieved they hadn't talked to Carl about the possibility of adoption yet.

Carl hopped down from the bed. "Wanna see my book?"

"Sure. What book?"

He walked over to his dresser and opened the top drawer. "This baby book."

Carl sat in Jenny's lap and opened the book. On the first page, there was a photograph of Tara, wearing a shirt of Billy's, cradling newborn Carl in a dimly lit room, at what must have been the home they shared. Jenny thought of what she'd learned in photography class years ago, and she didn't just see Tara and Carl in the picture. She saw Billy, and the complete pride and awe and love he felt photographing his new wife and baby.

"See," Carl said, pointing, "Tara *is* my mom."

Jenny had her arm around Carl's shoulder. She moved her hand to the top of his head and let it rest on his soft hair. "Yes, she is."

Carl flipped to the last page of the book. He was in a red sleeper by a Christmas tree in this house. Jenny had never done the math before, but now realized that Carl's first Christmas was spent here, alone with Billy. The book was only about twenty pages long, and his mother was already gone. She felt like she would cry, but she didn't want to in front of Carl, so she held it in. Her chin was bunched up and quivering, and when Carl looked up at her, he reached his hand out and touched it. "Jenny, your chin looks like a nut. Why does your chin look like a nut?"

"A nut? What kind of nut?"

"The big round one with dots in it."

"A walnut?"

"Uh-huh."

Jenny touched her chin and pretended to smooth it out and smiled at him. "Is this better?"

"Yeah, it looks regular now."

"Help me pack a snack for the road?"

"PBH?"

"Sure."

Carl hopped up and went into the kitchen. Billy came into the room and saw Jenny on the floor, the book in her lap, the trouble on her face, and said, "Are you okay? What's wrong?"

Jenny lifted the book and struggled to find the words to communicate what she was feeling and why. "Well, it's so many things. I just saw a photo you took of Tara and Carl in the home you lived in together. It was so warm and sweet, and well, you know, I can tell what it meant to you, what they mean to you, from the photo. And then, by Christmas, it was over. You were here and Carl was without his mother."

Billy sat next to her on the floor and put his arm around her shoulder. "Do you want to know why I took these pictures? Why I made this book? I wanted Carl to be able to see his beginning. I wanted him to know he was loved. But you're reading way too much into the picture of Tara. We were already having problems and we knew so little of each other. The photo is not the intimate moment you imagine; it was taken solely for Carl. And you know what else? It may seem sad that we spent that first Christmas here alone, but it wasn't. The two of us had settled in together, and I knew we were going to be happy."

Jenny covered her face with her hands and thought about Billy sitting alone, putting together the origin story of a family that had already fallen apart, and somehow still believing in the happy ending.

Billy put the book away and they joined Carl in the kitchen. Carl had put cookies, chips, and an apple on the kitchen counter. When Jenny saw him slathering peanut butter and honey on bread, she felt like she would cry again, and knew it was time to go. Billy said they would come up in two weeks, unless they all ended up in Bakersfield sooner for the birth of Heather's baby. He handed her a Mary Ellen Mark book from the bookshelf in his bedroom. He'd placed a bookmark at the section on a childbirth she photographed.

Jenny zipped the book into her bag and knelt and held Carl's face in her hands. "You, I'm going to miss like crazy," she said.

"Me too," said Carl.

Billy kissed her goodbye and said, "We'll be up soon."

As she opened the door to her car, Billy reached out and held onto her elbow. He looked at her long enough for her to know that he might know. "Is everything okay?"

"Uh-huh."

"Are you sure?"

"Yeah."

She kissed him again and got in her car and drove away. She slowed as she rounded the corner and took a last look at Billy and Carl, standing in the street, both still waving goodbye.

On the drive home, she kept thinking about Billy lying to her that Christmas Eve in Bakersfield, how he'd done so to protect his new family. This specific rejection went to the core of all the troubles she already had. It had always been difficult to believe anyone loved her the way Billy did. That night, those doubts became valid. Usually, she blamed herself for things that went wrong. It was her fault she'd never see Billy again; if she'd just opened the door and let him in, none of this would've happened. She had a deep need for closure, for things to end well. Billy's refusal to see her left her in a horrible limbo. That one night validated all the terrible things that held firm to a small, shadowy place inside of her. *He never loved you. This is all your fault. You will never be able to move on.*

She thought about Billy suggesting that they wait another year and began to wonder if she'd rushed him into something. She thought of Tara in the kitchen and the way she looked at Billy. She thought of Carl sharing his baby book, and how happy he seemed that his mother had come to see him, that she might live by him. She remembered her own mother's words: *You're playing house. He's using you. You look so stupid.* As she drove, she felt that little suit of armor Henry talked about. It was back, wrapping her arms and legs and the center where her heart lay.

Chapter Eighteen

APRIL 1991

When Jenny got home that night, she went into Carl's room and sat on his bed. The room had transformed over the last few months, into a space he'd made his own. His t-ball team picture hung on the bulletin board. The drawers were filled with his pajamas and sweatshirts. He'd left his tool belt and a pile of rocks next to Saint Teresa on his table. Chico lounged on the end of his bed, waiting for him to return.

Jenny went into her own room, picked up the phone, and called Henry. She did so half-heartedly, knowing he wouldn't answer. Over the last several months, she'd written to him about Carl's room and her budding relationship with the boy she believed would be her son. She'd written about Billy and all their plans, chronicling the beginning of their life as a family. She thought he'd be so proud of her for opening herself up, for taking this leap, but he just never wrote back. He never acknowledged the care package she sent after his trip in September. He never thanked her for the leather journal she so carefully selected. He never answered the long letter she wrote him after Christmas, telling him about seeing his mother at church, expressing her sorrow for not being more honest with each other. He never responded to the letter she wrote telling him she was getting married.

What made his failure to respond even more painful and confusing was the fact that, in her worst times, Henry had always been there for her. When she had valley fever, he visited nearly every day. After Nonna died, he looked through prayer cards with her, fell asleep beside her, and helped her hold a memorial service on her rooftop. All the times her mother came after her, he was there, reassuring her, telling her to put her voice out of her head. In the days following the party at Kyle's house, he removed a screen from the kitchen window to get to her, when she'd locked everyone out. Driving away to college, she believed she could leave everything behind, as long as they were together.

His friendship had been constant and without fail since they were children. He knew more about her life than anyone else. It hadn't been a conscious choice to open herself up to him. It was a byproduct of his natural intuition, and the fact that their bond was formed when they were very young. The length and closeness of their friendship had attuned them to each other, and not much had to be actively revealed. She kept writing to him even though he never wrote back. It was a sign of her commitment to not give up on him, a demonstration of faith that their friendship would endure. She would not accept his departure from her life, and she wanted to be sure he knew that.

When the phone rang later that night, she thought it would be Billy and wondered what she would say to him. Instead, it was Heather shouting, "Guess who's having Braxton-Hicks contractions!"

Jenny smiled at the sound of Heather's happy and excited voice. "I forgot what those are."

"It's when your stomach squeezes into a hard ball and it gets you ready for actual labor."

"So, does that mean you're close?"

"No. My doctor says some women have these for weeks. So, how are you? What's up?"

"Nothing much. I just got back from Billy's. I'm fine."

"What's wrong? You sound funny."

"Nothing's wrong."

"Jenny, what is it? I can hear it in your voice. The way you said 'fine' did not sound fine. Something's wrong."

"Can we just talk about your baby some more?"

"What's going on?"

Jenny sighed and said, "Billy's ex-wife is back. She just showed up at his door on Saturday."

"So? They're divorced, and Billy loves you."

Belonging

"I just feel like maybe we should take a break, slow down. We were moving so fast. I feel like I need to step away, be alone for a while."

"What are you talking about? The last thing you need is to be alone. Jenny, you're pushing love away."

"Don't worry about me. Get your rest. Take care of yourself and I'll see you soon, okay?"

"And now you're shutting me out. Don't do that."

"I'm not. I'm just tired. It was a pretty draining weekend."

"He loves you and you're running from it. Does he even know, or have you shut him out too?"

"I don't know what he knows. I just need some time away right now. I need some time to figure things out."

"Jenny, what's there to figure?"

"I was prepared to change my whole life for him—give up my house, my job, move, become a parent. What if I do all that and this doesn't work? What if he decides to go back to Tara so they can be a family again?"

"I don't understand how you think that's possible."

"He's hurt me before. Two times actually."

"Well, you're the only person hurting you now."

When they hung up the phone, Jenny thought about what Heather said, and a part of her knew she was right. But another part of her kept finding ways to validate her worst fears. When she told her dad on Christmas that she wouldn't be coming back, she thought he might try to call her or see her, convince her to stay in his life—*he was her father*—but she hadn't heard from him at all. He'd blandly accepted her exit from their family with the same resignation that defined him. And she never thought Henry would leave her, but he had, without a word. It had been eight months of unreturned phone calls and unanswered letters. Her best friend in the world had just discarded her. And then, of course, there was the fact that Billy had done this before—made a conscious decision to leave her behind, even though he still loved her.

At lunchtime the next day, Jenny sat at her desk, unwrapped a tuna sandwich, and looked through her messages. Billy had called three times since she'd been back, but they hadn't talked since she left his house. This was completely unusual for them. They always talked before they went to bed at night, and typically spoke to each other several times a day. She threw her sandwich in the trash and dialed his number. She was relieved when she got his answering machine and left a message that she'd be in court the rest of the day, but they could talk tonight.

At home, Jenny took out the Mary Ellen Mark book and opened it to the chapter on photographing childbirth. She studied the photographs: the baby wet and crying, the mother's expression of both pain and joy, the father looking proud and uncertain at the same time. She searched the father's face and realized it was a look Billy often took on, and wondered if fatherhood, by its very nature, made men both proud and uncertain.

Late that night, after she was in bed, Billy called. "Sorry it's so late," he said. "I wanted to get Carl to bed before I called again. I think we need to talk."

"Yeah, we do." Jenny closed her eyes and pulled her knees to her chest.

"I knew you weren't right when you left. I knew it. And now, we haven't even talked. Can you tell me what's going on? I really don't understand what you're doing."

Jenny sat silently, feeling a rush of tears, and holding them back. After a long pause, she said, "I'm not sure either, Billy."

"What does that mean? You're not sure what you're doing? That makes no sense."

"I think we need to slow down, maybe take some time to look at everything. Can we just—"

"There is nothing to look at. We should be together. We should've never been apart. I thought you knew that."

"Well, but we were, and we can't really ignore that. You had a whole other family, and maybe that's something you need to think about. I mean, what if you could have your family back? Would you still want this? I guess I'm not sure."

"Jenny, nothing has changed between you and me. We are a family. I don't want a family with Tara. How can you do this to us? I mean, you just left our house and planned on…what? Leaving all your things in my closet for us to see every day and just not come back?"

Belonging

"It wasn't a plan, Billy. I just don't know what to do. And you even said you could wait another year. You said that before this even happened."

"I said we could wait a year if that was best for you. I don't want to wait a year. I was trying to protect you."

"I don't need anyone to protect me."

Saying these words felt so natural, so central to who she believed herself to be. She'd been repeating this phrase and holding onto this feeling since the year she had valley fever and Nonna died. *She didn't need anyone.* It was a self-reliance and independence that at times probably saved her, but it had become both a strength and a weakness. It was an automatic stand that kept anyone from getting too close, and it was so contrary to what she wanted. It was as if her desire to share her life with Billy, to love him, to have him love her back, to start a family together, was at direct odds with a part of her that was intensely committed to needing no one, to being alone.

She heard Billy's screen door slam and realized he was going outside so Carl wouldn't hear his raised voice. "When you did this before, when you shut me out and just left, I thought it was because what I did was so horrible, you had no other choice. But now I know it's just what you do. You walk out. You keep people away who love you. We were really happy. I don't understand why you're doing this. It's like you're cutting off your happiness yourself before anyone else can do it for you."

"Well, that may be true, but I've had plenty of other people cut off my happiness before—including you."

The minute she said it, she wished she hadn't. Billy didn't say anything for a minute, and she knew he was stunned by the cruel shot she'd taken at him. When he finally spoke, he said, "We're never getting past it, are we? I mean, you're still holding on to it—after everything. What can I do?"

"I don't know, Billy. Maybe you can let me be alone for a while."

"Why? Why would you choose to be alone? You can trust me. I will not hurt you! Don't you know that? Christ, you know what? I don't deserve this! Neither do you! Neither does Carl, who also loves you, by the way!"

"I love Carl too. I love him as if he were my own child. But he's not, is he?"

"Please don't do this."

Jenny just sat there and said nothing.

"Are you there?"

"Yeah. I'm here and I'm alone and I can take care of myself. I always have, right?"

Her words came out calmly, evenly, completely disconnected from her actual feelings. It was such an old groove, declaring her need for no one, worn in from a time before she could say words. She said it without even a conscious thought. Inadvertently, she was declaring her independence once again.

"I'm coming up to see you. This is not happening over the phone."

"No, Billy."

"Are you serious? You seriously don't want to see me?"

"I didn't say that."

"Then what *are* you saying?"

"I'm saying I need some time, okay?"

"We're engaged. Did you forget that? Or do you just not want to get married anymore?"

Jenny could see herself sitting there in her bed saying words she couldn't believe were coming out of her mouth. "I don't know."

Billy paused for a long time. "Well, I guess that's all I need to hear."

She started to cry, and Billy said, "How did we get here?"

Jenny wiped the tears from her face. "I don't know."

They were quiet, and then Billy said, "Why don't you call me when you know something?"

Billy hung up the phone, putting an end to the conversation that was going nowhere. When she heard the dial tone, she got an image in her mind of Billy in the front yard of Lupine Lane, slamming his bat against a tree, while she just stood by and watched. She ached for Billy so badly that she felt it physically in her chest, like someone had opened her up and placed her heart in a cage. She wondered if she'd actually done it this time—been cold and detached enough to make him give up on her for good. She thought about what she'd done and why, and without explanation, as she was finally dozing off, she saw herself as a small child, standing on a stool, holding a stuffed rabbit in one hand, reaching for an old box of cereal with the other. Her father was out of town and her mother was crying upstairs. She couldn't reach the shelf, so how old was she? Two? Three? She saw herself take the cereal down from the shelf and eat it straight from the box.

She went to sleep with the phone in bed next to her, hoping it would ring, and Billy would say the right words and magically fix everything. But when she awoke the next morning, the phone was still beside her. She mindlessly got dressed, made some coffee, and fed Chico. She drove to the county jail, where she spent the morning meeting with clients. Arriving at her office around lunchtime, she stopped at the front desk to pick up messages.

The receptionist said, "There's a guy who's been calling you all morning."

"Oh, is it Billy?"

She looked at Jenny's messages, shook her head, and said, "No. Henry Hansen."

Jenny put a hand to her mouth and reached for the messages.

"He said he'd call back."

"If I'm not in my office, page me, okay? Find me. I have to talk to him."

Back at her desk, Jenny picked up a stack of exhibits and stared at the first page without comprehension. She could only think of Henry. A short while later, the receptionist buzzed her and said, "It's him again."

Jenny picked up the phone, "Henry?"

"Hi there, sweetheart."

"Oh my God, Henry. Where are you? Where have you been?"

"I'm at home. I was thinking it might be time for you to make that visit we talked about."

"Wait a minute. Why haven't you called me? Where have you been?"

"I've just been here, at home."

"And you just didn't answer any of my calls or letters?"

"Yeah, I didn't."

"Why? What's going on?"

Henry didn't speak for a long time. He took a deep, audible breath and exhaled. "I'm sick, Jenny. I have AIDS. And now they are saying I don't have long to live."

Jenny put her head on her desk and began to sob with her face on a pile of papers. "How long have you known?"

"I found out just before I came home and saw you."

Jenny thought of his solemn goodbye the morning he left Santa Clara and realized he thought they were spending their last moments together.

"I don't understand. Why didn't you tell me then?"

Henry hesitated. "Well, there's a lot we've never talked about. Plus, I was hoping I'd never have to—I thought there could be a mistake, or a cure, or good enough drugs to let me live a long time. You know, denial."

Jenny cried into the phone, "So you decided to just leave?"

"I didn't want you to know I was sick. Fuck, I didn't even want to tell you I was gay. I thought it was best to just go away. You made it very hard on me, though. I should've known better, but I didn't expect your level of persistence. I had to stop listening to your messages. I hated hearing your worry and confusion, knowing it was caused by me. I loved your letters, though." Henry paused and then said, "You're getting married."

A whole new wave of sadness crossed over her. She took a breath and said, "Why did you decide to call me now?"

"Because I don't want to die and have you just hear about it. I remember what it was like when Nonna died, and you didn't get to say goodbye or even go to her funeral. And I know what it was like for you when Billy was getting married, and you couldn't say goodbye to him. And I thought, here I'd be, one more open wound on your heart. One more person who disappeared without a goodbye. I don't want to be that. Plus, selfishly, I really want to see you—and I want us to say goodbye."

The thought of not ever seeing Henry again sent her into a panic. She didn't know how much time he had and was afraid to ask. "When can I come? Can I come now?"

"You don't have to come now. But you can. My dad wants to pay for it. His office will arrange everything. It's my fault he never called you back. I wouldn't let him."

Belonging

"Your dad," Jenny put a hand to her forehead. "Oh my God. Your dad. When did you see him last?"

"He was here for about a month and just left a few days ago. Christopher's been here too."

"What about your mom?"

"No. She knows though."

Jenny thought of Christmas Eve, and now understood the sick feeling she had when Henry's mother asked when she'd last talked to Henry. "I'm so sorry."

"The letter you wrote me after Christmas—it was very sweet, and brave. You should know that I live with someone."

"Okay."

"His name is Mateo, and we've been together since I first came to Brussels."

Jenny closed her eyes and said, "I'm really glad I'll get to meet him."

"I don't want anyone to know I'm sick, at least not yet. Can you keep this private for now?"

"Of course. I won't say anything."

When Jenny got home that afternoon, she took out the passport that Henry insisted she get and she had never used. She took clothes from her drawer without knowing or caring about the weather. At the last minute, she decided to put her camera in the bag. When she was done packing, she called Heather. "I'm going to Brussels to see Henry," she said. "Please don't have the baby without me."

"Wait. What? You're going to Brussels? When? Why?"

Jenny quickly thought of a lie and said, "We've been trying to plan this trip forever, and now he has some time off work. His dad got me a flight and I'm leaving tonight."

"What do you mean you're leaving tonight? Jenny, what's going on?"

"Nothing's going on. I'm just going for a short visit."

"But why now? The baby's coming soon. Is everything okay? Is Henry okay? Did he tell you why he hasn't been answering your letters or calls?"

Jenny hesitated again and said, "Um, yeah. I can't really talk about it now, though. Just don't have the baby without me."

"I hate this. I wish you'd tell me what's going on."

Jenny didn't offer anything further.

Heather sighed. "Okay, I'll put myself on bed rest if I have to."

"I'll call you right when I get back."

"What about Billy? Have you told him?"

"No."

"Jenny! Don't you think he should know?"

"He'll push me for answers, and I don't have any. I miss him and I miss Carl, and the last thing I want to be is another person walking out on Carl."

"You sort of are, though. I mean, you did."

Heather's words hit her with such force, she stopped breathing. She knew it was true, and she hated herself for it. How could she be another person walking out on Carl? She started to cry into the phone and said, "I don't know what to do."

"I know, honey. I wish I could help you."

When she hung up the phone, she looked around her room—the half-empty closet, the photo of Billy and her at fifteen, Mary, Mary, and Mary. She picked up the stack of photos by her bed, pictures she'd taken of Carl that she'd planned to hang in his room. *Carl holding Chico in his lap. Carl running through a flock of shore birds. Carl holding up a sand crab. A close up of Carl's eyes as he peeked into her lens to show her his eye freckles.* She knew that Heather was right. She dialed Billy's house, having no idea what she would say, but she owed it to Billy and to Carl to not just disappear. When Carl answered the phone, she said, "Hi, buddy! How are you?"

"Hi, Jenny! When are you coming back? I had a game today. I got three hits."

"I'm not sure when I'll be back. I have to go on a trip very far away. Good job in your game. I bet your dad was excited."

"He was. And my mom too!"

She heard the words, but how could they be true? She didn't want to cry, so she took a breath and said, "That's great, Carl. I bet she was really proud."

"Yeah. Oh, and guess what. I slid into home and my whole pants got muddy."

"You slid into home? I thought there was no sliding in t-ball."

"There's not. My dad talked to me about it later. My pants were so muddy!"

Jenny heard someone in the background ask Carl who was on the phone, and she heard him say, "It's Jenny and I'm talking to her now."

"Who's that, Carl?"

"Megan. She thinks I need to take a bath, but I'm on the phone."

"Oh, your dad's not there?"

"Uh-uh. He's out with my mom."

Jenny felt sick. Billy was out with Tara. Tara had been at Carl's game. She steadied her voice and said, "Oh. Okay. Well, I'm glad I got to talk to you. I miss you a lot."

"I miss you too. When are you coming home?"

"I'm not sure. I might not see you for a while, but I'll be thinking about you."

"Hey, guess what, Jenny!"

"What?"

"The grunion are running. I get to stay up late to see them."

"You are so lucky. I want to hear all about it when I get back."

Chapter Nineteen

MAY 1991

Henry was sitting on a bench near the front door when Jenny arrived at his flat in Brussels. As he stood to greet her, she could see that his already-thin frame was twenty pounds lighter. His hair had returned to his natural auburn color and was cut short and boyish, the way he used to wear it when they were ten. His bright turquoise eyes now appeared almost startling in his thin face. He hugged her for a long time. She laid her head on his chest and wept.

She looked up at him and tried to smile. "I used my passport."

"Who'd have thought you'd use it like this?"

"I'm so glad I'm here."

"Me too."

"You're so thin. How do you feel?"

"I feel like myself, except less hungry and more tired."

Mateo appeared in the doorway, and somehow, he looked exactly like Jenny had imagined: tall and muscular with large brown eyes, full lips, and an olive complexion. He wore loose jeans and an oversized rugby shirt, and his hair was dark and curly and fell just above his shoulders. When Henry introduced them—*this is my best friend, this is my boy-friend*—she was moved by his honesty and the express acknowledgment of both relationships.

Henry showed Jenny around the brick-walled flat he shared with Mateo, pointing to photographs in the hallway from their travels. When he got to his bedroom, he sat on a chaise and motioned for Jenny to sit beside him.

Belonging

"The doctors say I should start looking into hospice."

"When?"

"Soon."

Jenny was silent. She couldn't bring herself to ask all the questions she had in her head. *How much time do they say you have? Will you see your family again? Will Mateo get sick too?* She turned toward him and placed a hand on his knee, ready to talk, but no words came out. Finally, she asked him, "Will you go back home?"

"Home? You mean Bakersfield? No. I've said goodbye to our hometown. I'll be buried here. We picked a spot in the countryside outside of the city. I'd like to show it to you. It's a nice drive. Let's go tomorrow."

Henry closed his eyes for a moment and laid back. Jenny was relieved his eyes were closed, so he didn't see the darkness that crossed her face when he said he'd picked a spot to be buried.

When he opened his eyes, he said, "Thanks for coming," and squeezed her hand.

"There's something I have to ask you," she said.

The question had been brewing since high school. She wanted to know why he thought he had to keep secrets from her, why he drew a dividing line about his personal life, going as far as ditching her completely to keep her from knowing the truth. She wasn't sure how to ask that question, though, so she settled on, "Can you tell me why you didn't want me here before?"

Henry sat up and said, "Well, I don't think you'll understand, but honestly, I was afraid and ashamed."

"I sort of do understand. I saw your mom in church. I saw those boys attack you. I saw your family that day in your yard. It makes sense that you would feel that way. But then there's you and me. Our friendship goes beyond all that. You know everything about me, including my own shame. You have to know I would never do anything other than love you. Why did you feel fear and shame with me?"

"Well, that's the thing. It had very little to do with you and me, with our friendship. The moment I realized I was gay, I felt like the only way I could stay myself and keep my relationships with my family and friends was to hide it from everyone. I had a loving family and good friends. I couldn't risk losing all of that, so I decided to keep it hidden. And, you know, we lived in a place that reinforced this belief. I thought it was the only way to keep the life I knew and loved."

"And your worst fears came true when your family found out."

"Yeah, just like that, my mother didn't see me as myself. I was some freak or sinner that needed to be saved. I wasn't her son anymore."

Neither spoke for a while, and Jenny thought about how she knew exactly when Henry began hiding, pulling away from her, and she'd also suspected why. They were teenagers, and she didn't push him. She recognized his need to keep things hidden, to maintain a steadfast separation of their friendship and his love life. She wondered what would have changed between them if, at any point during those years, she had asked questions.

She let go of his hand and said, "What do you think would've happened if I said something after being at your house that day?"

"I don't know."

Jenny let a beat go by. "Henry? What did happen that day?"

Henry shook his head and said, "I can't believe you were there. It was bad enough with no witnesses, and then you wandered up the driveway, and in my mind, you were the worst possible witness."

"See, I don't get that."

"You were my best and most loyal friend, and I could not risk losing you."

"Was that your boyfriend in the car?"

"Yes. I met Lance in L.A. He drove down to surprise me. I'd lied to him too. He didn't know my family didn't know. Timing being what it was that day, my mom showed up to pick up Christopher, and the whole thing came tumbling out. My dad didn't know what to say, my mom flipped out, Christopher ran outside, and you were there. I wished I'd been able to tell them in a different way. My dad worked hard to understand. It was difficult for him at first, but he really tried, and that helped a lot."

"What about your mom?"

"You know most of what happened with my mom. She decided I was going to hell and tried to ship me away. She tried to keep Christopher away from me too. It was about as hurtful as you could be to a person.

Belonging

Worse when it's your own mother." Henry looked at Jenny and said, "But you know all about that."

"I do know all about that and I wish I could've been there for you the way you were always there for me."

Henry reached out and touched the top of Jenny's head and said, "Look at us, just a couple of orphans."

Jenny offered up a sad smile, aware of Henry's habit of using humor to get out of difficult conversations, and marveled at the fact that it still sort of worked. She reached for his hand and held it. "Can you tell me what happened with Lance?"

Henry's voice grew quiet, and he said, "We were together on and off during our first year at USC. I heard he died last summer."

Jenny thought about the way Henry often disappeared on the weekends that first year in college. She squeezed his hand. "I'm so sorry."

Henry looked out at the city lights in the distance. "They say I might go blind. It's a pretty cruel twist, don't you think?"

Jenny drew in a quick breath. She observed the brightness in his aquamarine eyes and tried not to think of them going dim. She touched the scar above his left eye and thought of the night she held a towel over his wound and felt the hot gush of his blood run down her arm. She wished, of all things, that they could go back—to a time when that was the worst thing that had ever happened to him, to a teenage summer when they believed they had all of life stretched out before them.

That night, Jenny was restless, in a different time zone. She thought about why Henry invited her to his home: so they could say goodbye, so he didn't just disappear from her life. It was noble and kind and thoughtful, and she was moved by his deep understanding of what it would have done to her to just never see him again. Now, she saw that his invitation was more than he'd been able to express. He wanted her to meet Mateo, see where he lived, be fully a part of his life. They would create another set of memories to store next to the volumes she already had on her mental bookshelf. This would be the last volume—after the libraries and bars and mosh pits of college; after the movies, music, and heartbreak of high school; after the playground in elementary school, where no one understood why her best friend was a boy and his was a girl.

She thought about Henry's visit in the fall and understood it was his way of getting in the last word, of telling her how he'd like her to live after he was gone. She thought about how unbelievably sad it would've been if she'd just never heard from him again. She would've been completely blindsided by a phone call out of the blue that Henry had died. She thought, *I'll still get that phone call someday, and it'll still blindside me.*

On the drive to the cemetery the next morning, Jenny took some photos of Henry, one hand on the steering wheel and one extended out the window, feeling the wind, a blur of green and blue behind him. As she looked at him through her camera lens, she struggled to keep her mind from jumping forward to dark thoughts of getting sicker, of hospice care, of dying at twenty-seven years old. She was caught in a quandary of staying positive on the outside—for Henry, and for their day together—and feeling morose and panicky on the inside. She silently prayed for the grace to sit beside Henry and be the friend that he needed. While her eyes were closed in prayer, Henry reached over and patted her on the knee and said, "Let's talk about your wedding. I wish I could be there. I always thought I'd be a bridesman. I had such good outfit ideas."

Jenny opened her eyes and turned toward the window, wondering what to say. Henry witnessed her brief flash of alarm and said, "Oh no, what have you done?"

"Me? Why do you presume it was me?"

"Because I read every one of your letters. I know it wasn't him."

"Okay. You're right. I told him I needed some time apart, and I don't think we're getting married anymore."

"Why?"

"His ex-wife came back. And when I saw them together, something changed for me. I had been planning to give up my job, house, everything, so that I could marry Billy and be a mother to Carl, but guess what—Carl already has a mother and what kind of mother would I be anyway? And maybe I don't completely trust Billy. So, I went home, and I told him I needed some time and that I didn't know if I wanted to get married. He was so mad at me. I called him right before I left to come here, and he was out with her. And Carl seemed happy that she was with them. And maybe that's the way it's supposed to be."

Belonging

Henry raised his hands, as if fending off the onslaught of words and said, "Oh, dear. I've got my work cut out for me. Did I mention that I'm dying? I may not have the strength to shake sense into you."

"You're not funny. I'm not here to talk about me and the mess I've made of my life. I'm here to be with you. You don't have to solve anything for me. Let's just drive and be together."

"I'll just say one thing about this, okay? I've witnessed the entirety of your relationship—the sweet part, the terrible part, all of it—and it's become very clear to me that he loves you in a way that is so complete and so real and so old that I don't know how you could ever doubt it."

Jenny tried to let the words sink in, but instead, deflected them. "Old is easy. It's a memory. It's nostalgic."

"Jenny. At some point in time, you gotta let it in. I understand. Believe me, I do. But it's time to stop doing this to yourself."

As Henry spoke, she remembered what Heather said. Her two best friends believed this was her choice, that whether she was aware of it or not, she'd chosen to step away from the love she'd always wanted.

"Let me ask you this. How much have you told him about your childhood, what it was like with your mother?"

Jenny shrugged. "Hardly anything."

"But he was with you when you left Christmas Eve?"

"Yes." She smiled at him. "We leapt from the roof together."

"And he knows you don't plan to return?"

"Yes."

"Doesn't he ask why? Don't you talk about why?"

"No, we don't." Jenny sighed and threw up her arms. "Can we please talk about something else now?"

"We could just talk about me dying some more."

"I wish I could punch you."

"Same."

"He never asked me why I left."

"Why not?"

"I don't know. Maybe for the same reason I never asked you things I thought you didn't want me to know."

"I think you need to tell Billy. I think it will only bring you closer, like you and me." He patted her knee and smiled and said, "Let's shed our shame together."

They had finally admitted the survival strategy the two of them had individually mastered. Henry had wanted to remain himself, protect the relationships he'd formed, and keep his old life and identity. Jenny had wanted to appear whole, independent, and not damaged. Henry was nearing the end of his life and had a clarity that she did not possess. He was insistent that the only way to have the love and family she always wanted was to let Billy see and know all of her, and she was beginning to believe him.

Henry turned down the long dirt road leading to the cemetery. They drove until they reached a line of Elm trees and a small white wooden fence. They parked and stepped out of the car, and Henry wrapped his arm around Jenny's shoulder as he bent down to open the gate. They paused by a headstone that read: *love never dies.* It reminded her of Henry Drummond's proclamation in *The Greatest Thing in the World*, the book she'd sent Henry in the fall—that eternal life is inextricably bound up with love. She thought of his simple explanation that we want to see tomorrow *because there is someone who loves you, and whom you want to see tomorrow, and be with, and love back.*

When they reached the spot Henry and Mateo had reserved, Henry sat down on the empty patch of grass. "This is it," he said, and stretched himself out like a corpse. "How do I look?"

Jenny sat next to him, collapsed into a ball, and wept. Henry pulled her closer and said, "Come on, this has to stop. Sit up. Look around. You love cemeteries. Don't you think this is a nice place to be for eternity?"

Jenny wiped her tears and said, "You're not going to be here, Henry. Just your body. That's all. You'll be with Mateo and me and your dad and Christopher and all the other people who love you."

"What do you think I should wear? Keep in mind, it could be hot."

"Henry! Stop! Stop pretending this is all some big joke! You're not going to hell!"

Belonging

"How do you know? I mean, really, how do you know? None of us really knows anything about the afterlife. Maybe there is nothing. Have you ever thought about that? Maybe it is just here, gone, that's it."

"That's why it's called faith. We can't know. But I know I feel Nonna every day. I see her almond eyes and her hair set for bridge. I smell her gardenia perfume and Coffee Nips. I still hear her voice."

Henry lay back with his head in her lap, and Jenny rested her hand on his hair. "I know you will still be with me, just like Nonna. And I know with every stitch of my faith that you are not going to hell."

"I wonder what I'll look like when you see me."

Jenny looked up at the sky and said, "I think I'll see you at your happiest age. What do you think that would be?"

"Maybe the year we moved into our house on the golf course. Or maybe our senior year of college? We had some very good adventures that year. Or maybe just after I met Mateo."

"I don't even know when you met Mateo."

"We met just after I got to Brussels. We've been together ever since."

"How did you know you loved him?"

Henry sat up and touched the grass. "Mateo is a very caring and humble person. He's very open and secure. He doesn't know shame. He was exactly who I needed, and somehow, I was who he needed too."

Jenny nodded, "Mateo means '*gift from God.*'"

They sat and listened to the sounds of the creek and the chickens roaming amongst the tombstones and Jenny said, "This reminds me a little of Bakersfield."

"Oh, great."

"The beautiful part—like out by the river in the late spring. It smells like lavender here."

Henry took a deep breath, "You smell lavender. I smell dirt."

He stood, brushed off his pants, and announced that he was ready to go. They walked up the gravel path toward the road. Henry had his hands stuffed in his pockets, and he was looking at the ground, when he said, "You love his little boy."

She put a hand to her heart at the mention of Carl. "Yes, I do."

"And you love Billy like you've never loved anyone."

"Yeah."

"You're going to be a wonderful mother."

"Thank you."

They spent the next few days wandering in the city, napping together, sitting on his balcony, sharing food and stories, sunrises and sunsets. Then, one day Henry opened his desk drawer and took out the leather journal Jenny sent him in the fall. He handed it to her and said, "Here, have a look. I filled it over these last several months. I've been writing about everything."

Jenny smiled at him, "Did you make some of it up? Or is it just true stuff this time?"

"All true. One hundred percent. Cinnamon is not mentioned once. I started writing the day it arrived in the mail. My first entry is about our visit. I'd like you to read it."

Jenny took the book from Henry and sat down at his desk. As she opened to the first page, Henry left her alone.

September 2, 1990

My last visit with Jenny. I went to see Jenny in Santa Clara. She has a light-filled house near an old Spanish mission. Her Marys are everywhere—the mother of God looking down from every shelf and wall. Maybe for the first time, I understood why she has always surrounded herself with Mary. I used to think it was because she wanted a mother, but it's more than that. Mary had courage and faith to trust her journey, with no one to validate her. I think that's really why Jenny relates to her so much—she's never had anyone to guide her. She has to trust herself and God.

She had country music playing in her house, just like when she was a teenager living in Bakersfield. She said she listens to it because of the hope and longing, that she loves the bittersweet stories with happy endings. I was thinking that there are a whole bunch of country songs that are just plain sad—about lost love, dead soldiers, and what might have been, but I didn't tell her that.

She told me about seeing Billy, and I could tell that she was both hopeful and afraid. I want her to be happy. I wish I could be sure he'll make her happy, but it's hard to forget that summer. Then again, we were teenagers, all of us making mistakes that should be forgiven. I know she loves him, has always loved him, so I encouraged her to put her fears aside and give him a chance.

I didn't tell her I was sick. Even after all we've been through together, there has always been a part of my life I don't want to share with her. It's ironic that I've asked her to be fearless, when I have not been. I wanted our last night together to reflect the sincere, reliable love that we've shared since we were children, for there to be the nice ending that Jenny always requires. I acknowledge that the nice ending was not very honest. I knew I was saying goodbye to her, but she did not know she was saying goodbye to me. I will have to come to terms with how much that will hurt. I know she'll be sad and confused as to why I decided to leave this way, and why I stopped communicating with her. There's just no other way. I won't be able to carry out the charade of being Henry for much longer, and I have to take care of the end of my life. I wish she could be part of it, but I just can't do that.

I'll ask Christopher to tell her the truth after I'm gone. Maybe I'll even have him give the journal back to her—filled—so she will understand a little of what it was like to be me. I hope she forgives me for leaving her. I hope she remembers all the fun we had together. I hope she is fearless. I hope she makes her own happy ending.

When Jenny finished reading, she wiped the tears from her cheeks, and continued to flip through the journal. Page after page was filled with Henry's scribble. Tucked somewhere in the middle, she was surprised to find a prayer card, worn and used, like it had been held or carried for a very long time. On the front was an image of Saint Francis, a bird on his shoulder, light surrounding him. On the back were the words: *All the darkness in the world cannot extinguish the light of a single candle.*

Henry came back into the room, and Jenny closed the book and said, "Thanks for letting me read it. I'd love to read it all. There's so much about this last year I'd like to know."

"Well, you can. I'm giving it to you."

"Henry, you can't."

"Yes, I can. You gave it to me—I just added the words. I want you to keep it now. It's not all sad and about dying. Some of it is. But mostly, it's filled with our stories, and this way, you'll always have them. Call it an early wedding gift."

Jenny put her head down and said, "I don't know that I'll be having a wedding. Could it be something else?"

"It could be my death day present, you know like a birthday present, but a death day present." Henry was laughing at himself, cackling even. Then he stopped and put his hands on her shoulders and said, "Come on, don't you think I'm funny anymore? You used to think I was really funny."

"You're still funny. The morbid humor is hard for me, though."

Henry sat on the couch, and she curled up next to him. He held her and said, "What do you want? Do you want to marry him?"

"Of course."

"Then, I think I should send you home."

Jenny sat up straight and said, "I don't want to go home yet. I want to stay here with you a while longer."

"Well, that's sweet, dolly, but I think we've done what we need to do, and I would be so happy to see you go be happy."

"I don't even know if he still wants to marry me. He was with her last time I called him."

Henry put his fingers in his ears and started humming loudly.

Jenny took his fingers from his ears and said, "I'm not ready to go."

"I think you are. We've had a nice few days together."

Jenny rested her head on Henry's shoulder and was quiet for a while. "I do have to get home for Heather's baby."

Henry took the journal from her lap and turned to the back page, where he'd written the lyrics to a song. Jenny recognized them right away—a previous generation's anthem to a young woman making it on her own in the world. She smiled at Henry and said, "Mary Tyler Moore via Hüsker Dü."

Henry nodded. "Do you know where the name Hüsker Dü came from?"

"No, where?"

"It's the name of a Danish board game. It means 'Do you remember?'"

Jenny blinked and nodded her head, and they sat there for most of the night, talking about all they remembered. Their history together spanned nearly their entire lives. Racing to the end of the grass on the playground in kindergarten. Listening to Henry read from his journal when she was home with valley fever. Staying with her the night that Nonna died. Being swept away in Henry's conga line at the junior high dance. Listening to "Far Away Eyes" in her bedroom. Summers spent at Stockdale 6 and every single movie they saw there. Driving through the fog listening to Tom Petty. Sitting by a kidney-shaped pool, talking about leaving town. Watching *The Graduate* and deciding to go to USC together. Packing up her room after she and Billy broke up. Waving their arms in the air in the mosh pit at Hüsker Dü. Sneaking into Robert Palmer, X, and the Red Hot Chili Peppers. Standing on the library steps, listening to Bishop Tutu speak about South African apartheid. All the drives over the Grapevine together. Sitting on the fire escape of the Padre Hotel on their last Christmas vacation. Walking through campus the night they watched Bud and Deanie break each other's hearts. All the sunsets from their rooftop in L.A. His visit to Santa Clara in the fall, when he told her not to fast-forward to the end.

They talked about what they hadn't shared—the last nine months. Henry told Jenny about getting diagnosed, the doctor appointments, the pain, and the planning. He told her about telling his dad and brother, and what it was like contemplating leaving Mateo and the life they'd built together. He told her what came before—the travels, concerts, late nights with friends, falling in love with Mateo, finding this flat. Jenny told Henry about all the weekends with Billy and Carl, how she planned to adopt Carl, Billy's proposal, how happy they'd all been. She told him what came after—the way she'd fled, the fears and doubts she carried, even after all this time. Melancholy and joy, hope and longing, all woven together.

"I love the journal," Jenny said.

"I loved it too."

They fell asleep next to each other, Henry's arm wrapped around her, holding onto the section of hair that she used to wear in braids.

The next day, when it was time for Jenny to leave for the airport, she held onto Henry and would not let go. When he finally pulled away, she reached for his face, held it in her hands, and looked at his turquoise eyes. Emily's plea at the end of *Our Town* sat right there in the middle of her chest: *Let's look at one another*. It was time to say goodbye. She'd made such a big deal of what it meant to not say goodbye; she knew exactly what that felt like. It was always with her, the nagging feeling of things that were unsaid, of love unexpressed. So here was her chance, and she had no words. It occurred to her that, with Henry, the love between them was certain and spoken; it always had been. Henry rested his head on her shoulder, and they held onto each other again. He pulled a strand of hair from her face where it had stuck to the wetness from her tears, and said, "You're my best friend." And she said, "You're mine." She kissed him once on the forehead and once on the nose, and said, "I will never forget you. I know you by heart."

Jenny forced herself to pick up her bag and walk out the door, understanding the finality of her exit. She felt nauseous and empty and despondent. She had an overwhelming longing to go back to their childhood, to hot summer days at Stockdale 6, to Mr. Hansen baking in the kitchen, to Henry falling asleep beside her in her tangerine bedroom—to days when they had all the time in the world together. When she got down the stairs and into her cab, she looked back at Henry standing in the window waving at her. The sky was bright and clear, and sunlight circled his diminished frame. As she turned the corner out of sight, she thought about the prayer card she'd found in Henry's journal and believed she understood why it was there. In times of darkness, each had always been the light for the other.

On the flight home, Jenny opened Henry's journal to a spot where he had left a bookmark. It was an entry from October: *Jenny keeps sending me lists of things to talk about. The lists are filled with happy things—the beach, stars, Billy, and Carl. I have no idea what grunion are, though.* She flipped to a page from December: *My dad is here, and he won't stop cooking. How many jarred pickles, peach melba jams, and peanut butter cookies can one sickly fellow eat?* She turned to a page from February. *Jenny called again. Mateo thinks I should tell her the truth. He says she deserves better.* She turned to a passage from the day he decided to call her. *Jenny sent me a book last fall that I didn't want to read, but I finally did. In the end it says, "You will find as you look back upon your life that the moments that stand out, the moments when you have really lived, are the moments when you have done things in a spirit of love...Love never fails. Love is happiness. Love is life." I'm calling her today. My one-sided goodbye was not in the spirit of love. We both deserve better, and also, I really want to see her again.*

She turned back to the first page of the journal and read it straight through, crying and laughing alternately. As she read, she began to understand the pain he'd lived with for much of his life, pain he'd hidden entirely from her. She began to understand why he kept secrets, going as far as abandoning his best friend to hold onto them. She lingered over Henry's wish for her. *I hope she is fearless. I hope she makes her own happy ending.* On the last page, she read the Hüsker Dü lyrics again, and realized it was both an acknowledgement of one of their favorite memories and a show of faith that she would, after all, be okay without him.

When Jenny arrived home early the next morning, she was stoic, all emotion drained from her. She thumbed through her mail and played her phone messages. There was one from Heather, telling her that the baby was still waiting for her to get home; one from Aunt Hope, checking on her; and one from Uncle Gino, who wanted to tell her that Alice Cooper came into the antique store that day. There were none from Billy.

She wondered what Henry was doing now and thought about the courage it took for him to finally fully show himself to her. He'd opened the door all the way, allowing her to experience his home, meet Mateo, be part of the life he'd created away from the expectations of people he'd left behind, and the place they grew up. She now realized they both had always been afraid in some way. It may have even been the heart of their early bond—an unspoken truth that they each implicitly understood about the other. Now, in anticipation of the end of his life, Henry did the very thing that terrified him the most. He put his whole life on display, everything he'd ever hidden. *This is what happened in my family. This is what I was afraid of. This is Mateo. This is my home. This is who I am. Please read my journal and understand.* He was fearless, and she was inspired to follow his lead.

She went down the hall to Carl's room, sat on his bed with his pillow in her lap, and thought about all the stories she'd made up about motherhood. She'd always imagined a mystical bond and incomparable love. The fact that there was seemingly no bond or love between her and her own mother made the fantasy that much greater, the role that much more important. Looking around the room she'd made for Carl, she finally understood that the bond and love she'd imagined wasn't exclusively the result of giving birth. There are women who give birth who never feel that way. There are women who adopt children and love them as if they'd always been part of them, and she knew this was exactly the way she felt about Carl. Despite her fantastical thinking about the meaning of Tara being Carl's biological mother, she knew he belonged with her, not Tara. She looked over at his pile of books and thought about how he sits right in the crook of her arm when she reads to him, and how it's a perfect fit, like two pieces of a puzzle.

She thought about Billy and imagined how hard it must have been for him to love someone who could just never fully take it in. She wondered what it would be like to be with him now, and simply accept the love that had always been given. She walked out to her back porch and looked out at her garden. The seedlings she and Billy planted in November were

Belonging

now thriving plants, heavy with ripe tomatoes. Uncle Gino's rosemary had grown so much that Chico was lounging in it, his ears peeking out above the green. Nonna's roses had found yet another home, the stalk having grown into a small bush. Jenny lifted Chico and put her nose against the fur on his neck. He smelled just like the rosemary. She went into her house, sat at the kitchen table, and wrote to Henry. She thanked him for everything he shared with her—his home, his journal, his love, the truth. She told him how much she loved him. She leafed through her copy of *The Greatest Thing in the World*, looking for the passage Uncle Gino showed her when Nonna died, and wrote it at the end of the letter: "*To love abundantly is to live abundantly, and to love forever is to live forever.*" Then she wrote, *We love each other abundantly and I promise you will live forever.*

When she finished her letter, she called Billy. She wanted to be with him and Carl. She wanted to tell him everything she'd kept from him for so long. She wanted him to know her completely. She wanted to accept the love that had so consistently been given. When his answering machine picked up, she hung up and decided that tomorrow she would wake up with the sun and drive to him, regardless of the concerns, worries, and bad thoughts that had consumed her, because she really was not afraid anymore.

Chapter Twenty

MAY 1991

The next morning, a few minutes before Jenny's five a.m. alarm went off, Heather called to say she was in labor. Jenny was only half-surprised. On the plane home from Brussels, she thought, *Heather will probably have the baby right when I get home.* And whenever her grief felt too big to hold, she'd tell herself, *Soon I'll get to see a baby being born.* When she locked up her house in the pre-dawn, she thought about her plan to drive down the coast to see Billy. It was too early to call him, so she decided to wait until she landed. Rickey had booked her on an early morning flight to Bakersfield from San Jose.

Uncle Gino was waiting at the airport for her, wearing khaki shorts and an olive-green shirt that matched his eyes. His silver ponytail was longer, and he wore a small gold hoop in his left ear, making him look a little like an old pirate. He shuffled over to her, grabbed her bag, and kissed her on both cheeks.

"Thanks for getting me. Did she go to the hospital yet?"

"Yes, but she said to tell you she's only two centimeters."

Jenny touched Uncle Gino's earring and said, "I like this new style."

"I found a wonderful collection of hoops from the seventies at an estate sale. I had to try them."

Jenny climbed into Uncle Gino's car and the smell of the vinyl seats and the bag of soil in the back made her think of all the times they'd driven out to the antique store or the nursery or the bakery downtown. Uncle Gino chattered the whole way—about antiques and his garden, the trip to Cambria he was planning for the summer, the colorful honeybee hives they passed along the road, the receiving blanket he was bringing to the hospital. It was handmade by Nonna, and he'd kept it in a hope chest for twelve years. When they stopped in the hospital parking lot, he turned to her and said, "You seem quiet. Are you okay, dear?"

"Yeah, just tired. I've been traveling a lot."

"You look a little sad. Here, this will cheer you up." He reached for a bag in the back seat and handed it to her.

Jenny opened it up. It was filled with old prayer cards. She pulled out a handful and looked at them. "Uncle Gino, thank you. These are so beautiful. I'm going to read every single one."

"The mortuary down the street was moving, and they left these behind. I remember you carried around prayer cards in a shoe box when you were a girl."

"I still have it. I can't believe you remember that."

"My long-term memory is excellent. But don't ask me what I had for breakfast this morning."

"You had oatmeal." Jenny reached out and tugged on his sleeve. "There's a little on your shirt."

Uncle Gino looked down and picked off a patch of dried oats.

In the hospital lobby, Jenny found a pay phone and dialed Billy's number. When she got the answering machine again, she imagined Billy and Carl flying a kite on the beach while the phone rang inside their warm home. She waited for the beep and said, "Hi. It's me. I'm in Bakersfield because Heather's having her baby. I was going to drive out and see you this morning, but I can't do that now. I've been thinking about you a lot, and I miss you. Both of you. I love you. Well, okay. I'll call back later. I'm going to see a baby be born now."

When she hung up the phone, she wiped the tears from her cheeks and took the elevator to Heather's third floor room. She had about twenty seconds to compose herself and put on a smile. She held onto her camera and thought about how her first pictures of Heather's baby and her last pictures of Henry would be on the same roll of film.

When Jenny walked into Heather's room, Rickey kissed her on the cheek and said, "You made it."

"I wouldn't miss it."

Heather was wearing a mint green hospital gown, her cheeks were pink, and her hair was pulled back into a ponytail. Jenny hadn't seen her in months and couldn't believe the size of her. She hugged her and sat on the side of her bed. "How are you doing? How many centimeters?"

"They haven't checked me in a while. I got to four. They gave me my epidural. That's why I feel better now."

Heather held onto Jenny's hand and said, "Was your trip okay?"

Jenny felt a heaviness at the mention of her trip, but she smiled and said, "Yeah, it was. I'm glad I got back here in time. I have work to do!"

She hung her camera around her neck and went out into the corridor to take pictures of everyone waiting in the hall: Uncle Gino clutching Nonna's receiving blanket. *Click.* Aunt Hope twisting a strand of pearls around her neck. *Click.* Uncle Joe resting his hand on Aunt Hope's shoulder, looking toward the hospital room door. *Click.* As she composed photographs, she thought of how she was taught to *find her eye.* She remembered when she began documenting her time at home with valley fever. The camera became something else then. It became a way for her to notice a particular moment and store the feeling that made her press the shutter. Looking at the images later, she was put squarely back in the scene. When she looked at photos she took of Uncle Gino in the antique store, she could feel the ceiling fan, hear the oldies station, and see his side-to-side shuffle as he put things on shelves. When she looked at photos of Heather in her childhood bedroom, she could feel a touch of sunburn on her cheeks, smell homemade biscuits, and hear Gregg Allman on the radio. She imagined that someday she'd look at pictures of Henry driving through the countryside in Belgium and be able to smell the lavender, feel the wind blowing, hear his laugh.

After the nurse checked Heather again and said she was at nine centimeters, Jenny went back into the room. Rickey had his hand on Heather's head, and Heather had her eyes closed and her knees up, draped under a sheet. *Click.* Heather opened her eyes and asked Jenny to sit beside her. Jenny put down the camera and sat on the edge of her bed.

"I'm scared," Heather whispered. She held onto Jenny's arm and pulled her closer. "I feel sad. I'm not supposed to be feeling sad. But I do. I feel like one part of life is ending."

Belonging

"Heather." Jenny placed her hand on Heather's cheek. "A part of life *is* ending—the part that has dreamed of this family since we were little girls. You're just overwhelmed right now. Overwhelmed and hormonal. I promise. Come on. You're about to meet your baby!"

Heather squeezed her hand and nodded. Rickey moved to Heather's side, kissed her, and whispered something in her ear. Jenny started taking photos again: Heather's face next to Rickey's face; Heather's hand holding Rickey's hand; Aunt Hope quietly sitting in the corner of the room; the waiting bassinet and the lavender sleeper.

Looking around the room, filled with anticipation and love, Jenny thought about what it meant to be here with Heather, Aunt Hope, and Uncle Joe. Heather was the trusted and loyal confidante she could always rely on to tell her the truth. Aunt Hope and Uncle Joe had provided the model of home and family that she most admired, and they made her a part of it. She was incredibly moved to witness and document the beginning of the next generation of this family she loved so much.

When the doctor came in a few minutes later and told Heather it was time to push, Jenny took a series of photos of the doctor easing the baby's shoulders out and then the rest of her tiny body. She photographed Rickey cutting the cord and saw fatherhood appear on his face, pride and uncertainty replacing his usual carefree manner. She photographed the doctor handing the baby to Heather and Heather meeting her baby's eyes for the first time.

Heather said, "There you are, Hope Marion."

Jenny zoomed in on the baby's face, pink and squished with tiny, raised fists beside her ears, and noticed that her lips were exactly the shape of a heart. She took a photo of the baby looking upward, her mouth open like a little bird, Heather's hand cupped around her head. She took a series of photographs she hoped would collect the joy of all these people, the feeling in the room, so that this day could be kept and held. Uncle Gino beaming as he greeted his sister's great-granddaughter. Aunt Hope swaddling her namesake in the receiving blanket from Nonna. Uncle Joe with tears in his eyes. Heather rubbing her index finger along the baby's pink cheek. Rickey scooping up the baby, carrying her to the light by the window, and singing to her.

Jenny had been behind the camera the entire time, but stepped away so that she could see without a lens in front of her when she heard Rickey start to sing her favorite old Kenny Rogers song to his daughter, the one about a girl who brings out all the colors in his life.

She stayed for a while longer, taking pictures of all the relatives coming to meet the baby, and when it was time for Heather to rest, she put her camera down and said, "You did so good. Hope is an angel and is so lucky to have you for her mom."

"Thank you. You've been taking pictures forever. You haven't even held her yet."

Jenny washed her hands and scooted into the hospital bed with Heather. She held the baby and lightly touched her eyebrows and nose. She rubbed her fingers over her ears and said, "She has furry ears."

Heather laughed. "She has a furry back too. At least it's blonde fur."

"She's so pretty. She looks like you." Jenny stared at the sleeping baby, feeling the weight and heat of her tiny body in her arms. "I'm going to spoil her, you know."

Heather smiled and said, "I know."

"And I'll tell her the story of her birth, how I saw it with my own eyes, how she entered the world without a peep, practically smiling."

Jenny held the baby's face against hers for a minute and felt her warm, soft skin. As she held her, she wondered if there could be anything in the world that felt better.

Driving out of the hospital parking lot later that afternoon, Jenny saw her father drop her mother off at the entrance. She hadn't spoken to him since she called on Christmas Day to say she wouldn't be coming back home. After photographing the birth of Heather's baby and watching Rickey cradle and sing to his newborn daughter, a part of her wanted to follow her dad and climb into the front seat next to him, to have them say things to each other, to look at one another. But a bigger part of her knew that would never happen. After all, she realized, it had been easy to separate from her parents; she never had to decline any overtures or attempts to bring her back into the fold because there simply were none.

Belonging

When Jenny arrived at Henry's house, she felt a rush of nostalgia, which she attributed to the smell of orange blossoms, the warm weather, and the sounds of lawn mowers and golf carts. Bakersfield in May.

Christopher opened the door and embraced Jenny. His resemblance to Henry snuck up on her, and she felt like she would cry. As she held onto him, she asked, "How are you doing?"

"I'm pretty sad. It's nice to see you, though. Come in. My dad will be home soon. I know he'll want to see you."

Jenny followed Christopher into the house. "Henry said you and your dad were in Brussels for weeks. That must have been so hard. How's your dad?"

"He's just keeping really busy."

"What about your mom?"

"She's pretending like none of this is happening. She hasn't spoken to Henry. She hasn't acknowledged his illness. It's crazy."

"I'm so sorry."

Christopher walked into the living room, motioned to the couch, and said, "Have a seat. Want some iced tea or something?"

"Sure."

Jenny watched as Christopher went through the sliding glass door to retrieve the glass jar of sun tea. She was overwhelmed by the memories in the house. Not a thing had changed, it seemed, since they were teenagers. The basketball hoop in the driveway, the pale-green shag carpeting, the plaid armchair she sat in. The house even smelled like it always did, like lemony furniture polish and cookies. A part of her expected Henry to appear in the hallway with his headphones on and the keys to his MG in his hand.

Christopher handed Jenny a glass of iced tea and put a plate of cookies on the table. "My dad made these. They're some kind of persimmon." He sat down across from her and said, "You're here for Heather's baby, right? Girl or boy?"

"A girl. Hope Marion. She was just born a couple of hours ago. Perfectly healthy and beautiful."

"Well, that's happy news."

Jenny took a deep breath and tipped her head to one side. "Yeah."

Christopher took a drink of his tea and set it down on a macramé coaster. "I'm glad you could stop by. Henry asked me to give something to you."

He went down the hallway toward Henry's old room and returned a moment later with a large cardboard box in his hands. Jenny recognized it immediately. She looked inside—all of her photos and letters were there. She reached for the small gold box Billy had given her in eighth grade and opened it. Inside were the three black and white photos from his photography final, a piece of binder paper folded up into the size of a Saltine, and her little garnet ring. As she held the box, the heavy cloak of regret she'd carried for so long began to fall. She would finally be free from the sadness over the angry, impulsive decision she made in August of 1982, to throw everything away.

She looked up at Christopher and wiped the tears rolling down her cheeks. "Where was this?"

"Henry's closet."

She remembered how Henry had asked her if she really wanted to get rid of everything and telling him she was certain that she did. She'd watched him set the box on the curb with the garbage, but then, he came back and took it? She wasn't sure how he did it, but she was pretty sure why. He always knew the exact meaning she would attach to something— whether it was an encounter with her mother, a movie they'd seen togeth- er, or a gift she'd received. Jenny would think, *How does he know exactly how I feel?* She remembered showing the box of photographs to Henry the day Billy gave it to her. He understood that the gift symbolized the beginning of something new and meaningful. So, on the day she wanted to throw it out along with all of her other memories, he knew what it meant to her. He knew, even when she was too blinded by anger and sadness, that someday, she would want it all back.

When she heard Henry's dad at the door a little while later, she walked to the entry to greet him. He put his briefcase down and held his arms open. She hugged him and he kissed the top of her head. "I was wondering who that cool Cadillac belonged to."

"It's Uncle Gino's. How are you doing?" she asked.

Belonging

He sat down on the couch next to Christopher and reached over and held onto his knee. "How am I doing?" He looked up at the ceiling. "I wish I could help my son and I can't, so I feel pretty inadequate. Day after day, I'm just getting by."

"I'm so sorry. I can't stop thinking about him. I can't imagine what it must be like for you."

"You know what it's like? Every day, I go to work, I make dinner, pick up the dry cleaning, bake something—anything, and I feel like I'm in the middle of a bad dream. I'll be in the checkout line at the grocery store or at a red light, just long enough to stop somewhere, and it hits me, and I think, it can't be true."

"I feel like that too. Thank you for sending me to see him. I can't tell you what it meant to be able to spend those few days together."

"You're very welcome."

They sat for a while in the quiet living room, listening to the golfers behind the house, sharing some memories, some hope, and offering each other whatever comfort they had to give. When it was time to leave, Mr. Hansen carried her box to the car, and they promised each other to always stay in touch.

As the sun started to set on the long day, Jenny drove out to Heather and Rickey's home on the river. She turned the radio on, and Merle Haggard was singing "That's the Way Love Goes," a song that Nonna didn't live long enough to hear, but always made Jenny think of her, nonetheless, because of its simple, timeless lyric that ties love to both God and music. She passed two signs posted at the mouth of the canyon. One announced in English the number of people who drowned in the Kern River since 1968. Beside it, a sign said the same thing in Spanish. She rounded a narrow corner and saw a group of colorful rocks around a wooden cross on the side of the road. She wondered if the memorial was for someone who drowned in the river or someone who crashed on the winding canyon road.

When she arrived at Heather and Rickey's house, Jenny grabbed her bag and her box and brought it to the guest room. She took out the little gold box, opened it, and laid each picture out on the bed. There was the photo of the little boy who, at the time, was probably Carl's age. Billy captured the angst and humor with the eye of the father he'd become. There was the old man and woman on the bench. Billy saw the gentleness and bond and history between these two people. Then there was the picture of her. It was astounding to her now. They were children when he took this picture, but somehow, he'd captured this moment of recognition—her eyes revealing that he meant something to her, the click of the shutter revealing that she meant something to him. She reread the note, with its sweet, innocent enthusiasm—the anticipation of their summer before high school. She picked up the ring in the bottom of the box and slid it on her finger atop Nonna's ring—her promise ring and engagement ring together on her left hand.

She put the pictures and the note back in the box and went out the sliding glass door in the back of the house. She walked through the landscaped yard, opened the gate that led to the river path, and found a spot to sit and watch the sun go down over the valley. Alone in the stillness of the early evening, the emotion of the day and the place caught up with her. She cried for Henry and her inevitable loss. They had said their last goodbye. At the time, she'd done her best to hold her sadness inside, so they could get through their final moments together in a way that honored the love and strength they'd always given each other; but now, alone on the riverbank, she could no longer hold it in. She cried for Billy and Carl and the emptiness she felt without them. She'd walked out on the most joyful life she'd ever known, and she wasn't sure if she would be able to get it back. She cried for Heather and Hope and Rickey, recognizing the weight of the day—the beginning of their family. She'd seen the start of a new generation, a family formed before her very eyes. Sad tears and happy tears at once. An immeasurable longing and a baby named Hope.

She didn't know how long she'd been there when she heard the gate open. She figured it was one of the caretakers and didn't bother to look back until she heard footsteps directly behind her. She turned and saw him and said, "Billy."

He sat down and put his arms around her and pulled her close to him. He was warm and his cotton shirt was soft, and she could feel his heart beating. He kissed the top of her head and held her for a long time. He lifted her chin and wiped her tears and looked at her in a way that was so certain and so familiar.

"I need to tell you—well, I need to tell you a lot of things, but mostly that I love you and I'm sorry," she said.

"I love you too. And I'm sorry too." Billy kissed her again, held both of her hands, and said, "There's stuff we need to talk about."

"I know."

"I know you called when I was out with Tara. She called a couple days after you left. She said she was coming back after her trip to L.A. and wanted to spend more time with Carl. I let her come to his game. And I let her come to our house after."

"How was that?"

"It was really hard and sad. Carl offered to show her his baby book. It was almost like he was trying to prove it to her, that she was his mother. It was difficult to watch, and I started to worry about him, that he might have some expectations."

"I worried about that too."

"I know you did. I asked Megan to come over that night to stay with Carl so I could take her somewhere and figure out what she wanted. I told her, if she really wants a part in Carl's life, it can't be a random appearance every few years. I also told her we're getting married soon and you are going to raise Carl with me."

"I am."

Billy handed her an envelope and said, "I brought you something."

Jenny opened it, and inside was a black and white photograph of her and Carl on the beach. She is sitting in the sand, and Carl is in her lap, facing her, rubbing her hair under his chin. They are mid-conversation, both smiling, looking at each other. Jenny was taken by how much it looked like he was her son in the picture, how much it looked like she was his mother. What was it? Something she couldn't define, but Billy had managed to capture—the tender recognition that they would be mother and son, that they belonged to each other.

"I don't want there to be any surprises, so I have to tell you that I don't know what she plans to do—if she'll be back in ten days or ten years.

I want you to know, though, it doesn't matter what she does. It matters what we do," Billy said.

"I know. I know that now. I want to explain what happened that day. I need you to understand. Tara arriving was unnerving to me, but I thought I could handle it. I thought I did handle it. But then you told me about the lie, and I was very shaken. And right after that, you decided to talk to Carl alone about his mother's visit. I was stunned and hurt that you didn't want me there. We'd already been planning adoption, and you didn't want me with you? And I know you said it was a mistake, but by that point, I'd already closed down. I love you so much. I loved Carl at first sight. I was afraid that my love and trust were misplaced and hurried, that I didn't belong. I had my mom's voice in my head too, telling me that I was only convenient, that you don't really love me, and I guess I let myself believe it."

"Your mom said that? When?"

"Christmas Eve, after you and Carl left."

"Why didn't you tell me?"

"There are a lot of things I've never told you. On Christmas Eve, when my mother hurt Carl, you accepted that it was an accident. Carl was okay, and you were able to let it go. But I couldn't let it go, because to me, it was so much more than that. It was every day of my childhood. My mother was dangerous—either drunk or angry or both. I had to learn to stay out of her path when I was even younger than Carl. And I couldn't go home with you that night because I couldn't leave my dad alone with her. That's the terrible bind I was in growing up—fearing her and protecting him. I'm just beginning to understand the effect it had on me, the lack of trust it bred, the way it made me feel about myself."

"Why have you never told me any of this?"

"Because that's not who I wanted to be. I didn't want you to see me as this girl from a messed-up home that you had to rescue. I didn't want you to pity me. I didn't want you to think I was damaged. You were right when you said that I just flee. That is what I've done, but I don't want to anymore."

"Jenny, I wish I had known." Billy shook his head. "I should have known."

"There was no way you could have. I was so good at hiding things." Jenny paused and said, "Why did you come to my window on Christmas Eve?"

"I just wanted you with us."

"That's all?"

"I wanted us to wake up together on Christmas morning. I didn't understand that you were leaving for good until we were out on the roof, and you were saying goodbye."

"Didn't you wonder why?"

"I did wonder. But it also didn't surprise me. I guess I saw enough, but I never actually let it sink in, what it meant to be living in that house. I'm sorry for that."

Once Jenny had begun sharing, Billy started to piece together all he'd witnessed over the years, and he began to share too. Eventually, he would tell her all the things he saw, wondered about, and never questioned. When she was home with valley fever, he saw the mess of the house and noticed the absence of her mother. In high school, he witnessed her always gathering food. She ate dinner at his house all the time, and he never once had a meal at hers. When he dropped her off the night Henry got jumped, he knew she was afraid of what awaited her inside. He saw her mother grab her by the arm and take her from the pool at the Fourth of July party. He saw the aftermath, the darkness, and named it "the hole." He knew her parents were rarely around. He knew Henry's dad is the one who shepherded her college applications. He saw the sadness she often carried. He knew that she'd stayed away from Bakersfield for years and that only Heather's wedding brought her back. He witnessed her mother land on Carl on Christmas Eve, and raise a glass to the room, making a joke of it. Billy realized that there was a lot he noticed and never spoke about, and also, a lot that he missed.

Their relationship as teenagers worked well because he provided a consistent, pragmatic type of care. He didn't ask too many questions, and she didn't want anyone to dig too deep, so it was a perfect fit. But they weren't teenagers anymore, and they would need a different type of relationship now, one that allowed questions to be openly asked and honestly answered. There would be no more secrets, no more flight, no leaving each other. They would make new promises, once again.

For her part, Jenny vowed to tell Billy everything she remembered about Lupine Lane. She would tell him about lying in her room as a toddler with a tube on her arm, willing herself to disappear. She would tell him about the comfort of living at Nonna's and the terror of having her mother return in the middle of the night to take her back. She would tell him about her teenage years, when her mother shifted from neglect to intrusion, and began calling her *trashy* and *slut*. She would tell him what it was like to be a child always scanning for trouble or a shift in her mother's mood, about having to care for her father. She would begin to explain "the hole," the need to isolate and to flee, and her conscious choice to not go there anymore. All of this would take time, though. It would be a slow unfolding of memories, the sharing of which she hoped would finally remove any space between them.

"I will never leave you," he said.

"I will never leave you." Jenny looked down at the photo of her and Carl. "I don't want to be apart anymore, and I don't care where we live. I want to marry you. I want to be Carl's mother. I want us to be a family."

"I want that too."

Billy took her hand and looked at the garnet ring on her finger and said, "You're wearing your promise ring. I haven't seen it. I thought you might have thrown it out with everything else."

"Henry saved it for me. He saved my pictures and letters, too, my whole box of memories. He kept it all for me."

Jenny promised herself that she would also tell Billy all about Henry, their years of friendship, and days of saying goodbye. She would tell him about the bond they formed as small children, unlikely allies that would become inseparable. She would tell him how Henry was so attuned to her suffering and hiding, because he was also suffering and hiding. Both had experienced the rejection of their mothers. Both kept secrets due to the shame they felt. Henry kept secrets from her for the same reasons she kept secrets from Billy, and then he showed her how to let them all go. One day, she would tell Billy the whole story of her friendship with

Belonging

Henry, how he showed her to be unafraid, what his abiding love meant to her, how it brought her back to this place.

Jenny put her head down on Billy's shoulder and looked out at the riverbed, which now, after the winter and spring rains, had a shallow stream of water running through it. The air was still and warm and smelled like the dusty riverbank. The only sounds were the trickle of water and the low hum of the country music station from inside the house. Jenny held out her hand and looked at the rings on her finger. She thought about all the love and hope and history they held. The garnet ring held the longing of their youth—a symbol of their first articulated desire to never leave each other. Nonna's ring held the promises that Nonno and Nonna made on their wedding day in 1937. When Billy gave this same ring to her, it took on another meaning. It represented their hope for a life together and bound her history to what would follow. She held it all on her hand—the past, present, and future.

PART THREE

PART THREE

Chapter Twenty-One

JUNE 2017

In the spring of Uncle Gino's ninety-fourth year, he summoned Jenny to his old yellow house to be by his side as he received his Last Rites. She left her home at daybreak and drove four hours south, all the while thinking of Uncle Gino, saying silent prayers for the commending of his soul to heaven. On the I-5, she passed signs that read *Congress Created Dust Bowl* and *Is Growing Food Wasting Water?* posted in brown fields that used to be green. As she neared town, there were housing developments on land that once held oil fields and orchards, dairy farms and stables. Only the oil derricks remained, bobbing up and down as houses went up around them.

When she arrived at Uncle Gino's house, everything was blooming in his garden—daylilies and daffodils, tulips and daisies, iris and lavender. A rosebush he had trained to reach up and over the arched entrance of his yellow Victorian was in full bloom, the vines heavy with pink blossoms. The landscape was so manicured and vibrant, it looked like something out of a fairy tale: blue sky, yellow house, pink roses, flat green lawn. Had it been a different day, he would have been waiting for her in the doorway or in the rocking chair on the porch, and they might have decided to spread out a blanket on the grass and have lunch outside. She paused on the sidewalk in front of the house and marveled at how the garden thrived, even as Uncle Gino was living his last days.

Jenny was met at the front door by Uncle Gino's caregiver, a young woman she'd hired last September after Uncle Gino returned home from spending the summer with her. The caregiver led Jenny down the hall

239

to Uncle Gino's bedroom. He had fallen asleep sitting up in his bed, glasses on the end of his nose, a photo album in his lap. She referred to her notebook and updated Jenny on his condition. *Mr. Vitelli has grown quiet over the last few days, sleeps much of the time, is not eating much. Mobility has decreased, but able to walk with assistance. No noticeable cognitive impairment. Enjoys listening to music and looking at his photo albums. Prefers windows to be left open. Recently, speaks aloud in his sleep, to Honey Bea and Marion. Has expressed need to see Jenny. Per his request, Last Rites have been arranged with Catholic Church.*

The caregiver handed Jenny her notebook and told her to call with any concerns; Uncle Gino had asked that she be given the day off. Jenny thanked her, said goodbye, and sat in a chair by Uncle Gino's bed. She touched his hand and whispered, "Uncle Gino, it's Jenny. I'm home." When he didn't stir, she picked up the photo album and looked at the open page. There were black and white images of their large Italian family gathered on the porch of this house almost one hundred years ago. She recognized Uncle Gino as the baby in the photos, and the gangly, brown-eyed girl holding him as Nonna. She looked at the baby in the book, and then the old man in bed, and bent over and kissed his forehead. She thought about what the caregiver said. It made her sad to think of Uncle Gino quiet and uninterested in food. She was deeply moved by his desire to listen to music and feel fresh air, by his speaking in his sleep to his wife and sister.

While Uncle Gino slept, Jenny wandered into the living room, where music was coming from the mid-century stereo console. *The Dorsey/Sinatra Radio Years* was sitting out, and she realized he was listening to his favorites from the 1940s, just like they used to do on summer afternoons in the antique store. While "The Song Is You" played, she thought about what it meant to have a caregiver open the door to this house instead of Uncle Gino. He had been waiting at the door her whole life—her grandmother's baby brother, the holder of their family history, the last link between generations.

Jenny returned to his bedside, hoping he'd wake up and they'd have some time to talk before the priest arrived. She looked out at the garden and thought about how she knew every tree in his yard, every room of

240

his house. It had been a central part of her life for all of her fifty-three years. She thought about all of the other houses she and Uncle Gino held in their memory: Nonna's sprawling, immaculate ranch style house on the west side of town; the tragedy that was Lupine Lane; her own home two-hundred miles north, where Uncle Gino had spent his last ten summers. They carried these houses within them, and the meals prepared in the kitchens, the music played on front porches and back patios, the flowers growing in the gardens, and traditions born just from doing the same thing in the same place every year.

When Uncle Gino awoke to Jenny sitting beside him, he smiled and said, "*Mi passerotta.*"

Jenny put her hand on his cheek and said, "How are you feeling?"

"I've been a little weak, but I feel better today. I'm so happy you're here."

"Me too."

"How are the children?"

"Everyone is good. They all send their love."

"Is the priest coming this afternoon?"

She nodded. "In about an hour."

"Good. We have some time. There are some things we have to talk about. Can you hand me my folder on the dresser?"

Jenny retrieved the folder and handed it to Uncle Gino. It looked like something she'd find in his antique store, made of aged leather, with an ornate gilt border and *Gino Vitelli* embossed in cursive script in the bottom right corner.

He opened it, took out a document, and said, "This is a copy of my will. You know I'm leaving you the house and the store. This house is our family legacy. I hope it gives you something to hold onto when I am gone, to preserve for your children and their children, the way that your great-grandparents preserved it for us. And the store, well, I feel like it's always belonged to the two of us. But I also want you to feel free to do what you want with them. I know your life is not here, so I don't want them to be a burden."

"Uncle Gino, they would never be a burden. Thank you for entrusting me with this home and your store. I will take very good care of both."

"Well, I don't want you to think you have to keep a little museum in my honor. You can probably get good rent on the house. People are moving downtown again, young people."

"Okay. I'll keep that in mind."

Uncle Gino turned the page. "I put my funeral arrangements in here. You know where my plot is, next to Honey Bea."

Jenny nodded, reached for his hand, and held it.

"I've planned a private graveside service and selected the music and readings." He handed her a prayer card. "I would like you to read this Saint Teresa poem, and play 'Peace in the Valley'—the Randy Travis version. And I want a closed casket, okay? I want you all to remember me in life."

A part of Jenny was squarely in the room with Uncle Gino, listening to his words and aware of the weight of the moment. She was intent on fulfilling his request to remember him in life—pulling weeds in his garden, standing behind the counter at the antique store, the last person on the dance floor at a family wedding. But a part of her had wandered off, in disbelief that they were talking about something that, by definition, would occur without him by her side. Uncle Gino's presence in her life was a given. There had never been a Jenny without an Uncle Gino. He told her all about their heritage and showed her how to make Nonna's recipes. He took her to church and the cemetery and helped her understand the meaning of both. He taught her about antiques and outsider art, growing roses and tomatoes, Saint Teresa and honeybees. He'd always been the one to give her life context, sharing his home and garden, his memories and faith.

"The wake should be here, in the backyard. I had some new lights strung across the patio in the fall. And can you play old Italian music on the stereo?"

"Of course. What should I serve?"

"Just the usual, like any holiday. Rigatoni, green salad, garlic bread, and would you mind picking up some pickled tongue? And frosted smiley face cookies?"

Jenny smiled. "I'll take care of all of that. You've thought of everything."

Belonging

Uncle Gino closed his eyes and then opened them and looked out toward his garden.

"Have you been outside lately?" Jenny asked.

"Not past the front porch."

"Everything is blooming. Your garden is so beautiful, and the wisteria, and the roses over the arch."

Uncle Gino continued to stare out the window and didn't seem to hear her. He let go of a heavy sigh, held up the leather folder and said, "There are some letters in here for you." His voice trailed off and he began to cry.

Jenny was alarmed by his tears, his sudden shift in demeanor. While he spoke about his own funeral arrangements, he was solemn and purposeful, and even maintained a bit of the cheer that was so characteristic of Uncle Gino. Now, he was filled with an anguish and sorrow she did not recognize or understand.

"I promised myself that I would give these to you when the time was right, but in forty years, the time has just never seemed right, and now I don't have any more time."

"Letters from who?"

He shook his head and held tight to two envelopes clipped together. "Before you read these, I want you to know how sorry I am. I am so very sorry that I didn't give them to you sooner, and I hope that you can find a way to forgive me."

Jenny began to feel sick to her stomach and her forehead throbbed, her body anticipating an awful surprise. She took a breath and reminded herself of where she was—in the room with Uncle Gino, on the day he would receive his Last Rites. Whatever it was he was sorry for, whatever these letters held, they would get through it, and she needed to preserve the peace and prayerfulness of this afternoon together.

"Uncle Gino, I can't imagine what you think you need forgiveness for, especially from me." She put her hands on his cheeks and looked at his eyes, her gaze unwavering. "Whatever it is, it's okay. I promise. You are forgiven. I forgive you, whatever it is you think you need forgiveness for."

A car pulled up in front of the house, and Jenny walked to the window. "Father Thomas is early. Do you want me to ask him to give us some time? I can get him a glass of iced tea or something?"

Uncle Gino shook his head, closed the folder, and put it on his bedside table. "We shouldn't keep him waiting. Just bring him back."

Jenny dabbed at the tears on his cheeks with a handkerchief. She took his black plastic comb from his dresser and combed his gray hair off his face. She buttoned the top button of his pajama top.

"You sure?" she said.

He nodded, and she turned to leave his bedroom.

"Wait."

Jenny stopped and turned back to Uncle Gino.

"I want to be sure that you know, I wish I had done things differently. I just didn't know how, and I am so sorry."

Jenny returned to his bedside and straightened the quilt across his lap. "Uncle Gino, I don't know what these letters are that have you so upset. I do know that there is nothing in the world that could change my love for you."

She held his hand and waited to see if he wanted to say more. There was a knock at the door, and Uncle Gino said, "Thank you, dear. I think I need to see Father Thomas now."

Jenny greeted Father Thomas and led him back to Uncle Gino's room. He had been to Uncle Gino's home many times, often in khaki shorts and a short-sleeved shirt, to help cook for the church's annual pasta feed, to lead a men's prayer group, to have coffee on the front porch. Now, he approached Uncle Gino's bedside in full clerical attire. He greeted him by holding both of his hands and bowing his head. They chatted for a bit, and then Father Thomas asked Uncle Gino if he was ready to begin. Uncle Gino nodded and Father Thomas made the sign of the cross and offered a blessing. He asked Jenny to leave the room, so he could hear Uncle Gino's final confession. She left them alone and went outside to wait in the garden.

Walking through the rows of flowers, Jenny couldn't stop thinking about Uncle Gino's despair, how full of regret he seemed as he spoke of the letters. Her mind was working, spinning, figuring. Who were the

Belonging

letters from? Why was he so troubled by them? Why did he think he needed her forgiveness? Eventually, she made a conscious choice to put these thoughts aside. She continued to wander up and down a row of rosebushes, deliberately observing the different smells and colors. As she did, she decided that later today, when the priest left, she would get Uncle Gino outside to see and smell his garden.

After about thirty minutes went by, she became uneasy again. Time was precious, and she wanted to be in the room with Uncle Gino. Why was his confession taking so long? He had lived a humble and quiet life of faith and service. As a young man, he returned from World War II and married Honey Bea, and they lived a few short, happy years together. After Honey Bea died, he poured himself into renovating and restoring his family home, rented an old warehouse space on Q Street, and opened the antique store. He volunteered at the church, had a nice group of friends he'd known since childhood, and never remarried.

Jenny settled into her chair, next to Uncle Gino's empty chair on the front porch and thought about packing up his house. It just didn't seem possible. Because of Uncle Gino's careful preservation, this house had become a time capsule, a representation of what life was like for the early Italian immigrants in the valley. The original picnic tables and arbor were there. The arbor was heavy with wisteria blossoms and new lights. Large antique vats that once held olives, and barrels that once held homemade wine, sat on the back patio, now planted with herbs, peppers, and tomatoes. The love that Uncle Gino poured into the flowers he grew, the food he served, the family photos he framed, could not be dismantled. Would she end up with a little museum, just like he said? She knew how impractical and sad that would be. Uncle Gino, the life force behind it all, would be gone, and the house would register that void. There was no question, though—she would never sell it. She would keep it for her children, and they would keep it for their children, and it would stay in their family.

As she sat there reflecting, Father Thomas opened the front door and asked her to come back in. When she walked into the bedroom, Uncle Gino looked tired. His cheeks were pink, his eyes damp. She sat beside him and held his hands and said, "Are you okay?"

"I will be, dear."

245

Jill Fordyce

Father Thomas anointed Uncle Gino with oil, said that he had been cleansed of all his sins, and his soul was purified in preparation for his entrance to heaven. He placed a communion wafer in Uncle Gino's mouth, said it would be food for his journey, and asked that they pray together. He offered a reading from the First Letter of John: "*We know that we have passed out of death into life, because we love...*"

When the Last Rites were complete, Jenny held her hands to her face and softly cried. She was not prepared for the loss of Uncle Gino's physical presence—the sound of his voice, the shuffle of his walk, the feel of his warm, rough hands. Father Thomas touched Jenny on the shoulder and said his goodbyes. Alone in the room with Uncle Gino, she asked if she could get him anything, a cup of tea or water?

Uncle Gino shook his head and said, "I'd like to go out to the garden now."

Jenny slid his slippers on his feet and helped him up from the bed. She offered her arm and he held it, and together, they went out to his garden. At the front door, they paused under the pink roses that hung over the arched entrance, observing the years of care that created this living entry to his home. As they walked through the rows of flowers, Jenny was quiet and careful to let Uncle Gino lead. He took his time, touching leaves and smelling blossoms. He pulled a sprig of rosemary from the hedge that grew along his fence line, closed his eyes, and held it to his nose.

"It's all right here," Uncle Gino said, opening his eyes and holding the sprig up for Jenny to smell. "It's my garden. It's Sunday dinners at Nonna's. It's a field by the sea in Italy."

Jenny closed her eyes now and took in the familiar smell. She was aware of the buzzing of honeybees, the feel of the sun, Uncle Gino beside her. She remembered walking through this garden as a child, picking tomatoes and pulling sprigs of rosemary. She remembered Nonna in a checkered apron stirring a pot on the stove. She imagined the large Italian family she'd known only from pictures, standing in rows of green with purple flowers.

Jenny opened her eyes and said, "Yes, it's all those things."

They walked around the entire yard and ended up on the back patio together, sitting under the wisteria arbor. Uncle Gino pulled a ripe tomato

246

from a vine growing in a wine barrel and smelled it too. He turned to Jenny and said, "Could you do me a favor, dear, and turn on the lights on the arbor?"

Jenny went inside and flipped the light switch. She took a small plate and a paring knife from the kitchen counter, sat back down next to Uncle Gino, and cut up the tomato he'd pulled from the vine. Under the lights, they each ate a small wedge of tomato and listened to the sounds of the end of a spring day—mourning doves, a lawnmower, the grandfather clock striking five times. When Uncle Gino said he was ready to go back inside, Jenny brought him into his bedroom, took off his slippers, and tucked him into bed like a child.

"I love you abundantly," he said.

Jenny marveled at his memory, recalling the passage he'd underlined in *The Greatest Thing in the World*, the book he'd given her when she was just a girl. *To love abundantly is to live abundantly, and to love forever is to live forever.* She kissed his forehead. "I love you abundantly too."

"I've loved being the old man carrying the firewood."

As the afternoon light faded, shadows from a grand old California Sycamore tree fell over the room, as it had done for nearly a hundred years. Uncle Gino closed his eyes and did not open them again. Jenny touched his cheek and held his hand. She bowed her head, wept, and prayed. She felt both incredible loss, and also gratitude, that she was with Uncle Gino for the end of his long and precious life.

In the early evening, Jenny watched as paramedics lifted Uncle Gino onto a gurney, covered him, and removed him from his home. She followed them outside and stood in the front yard until his transport turned the corner out of sight. She sat down on the front porch, beneath the pink roses, and sobbed. She sat there for a long while, reluctant to go back into the house. Everything inside was now past tense: *this was Uncle Gino's record collection, these were his slippers, this was his home.* When she finally did go in the house, she didn't know where to begin, what to do.

She went into Uncle Gino's bedroom, put his slippers in the closet, and made his bed. She folded his quilt and held his pillow. She stared at the folder he'd left on his bedside table. She wanted to open it, to know why Uncle Gino had asked for her forgiveness, what was in the letters, who they were from. But her worry was stronger than her curiosity. She understood that whatever the letters held could not be put back, and that, given Uncle Gino's deep remorse, whatever it was could break her heart. She wanted to remain in the peacefulness of her last day with him a little longer. She wanted to hold on to the feeling of walking through the garden together, sitting under the arbor, and sharing a tomato he had grown from a seed. She left the folder there and went into the kitchen.

Jenny washed and dried the paring knife and the plate and put them away. She filled a bowl with milk for the stray cats that Uncle Gino fed and put it on the back patio. She turned off the lights on the arbor and went into the living room. She thumbed through Uncle Gino's records, looking for something to replace the heavy silence. When she came upon the 45 of Billy Mize's last single, she smiled. It was a song that Uncle Gino loved. She dusted it off and dropped the needle on the vinyl. Right away, the twang of the pedal steel guitar transported her back to the year it was released—1977—and she could see herself walking the aisles of the antique store with Uncle Gino, dancing with Nonna on her back patio, going to the movies with Henry. She closed her eyes and imagined them sitting in the room with her now, and let the melody put her back in a time and place where she could extend her hands and they were all within reach.

When the song ended, Jenny went back into Uncle Gino's room. Although she was afraid to read the letters, she felt an overwhelming need to understand. She and Uncle Gino had an extraordinary bond, nurturing and vibrant. He had always cared for and believed in her. They'd had so many long, weighty conversations, especially over the last ten summers, when he'd fled the heat, and spent June, July, and August at her home in Northern California. The possibility of secrets between them never occurred to her, but he'd kept these letters from her for forty years. He'd experienced agonizing remorse on the last day of his life, and it was her forgiveness that he had sought. As she retrieved the leather folder from Uncle Gino's bedside table, she remembered Saint Teresa's advice to those who were troubled: *go someplace where you can see the sky and take a walk*. She closed up the old house and drove to the bluffs, a lookout in the northeast part of town, where she could walk a path and have an unobstructed view of the night sky.

On the drive, she was filled with a familiar longing to go back in time. She wished she were a teenage girl, working at the antique store on a Saturday, with the oldies station on, and Uncle Gino humming along behind the counter. Or that it was last summer, when she woke up every morning to Uncle Gino sitting at her kitchen table with the newspaper and a bowl of fruit. Or even earlier today, when they'd walked through his garden, and shared a last meal of sorts—a tomato he'd grown in a barrel left behind by her great-grandparents.

Jenny parked on Panorama Drive and took the leather folder from the passenger seat. It had only been hours since she stood in the yard and watched the ambulance round the corner. Whether she was ready to read the letters or not, she wasn't sure. She expected that whatever they held would be deeply unsettling. She walked for a while, holding the folder against her chest, looking out at land and sky. There was a waxing crescent moon and Venus was dim and fading. Her hometown was stretched out before her: farmland and oil fields, crisscrossed by the canals and the Kern River, the old downtown, the horizon dotted with lights.

Looking out at the landscape, she recalled the day the epic dust storm ripped through the town, when fierce winds unearthed spores of a fungus that lived in the soil. She'd breathed it in, allowing the fungus to blossom in her lung, make a host of her body, take over her life. She feared that opening the letters would be like the raging wind, dredging up long-ago buried secrets, allowing them to take root inside of her and make her sick. Now, however, she had a choice. She could hold her breath. She could leave its contents buried. She could refuse to read the words. She thought about this only for a moment, and then she rubbed her fingers over the name *Gino Vitelli* in golden script, etched across the bottom of the old leather folder. Uncle Gino said these letters belonged to her. He was filled with regret for not giving them to her sooner. Whatever they held, he needed her to know. She was as sure of this as she was of his abundant love. So, she took a deep breath, taking in the smell of the evening air, soil and citrus, asphalt and dust, and settled on a bench beneath the palm trees. She said a silent prayer, opened the folder, and looked inside.

Chapter Twenty-Two

JUNE 2017

Jenny took out the first document in Uncle Gino's leather folder. It was his will, where he had dictated his own funeral arrangements and bequeathed his home and antique store *to my grand-niece, Jenny Hayes Ambler*. Beneath the will were two envelopes clipped together, and a sticky note in Uncle Gino's handwriting. The note instructed: *Read the letter addressed to your mother first*. Jenny unclipped the envelopes and looked at them. One said only "Jenny," written in Uncle Gino's handwriting. The other was addressed to *Miss Janice Moretti* at Nonna's house, the home her mother grew up in. It was from *PFC Gary John Rossi*. There was an APO number beneath his name, an airmail stamp, and a postmark that read *U.S. Army Postal Service*. She opened the envelope addressed to her mother and began to read.

> *July 12, 1964*
>
> *Dear Janice,*
>
> *I arrived in South Vietnam this week, and it was suggested that we write "just in case" letters to people we love back at home. It feels strange for a lot of reasons to be writing this to you. First of all, I hope it is never sent or read, since that will mean the worst, that I am never coming home to you, my family, our child. But also, I don't even know what my role in your life, or the baby's life, will be anymore, since you and Bob Hayes are married now. I'm guessing that's why you haven't*

250

responded to any of my letters, and I do respect that. Hopefully, we will see each other again, and I'll get to hold our baby, but the idea of this letter is to say the things I would want to say to you and the baby if I never come home. That is a tall order for a simple man, but I will do my best.

To you, I want to say that I'm very sorry things didn't work out for us. I will never regret our time together, and only wish it could've been longer. I certainly don't regret the baby, but I imagine that there is a part of you that might, given that we were not married or even together anymore, and you were left alone and pregnant when I was deployed. I'm sorry for what you must have gone through alone. I figure that's why you married Bob in such a rush, and I want you to know that I don't blame you for it. I'm sure it seemed like the best you could do for yourself and the baby, making sure that he or she arrived with a father. I want you to know that, as you requested, I haven't told anyone, even my parents, and I sincerely hope that is what is best for you, Bob, and the baby. I know that Bob is a good man and believe he will be a good husband and father. If I am gone, I would like to express my gratitude to both of you for raising our child. I wish things had been different. I wish you and the baby would be waiting for me to come home. I wish I was coming home, but who am I to question this path that the Lord made for us?

I still say the prayer we memorized in Sister Margaret's class every day. In ninth grade, they were just words we had to say before we turned in our homework. But somehow, the words have stayed with me, especially here, so in case you forgot, I will leave them with you now. "May today there be peace within. May you trust God that you are exactly where you are meant to be. May you not forget the infinite possibilities that are born of faith. May you use those gifts that you have received, and pass on the love that has been given to you."

I will always love you, Janice. I hope you don't forget me. What follows is my letter to the baby.

Love,
Gary

———

Dear Baby,

First, I want to say that I am so lucky that you were born, my only child. I don't even know if you are a boy or a girl or when your birthday will be. Your mom says you are due in August. I wonder what you will look like, what color of eyes you will have, and if you will have the two dimples under your lower lip like me. My mother calls them "God's stamp of approval." I want to know all about you, but the idea of this letter is that we will never meet, at least not here on Earth. I am writing this letter to you in case I don't come home from the war. It is a terrible thing to think about, that I will never get to hold you, but if that happens, there are some things I want you to know.

As I write this, I guess I'm not sure what you even know about me or my family. I hope your mom tells you about me when the time is right, but it's hard to know when that would be, given the circumstances. My full name is Gary John Rossi. I am currently nine-

teen years old. I am the only living child of Anthony and Maria Rossi. I had a brother, Stephen, but he died when we were young, and I don't remember much about him. He was two years older than me. I was born and raised in an old Spanish house on Mt. Lowe, just around the corner from your mom. My dad was in the Army in WWII and came back home and opened a furniture store, which he still owns today. My mom is a homemaker, volunteers at church, and goes to Mass almost every day. In high school, I played every sport, and I was pretty good. I enlisted in the Army because I wanted to follow in my dad's footsteps.

I want you to know that I loved your mother very much and if things had been different, I would've married her, and we would've raised you and had a big family together. When we were in high school, we made all sorts of plans. Although it's sad for me to think about now, I'll say them here so you can imagine what it is we wanted for us, and for you. We planned to live in a big house, near our families, and I would eventually take over for my dad at the furniture store. Your mom would raise our children, be part of the charity league, host great parties, and learn to cook like her mother. We would have a swimming pool and a rose garden and Sunday dinners after church for all our family and friends. We would go to Hawaii and Italy someday. These probably seem like pretty standard dreams, but what more could a man want than good health, a family, a garden, good food, friends, travel? I'm sorry that the life we planned didn't come to be. Your mom and I broke up before I went to boot camp. She didn't want me to go, and I can't say I blame her, but it was something I felt I needed to do. If I'd known about you,

I would not have gone. I would've stayed. But neither of us knew until after I was deployed. I learned about you in a letter from your mother.

If you are reading this, I didn't make it home from the war, and my old friend, Bob, has taken my place as your father. I am grateful that you and your mom have such a gentle and good man to take care of you. I've known Bob Hayes since elementary school, and he was always a good friend, athlete, craftsman.

There are a lot of things I will miss if I don't make it back home. I will miss my mom and dad and my dogs. I will miss fishing and playing baseball. I will miss my mom's cooking and the smell of my dad's pipe. I will miss my house and yard and swimming pool. I will miss country & western music and my truck. I will miss the view of the canals and the oil fields from the bluffs. I will miss your mother. Most of all, I will miss being your father. I imagine holding you all the time. I'm imagining it right now, so maybe you can imagine it too, and that way, we will be together.

Since I won't be around to raise you, I spent some time thinking about what I'd want to teach a child, what I know to be true, and it is really only this: trust in God and love people. If you trust in God, and the path he's made for you, it will make your whole life a lot easier, because you won't have to go around believing it's all up to you. Loving people is pretty self-explanatory. I mean, what is life without people to love? Right now, I'm sending you all the love I have, and I hope that love will stay with you all of your life.

Love,

Dad

Belonging

Jenny felt nauseous, her face grew hot, and her hands began to tremble, as she studied the handwriting and took in the words of this young man who, it seems, was her father. For several moments, she sat there, her body shaking and stunned, her mind stuck and foggy. She couldn't even cry. Her thoughts began to race. So many different dates and times and memories flooded her. She went back through the letter and tried to understand the timeline. It was written a month before she was born. Her mother was already married to her father. There was no doubt that the baby Gary was writing to was her. She kept going back to certain details—*he had written many unanswered letters to her mother; he never told anyone about the pregnancy; he knew her father.* She touched the space below her lower lip and felt the two dimples. She tried to imagine what Gary looked like. She kept seeing her own son, Will, who also had "God's stamp of approval" beneath his lower lip, and she began to sob.

She read the letter two more times, taking the information in, wiping the warm tears from her cheeks. Bob Hayes was not her father. Her mother had been a pregnant, unwed teen. Her biological father must have died in Vietnam. As sad and confusing as it was to have the history of her own life leveled by the contents of the letter, in a way, everything made so much more sense now—her childhood, her parents, and even herself. She reflected on the essence of the young man who wrote this letter, so clear to her from the words he put on the page. *He was guided by his faith. He loved his family. He was generous and kind. He was grateful she was born. He longed for this very view above town.*

Jenny remembered Uncle Gino's bowed head and downcast eyes and understood his regret. Somehow, he'd come into possession of this letter, and he'd never been able to share it with her. She understood the pain that must have caused him, to have always taken great care in teaching her about her heritage, to have entrusted her with the legacy of their family home, only to withhold the fact that she had a whole other family. She opened the second letter, addressed to her in Uncle Gino's handwriting, and began to read. On the top of the page was the date, and she recognized it as his own birthday, several years ago.

Jill Fordyce

April 15, 2013

My dearest Jenny,

Today, I turned ninety years old. I spent my birthday troubled by the idea that my life is coming to a close, and I am holding onto something that belongs to you. I have kept the letter from your father, Gary John Rossi, for decades now. Although you are the dearest person in my life, I have failed you, and I hope you can forgive me. I am writing this down now so that you have a record. My memory is strong, but my penmanship seems to get worse with each passing year.

Gary is buried at Union Cemetery, not far from Nonna and the rest of our family, and I thought about bringing you there many times. I wanted to be able to tell you the truth. I never did, and I will try to explain why. When you were young, there were so many reasons. I didn't want to add another burden to your life. You'd been so sick. You lost Nonna. I was afraid of what your mother would do. This was her secret, and you already lived in such tumult at home. I also worried about harming your relationship with Bob. I don't know if Bob is even aware that he's not your biological father.

When you became an adult, I thought again, many times, of giving you the letter. I always decided against it, though, not wanting to disrupt the peaceful home and family you'd finally made a reality. Every time I planned to share this with you, I thought better of it. I wanted to protect you. There was no right time. Now, I wish that I'd done better by you. I hope that someday, we can talk about this. But if, for some reason, that does not happen, what follows is everything I know about Gary's family, his relationship with your mother, and the day we learned of his death in Vietnam.

Anthony and Maria Rossi and their two boys lived just around the corner from Nonna. Maria and Nonna swapped recipes, and Anthony often helped Nonna out in the yard after Nonno died. As you know from the letter, they tragically lost their son, Stephen, as a child. Gary was your mother's boyfriend all through high school. He spent a lot of time at Nonna's house when he and your mother were teenagers. I remember him from that time—tall, handsome, polite. Soon after Gary joined the Army, your mother began seeing Bob, and they eloped just a couple of months later.

We were at Nonna's house the day Anthony and Maria learned Gary had been killed in Vietnam. News spread quickly through the neighborhood and soon reached us. It was April 14, 1966, just after Easter Sunday. Although Nonna and I didn't know at the time that Gary was your father, it was a deeply affecting loss. We all knew Gary as the young boy who grew up around the corner from Nonna, as Anthony and Maria's son, as your mother's high school boyfriend, and so young—only twenty-one. Your mother was inconsolable. While Nonna tried to comfort her in the house, I walked with you through the rose garden. You were not quite two years old, and you carried a stuffed rabbit with pink eyes that had been in your Easter basket. I tried to distract you from the sound of your mother's cries coming from the house by having you smell all the flowers and tell me the names of the colors you knew. After that day, your mother was never really the same.

I discovered the letter in Nonna's safe deposit box shortly after she died. I don't know the circumstances of how it came to be there. Nonna never told me about the letter and never told me that Gary was your father. I know if she had lived longer, though, she would've told you the truth. Please don't fault Nonna. You were only thirteen when she died.

Anthony and Maria were at Nonna's funeral. I remember seeing them there. After I read the letter, I understood why your mother wouldn't let you attend the service. You bear a striking resemblance to their family, and your mother could not let them start asking questions. This is one more regret I carry—that you were never able to meet your paternal grandparents, and they were never able to meet you. They've both been gone for years now. I saved information about them for you—obituaries, news clippings, some old photos, recipes in Maria's handwriting. It's all in the roll top desk in my office at the antique store.

As I write, it occurs to me that this is my own "just in case" letter, written in case you and I never have this conversation. Although we will no longer be able to talk in the traditional sense, if you seek me out, I promise that I will always be around and ready to listen. You are resilient and strong, and you are surrounded by a family who loves you. I know you will be okay. I've been saving this prayer card for you, a beautiful old Saint Teresa. I love you and I'm sorry. I hope that you will forgive me.

All my love,

Uncle Gino

Jenny took the prayer card from the envelope. On the front was a unique image of Saint Teresa—primitive and bright. She holds a book and a feather pen; a golden arrow pierces her heart, showing the light from within. On the back, it read: *What a burden I thought I was to carry—a crucifix, as did He / Love once said to me, "I know a song / would you like to hear it?" / And laughter came from every brick in the street / and from every pore in the sky.*

So many different sorrows now washed over her. First and foremost, there was sorrow for the loss of Gary John Rossi, the father she never knew. After seeing his handwriting, reading his words, and understanding his faith, a picture of this teenage boy emerged, and she was tormented thinking about his youth, his innocence, and the way he died.

There was the sorrow she now felt for her mother. For the first time, she understood what Janice's young life must have been like. She was forbidden from going away to school. She watched the man she loved leave to war. She became an unmarried, pregnant teenager in her traditional Catholic community. She made a desperate choice to marry a man she didn't love. She had to grapple with Gary's death at twenty-one years old. She had a child who was both a constant reminder of the love she'd lost and the life she would never have. She spent years blaming Nonna, and Nonna's sudden death left her without the opportunity for forgiveness or healing. She turned to alcohol to drown her anger, disappointment, and heartbreak, and whatever faith she had earlier in life was lost.

There was the sorrow Jenny felt for her father, Bob Hayes, who she suspected must have known she was not his child. He endeavored nonetheless, to care for her the best that he could, and in a way, the knowledge that he was *not* her father made her feel closer to him. His failings were easier to excuse and accept, given the nobility and kindness of loving her like she was his own.

She thought about the words on the prayer card—burden, love, song, laughter, and sky. She put the letters back in the folder, wiped the tears from her cheeks, and began to walk along the grassy bank of the bluffs. While she walked, she took her phone from her purse and called Billy. When he answered, she imagined him standing in their home, their four children gathered around the stone fireplace, the cat asleep in a chair, the windows open to green fields and blue sky. Jenny said *goodnight* and *I love you* to Billy, who passed the phone to Carl, and then to Mary, both now adults living on their own; and then to Will, a junior in college; and then to Summer, their last child at home, and she said *goodnight* and *I love you* to each of them too. Tonight, her children were gathered in their childhood home, and in a few days, they'd drive to Bakersfield together for Uncle Gino's funeral.

Jenny took one last look at the view from the bluffs, before leaving for Heather and Rickey's house, where she'd be staying until after the funeral. As she drove through the canyon, the moon hung above the mountains, so perfectly curved and yellow in its waxing crescent phase. She thought of how her children used to call this a *shining sliver of moon*, a phrase from one of their favorite books. At Heather and Rickey's house, she was greeted at the door by Hope Marion, who hugged her tightly, and led her to the back patio, where Heather and Rickey and their three other children had been waiting up for Aunt Jenny to arrive. They sat around and told stories about Uncle Gino until after midnight and agreed to continue over coffee in the morning.

In the guest room, Jenny put the prayer card from Uncle Gino on the nightstand, got into bed, and tried to sleep. Unable to settle, she closed her eyes and imagined herself standing in front of the picture wall in the upstairs hallway of the home she and Billy built together, where they lived and raised their family. With her eyes closed, she could see the framed photos on the wall. *Nonna in her garden. Uncle Gino and Jenny at Heather's wedding. Jenny, Henry, and Billy standing in front of Stockdale 6. Henry driving down a country road in Belgium. Jenny and Billy on Billy's front lawn when they were fifteen. Their wedding photo in front of Mission Santa Clara. Jenny and Carl on the beach in 1990. Billy, Jenny, and Carl on the courthouse steps on the day Carl's adoption became final. Billy, in a hard hat, standing in front of a bridge he designed. Jenny, holding a newborn Summer, with Carl, Mary, and Will gathered around her. Carl, receiving a medal for rescuing shorebirds at Refugio State Beach. Mary in a graduation gown on the lawn in front of Doheny Library at USC. Will as captain of his high school football team. Summer on stage in the youth theater production of* Our Town. In the center of the photos is her old painting from Uncle Gino's store.

As she began to feel sleepy, she saw Henry standing beside her in front of the picture wall. He was college-aged, tall and healthy, wearing jeans and a Tom Petty t-shirt. Since the moment she put down the letters, she'd been waiting for Henry to appear. He was the person who would most understand how and why people kept secrets, concealed a part of themselves, erased a personal history. He would also know the freedom and autonomy that came with the secret being unearthed. Half a lifetime ago, he'd shown that to her. The lesson was so vital and clear, it became part of her then. She wanted Henry to know that learning the truth about her family, while shocking, had not devastated her. In some ways, it had made her feel whole and free. In her half-sleep, she watched as Henry took his time studying the photos that chronicled her life, with and without him. Then he turned to her, kissed her once on the forehead, once on the nose, and he was gone.

Three days later, Jenny arrived at Uncle Gino's house before the sun came up. She made a pot of coffee, poured milk in a bowl for the cats, and put it on the back patio. She counted the jars of rigatoni sauce and the plates of pickled tongue and arranged frosted yellow smiley face cookies on a silver tray. She turned on the patio lights and placed votive candles, potted rosemary plants, and bowls of Uncle Gino's tomatoes on the long tables under the arbor. She filled a basket with the prayer cards she'd made for Uncle Gino: a photo of him in his garden, and the words: *To love forever is to live forever.* She went back inside to find the old Italian music Uncle Gino asked to be played, setting aside Dean Martin, Jerry Vale, Sergio Franchi, and Tony Bennett. She smiled when she happened upon a signed copy of Alice Cooper's *Lace and Whiskey.*

When she was done with her tasks, she allowed herself to be still for a moment. She picked up a photo Uncle Gino kept in an ornate silver frame on his coffee table. She's in her wedding gown, Billy is waiting at the end of the altar, and Uncle Gino is giving her away. As she looked at Uncle Gino in the photo, she felt his absence in the house, the quiet and emptiness that came with transcendent loss. She'd experienced it only twice before. Once, in her childhood bedroom, looking at Nonna's empty cot after she died. And again, in September of 1991, when she answered the phone in her kitchen in Santa Clara, and Henry's dad told her that Henry had died in Brussels that morning, a few months before his twenty-eighth birthday. She put on the Jerry Vale album she'd just set aside. When "Arrivederci Roma" filled the empty house, she held onto the picture and said a silent *arrivederci* to her much beloved Uncle Gino.

She took scissors and twine from a drawer and went outside to the garden. She walked through the row of rosebushes, one of which had originally been in Nonna's garden, but lived today in both Uncle Gino's, and also, in her own. She cut roses and stalks of rosemary, symbols of togetherness, love, and remembrance, sat on the porch, and tied them together into a dozen small bouquets to leave on the graves of all her relatives. After, she walked around the yard and gathered a few of every-thing that was blooming—yellow daylilies and daffodils, white tulips and daisies, purple iris and lavender, and roses of every color—and tied them together into one more bouquet.

When she was done, she turned on the hose and filled a bucket with water. She placed the bouquets in the water and sat down on the front porch, looked out at the orange and pink sky, and felt the coolness of day-break on her skin. The twist of the spigot and the spray of water caused a rush of memory. She closed her eyes and imagined Uncle Gino there, water pooling around his feet on the lawn, bending down to pluck a weed. She put her hand on her heart and told him that she understood. She accepted that he had never given her the letter because of fear that it would upend her life, and she forgave him without question. She was grateful he'd written his own letter, that he'd saved information about the Rossis for her, and that he acknowledged that she would be okay. She *would* be okay. She hadn't been in "the hole" in nearly thirty years. She never thought of disappearing or fleeing. She could attribute this to age or faith. But it was also because of the love and care she'd received from Uncle Gino, Nonna, her father, Aunt Hope, and Heather. It was because of Billy's unwavering love and commitment, and the home and family they created. It was because of Henry who, years ago, taught her that she never had to hide any of herself.

She silently thanked Uncle Gino for her newfound clarity. The letters had put the whole of her life in perspective. For the first time, she un-derstood something about her mother—the trauma she'd experienced, the moment in time when she became broken in a way that she was never able to repair. She saw herself at two years old, on her bedroom floor with a tube on her arm, the stuffed rabbit at her side, and realized that her earliest memory of fearing her mother, the earliest memory of abandoning herself, coincided with Gary John Rossi's death in Vietnam. She understood her father's role, perhaps why he subjugated himself to her mother. He'd always been her second choice, and he likely knew that. She was also just beginning to see herself as someone with a lineage that made sense, a father with whom she shared features, who recited prayers, who cared about the same things that she did. She now understood that a series of events that took place before she was born created the shame and sadness that hung over her childhood. Knowing the truth made her see, at last, that none of it had ever been her fault.

This understanding brought up the inevitable, that she had to go back to Lupine Lane, and she needed to see her parents. It was something she'd thought about many times over the years, what it would be like to stand in that house without fear, to look at her parents in the context of a life fully lived without them. When she left home almost thirty years ago, she asked Billy to stay out in the cold with her on the rooftop so that she could say her own goodbye, conclude, and feel complete. But the truth was, there was always a part of her that wished she'd done something other than just flee out a window on Christmas Eve. Uncle Gino's letter had given her the reason to go back. She would now be able to acknowl-edge—instead of ignore—the wounds that created their family.

Jenny placed the bucket of flowers in her car and looked back at Uncle Gino's house—once her great-grandparents' house and now her house. She knew she would never sell it. Maybe she would rent it to a young couple who could tend to the garden and help at the antique store, but it would remain in her family forever. It would always be a physical representation of her immigrant great-grandparents, of their ambition and self-reliance, of their faith and generosity—their intent to create a place to belong. Jenny could imagine them there, surrounded by family, neighbors, and friends, serving a warm meal under the arbor, drinking homemade wine, and dancing to Italian music.

As she drove away, she turned on KUZZ. The morning news led off with a story about a woman's body being found in the Kern River, about a quarter mile east of the China Grade Loop. The DJ repeated the frequent warning to stay out of the river, and then cued up Miranda Lambert's new song. It was full of loss and longing, and Jenny listened intently for any hint of hope. As she drove, she made note of all the changes in the landscape around her.

Stockdale 6 Theatres closed on May 7, 2000 and was now a Dollar Store. During its last week, the marquee read, "Thank you, Bakersfield for 25 years!" The Padre Hotel had been renovated and was once again an opulent centerpiece of the old downtown. The iconic gold "Bakersfield" sign had fallen into a state of disrepair in the late 1990s and had to be demolished. A smaller version was erected on Buck Owens Boulevard and Highway 99, reportedly paid for by Buck himself. A portion of 7th Standard Road out by the airport was now called Merle Haggard Drive. Merle died on his birthday the previous spring. On his final visit to Bakersfield, he watched as the boxcar he grew up in was lifted from its foundation and transported to the Kern County Museum, where it would be lovingly restored and kept in posterity. His last song, called "Kern River Blues," was about saying goodbye to Bakersfield and lamenting all the changes that had taken place: the expansion of the city limits, the closing down of all the old honky-tonks, and the Kern River going dry. Due to historic rainfall in the year after Merle's death, the Kern River was now flowing through town in places Jenny had never seen water before.

Chapter Twenty-Three

JUNE 2017

When Jenny finally stood in front of 822 Lupine Lane, she stared up at the house. The paint was peeling and a few of the shutters were missing. The picket fence that used to surround the front yard lay in sections at her feet. The air was hot, and it smelled like summer—lemons, grass, and dirt. The conflicting feelings that always arose at the edge of this yard were there. The house itself appeared eerie and airless, and evoked such dread that it felt like she could be sucked inside and suffocated. But outside, there was the flat green grass, the bending birch tree, the pink cinder block fence, and the lemon tree dotted with lemons the size of oranges, its shiny dark leaves and bright yellow fruit out of place against the dilapidated house. The land itself, the earth she stood on, the air she breathed, made her feel heavy right in the center of her chest, the way it felt when you'd missed someplace and you finally returned.

Jenny wanted to feel what it was like to stand on the lawn and pull a lemon down from the tree. She wanted to hold one in her hands and rub off the dirt, hold it to her nose and smell it. She stepped onto the lawn, looked up at the umbrella of leaves and branches above her, and picked a ripe lemon. When it came loose in her hand without even a tug, she began picking more lemons. She was filling her sweater with the fruit when she saw a light turn on in the upstairs hall. She returned to her car, put the lemons in the passenger seat, and sat to gather herself. She hadn't been to this house since she leapt from the rooftop twenty-seven years ago. She had never talked to her parents about her childhood or why she left. They were difficult to confront about anything—her mother, vicious; her father, helpless—and she was about to ask them about a secret they'd kept since before she was born. She felt anxious anticipating what would unfold, once she told them what she knew. She said a silent prayer for strength and grace, walked across the grass to the front door, and knocked.

When no one answered, Jenny went to the back gate, pushed it open, and walked toward her father's workshop. The backyard had turned to overgrown weeds and patches of dirt. The door to the workshop was open, and when she stepped inside, the smell of sawdust and smoke brought memories of her father. She heard shuffling through the weeds, and then there he was, an old man, standing on the back patio. He was holding a piece of toast on a paper towel in one hand and a mug of coffee in the other. He wore wire rimmed glasses, and his body was soft. His hair and mustache were both white, and the unruly patch of hair that she used to pat down when he needed a haircut was entirely gone. He was dressed in brown pants and a white t-shirt, and he looked so different, so much smaller and so much older. Seeing him now, she understood that she'd missed as much of his life as he'd missed of hers.

He was startled when he saw her standing in his workshop. At first, he looked surprised at the notion that anyone was standing there, but then Jenny watched a different type of alarm take hold. It was the alarm of looking at his middle-aged child, who he hadn't seen more than a handful of times since she was in her twenties. She walked toward him and said, "Dad, it's me, Jenny. I'm sorry, I didn't mean to startle you. No one answered the front door, so I thought I'd see if you were in the workshop."

He squinted at her and said, "Jenny?" Then he looked down, shook his head, and said to himself, "No, no."

Jenny put her hands on his shoulders and looked right at him and said, "Yes, Jenny. See?" She opened her eyes wider, reasoning to herself that, if he could see her eyes, he'd know her. Her father nervously looked back toward the house, toward the sound of a TV. Jenny gave his shoulders a small squeeze. "Dad, are you okay?"

He smiled as if remembering something, and said, "Sure, I'm fine. You just surprised me out here. Come on in, and I'll get you some coffee."

She followed him into the house. The same smell was there—dirty laundry, cigarette smoke, candles that were too sweet. She instinctively

Belonging

left the door open behind her, making sure she'd have some air. Her father pushed some old newspapers and mail off the kitchen table. "I didn't know you were coming, or I would've cleaned up."

Jenny took a seat and watched her dad take out his red jar of Taster's Choice instant coffee. She wasn't sure if she'd seen one since she left this house. He scooped a spoonful of the brown crystals into a mug, poured water from the tea kettle, and said, "Do you like milk in it? Sugar?"

"Just a little milk."

He poured some milk in her coffee, handed her the warm mug, and sat down across from her. His hands shook a little, his nails were dirty, and his knuckles were swollen from age and arthritis. He stared at the open door to the patio, a worried look on his face.

"What's wrong? Do you want me to close the door?"

"There are so many flies."

Jenny got up and closed the door. "I came home for Uncle Gino's funeral. Are you and mom going?"

He shook his head and said, "I don't think so."

He took a sip of his coffee and looked down at his hands.

Jenny said, "Dad, can you look at me?"

When her dad finally looked across the table at her, she observed his mannerisms, his formality, the dimness of his eyes, and understood that a part of him might be gone. She thought about the memories they shared, and how strange it was that they might now only be held by her. He was the only other person who knew what it felt like to go to sleep and wake up here, who knew the sound of the whoosh of the air conditioning and the birds on the roof, who knew the way the shadows moved across the yard in the late afternoon. He was her only witness to what went on in this house, the only other person who understood the terror of displeasing her mother, the constant feeling of uncertainty that existed within these walls.

Jenny asked, "Is mom upstairs?"

Her father nodded and said, "Do you want to see her?"

"Yes. Should you go get her or should we go up?"

"It'll be easier if we go upstairs. It's hard for her to come down. One of her legs is much smaller than the other now."

"What do you mean? Why?"

"The doctor says it atrophied. She tore something in it a long time ago. She had a bad fall, and it just never healed."

Jenny put their coffee cups in the sink and followed her father to the stairs. The stairwell was darker and smaller than she remembered. More than anything she'd seen in the house so far, it carried with it a feeling of isolation, loneliness, and dread. At the top of the staircase, she looked to the right, toward the open door to her tangerine bedroom. It had become another place for piles—old clothes, boxes, magazines. The morning sun made shadows on the walls. Time and decay had turned them to the color of a bruised orange.

Standing beside her father, Jenny had her first glimpse of her mother. She was dressed in a black tank top without a bra, her breasts low and loose, and black cotton leggings. Her body appeared both small and heavy simultaneously, a round belly and full thighs over tiny bones. She wore the same short haircut, frosty lipstick, and gold hoop earrings that had been her signature style for decades. It now looked out of place, almost costume-like, on the old woman she'd become. It briefly occurred to Jenny that age and infirmity would make her mother incapable of doing harm. But all the memories were there, living inside of Jenny's body, and her heart was beating too fast. She reminded herself to be present and unafraid.

Her father said, "Jenny's home."

Jenny walked to the edge of the bed and said, "Hi, Mom. I'm home for Uncle Gino's funeral."

Her mother reached for a cigarette on her nightstand. "You mean to collect your inheritance?"

At first, Jenny was surprised that she knew about Uncle Gino leaving her the house and the store. But she remembered how her mother had always maintained channels of information, how she reveled in town gossip.

Jenny shook her head. "I don't know why you would say that. I love Uncle Gino."

"Well, my grandparents—who you never even knew—intended for the house to be passed down from one generation to the next." She lit her cigarette and continued, "But Uncle Gino decided to skip over Joe

Belonging

and me. Of course, Joe doesn't care, he has all the money in the world. That house was supposed to be mine, not yours. Just like Nonna's ring."

Jenny looked down at the ring she'd worn on her left hand for nearly thirty years. "Did you want to live in the house?"

"God no. Your father can't work anymore. I'd like to sell it."

Jenny's father sat down on the edge of the bed. Her mother ran a hand over his back, looked at Jenny and said, "He has some memory loss now. Did you notice? The doctor says it was probably caused by stress. He asked if he'd ever suffered a big trauma, like the death of a child."

Her father looked out the window toward the yard. Her mother's eyes were excited and flashing. It was that same confusing combination—something awful said with apparent glee. It was a look Jenny knew well, and she understood that her mother was coming for her. "And I told him, yes, his daughter abandoned him years ago and she might as well have been dead."

Although the cruelty of the words was staggering, Jenny remained still and accepted them for what they were—the desperate claim of someone who lived a bitter, untruthful, and faithless life, not because of her, but maybe in spite of her.

Jenny said, "I left here to save my life."

Her mother snapped back, "At the expense of his. Why are you even here?"

As Jenny thought of what she would say, she studied the room. Old tabloids and gossip magazines were in piles on the bed and the floor. Fast-food wrappers and brown prescription bottles were on the nightstand. Her mother was sitting on the bed with one leg visibly smaller than the other, and her father seemed only vaguely aware of the exchange happening in front of him. The only sounds were the ones she remembered from her rooftop—air conditioner units, lawnmowers, birds.

In the quiet filth of the room, Jenny took a breath and began. "Uncle Gino gave me a letter before he died." She looked directly at her mother. "It was a letter to you and to me, from Gary John Rossi."

Jenny's mother turned to her father, startled, and said, "How dare he. He had no right. That letter belonged to me."

"The letter was to both of us. It belonged to me too. Uncle Gino wanted me to know the truth. He wanted me to understand. That's why he gave me the letter."

Jenny's father sat wide-eyed, like he'd seen a ghost. Jenny sat down and put her arm around him. She could feel that he was trembling. She held onto him and said, "You know this, right? You know what I'm talking about?"

Her father glanced toward her mother as if asking permission, and her mother turned away. He nodded at Jenny, got up, walked across the room, and retrieved an old shirt box from his closet. Her mother yelled, "Bob, stop!" But he didn't stop. He took the box down from a shelf, set it on his dresser, and opened it. Inside were old letters and photographs, and he thumbed through them until he discovered what he was looking for. He found the black and white photograph of a young soldier in his combat helmet and handed it to Jenny. Her mother sat in stunned silence.

Jenny studied the boy in the photo, his big brown eyes, bold eyebrows, olive skin, broad smile, two dimples below his lower lip. As she imagined, he looked very much like her son, Will, who was about the same age now as the young soldier in the photo. She turned over the photograph and saw the date on the back—January 1964. Seeing his face for the first time, she began to cry, and now her dad held her and said, "This is Gary John Rossi, your father. I'm sorry we never told you the truth."

Jenny wept as she stared at the picture. There was an immediate recognition and affection. They shared the same eyes, lips, olive skin, eyebrows, and "God's stamp of approval" below their lower lip. Her resemblance to Gary was so great that she finally understood why it was her mother would never even really look at her. Seeing his face brought the heaviness of the loss directly to her now, and she felt the tragedy of his death all over again.

Her dad looked at the photo she held in both hands and said, "He was a good friend. We grew up together."

"I know that, from the letter."

"He was the best first baseman in the county. And a good fisherman too."

Belonging

Jenny was struck by the poignancy of watching her dad recall the boy who was her father, and the love she felt for both of them.

"I wanted to tell you many times, but Mama said it was best to leave it alone."

"Have you always known?"

"Since the day you were born. I thought you were early, but the nurse said, no, you were right on time, and we'd only been married six months, and—" He hesitated, and added, "It just wasn't possible. And then I saw you and, well, you have the picture. The shape of your eyes and the color of your skin." He smiled and touched her on the head and said, "You were such a golden little baby."

Jenny's mother, unable to tolerate this scene—a narrative she could no longer control—stood and said, "You got what you came here for. Now leave us alone."

Jenny walked around the side of the bed, toward her mother. "I don't know why you're so angry at me. I know you must have suffered. I know it wasn't your plan to deceive me. I believe you did what you thought was best, at least at that time. And I forgive you. So, what is it? You can't even look at me and talk about this? I'm a middle-aged woman with grown children. Can't we just talk about this?"

"You forgive me? Should I thank you? And don't pretend to care about me. There was never any bond between us."

It was a devastating admission. *There was never any bond.* She said it without shame or remorse, as though she believed that Jenny, as a child, was responsible for this failure. While Jenny pondered the words and thought of her own children, her mother said, "Ever since you were born, the world has revolved around you. And the minute you could leave, you did. And still, you got it all, didn't you?"

Her mother had finally admitted the truth, the reasons behind her lifelong resentment. She could never let go of the idea that she'd been trapped—in Bakersfield, in motherhood, in marriage. In her mind, she'd been deprived—of freedom; of education; of the love of her life, the father of her child. Against her wishes, Gary had enlisted in the Army, leaving her alone in Bakersfield, unwed and pregnant. When he died in the war, her hopes for a different life were taken from her—permanently, irrevocably. She was left married to a man she didn't love, with a child who looked like her biological father. She found a way to blame Jenny for all of this. It was the ultimate unfairness that this child, who caused her to lose everything, somehow ended up with everything she thought she wanted.

Despite how painful it was to hear, Jenny was grateful that she could finally make sense of the bitterness, the anger, the jealousy. She studied her mother's face and eyes, and this time, she could see all of her. The desperate girl trying to get out of town. The pregnant teen eloping with a man she didn't love. The newlywed who was handed an infant she didn't want or know how to care for. The young mother who learned that the man she loved was never coming back. The happy drunk laughing on the front porch. The angry drunk spewing her rage. This old woman, made up and crippled in her dark bedroom beside her husband, who some days remembered her, and some days might not.

Jenny shook her head. "I don't want to fight with you. I was hoping we could just acknowledge the truth. I'll just go now."

Jenny's father reached for her hand and said, "I love you just the same. Do you love me the same?"

Jenny put her arms around him. "Of course I do." There was a knot in her stomach as she realized that her dad had always known the truth, but nonetheless, stayed, did his best to be her father, and undoubtedly loved her. He'd been there for her, but he'd also always been there for her mother, every version of her, from the time she was nineteen years old, and Jenny knew that is where he would remain. When she let go of him, she held out her hand, and said, "Will you walk me down?"

Her father glanced at her mother and heeded the warning she gave with merely the narrowing of her eyes, a slight flare of her nostrils. Bowing his head, he silently declined Jenny's request, leaving her hand open and extended. She placed her hand on top of her father's head, touching the warm patch of skin that used to be covered with coarse, dark hair. She understood why he could not walk her down, why he had to stay. He'd already taken a bold stand against her mother, one that could cost him dearly, and he'd done it for her. He'd placed the photo of Gary in her hands, knowing that it was an irreversible action, one that was in direct contradiction of an edict issued by his wife, an edict that spanned and

Belonging

controlled the entirety of their life together. Understanding how vulnerable her father was, and knowing that she'd be leaving him behind, Jenny let her hand linger there. She hoped her touch would convey all the love she felt for him, would acknowledge what he had given to her. Despite all the reasons to leave, he did the best he could, and he stayed. He had, unwittingly, set the example of loving and caring for a child who was not your own, a foundational lesson that changed her life. She kissed the top of his head and said, "Thank you, Dad. I love you," and turned and walked out of the room. In the hall, she looked back at him, framed by the doorway—a still life of an old man slumped and hollow—with one hand over his heart, as if he was trying to hold onto her there.

At the bottom of the stairs, Jenny pushed open the front door and walked outside. She took a deep breath and felt the sunlight and fresh air on her face. The sprinklers were on in the front yard—circular swirls of water spraying the lawn. She took off her shoes and walked through them, getting her skirt damp. Turning back to take a last look at the house, she thought of Uncle Gino's wish for her: *release your burden, accept the love, listen to the song.* She remembered the prayer Gary recited in his letter to her mother and said everyday: *may you not forget the infinite possibilities that are born of faith.*

Standing in the street in bare feet, blades of green grass stuck to her ankles, she accepted that the desire for peace and closure, for understanding and forgiveness, resided only within her. And as if grace itself had settled over Lupine Lane, she finally understood that was enough.

When Jenny arrived at the cemetery that afternoon, she parked next to the elevated cross where all her relatives were buried. A tent had been set up over the burial spot Uncle Gino reserved next to Honey Bea in 1953. She remembered how Uncle Gino always walked the block as a way of acknowledging his ancestors, and she would now do the same. She took the bucket of flowers from her car and walked along the path toward the tent, leaving a small bouquet of rosemary and roses on the graves of each of her family members, including those she never knew, on behalf of Uncle Gino, remembering how he used to touch every stone.

Jenny plucked a few weeds and dandelions that had grown around Nonna's grave, sat against her headstone, and closed her eyes. This was the first time she'd talked to Nonna since learning about her father. She told Nonna that she didn't blame her, that she knows she did her best, and that thirteen years of her love had sustained her for a lifetime. She left a small bouquet and walked to the shaded area just west of Colonel Baker's stone, and there, she found where the Rossis were buried—her grandmother, Maria Teresa Rossi; her grandfather, Anthony John Rossi; and her uncle, Stephen Anthony Rossi, who died as a child, and whose gravestone read, "*From mother's arms to the arms of Jesus.*" She left a small bouquet on each. She arrived next at the small inset gravestone that read: *Gary John Rossi, October 10, 1945–April 12, 1966, loving son, American hero, U.S. Army, "Blessed are the pure in heart, for they shall see God."*

Jenny sat in the grass next to his grave, brushed off a few leaves, and touched every letter of his name. She thought about the words that someone, maybe his mother, had chosen to leave on his gravestone. They sounded like words she would have chosen herself to describe the young soldier who wrote about his desire for family, a rose garden, and Sunday dinners after church, whose advice to his unborn child was to trust God and love people. She held the picture her dad had given her and studied it—a teenage boy whose big dark eyes and sweet smile were incongruous with his combat hat and fatigues. His face was so deeply familiar to her. She felt an incredible sadness for the loss of his young life, for the way he died. She resolved to learn everything she could about him—his childhood, the Rossi family, his time in Vietnam, his last day.

The sadness and loss lived alongside gratitude and hope. She knew from his letter that he carried a strong faith. Somehow, despite losing his life at twenty-one years old and never getting the chance to meet his child, he passed on this faith, and he started a family that carried it forward today. For the first time, Jenny understood that her birth wasn't the horrible mistake her mother believed it to be. It was part of a singular design, to make sure that Gary, his love, and his faithfulness, endured. She placed a bouquet from her basket on his grave and left a prayer card with a picture of the risen Christ, his arms extended, light surrounding him, that read: *Behold I am alive forever and ever.*

Belonging

Jenny walked back to the tented area on the other side of the cemetery. She took a seat in a white plastic folding chair by the fresh hole in the ground, closed her eyes, and breathed in the smell of dirt, grass, rosemary, and roses. Her eyes closed, she focused on each sound: the cooing of a mourning dove, a faraway lawnmower, church bells, and the clucking of chickens from a nearby yard. She imagined everyone she'd lost there with her, just across the way, all dressed for the funeral: Nonna and Nonno; Henry and Mateo; Honey Bea and Uncle Gino; Billy's dad; Maria and Anthony Rossi with their young son, Stephen; and Gary John Rossi, who she saw in his helmet and fatigues, just like in the picture her father had given to her. Sitting with the sun on her face, feeling a warm breeze, she felt the love of them all.

Jenny thought about what her mother said—that there was no bond between them—and understood that it was her way of telling her, once again, that she did not belong. The letters told her why: she was untimely, inconvenient, not wanted, and a reminder of the tragedy that had left her mother without hope, without faith. But despite this, Jenny was born into a family that embraced and celebrated her—Uncle Gino, Nonna, Aunt Hope, Uncle Joe, and Heather. She was a descendant of her Italian great-grandparents, who'd made a home in the middle of California, and left a legacy of gathering—of food and music and crowded tables under the arbor. She'd inherited their home, filled with generations of memories, and a rose garden that would bloom for her children. She was born into this place that she intuitively felt was a part of her, where she loved the smell of the fog, grass, and swimming pools; where the river carried a rich history; where the songs were about finding home. She took this rooted feeling, and she and Billy created their own family, one where children never had to question whether they belonged; they felt it even before they took their first breath.

Soon, she could hear the arrival of cars and people. She greeted Aunt Hope and Uncle Joe, Heather and Rickey and their children, Mr. Hansen and Christopher, Billy's mom, Father Thomas, and finally, her own family. When she saw Billy walking toward her with their four grown children, all the fragments of herself came together and formed a solid, light-filled whole. She embraced each one before they took their seats next to her. As the service began, Billy took her hand and held it. After Father Thomas gave his blessing, Jenny looked to her right, at Summer and Mary, and to her left, at Billy and Will and Carl, and stood to recite the Saint Teresa poem Uncle Gino had selected for her. As "Peace in the Valley" began to play, Jenny placed her last bouquet, the one made up of every blossoming flower in Uncle Gino's garden, on top of his coffin before it was lowered into the ground.

As she said a final goodbye to Uncle Gino, she silently thanked him for the letters, for sharing the truth, for all he'd taught her, for all the love he'd given her. She thanked him for the summer days in the antique store, for the trips to the bakery, for all the prayer cards. She thanked him for teaching her how to send love to people no matter where they are and for helping her to understand that *to love abundantly is to live abundantly, and to love forever is to live forever*. When Jenny turned away from Uncle Gino's grave, Carl was there, standing behind her, tall and blond, so much taller than her. He reached for her hand. "I know how much you'll miss him, Mom."

Jenny held onto his hand and squeezed it.

"But you know, he's never really gone. We can send him love, and he'll send it back. He'll be right here with us, always," Carl said.

Jenny smiled at Carl, a grown man, repeating words she'd told him as a ten-year-old boy when their beloved cat, Chico, died; and again, as a teenager, when they made a family trek to a graveyard in the Belgium countryside and she told him all about her best friend, Henry; and again, as a young adult, when they lost Billy's dad in 2011. She hugged him and said, "I know."

As Carl held Jenny by Uncle Gino's grave, Billy and the rest of their children gathered around them. Together, they formed a circle, their arms branched out like the canopy of the old lemon tree, between them only sunlight and shadows.

Acknowledgments

I love acknowledgments. I read them in every single book I pick up. I always want to understand the journey, the people, how someone puts their fingers on a keyboard one day, and then years later, after receiving so much love, support, belief, and encouragement, holds a book in their hands. Writing may be a mostly solitary experience, but bringing a book into the world is anything but; I wish I could write a chapter of acknowledgments.

First, thank you to my husband Craig, who never wavers in his belief in me, and whose hard work, ambition, and commitment to our family has made my writing possible.

To my children, Jennie, Jack, Daisy, Will, and Hope, who are my inspiration.

To my sister Julie Alonso, artist, patient listener, honest reader, the best head cheerleader, the person I've known the longest, the one who shares all the memories. I am so grateful for you, your complete faith in the book, and the very best notes in the margins.

To Carol and Larry Fordyce, who have treated me like their own since I was a teenager and taught me the most about belonging.

To my dear friends who read early versions and have provided so much love and support: Jackie Thompson, Molly Perry, Peggy Scholz, Gail Goldman, Denise Roy, Rob Shannon, Nina Manny, Patty Quinlan, Whitney Weddell, Whitney Arnautou, Claudia DeNuccio, and Amy Platz.

To Debra Englander and everyone at Post Hill Press for their belief, collaboration, and care.

Jill Fordyce

To Malena Watrous and Stacey Swann who, as teachers and editors, provided their generous insight, guidance, and encouragement.

To Jennifer McCord, who uniquely understood what I wanted this book to be and patiently helped me make it so.

Finally, no one would be reading this book without the efforts of the most faithful, enduring, kind, and brilliant agent, Mel Parker.